# BROADSWORD

# Broadsword

### a novel of love
### amidst the chaos

## Roger Glasgow

Petit Roche Press
Roger Glasgow
www.broadswordseries.com
r.a.glasgow@comcast.net

ISBN: 978-1-7343011-0-6 (ebook)
ISBN: 978-1-7343011-1-3 (paperback)

Book and cover design: H. K. Stewart

This book is a work of fiction. Names, characters, places and occurrences are either products of the author's imagination or are used fictitiously. Any resemblance to actual persons or occurrences is purely coincidental.

Printed in the United States of America

This book is printed on archival-quality paper that meets requirements of the American National Standard for Information Sciences, Permanence of Paper, Printed Library Materials, ANSI Z39.48-1984.

To my wife, **Jennifer**

*A patient listener and constructive critic*

# TABLE OF CONTENTS

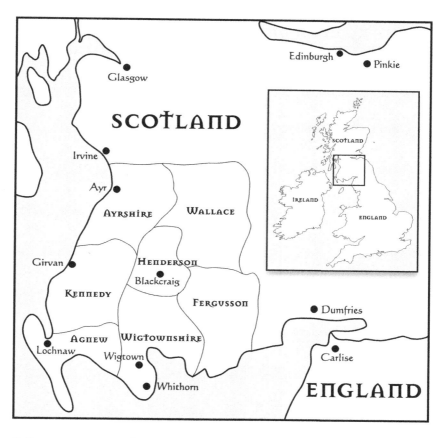

Map of the Shires of the Region, 1550s

# Henderson Family Tree

Colin Henderson
    m. Mairy "Grannie" Wilson

        c. Hugh Henderson
          m. Ann Wallace
            c. Andrew (Andy) Henderson
              m. Helen Agnew
                c. Colin Henderson
            c. Mairy (Ree) Henderson
            c. Joseph (Joe) Henderson
            c. James (Jamie) Henderson
              m. Ally Agnew
                c. Grace Henderson

        c. John Henderson
          m. Jean (?)
            c. Innis Henderson

        c. Richard Henderson

        c. Malcom Henderson

# Agnew Family Tree

Andrew Agnew
  m. Agnes Stewart
    c. Helen Agnew
      m. Andrew (Andy) Henderson
  m. Rachel Fergusson
    c. William Agnew

Gilbert Agnew
  m. (?)
    c. Blair Agnew
    c. Margaret (Maggie) Agnew
    c. Ally Agnew
      m. James (Jamie) Henderson
        c. Grace Henderson

# Preface

BROADSWORD is a work of fiction. Accounts of some historical events and people were included to help set the context in which the story unfolds. For example, some of the battles actually occurred, such as the notable battle of Pinkie Cleugh, but all details of the battles are fictional. Also some of the characters in the story were real people, such as the Agnew brothers and the Catholic Archbishop James Beaton, but all the events and dialogue is wholly fictitious. Blackcraigshire, home of the book's principal protagonist family, the Hendersons, is an imaginary shire set in an actual geographic place (mountainous area of Southwest Scotland).

My inspiration to write this book came from the circumstance that my ancient surname ancestors lived in Southwest Scotland during the times covered, and I have often wondered what their lives were like. This book is an attempt to capture a semblance of those times. The surname "Henderson" for the lead family was chosen because it is the historical name of a known Scottish border clan of the era, not heavily involved in "reivering" (raiding and plundering). "Reivers" normally stole livestock, but also at times looted household goods, kidnapped prisoners for ransom and occasionally committed more serious crimes such as extortion, arson and murder.

The reivers were products of the near constant unrest resulting from warfare between the English and Scottish kingdoms that raged across the common border from the thirteenth through the sixteenth centuries. From west to east, the border ran along the Solway Firth, and then roughly followed the course of Hadrian's Wall built by the Romans when they invaded Britain in the first century A.D. The story told by this book takes place in the mid-1500s, mostly in Southwest Scotland.

I chose this time in history because it teemed with many events that changed the world. Scotland was undergoing unparalleled violence and foment—clan vs. clan, Protestants vs. Catholics, highlanders vs. borderers, nobles vs. monarchs and Scots vs. English. Mary, Queen of Scots, throughout her tragic and tortured life, was connected in one way or another with much of this disorder. She was only six days old when her father, King James V of Scotland, died in December 1542. Mary's mother, Mary of Guise, was French and took Mary to France, a long-standing ally of Scotland. James Hamilton, the second Earl of Arran and a Scotsman, served as young Mary's regent, until the regency devolved to Mary's mother.

Upon the Scottish king's death, England's King Henry VIII sensed an opportunity to force a pact with Scotland. He wanted to add to his domain and crush the Scots-French alliance. He proposed a marriage of infants—his four-year-old son, the future King of England, Edward VI, to the infant Mary. King Henry promised Scotland's continued independence after the marriage, but Arran and other important Scottish lords became suspicious that he actually planned to rule it as a vassal state. They also suspected he would move to impose the Anglican form of Protestantism upon the Scots and halt the Calvinist Reformation in Scotland. After preliminary discussions, the Scots rejected the marriage proposal, and King Henry decided to force the issue with a brutal military invasion of Scotland. History would dub the resulting conflict the "rough wooing" war.

Henry put the English army under the leadership of Edward Seymour, the Earl of Herford and Duke of Somerset. Somerset was the eldest brother of Queen Jane Seymour, Henry's third wife and the only one of his six wives to bear him a son—Edward. Henry's plan was to move about 30,000 English troops up the eastern coast of England and capture the Scottish capital, Edinburgh. To soften Scots' resistance, Henry sent an advance contingent of about 5,000 troops to the borderlands to scout, raid, plunder, kill, terrorize and generally keep the Scots harried and disorganized. The Henderson family was unavoidably caught up in much of this chaos.

# I.

# REIVERS

## SCOTS BORDERS REGION, 1546

JAMIE Henderson carefully made his way down the steep terrain toward the River Cree, keeping a sharp eye out for loose rocks that might send him tumbling. A fall on the glacier carved bluff that oversaw the stream would almost certainly cause painful injuries, possibly even death. The river at this point made a precipitous drop before flattening out onto the floor of a small grassy glen. This was the eleven-year-old lad's destination. It was the best place to check on the salmon spawn. Jamie proceeded cautiously, watching where his bare feet fell.

He topped a slight rise and looked out. The sun low in the western sky on a clear late October afternoon framed a spectacular golden vista. Jamie tarried for a moment enjoying the view. This vantage point never failed to give him a sense of quiet tranquility. He could see the blue-green rivulet snaking through the valley below and peered intently for any movement in the river's shallow shoals. Ripples could be seen sparkling and glinting from the sun's rays, but he was too far away to see any fish. He moved down the slope until he came out in the valley and walked through knee-high grass toward a line of willow bushes on the river's banks. Pushing the branches aside, he found himself staring at wriggling, pulsing water that seemed alive.

Jamie was astounded. Salmon, fighting their way upstream, packed the water from bank to bank. Many were so big their dorsal fins protruded above the water line like waving flags. *Mother of Mary, I've never seen so many salmon in one place! There's more fish than water.*

He sat down and continued to look in amazement at the massive run of finny warriors. After a while, with the western sun warming his face and the movement of struggling fish having a hypnotic effect, he lay back and soon dozed off. Abruptly, he was awakened by loud snorting, huffing and splashing. He rolled over on his side and cautiously looked downstream. A column of horsemen, a dozen or more, were crossing over the Cree to the side he was on. Some of the horses stopped and drank. Others perked their ears and looked in his direction. He could not tell if they saw him, but he was relieved that the riders were not looking his way. Less than 30 yards away, they were big men, heavily armed, and did not look friendly. If the horsemen turned left and continued upstream, they would ride right by him. He flattened himself to the ground and held his breath.

As Jamie had feared, the lead rider guided his horse out on the bank and turned left. Jamie realized he would have no chance to escape if he got up and ran, and would be seen if he moved. His only choice was to lie where he was, remain as still as possible, and pray the grass and willow branches would provide enough concealment. Barely breathing, he could see the horse hooves plop just inches from his body as the men rode by one by one. It seemed an eternity as he waited for the last one to pass. Gritting his teeth, he feared at any moment one of the horses would stop and he would hear: *Hey there, boy! Stand up so I can see you.* Thankfully, just as his lungs felt they would burst, the last of them rode by.

After they had all passed, Jamie convulsed into a spell of trembling and shaking so severe he worried his bones might rattle and give him away. After several minutes he got to his knees, crawled a short distance, and peeked around the bushes. The line of horses was moving upstream in a slow walk. Riders were turning their heads from side to side as if looking for something. *They must be reivers looking for cattle to steal,* he thought. *Thank God ours don't graze out this far.* Still, they were dangerous-looking men. He had never seen any of them before. He needed to warn his Paw, Hugh Henderson.

Getting to his feet and stooping low, Jamie ran toward the slope where he had come down into the glen. He started up the incline, keeping a steady pace and dodging behind trees and large rocks when he could. About half way he stopped behind a tree and looked out. The column of riders had stopped, and several of them were looking his way. The lead rider lifted his arm and seemed to be pointing. Two of the riders at the head of the line suddenly peeled away and headed in his direction at a gallop.

Jamie's heart leaped. *They're after me!* He took off at a dead run. Home was probably two miles distant, and he would have to run uphill over rough, rocky ground for most of it. He was barefoot but that didn't register on him. He must warn his Paw and the rest of the family. When he reached the top of the steep incline, to where the trail turned off toward the bastle house where he lived, he stopped behind a big shelf of rock and looked back. The two horsemen were nowhere in sight. Jamie cupped both hands to his ears and waited awhile, listening. The only sounds he heard were from the rushing water of the Cree and the whistling of wind in the tall trees.

✦ ✦ ✦

Hugh Henderson, as the eldest son of the late Colin Henderson, inherited his father's home, a well-built stone bastle house, as well as his position as the Laird of Blackcraigshire, a small council shire squeezed between the borders of southeast Ayrshire and north Wigtownshire. The land had been granted to the Hendersons as vassals of the Barons of Lochnaw many generations ago for the provision of exemplary military service. Situated inland near the beginning of the Galloway uplands, and continuing into the mountains, the land contained some fertile lowlands in the glens and a lot of rolling hills. The principal features of the shire were Glen Trool and, at its head, Loch Trool, located just below Ben Blackcraig, the highest elevation in Southwest Scotland. The loch was the headwater of the River Cree.

The lowland was mainly devoted to farming, livestock and grain fields, with the upland suitable for sheep and sparse plots of oats and wheat. Much of the land around Loch Trool was too steep and rocky to be arable and was clad in forest. The vast Agnew estate covered the rest of Galloway from the Rhinns peninsula in the west, to Wigtownshire in the east, and then north from Luce Bay to the start of the uplands.

The Henderson family raised beef and dairy cows, sheep and a few hogs, grew grain for human and animal food, and sold milk at the small market a few miles to the south on the Wigtown road. They also oversaw and collected rents from the several tenant farmers and crofters who worked the rest of the shire's arable land and raised a few livestock.

The Henderson bastle house was two stories tall, built of thick stone walls, with a well-fortified three-story pele tower at one end, designed for defense against reivers and other lawless bands that wandered about the wild borderland marches of Southwest Scotland. The lower level of the house had a dirt floor and was used as an animal barn where dairy cows were milked and fed. A surrounding barmkin rock wall served as a corral. The second floor had a hearth and was used for human habitation. There was an overhead half-loft for sleeping. The house had no windows, only slits for lookout and shooting arrows if necessary. There was no interior stairwell. Instead, an exterior rope/rung ladder was used for access to the second level and could be pulled up at night and in times of emergency. Accessed from the second floor, the pele tower had a flattened round roof and castellated battlements. Arrows from longbows and crossbows, stones, hot liquids and other missiles could be rained down on attackers from this tower. The whole house was, in short, a miniature castle. Life on the border was perilous and often violent.

Hugh Henderson owned six adult Ayrshire dairy cows, fifteen black and white Galloway beef cattle, a small herd of Soay sheep, and three horses—two of them fine palfry riding horses and one pack horse. He also had two oxen for plowing, a few hogs and one border collie. All of them, except for one milk-cow called Bossie, and a herding collie named Trig, were soon to be stolen.

+ + +

As the fading light of dusk seeped into the glens and crept up the hillsides, the Henderson menfolk were finishing their chores.

Hugh's older sons, Andrew "Andy" and Joseph "Joe," along with Trig, had rounded up the livestock and corralled them within the barmkin. The dairy cows were herded into the barn area of the house to be fed hay and a bucket of oats each. They would be milked in the morning. The horses were fed a half portion of oats. Hay was pitchforked to the other livestock to supplement the wilting fodder they had grazed on during the day. Hugh had been out on horseback all day checking on his tenants. He had sent his eleven-year-old third son, James "Jamie," to check to see if the salmon had begun spawning on the nearby River Cree. Smoked salmon was an important food staple for the Henderson household.

Hugh's wife, Ann, and oldest daughter, Mairy, called "Ree," had a good blaze going under a large iron cooking pot hung at the hearth. They were busily cutting up vegetables and chunks of beef for a hearty stew. Hugh's mother, Mairy Henderson, known to the family as "Grannie," was tending an iron skillet that held a mix of milk, eggs and flour to make biscuits. Ann and Hugh's wee twins, now three months old, were sleeping contentedly in a large double cradle Hugh had constructed. In autumn the weather was usually warm during the day and cool to cold at night. With the pleasing warmth of the fire and the rich aroma of the food as it was being prepared, everything pointed to a pleasurable and comfortable evening.

Suddenly Jamie burst in, jerked up the outside ladder, fell to his knees and gasped, "Paw, Paw!"

Everyone in the house's small living quarters turned and looked. Jamie was on his hands and knees, coughing, wheezing and sweating, his face white and his clothing soaked wet. Hugh ran over.

"Son, what be wrong?"

"I saw horsemen, a bunch of them, heavily armed," he stammered.

"What, where?"

"Down at, at the riv .. river."

Hugh put his arm around Jamie's shaking shoulder. "Son, take it easy, come over here and sit down. Calm yourself a bit and we'll talk all about it."

Ann, was standing near, a look of concern on her face. The other family members had gathered around.

"Give him some room," Hugh said. They all stood back a bit. Grannie brought over a cup of water and handed it to Jamie.

After a couple of gulps Jamie's breathing slowed and his face gained some color. Hugh said in a soothing manner, "Now tell us lad, what happened."

"I was on the bank of the river looking at the salmon and, and … Mother Mary, the river was full of them, most I ever saw, more fish than water."

"Good, very glad to hear it," said Hugh. "Now what about the horsemen."

"Like I said, I was lying there on the bank looking at the salmon. Nothing else was happening. I guess maybe I dozed off, for suddenly I heard horses and men."

"Where," persisted Hugh gently.

"Crossing, they were at the shoals just below me. The horses were splashing and snorting. Some of them stopped to drink."

"The men, … were the horses mounted by the men you mentioned," Hugh probed.

"Aye, they were all mounted."

"Were they all armed?"

"I couldn't see all of them, but the ones I saw were."

"Had you ever seen any of them before?"

"Nay, not that I know of."

"Did any of them see you, do you think?"

"I don't think so. I laid still in the grass and bushes. They rode right by me. Then I got up and ran back up the mountain toward home. After I was about half way I stopped behind a tree and looked out. The men had moved further upriver. Then they stopped and appeared to be looking around. Two of them pulled out and started galloping their horses in my direction. I took off again. When I got to the turnoff, I stopped and listened—didn't hear anything. Then I came here as quick as I could."

"You did the right thing, Son. Whoever it was, sounds like they rode on. They might have been reivers out looking for stray cattle, or they might have been just a group of men scouting for fishing or good hunting grounds. Hard to say. Let's hope we don't find out. Now let's all get ready to eat."

They all lined up to wash their hands in a basin. Hugh hung back and spoke in a low voice to his oldest son, Andrew.

"Andy, why don't you take first watch tonight."

Andy nodded.

Bowls were filled with stew, the large skillet of hot biscuits was set upon the table, and everyone sat down to enjoy the meal.

Suddenly Andy called out. "Paw, horsemen coming!"

"How many?" Hugh asked, a panicked feeling suddenly in his chest.

"A lot, over a dozen in sight."

Hugh sprang over and looked out. Andy was right. There were many—too many to count quickly. *My God! Those must be the horsemen Jamie saw, they've found us. We'll be wiped out.*

"Reivers!" Hugh cried, "too many to fight off. We've got to get out of here!"

With a dozen or more reivers coming down on them, there was no time to tarry.

Hugh Henderson was a savvy, skilled Scottish chieftain—a warrior and landed knight, 39 years of age. He was near six feet tall, big boned, with broad shoulders, narrow waist and long legs. A handsome man, he was blessed with a square jaw and flashing, dark eyes beneath long black hair. When he was a lad of 14, Hugh's father had sent him off to Irvine, the Scottish military capital on the Ayrshire coast near Glasgow City, for training in the military arts. Many of Hugh's male ancestors had done the same thing over the centuries, and his own eldest son, Andrew, had recently returned from his two years of training.

But this was not a time to fight. Hugh's first obligation was to protect his family. The reivers probably only wanted the livestock, but much worse could happen, and had. First, he needed to get everyone out of the house. They couldn't hold off a horde of determined attackers for long. Fortunately, he had planned for such an exigency. The horsemen were approaching from the south, where there was a rough road with switchbacks ascending a steep grade, and a stout gate in the barmkin wall leading to the front of the house. At the rear of the house, a small square door was on the second level, barricaded with a sturdy iron crossbar. This could be quickly opened for escape purposes. Long ago, Hugh had constructed a long rope of braided leather with a loop on one end. The stronger family members could rappel down to the ground on the rope, while others could be lowered by looping the rope under their arms. The two small twins could be lowered in the cradle.

The reivers soon broke through the front gate, and were hustling to manage and herd the unruly livestock, which took some time. Others were pounding on the outside of the house. Apparently they had spied the main outside door on the second floor and were chopping holes to try to climb up to reach it. It would be hard to break down, but Hugh had no doubt they eventually would succeed. *They intend to rob the house as well as steal the livestock,* he realized. He barked instructions—pointing out that they couldn't save much—only what they must have.

First, he mentioned the gold guilders. The big coins would be difficult to carry in their clothing and could be accidently lost, or stolen by the reivers if someone was caught. Hugh instructed that they be divided up between the three boys, and swallowed. The coins could be recovered in their shitten later. He directed Ann and Ree to get the twins tied with a long cloth wrapped around the cradle, along with as much warm coverings as they could manage. Andy was to go down the rope first and help the rest at the bottom. Then those who needed the loop would go—Ann and Granny; then they would lower the twins, and finally, Joe was to skinnie down.

After Joe was down, Hugh planned to toss out all the weapons for Andy and Joe to gather up. They would certainly be needed. When their feet hit the ground, he emphasized, everyone should all take off up the trail toward the wood as fast as they could. They would meet up in a copse of oak trees higher up. Hugh would come down last and snap the rope loose to take with him. Everyone was to grab a warm shawl or blanket, and shoes. Who knew when they would get back and what might be destroyed.

"Let's go, *gang!*" he yelled.

The plan was executed to perfection. All got down, hurried up the trail and were soon covered by the wood. Fortunately, the livestock the reivers were trying to herd—horses, cows, sheep, oxen, hogs and the young offspring of many—did not cooperate, running to and fro, bawling, baaing, squeeling and in general raising a ruckus. This kept the reivers occupied and assisted the escape immeasurably. The collie, Trig, after first trying to keep the livestock contained in the barmkin, heard Andy's low whistle and ran to the back, where she obediently followed the rest of the family into the wood. Hugh let out a huge sigh of relief as he, Andy and Joe ran up the path with the weapons, and met up with the others. They had been lucky.

After a round of hugs and endearing murmurs, Hugh said quietly, "We have to keep going, and hurry!"

Night was coming on fast, the sky was clear, and a half moon was just beginning to rise. They needed to put some distance between themselves and the reivers. Fortunately, the reivers faced the same conditions and were moving in the opposite direction, trying to drive a herd of panicked livestock in the dark. In about a quarter mile the group would arrive at the grove of oak trees. At this time of year there should be a blanket of leafy cover on the ground.

Ann wore a linen sheath that was fitted over her shoulders and fell below her knees, cinched at the waist. Over that, she had a long shawl for a wrap and wore simple leather shoes. Though she was covered with clothes and a wrap, Hugh noticed with satisfaction how his wife's auburn tresses spilled over her erect shoulders, and how the firm round cheeks of her butt atop long shapely legs jiggled just slightly as she hurriedly walked ahead. Despite the dreadful circumstances, he couldn't help musing, *Too bad we'll be spending the night with family all around.*

Hugh wore a long woolen cape, cinched at the waist by a belt, breeches and leather boots, as he had been riding horseback around the estate just before the attack. The cape could be pulled up over his head in cold or windy weather for a hood.

Once they reached the oak grove, Hugh called for everyone to stop, rake up a pile of leaves to keep their bodies off the cold ground, and bed down for the night. There were warm blankets for the twins, and the other family members had woolen wraps of some sort. As they settled in for the night, all wrapped their bodies as best they could, and lay down next to each other to conserve body heat. The air was already cold and still, and would get colder as the night wore on. Hugh and Ann lay side by side with the twins wrapped and tucked between them.

Ann had worried that she would be unable to produce enough breast milk to feed both babes as they got older. The Ayshire milk cows they owned had produced plenty of supplemental milk. But they were now gone, victims of the raid. After everyone had settled down, and seemed asleep, Ann whispered to her husband: "They stole the milk cows. With the twins, how can I manage?"

Hugh was quiet for a moment, then replied: "Bossie—re-member, we took her to my brother John's a couple of months ago. Her calf is weaned and she is ready for breeding. John's got a good Ayshire bull. In a few months Bossie will calf and her utters will be full. Maybe we can retrieve her."

He touched his wife's cheek with his hand.

"Don't worry. It'll all work out."

Ann felt slightly better. Hugh was a good man. Always think-ing. He took good care of his family. Whatever trouble they faced, and there had been a lot over the years, he had always found a way to get them through. She gave him a kiss.

"I'm nay worried."

It would be a long night, and dawn would bring a fresh but un-certain future.

# 2.
# †RAGEDY

AS the Hugh Henderson family lay on their leafy beds in the chilly air a couple of hours after nightfall, the half moon slowly rose through high flimsy clouds, dimly illuminating the tree canopy on the hill and the environs beyond. Hugh awakened and arose quietly. He could see a reddish glow in the direction from which they had come. *The reivers have set fire to the house,* he realized. There was a lot of straw that would make a big blaze, and likely it had burned through the wood floor to the second story. *There wouldn't be much left but the outer shell,* he thought. They could repair it, but it would take a while. *And who were these reivers—a dozen of them, or more?* Hugh had never encountered that many.

*Maybe the English had invaded again and this had been a foraging party,* he speculated. Come to think of it, although not attired in military garb, they had looked better armed and had bigger horses than typical cattle rustlers. And what about John and his family? His house was higher up than Hugh's place, closer to the rugged uplands. Possibly, if they were just reivers, they had gotten all the livestock they could handle from Hugh and had left John alone. But, if they were military?

Hugh also worried about Ann and the twins. Since Ann's stillbirth of a daughter five years ago, they had thought her childbearing days were over. Imagine the surprise when Ann turned up pregnant. Double that for when she gave birth to twins, a boy and a girl they named Malcom and Helen. Eleven years had passed between the birth of Jamie and the twins. In addition to being much surprised, Jamie and the other siblings quickly grew proud and protective of their new sister and brother. They felt more like uncles and aunt than siblings. Such a seemingly God given gift, the twins held a special place in the hearts of both Ann and Hugh. But it was Grannie who took to the twins the most. She absolutely doted on them, always anxious for Ann to finish her breastfeeding so she could take them, hold and care for them.

Because of the attack of the reivers, no supper was had. Now the whole family was empty and hungry. Maybe they could go back to the house after daybreak and gather a few vegetables from the garden. In mid-autumn it had mostly turnips, potatoes, beets and a few cabbages. That might get them by for a day or two.

But they desperately needed milk, especially for the twins. Although Ann was healthy, at her age she could barely breastfeed one babe, much less two. The twins had been sickly lately; they were spitting up and often had diarrhea. *We should go to John's place,* thought Hugh. *There we can obtain milk from Bossie, or one of John's cows, maybe even stay over for a few days until we can get a decent shelter built further up the glen.*

Hugh went back to lie down beside Ann and the twins. Ann stirred.

"Any troubles?"

"Nay," he answered quietly, "tomorrow will be a long day."

The next morning broke cold and clear for the shivering family spread out on the hard ground. The sun was rising, and Hugh was sure that warmth would soon seep in. He, Andy and Joe and his older daughter Ree were all sleeping side by side a few feet distant.

"Waken my bairns, we have work to do."

The three arose slowly, stretching stiff limbs and yawning. Hugh dispatched Ree and Joe to gather up dry wood for a fire—but wait to start it, he cautioned. Andy and he would hurry back to the burned house to retrieve whatever they could find of value, and gather up any vegetables left in the garden. They had a hen coop, maybe they could gather a few eggs and catch a chicken or two for roasting.

"We'll meet back here in half an hour," Hugh said.

Hugh and Andy started the trek back down the path to the house. They proceeded cautiously, reluctant to discover the full extent of the damage and keeping a lookout for any lingering raiders. Both had sharp dirks under their belts in case of trouble. As they emerged from the wood into the clearing for the house, they saw it was still standing, but the fire had burned all the way through the second floor. Much of it had fallen down and lay in a smoldering, still smoking pile of debris. The reivers, along with the livestock, were gone. They checked the hen coop that was several feet away from the main house on the outside of the barmkin fence. It had been raided too; no chickens were seen, although they were able to round up a few eggs. *Strange,* Hugh thought, *reivers usually only wanted livestock.* He had never known of them stealing chickens. However, the garden was still intact, though trampled by livestock. They would be able to gather a decent number of vegetables.

A lean-to was attached to the house containing horse tack, oxen yokes, and other items of farming apparatus. It had not burned. The two men found a wooden scoop shovel and a long pole that they used in probing the smoldering debris of the house. About the only useful item found in the debris was the big iron cooking pot, charred but still intact.

The horse tack, saddles, plow, ox yokes and such were now of no use because the livestock, including the two oxen and three horses, had been stolen. But such equipment might be useful in the future, so they collapsed the sidewalls of the lean-to in order to conceal it. They then went to the garden and pulled up as many vegetables as they could, filling the cook pot. They hung the pot on the long pole, and balanced it on their shoulders. They also threw in a few still-glowing embers, and toted the pot and vegetables back up to where the others were waiting.

"Start the fire, we need to eat," Hugh said.

It was time to prepare the food and fill their stomachs. Water was obtained from a nearby burn and the vegetables were washed, diced and placed in the pot, along with the eggs, still in their shells. The pot was balanced on some flat rocks and placed over the fire and accumulating coals. Soon a fragrant broth was boiling over the fire. Stomachs would be satiated for at least one more day.

After all had eaten, Hugh directed everyone to head toward his brother John's place about four miles away. When they got near, the main group stayed in the cover of the wood while Hugh and Andy looped around to get a closer look.

"I hope not, but the same cowardly bastards that came down on us may have made their way to John's place," Hugh whispered.

They approached from the back of the house, staying watchful and walking slowly. John's place was a well built, one-floor cruch house with rock walls, a hearth, thatched roof over a timber frame and a packed earthen floor. There was a partition in the middle. One end was for humans and the other for animals.

Immediately, when the house first came into view, Hugh sensed that something was amiss. The house had not been burned, but there was no smoke coming from the chimney and no animals were about. In fact, there was no sign of life at all. The two approached cautiously, dirks at the ready. Nothing was seen, no movement, not even a rooster crowing or chickens scurrying about. They skirted the house so it could be seen from the front. An ominous sign came into view—the front door was wide open.

Hugh moved carefully a little closer and further to one side. Just inside the door he could make out a crumpled form on the dirt floor, maybe a pile of dirty clothing or bedding, he thought. He motioned Andy to come up, and as they got closer he realized that, *no, it was not clothing or bedding, it was a body.* Both rushed up and were sickened by what they found. The body was that of John's wife, Jean. She lay in a pool of blood, her throat slit and her belly gashed open end to end. She was seven months pregnant. The unborn babe never got to take a first breath.

Although no stranger to dead bodies, the gruesome sight made Hugh nauseous, a bile-like taste rising in his throat. He had to fight off retching. Looking quickly around in the dim light, Hugh could see that there were other bodies scattered about, horribly butchered, some still where they had lain in their sleep.

John lay next to Jean. He still had his nightclothes on. John's arms were slashed. He had several deep stab wounds to his torso, and his throat was slit open. A sgian dubh blade, covered in dried blood, lay next to John's right hand. The corpses of six Henderson children, ranging in age from 14 to 3, littered the floor, most in grotesque positions.

"My God Paw, they have all been slaughtered," Andy said in a quiet, subdued voice.

Indeed they had all been brutally slain. Hugh quickly surmised what had happened. A group of reivers, perhaps the same ones who had attacked his place last evening, had later that night slipped up to John's house when all were asleep. They must have crashed through the front door with dirks and broadswords drawn, and quickly commenced their grisly killing before any defense could be mounted. John had managed to grab his sgian dubh blade, and had fought fiercely to save his wife and the rest of his family. That would explain the slash wounds to his arms. But he was no match for several heavily armed men who had the benefit of surprise. He must have persisted for a while before the broadswords and dirks cut him to pieces. Jean had rushed to his side in a futile effort to help. That was why both of their bodies lay at the door entrance. The children had no chance at all, most struck down near where they had been sleeping.

Shaken to the core by the ghastly scene, Hugh and Andy staggered outside and fell to their knees. Andy was moaning piteously, while Hugh let out a dreadful sustained blood-curdling scream. His lust for vengeance was rising already. But against whom? His whole body was throbbing for vengeance, but his brain told him more investigation was needed.

"Stay here, lad. I'll go look around some more."

Clearly, the family had all been asleep and was surprised by the sudden attack. But exactly when did it happen? He looked around at the bodies. Their lips were still pink. He felt of Jean's arm; it was not cold, still somewhat warm. He lifted the body of one of the small children, a girl. It was stiffer than usual but still flexible. This happened after midnight, he reasoned, probably early morning, maybe four or five hours before Hugh and Andy got there. He called to Andy to check if there was livestock in the barn.

"Nay, none."

John did not own as much livestock as did Hugh, but he had a couple of milk cows, an Ayrshire bull, a horse, two or three beeves, and a few sheep. All but the sheep would be in the barn on a cold night. And what about John's dog, a hunting hound? He usually slept in with the family. Where was he, and why had he not set off barking before the intruders broke in?

Worst by far, if the reivers only wanted to steal the livestock, why did they savagely murder an entire family, asleep in their house, offering no resistance whatever? It just didn't make sense. *No,* Hugh thought. *These were not common reivers. These men were much more evil.* In Hugh's experience, that could only mean one of two things: One, an attack by a rival clan—but there had been no friction between his kin and another clan in a long time—or two, it had been the English; specifically—an invading English military force—but even they did not normally slaughter innocent civilians indiscriminately.

Hugh thought back to what he took as reivers who attacked his place the previous evening. They had been much better armed and better coordinated than your usual band of cattle thieves, and mounted on cavalry-sized horses. *English,* he thought. It must be part of an English army—a unit of cavalry sent ahead to forage for food. Evidently they also had orders to spread fear and terror throughout the populace as they went. They had shucked their military attire for civilian clothes so they would not stand out.

This area was in the West March on the Scottish side of the border. Assuming a sizable contingent of English soldiers, as it appeared, surely the March Warden would have noticed or been notified of their passing. Why hadn't an alarm been raised? Perhaps the warden also had been killed, or paid off for that matter. Hugh had heard the warden was corrupt.

Dejected and forlorn, Hugh and Andy slowly made their way back to the others. Hugh related the terrible scene they had found and his suspicion of what had happened. Everyone listened in stunned silence, broken only by shrieks of grief as the ghastly truth began to sink in, then sad sobs, sighs and finally, deathly silence. After a while, Hugh summoned his three boys to go back with him to bury the bodies. They had the scoop shovel, and Hugh figured more tools for digging could be found in John's shed. They were all anxious to get the gruesome task completed. There was no telling whether the English detachment, or whoever they were, might be close by still.

As Hugh and his three sons went about the macabre chore of gathering the bodies, stretching them out side by side at the burial site and wrapping them in whatever meager fabrics could be found, Joe made a startling discovery.

"Where is Innis?"

Hugh's oldest nephew, Innis, age 16, was not among the dead.

Hugh quickly sent his three boys out to look all around. Innis was nowhere to be found. Hugh did not have much time to puzzle over this strange situation. They needed to get the bodies in the ground. A big rectangular pit was dug, large enough to hold all the bodies side-by-side. The ground was soft, so the work went quickly. After the bodies were covered with earth, and a crude cross was erected, Hugh's glum unit walked in misery back to the rest of his waiting family. Hugh mentioned the mystery of Innis missing and held out hope he had survived somehow.

"Keep your eyes and ears peeled," he instructed them all. "Maybe Innis still be around somewhere."

Hugh reasoned they needed to get as far away from the lowland as possible. The main geographical features of Blackcraigshire were Glen Trool, the Loch, the River Cree and Ben Blackcraig, which towered over the entire area. Glen Trool ended at its southwest terminus in a narrow opening coming down from the Galloway hills, where a small burn flowed out of the loch and grew into the River Cree. The area around the entry to Glen Trool was forested, so unless one knew exactly where it was or blindly stumbled upon it, the opening was not likely to be noticed. In fact, except for a couple of Hugh's tenant farmers living up the glen who tilled the weak soil and ran a few sheep, humans seldom entered this domain.

The loch at the top of Glen Trool had clear, cold water and was teeming with salmon, trout and resident fresh-water fish. This, Hugh decided, was where they should go. If the recent dreadful happenings were what he thought, an English invasion, they should be safe there. The English armies would concentrate their efforts on the towns, the populated areas nearer the coast, and the castles of the aristocracy, not some hard-to-find glens and lochs in the uplands with sparse, if any, population.

The small group of Hendersons was already near the opening to Glen Trool, so they proceeded in that direction through thick woods. After they had gone a short way, maybe a half-mile, Trig suddenly stopped, stood stock still, her nose sniffing the air, her body quivering. Shortly, they heard a dog bark some distance away. It was a deep bay, like that of a hunting hound.

"I think I recognize that bark," said Jamie. "Sounds like Uncle John's dog, his old hunting hound, Smartie."

Hugh and Andy immediately started calling.

"Here! Here Smartie. Come!" After a while the dog emerged from the bush, tongue hanging out and tail wagging.

"Smartie," said Jamie, "Come here!"

Smartie did, licking Jamie's hand, wagging his tail even more vigorously. All gathered around, petting and praising the dog, when, shortly, the bush parted and out walked Innis, pale as a ghost and shaking like a leaf.

"Uncle! Oh God I be glad to see you. I need help. My family has all been killt!"

Hugh took the boy in his arms and soothed him as best he could. After a few minutes, Innis was able to tell what had happened. His father had asked him to arise early, well before first light, take the dog and drive the scattered sheep down to the barmkin for shearing the next morning. The womenfolk would need to spin the wool to make thread for looming new shawls and covers for the coming winter. He had left with Smartie early in the morning, after the rest of the family had gone to sleep, to find the sheep and start herding them home. He soon found the flock and started moving them back toward the barmkin. As he got near, Smartie stopped and started growling.

He could hear the sound of wood being battered and splintered, and made out the forms of several men bashing down the front door. Several more were holding a group of large horses nearby. The sound of shrill screams, cries and shouts pierced the air. He knew his family was being attacked, and his first instinct was to run and try to help. He ran a ways toward the house, but realized there were too many. He had no weapon and would undoubtedly be killed as well.

Shortly, he said, the men emerged from the house, herded the livestock out of the barmkin, and galloped off with the livestock in tow. The scared sheep had all scattered. Although there was a half moon, he was too far away to make out the features of any of the men and couldn't provide any useful information as to the identity of the savage killers.

"Nay need to go further, lad," Hugh said kindly. "We have been to the house and know what happened. Your kin have all been buried in a Christian manner."

Hugh attempted to console the young man, explaining that they knew the hurt he had in his heart. They had it, too. Hugh and his family had also been attacked, he said, likely by the same group of marauders. Fortunately, they had escaped, but were burned out and all their livestock stolen as well.

"We're headed up the glen for safety," Hugh told the boy. "You must join us."

"Aye, Uncle," said Innis. "Thank you."

# 3.
# THE LEAN-TO

THE small mournful group moved upward, through thick woods, searching for the high glade at the top of the glen. After about two hours of hard travel, Hugh shouted, "This way!" They emerged upon a narrow grassland with a few short shrubs scattered about.

Before they had gone far, Jamie, always acute of ear, heard the faint tinkling of a bell.

"Och, I think I hear a cow bell. Sounds like Bossie's."

Hugh started shouting, "*Sooo, cow soooo!*" in a high, shrill voice.

After a while the sound of rustling and louder tinkling was heard. It seemed to be getting closer. Then Bossie appeared, breaking through the brush, her belly distended with a new calf. Her yearling heifer was following.

"Bossie, we be so glad to see you!" cried Grannie. How happy and relieved they all were at this fortunate turn of luck.

*At least we now have a source of milk*, Hugh thought. Then, wondering, he asked Innis why it was that Bossie was not taken by the raiders with the rest of John's animals. Innis replied that Bossie could not get along with his Pa's milk cows, so they let her and her yearling out at night to forage. Hugh smiled in spite of himself, as the truth of Innis' story was evident. Bossie had always been the head cow of the herd, and jealously guarded her status as chief matriarch. No doubt John's cows took exception to Bossie's right to rule, and they had to be separated.

After a full day of travel, the Henderson band reached the top of Glen Trool and the banks of the loch. It was a monumental setting. Ben Blackcraig rose majestically above the deep azure waters of Loch Trool, around which stretched a forest of trees in colorful hues of red, yellow, brown and gold. At the top of the Ben stood Bruce's Stone, commemorating King Robert the Bruce, and his long ago victory at the Battle of Glen Trool. No one was able to appreciate the beauty of the place, however, as they were spent, physically and mentally.

They bedded down in a soft meadow and slept hard until dawn broke over the top of the Ben the following morning. As usual, Hugh was the first to rise, finding frost on the ground and fog rising from the loch. Again, he was thinking ahead. First, they needed to build a rough lean-to for shelter. It needed to be concealed and protected from the elements. Hugh found a grove of evergreens near the mouth of the loch that he thought would suit his purposes.

Hugh and Andy had found an axe and a scythe in John's shed. The ax would be useful for chopping down some sturdy saplings to construct a frame for the lean-to, and they could use the scythe to cut straw, which could be woven around the sides and packed with mud to keep the wind at bay. Closely set saplings on the top of the structure would support a raft of woven straw for a decent rain resistant thatched roof. Hugh chose a near vertical rock cliff face with southern exposure to serve as a back wall. This would help block the cold north wind and allow dawn-to-dusk sunshine for warmth. Everyone was assigned a job, and by nightfall the rudimentary lean-to frame was nearing completion. Piles of straw and clay were placed nearby that could later be fashioned into daub and wattle walls.

Housing was important, but more essential was food. Hugh calculated that the best bet for getting an ample amount of meat for so many would be to figure a way to catch fish from the waters of Loch Trool. They could make fishing line by unraveling woolen cloaks, but what about hooks of sufficient strength to land a big fish? Then he remembered the chain mail vests and hoods they had saved. A few metal links could be removed, then bent and sharpened into fish hooks. As a supplement to the fish, they could hunt wild animals and search the surrounding wood and fields for wild fruits, onions, berries and roots. It wouldn't be much, but enough to get by, or so he hoped.

After a few days had passed, things were coming together at the small settlement. Ree and Joe proved adept at fishing, usually catching three or four good-sized salmon or trout and a few smaller fish per day. Andy and his first cousin, Innis, were developing into good huntsmen, teaching new skills to the dogs, Smartie and Trig.

They were able to scare up and shoot some squirrels, grouse, and other game; even an occasional red deer. Plus, of course, they had Bossie for milk, which was essential for the twins. With everyone pulling together and a little luck, the Henderson family just might be able to survive until the danger passed.

One afternoon at dusk, Andy and Joe were out in the woods searching for game. They had come over a hill and were descending into a narrow glen. Suddenly a good sized red deer stag jumped from the brush and took off, sprinting away from them. Andy had his long bow in his hand and quickly notched an arrow, took fast aim and let loose. The arrow hit the deer in the left hindquarter, burying deep. The animal stumbled but did not fall. It continued to run, hobbling on the wounded rear leg. Andy and Joe ran to the spot where the deer had been hit, found blood on some leaves and stems, picked up a trail and followed it, running as fast as they could, keeping their eyes on the trail.

"I hit it in the hind leg, but a deer can go a long way before falling," Andy gasped between breaths.

After they had followed the trail a good distance, darkness overcame them and the blood droppings could no longer be seen. It was a big deer, fat from browsing on the plentiful acorns scattering the ground at that time of year, and would feed the family several meals. The skin could be stretched, dried and cured to make a nice rug for the lean-to's cold bare ground. Andy thought the stag would probably lie down in some cover, weakened from loss of blood, and hide there during the night. They should get up at first light and resume the search, he told Joe.

"We need to find that deer. The family is short on food."

Starting just before daybreak the next morning, the two set out with Smartie, the hunting hound, and found the spot where they had left off the previous evening. There was still blood, now dry, but adequate enough to follow with Smartie's help. Soon however, the blood splatters became more sparse, and finally disappeared altogether. Andy told Joe they should split up, each going a different way in the same general direction. Andy felt sure that the deer was near, weak from the wound, and they would find it. After several minutes, Andy heard Joe shout. Andy figured Joe had found the deer and hurried in that direction.

He broke through some brush into a small clearing. There was the deer, down with an arrow sticking in its ribs just behind the front leg, the best place to hit in order to bring down a large animal. Joe was over it, his back to Andy, near the animal's head and seemed to be pushing on something. He apparently had not heard Andy's approach. Andy walked around the deer's rear and Joe looked up.

There were arrows stuck deep in each of the deer's eyes, and Joe was pulling on one of them. Andy could see the animal's prone body twitching and quivering, and hear ragged wheezing. It was not yet dead. Immediately, Andy drew his sgian dubh from his boot, shoved Joe aside, placed his knee on the animal's neck, and sliced its throat, blood gushing forth.

Then Andy turned to his younger brother, with a dark, angry look in his eyes and a low rage in his voice.

"You shot this deer three times, did you? Once in the chest, and once in each eye? Tell me, how is that possible?"

Looking down at the ground to avoid Andy's eyes, with a slight quaver in his voice, Joe tried to explain.

"No, it jumped up and I shot it in the chest. It fell and I was trying to finish it off."

Andy was now even angrier.

"Holy Hell! You stuck arrows in both eyes while it was still alive! To finish it off? You expect me to believe that? I know what you were doing—you were torturing the poor animal, just like you did with those puppies. What the hell is wrong with you!"

Joe started mumbling something, but Andy cut him off.

"You have been hunting with Paw and me for years now. You're not that dumb," Andy screamed. "Once an animal is down, you cut its throat. You know that. We've told and shown you many times—first, stop the animal's suffering, and second, drain the blood so the meat will be fit to eat."

Joe just stood there looking scared, saying nothing.

"Now you've taken sick pleasure in making an animal suffer unnecessarily, and would have ruined the meat if I hadn't come along. I didn't tell Paw about the puppies, but I'm sure as hell going to tell him about this," Andy said, his face still white with rage.

Joe held out his hands. They were trembling.

"Please don't, I beg of you," he pleaded.

Andy walked toward him.

"You'll get one more pass from Paw, but no more from me."

He clenched his fist and smashed Joe's jaw, knocking him flat on his back. Joe was out cold for a few moments. Andy splashed his face with some water from a goatskin he was carrying, and Joe slowly came to, shaking his head and moaning.

"You didn't have to hit me," he said shakily.

"I don't want to ever learn of you doing such a thing again, do you hear! If I do, you'll get more than a fist," Andy growled. "Understand?"

Joe nodded.

"Now let's get this deer cut up and take it to the house."

# 4.

# BOSSIE

## LOCH TROOL—NOVEMBER, 1546

AUTUMN had slipped across the borderlands of Southwest
Scotland and was now in full force. This was especially evident in
the hills and glens around Loch Trool. A thick fog rose from the
loch each morning, and frost frequently hugged the ground. On
this morning a wizened and stooped old woman slowly made her
way up the steep side of a wooded hill on the south flank of the
Loch, in the shadow of Ben Blackcraig. She was wrapped in a tattered woolen shawl and grasped a knobby walking stick to navigate
around the moraine boulders and rotting logs. It had rained the
previous night. The air was filled with fresh and pungent smells—
conditions perfect for the sprouting of wild mushrooms.

Wheezing, Grannie Henderson settled down on a log to catch
her breath, placed her woven vine basket on the ground, and surveyed the surroundings. The fog was beginning to lift as the sun's
rays penetrated the hardwoods, now mostly bare of leaves. Here
and there she saw them, plump white canopies atop stubby stems
poking through the moist forest floor.

*Lordy,* she thought, gazing at the many white splotches scattered about, *there be a bunch o' them—chanterelles.* She hobbled to
the first cluster, lowered herself to her knees on the wet ground,
and began scooping the fragile fungi from the soft earth with her
fingers. Soon the basket was filled and she wondered what she
could use to carry more. *Me shawl,* she thought, *the sun has broken*

*through, and me shift should be warm enough. Maybe I can loop the shawl around one shoulder and under the other to make a bag.* Using the walking stick, she pushed her creaky knees off the ground to a standing position and unwrapped the shawl.

Suddenly she heard a high-pitched whistling sound. At first she could catch only faint snatches of it, but as she stood still and listened closely, she could make out a tune. *That be Jamie,* she thought, *he said he might go out and look for berries.*

James was in an open meadow below the hill where Grannie labored, just out of sight. He had found a patch of plump wild elderberries and was merrily whistling as he picked them. Grannie's heart filled with love and pride as she listened. Of all her grandchildren, Jamie was her favorite. He was energetic, dependable and above all, eternally cheerful. *Most Scot lads,* Grannie mused, *if they sing or whistle at all, tend to stick with the sad ballads. But not Jamie— nay woeful dirges for him. His tunes always be peppy and happy.*

Grannie finished tying the shawl and bent back to her work. She would return home to the family of nine with a bountiful harvest of tender mushrooms later in the day. Hopefully Jamie was having similar success with the berries. Food for the family was already in short supply and would dwindle even further during the coming winter. Everyone would need to utilize all their skills and resources to help the family survive. This was especially true for Ann, Grannie's daughter-in-law. She was nursing the wee twins, Malcom and Helen, and she could not produce enough milk to adequately breast feed them, so they had to rely on supplemental milk from Bossie.

Grannie was worried; the cow had not turned up for milking the previous day. Grannie's many chores included feeding and milking the animal. She was sure Bossie would show up that evening, but still, a troublesome knot of anxiety gnawed at the pit of her stomach.

In the early afternoon she found another log to sit on, unwrapped some hard oatmeal biscuits and dried venison strips from a cloth in her pocket and downed the modest meal with water from a goatskin. Then she turned back to the mushrooms. The basket was long since filled and the improvised shawl bag was filling fast.

Soon she would head back with her bounty to the primitive family lean-to. As she knelt down to her work, she heard Jamie yelling her name. He sounded excited, and there was a hint of panic in his voice. Grannie called back, stretching out his name in a high-pitched tone that would carry a long way.

"Jaammiee, Jaammiee! Oovver heere."

She hesitated a moment then called out a couple more times so he could follow the sound of her voice among the trees and boulders. After awhile she saw him jogging up the hill at a quick pace. She called again and started shambling toward him, aware it would be easier for him to spot a moving figure than a still one. They met in an open spot, both breathing hard.

"Let we sit," Grannie gasped, pointing to a nearby flat rock. "Somethin' be wrong?"

Between deep breathes, Jamie explained, "Ma says the twins are real sick. Ree came and told me while I was working in the berries. They need milk. She wants us to go look for Bossie before it gets too dark."

Grannie mopped her brow with the cloth that had held the food.

"Ye hurry on to the hut. I'll git thar soon as I can. Find us somethin' warm to wear. Here, take a drink 'o water afore ye go," she said, handing him the goatskin.

Jamie took a gulp, turned and sped down the hill, dodging and jumping rocks and logs with the grace of a stag. As he neared the hut, Ree came running to meet him. She was barefoot, her long copper-red hair flying out behind her.

"Did you find Grannie?" she asked, concern evident on her face.

"Aye," answered Jamie, "she's coming but she's slow as you know. How are the twins?"

"Ma breastfed them this morning after you left to look for berries," Ree said. "She couldn't produce much, and the twins were unable to keep it down anyway. Both are pale and listless. Ma's worried about finding the cow."

"We'll go out and search as soon as Grannie gets here," Jamie said. "She wants me to gather some warmer clothes for her. We'll also need Trig. Have you seen her?"

"The dog was around this morning," Ree said. "She usually stays nearby, often sleeps in the sun beside the hut. I'll see if I can rouse her."

"Och, the basket of berries, I left it on a big rock on the trail beside the burn at the first rapids," Jamie said. "Would you mind fetching it?" Ree nodded and left to look for Trig.

Grannie finally arrived, hobbling along on her walking stick. First she went inside to check on Ann and the twins, and to transfer her load of mushrooms to a larger basket. Then she donned a woolen shift, put on some sturdy leather shoes, and wrapped her long shawl around her. She knew of a high meadow where Bossie often went to forage. It was a ways off, but she thought they should start there. When she came out, Jamie and Trig were waiting.

It was mid-afternoon when the old woman, young lad and herding dog set off on the search. They walked around the south end of Loch Trool, waded across the burn, and up onto a path along a line of hills. After a mile or so, the path turned left and ran diagonally up a steep incline. The path was stony and closely bordered by heather and bushes with bare, bristling branches. Picking her path with the walking stick, Grannie led the way. She clutched the coarse woolen shawl close to ward off a chill wind that had come up as they gained elevation. After a difficult climb, they emerged upon a high grassy meadow. It was here they hoped to find the milk cow.

Glancing back over her shoulder, she checked to be sure that Jamie was still following close behind, along with Trig. Jamie had a tattered tartan cinched around his waist with a twisted rope. His legs, head, and feet were bare, the same condition he was in when picking the berries.

"Lordy, lad," Grannie scolded, "you did'na bring shoes ner a wrap?"

"I'll be all right, Grannie, I hardly ever wear shoes till the first snowfall anyway."

Grannie just shook her head. Jamie did often seem oblivious to the weather, and it had been warmer when they started. She hoped it wouldn't get worse. The cold wind that had come up out of the north wasn't a good sign. Trig trotted along beside Jamie.

She was black with white markings, four years old, smart and nimble—a perfect herding dog in any kind of weather.

At intervals Grannie and Jamie would pause and listen. Grannie cupped a hand to her ear, trying to detect the tinkling of the cow's bell over the rustle of the wind. Jamie rotated his head from side to side listening intently. Trig sat at their heels with her ears perked, seemingly aware they were listening for something.

Bossie was a hardy Ayrshire dairy cow that could get along on sparse fodder, the thin wild grasses, leaves and other vegetative matter common to the hills and glens of the uplands of Scotland, and still produce a good amount of milk.

"Jamie, lad, do you hear the cow bell?"

"Nay, Grannie, I don't hear Bossie's bell anywhere. You don't suppose she got it pulled off somehow?"

Grannie shook her head, "I would'na think so."

"Don't worry, we'll find her soon," Jamie said, trying to sound confident.

"We must," Grannie said. "The wee ones be sick and need the milk."

The family was then living in what they hoped would be but a temporary dwelling, a crude thatched hut deep in the hills on the southwest end of Loch Trool. Nine people crowded into the small hut. Winter was coming on and food to feed the family was already scarce. The twins in particular were not thriving well despite Ann's breastfeeding and the supplementation from Bossie's milk.

Since they had no hay or oats, they allowed Bossie and her calf to go out to forage during the day, but put them up at night in a corral built of saplings. Sometimes there were leftovers for the cow to eat, such as fruit cores, vegetable rinds and grains from the ends of cut straw. Bossie almost always came back to the corral around dusk, though at times they had to send the collie out to round her up. On rare occasion, someone, usually Jamie, would have to seek her out by following the sound of her bell and encourage her back home with the help of the collie.

Although in her late 50s, Grannie was an active, hardy and cheerful woman. Stooped in posture, with long grey hair and a wrinkled face, her only significant infirmity was a lame leg, the result of a fall from a horse as a teenager. Her husband, Colin Henderson, had been killed in a fight with the English a couple of years after Hugh and Ann were married. Since then, Grannie had lived with Hugh, her eldest son, and Ann. This arrangement was a common Scottish tradition. Grannie more than earned her keep, helping Ann birth and raise all her children. She performed chores of many sorts, both inside the house and out. Hugh and Ann, along with all four of the older children, adored Grannie, and respected her immensely as the matriarch of the family. Grannie loved them all in return.

After they failed to hear Bossie's bell, Grannie instructed Jamie to circle around to the right, and she would go left to look for the cow. They had to hurry, for it would be dark soon, and she could think of no other way to promptly cover the ground where Bossie might be. Jamie started out, and Grannie called Trig to stay with her.

After a few minutes, Trig stopped and stood in a rigid pose, ears perked forward. *She hears somethin'*, Grannie thought. Cupping her hands to both ears, Grannie rotated her head in a semi-circle, listening carefully. Yes, there was something, a bawling noise, which seemed far off.

"Jamie!" Grannie yelled. "Come here; the dog hears somethin'."

Jamie came running, and, settling in beside his grandmother and the collie, strained to hear. Yes, there was a faint sound like an animal crying, it sounded like a calf in acute distress.

"Grannie," Jamie said, "I think that's Bossie's heifer. She must be stuck or caught."

"Quickly, let's head toward the sound," Grannie responded, then cautioned, "be careful and keep the dog by your side. We don't want her to get excited and bark or run off."

The three moved to the edge of the meadow and along a tree line. The bawling noise suddenly stopped. After a while, they came upon an open area. Not far beyond was a lone oak tree, and hanging from a limb was a carcass. Nearby two men worked on the carcass with knifes. It was clear that an animal was being butchered.

"Be very quiet," whispered Grannie. "Sush!"

44

Peering into the distance, Grannie warned Jamie to stay hidden, and, for sure, to keep the collie quiet.

"I'll go down and see what's going on. Even if they're up to nay good, they surely wouldn't harm an old woman."

Jamie was concerned, but figured Grannie knew best, so did not protest. Grannie walked confidently toward the two men and the hanging carcass, thumping along on her walking stick. As she got nearer, she saw something stunning. Tied to a nearby tree was Bossie. The carcass must be that of her calf. Grannie had already been seen by the two men, so there was no chance for retreat. The men abandoned their work on the carcass and looked at her with surprised expressions.

Grannie thought fast, deciding that her best course was to continue walking toward the two men. She must not, she knew, show any emotion or alarm at the fate of Bossie, or her offspring hanging from the tree limb. Nor should she give them any indication she had kinfolk nearby. In a kindly, if bewildered voice, Grannie said, *"Hullo gud sirs, can ye help a puir lost auld widow?"*

The two men did not answer, but eyed her suspiciously. They were lean, hungry-appearing men, shabbily dressed, and had an ugly look about them. Passing around a large crock bottle, each was taking an occasional gulp.

"Why are you out here, old woman?" one of them said.

Grannie rapidly surmised that the men were dangerous, common country outlaws, most likely; not too smart, but treacherous. She decided to act addled.

*"May I beseech ye fer a wee scrap to eat?"*

No pity or compassion appeared in the countenance of either man, only animosity and greed. Grannie noted that they had started a fire, which was now beginning to blaze. She was sure they planned to make a meal of the heifer. Then she spied two dirks in ornamented scabbards lying on the ground. The dirks had gilded pommels. These were military grade weapons, not something found on peasants or simple yeomen. Possibly she was mistaken in thinking they were just common men; they had either stolen the dirks or were themselves military men. *What were they doing way out here?*

"Where did you come from? Do you have a home near," the bigger and older-looking of the two demanded, his yellowed teeth leering beneath a bushy mustache.

Since Grannie, an old woman, was way out in the wilds, the bandits were curious as to where she had been, suspecting that she might have a house nearby they could plunder.

Grannie felt trapped. She could not tell them where the family hut was located without endangering everyone else. So she pushed her half-wit act even further.

*"Naw, I have nay hoose. I'm but a puir lost widow,"* she answered in the most pitiful manner she could muster, hoping they would accept her story and consider her befuddled but harmless.

The two men stepped away a few feet and consulted in a low voice. Grannie could make out, "mustn't let 'er leave." Evidently they were concerned because she had seen their faces and could later identify them, so they could not let her go.

Abruptly, the bigger man picked up the unburned stub of a large limb from the fire and slammed it into Grannie's neck. She felt a hard sickening thud, followed by something cracking in her neck and a jolt of sharp pain. The blow knocked her sprawling to the ground. She was dazed and unable to move. Then she felt another deep cutting pain in her chest. The other man had stabbed her with his dirk, plunging it deep into her body, piercing her heart. Grannie flailed, convulsed and coughed, her life draining away.

Jamie looked on in horror, petrified by what he had seen from his hiding place. It had all happened so fast. His first impulse was to run to Grannie, but he could see it was too late. All that would accomplish would be to get himself killed, and maybe the dog also. Terrified as he was, he realized that his duty now was to protect the rest of the family. *What if the two men attacked them during the night? He had to warn them.*

Jamie took off into the woods, Trig at his heels, running as fast as his cold bare feet would carry him. They were over three miles distant from the hut, but he dared not stop.

He didn't think the men had seen him, but did not want to take any chances.

# 5.
# REVENGE

HALF an hour later Jamie arrived at the hut, wheezing and heaving, so out of breath he felt his lungs would burst. He plunged through the front opening and collapsed, unable to speak.

"Jamie, child, what's wrong?" cried Ann. "Where is Mairy?"

"Dead," he sobbed. "They killed her!"

Hugh, chieftain of the Henderson clan, leapt from his seat and ran over, followed by Andy.

"What! Where?" Hugh shouted.

By this time, Jamie had calmed some and was able to haltingly get the story out. Everyone listened closely as he, with tears streaming down his face, stammered what had happened. Hugh's chest filled with fury, as did Andy's. They both knew what had to be done. Hugh grabbed his broadsword, and Andy felt for his dirk, which was nearby in a scabbard.

"Quick!" Hugh said. "We mustn't let them get away."

They both took off running at top speed. After a half-mile or so, Hugh called out, "Andy, stop!" They were gasping for air and trembling from the sudden exertion.

"We have to slow down," Hugh said. "Hurry, but not get exhausted in the process. We need to be at full strength and ready when we get close."

Emerging from the wood, they skirted left where Jamie had said he and Grannie had gone. Soon, they saw a reddish glow in the distance.

"Quietly, let's slip up on them," Hugh instructed, "tread carefully and slow."

As they crept closer, they could see two men sitting on the ground around a low-burning fire. A glowing bed of hot coals provided dim illumination. Atop the coals was a sizzling haunch of meat.

"Bossie's calf," whispered Hugh.

The two men had their backs to Hugh and Andy. Passing a jug, taking a swill now and then, they were talking and laughing.

Hugh whispered, "Let's don't kill them immediately if we can avoid it. We need to get information first. I'll take the big man; you take the other."

They had reached a distance of only a few feet when the big man looked up. Hugh's broadsword was at the ready, and he brought it crashing down on the man's head, with the flat side of the blade downward. The man had no chance to get to his feet before the ponderous blow knocked him out cold.

The second man reached for his dirk, which was lying on the ground nearby. Andy smacked the pommel of his dirk into the side of the man's head, opening up a large gash and knocking him sideways to the ground. The man looked up, surprised and addled. He did not move, just looked at Hugh and Andy incredulously.

"Where'd you come from?" he finally mumbled, wondering how they had suddenly appeared out of nowhere.

"Where be the old woman you killed?" growled Hugh in a low menacing voice.

"But how did..." the man started.

"She was my mother," Hugh said, his eyes red with a mixture of sorrow, rage and hate. The man on the ground turned white. They had killed the mother of the man who now held a broadsword over his head.

"We didn't intend to kill 'er," the man pleaded unconvincingly.

Hugh grabbed the man's arm in a vice-like grip and plunged his hand into the hot coals, holding it there sizzling for a few seconds while the man screamed like a stuck pig. Then he pulled it out and stomped the man hard in the ribs, knocking the breath from him.

"Where she be?" he growled again.

The man pointed in the direction of some trees a few yards distant, where Bossie remained tied. Hugh walked over, sword in hand, and found the crumpled, bloodied body of his mother. Enraged, he started back toward the man, both hands on the sword grip, swinging it in the air around his head. Very shortly, the man's head would be lopped off.

"Paw, wait! We haven't questioned them yet," yelled Andy.

This jerked Hugh back to his senses. He stopped with the sword hanging in mid-air over the man's head. Shaking and pale, squeezing his scorched hand between his knees, the man looked up at the suspended sword. A wet stain crept down his trousers.

"You will tell me everything," Hugh said in a calm, even voice, seething underneath. *"Everything!"*

The man remained quiet, his face twisted into an agonized grimace. He seemed in shock, staring bewilderedly at his charred hand.

Hugh modulated his voice to a more subdued tone, "I can tell from your dirks and scabbards that you are military men and from your accent that you are not from these parts. You must be English soldiers who have deserted your unit. Am I right so far?"

"Ahh … Aye," the man acknowledged through gritted teeth.

"Who be your commander, and where be his army?" Hugh demanded.

"We were with the foot soldiers of King Henry's army," the man mumbled in anguish, shaking his scorched hand in an apparent attempt to subdue the pain. The King had sent an advance contingent to invade the Scottish borderlands, the man related.

"We were marching west, intending to sweep up the Ayrshire coast. They treated us badly so we left."

"How many troops in all?" Hugh asked.

"I don't know exactly," the man said, "I have heard a large army is being levied in London."

"How many in your unit?" Hugh asked.

"About 2,000," the man answered, squeezing his burned hand between his legs.

"How many cavalry?" asked Hugh.

"Not that many," the man replied shakily, tears of pain running down his cheeks, "maybe a hundred." He clarified he wasn't sure as the cavalry was scouting out ahead for targets. His unit was between Dumfries and Wigtown when the two slipped away three days ago.

"How'd you provision?" Hugh probed.

They had several ox carts they loaded with provisions wherever they could find them, the man explained. Also, they had a herd of sheep and cattle.

"From plunder, I presume," said Hugh.

"Aye," acknowledged the man weakly.

The man said he believed his contingent was the only one headed west, amplifying that most of the army was still in England. He had heard they planned to start moving the main army up the east coast toward Edinburgh in a few weeks.

The big man Hugh had hit over the head with the side of his sword blade was beginning to moan and move. The blow had not killed him. When he came to enough to speak, Hugh addressed them both.

"You two bastards killed my mother and deserted your army. Both warrant death. Would you prefer to be executed like men and soldiers, or die slowly as the coward killers of old women, tortured and cut to bits?"

The first one, still staring down at his seared hand, understood what the torture would be like, and nodded to the other.

"Execution," he said.

Hugh hauled both men to their knees, and ordered them to sit back on their buttocks, with their knees held tightly to their chest, wrapped by their arms. They did and their heads were quickly cleaved off with two mighty blows from Hugh's broadsword.

The bodies of the two men were stripped and left where they lay. *It would make it easier for the vultures to go about their grisly work,* Hugh thought bitterly. Hugh and Andy gathered up the dirks and scabbards, and whatever else they could use. They spied two sets of chainmail vests the men had apparently taken off due to the weight. Otherwise there wasn't much. The family was short on food, so they also took the cooked haunch and the rest of the calf carcass wrapped in the cloaks of the dead men for transport back home. Hugh asked Andy to fetch Bossie and coax her along the trail as they headed back.

Andy hauled the calf carcass and haunch over one broad shoulder while Hugh toted poor Grannie's limp and broken body so they could carry out the thankless task of giving her a decent burial.

The next morning, they cleaned Grannie's body and wrapped it in the best linens they had, topped by Hugh's ceremonial chieftain cape, which they had managed to save from the attack at the bastle house. They then carried her on a litter to the top of Ben Blackcraig where she could preside over the small family shire for eternity.

It was a cold day, and a ghostly pall of fog covered the mountaintop. Barely visible in the distance, perched high on a sheer cliff, was a primeval circular henge. Ancient stone slabs had been erected there long ago, now ghostly remnants of a revered place of a long forgotten culture. A small plot of ground was found in a flat area at the base of the henge, where they dug a grave. Prayers were said and Mairy Wilson Henderson was commended to God. Later, they would erect another slab as a marker for her final resting place.

But before that, Hugh had some critical decisions to make. A ruthless English army contingent was headed straight in the direction of his oldest and closest ally.

# 6.
# Lairds of Blackcraigshire
## 20 years earlier—Ayrshire, Scotland

HUGH'S father, Colin, in his prime, was about 5'10" tall, of slender but muscular build, with broad shoulders and long arms. He was a good-looking man with a long, chiseled face, aquiline nose, and dark, shoulder length hair. Col, as he was known, was proud of his position as Laird of Blackcraigshire.

Col had thirty or so tenant farmers in the shire and treated them firmly but fairly. Some had small land holdings, and others were laborers. All were obligated to pay tenancy fees to Col as laird, either in goods or specie, due at the end of harvest season. He had four sons, Hugh, the eldest, followed by John, Richard, and Malcom. Family lore held that, centuries before, the original Henderson ancestor was a high official in the court of the Scottish King David I, living in the royal burg of Glasgow City, and had been forced to flee to the hills of Galloway during a brutal Viking invasion.

Col was one of the most respected and feared of the Scottish chieftains in the region. He had trained his four sons well in the fighting arts, and together they made a formidable force. Col had always been a cavalryman, following in the footsteps of generations of Henderson men, and had practically raised his sons on horseback. All were outfitted with the best in arms and protective gear - broadsword, dirk, crossbow, chainmail vest, padded leather hacqueton, vambrace, steel helmets, and metal shields. This type of armor was lightweight, flexible, easy to don and remove, and versatile, either mounted or on foot.

The Henderson men were trained in all aspects of warfare techniques, and were particularly adept at fighting with the broadsword—a large, double-edged, two-handed military sword, four to five feet in length, weighing five to seven pounds. It took years of hard work to develop the skill, strength and durability to become accomplished at handling the sword. The Henderson fathers had historically started training their sons as soon as they could ride a horse, first using wooden swords, then moving up to blunt edged metal ones. By their early teens, the young men had usually become skilled enough to graduate to real swords. Training was dangerous and a requisite level of skill and strength had to be demonstrated before the use of real swords was permitted. At that point, the boys were sent to the Military College in Irvine on the Ayrshire coast for at least two years of more intense instruction.

Through it all, the Hendersons remained loyal to their benefactors, the Agnews of the Barony of Rhinns, who themselves owed fealty to the great Kennedy clan of the coastal plain and eastern uplands of Ayrshire. Upon call by the Agnews, the Hendersons were required to send as many as 30 fighting men, including at least 10 well equipped cavalrymen, to do battle. In practice, the cavalrymen primarily consisted of the Laird, his brothers and their grown sons. In one battle against an English force some two years after Hugh Henderson had married Ann Wallace, the old chieftain, Col Henderson, facing overwhelming odds, was killed after being impaled on the end of an English pike.

Hugh was 20 years of age and Ann was 18 when they were married at Ayr in the autumn of 1526. Laird Col and his wife, Mairy, were in high spirits. This was the first time one of his kin had married into the eminent Wallace family, then led by clan chieftain, Darrow "Dar" Wallace, the Earl of Carluke. The marriage vows were exchanged in Ayr at St. John's Church, the most illustrious place of worship in all of Ayrshire.

The wedding had been preceded by a week of celebrations, mostly held at the Ayr market square, taken over for the occasion by the Wallace and Henderson clans, where heaps of free food, wine, and beer were offered to all. Gaiety, frivolity, and drunkenness prevailed, a veritable bacchanalia worthy of Roman times. Some said the event had been blessed by the ghost of the old Roman Emperor, Hadrian, glad that he no longer had to face the terrible Scotti on the other side of his famous wall.

The market in Ayr was where Hugh Henderson had first laid eyes on the lovely Ann Wallace. While lounging lazily around the mercat cross with some friends on a summer afternoon, a heavenly apparition suddenly appeared to him, or so it seemed, as the strikingly beautiful Ann strolled casually in Hugh's direction. She was tall, erect of posture, her proud head held high, blessed with cascading auburn hair, big hazel eyes and pouty cherry lips. She walked right up to Hugh with a quizzical look on her face.

Hugh was instantly so smitten he was struck dumb. He couldn't say a word, not even "hello." His knees felt so weak he stumbled. Smiling, evidently aware of the effect she was having on him, Ann asked sweetly for directions to the apothecary.

"Do you know where there is a druggist?"

Hugh recovered from his stupor just enough to point and mumble, "Yon way."

Ann sauntered on in the direction he had pointed, glanced back over her shoulder, smiling again, as if at a baby or a dunce, and said, "Thank you."

She then disappeared inside the apothecary. Hugh was furious with himself. How could he be so stupid? He normally possessed good enough manners and ease at expressing himself; what had happened? One of the most beautiful young women he had ever seen walked right up to him and all he could do was fall flat on his face. *He must redeem himself,* he thought, *and fast.* Others had seen her, some of his buddies; how could they not? So he asked around and soon found out her name.

"She be a Wallace, daughter o' the Earl. Her name be Ann, I think," said one.

Hugh rushed over to the apothecary, hoping she would still be there. He had to talk with her. But on what pretext? And would the daughter of Earl Darrow Wallace of Carluke even give him the time of day? Sure enough, she was there, examining some items on a shelf.

Hugh approached and, pretending to have a sick stomach, asked, "I beg your pardon, do you ken something good for a queezy stomach?"

"Are you sick?" she asked.

Hugh confessed he wasn't really sick but just wanted to talk to her. "Nay, not really, just wanting to gab with you. I be quite well, actually."

"You don't say. You be a good gabbie already," she said, laughing.

So they joked and gabbed for a good while. Hugh finally asked if she had time to walk to the market and look around. He pretended he was looking for a new pair of boots. She did, and they spent the rest of the afternoon in this manner. When it was time for her to go, Hugh asked if he could see her again. Ann explained that she was there with her brother, Duncan. Her family lived at Blackmor Castle, a ways northeast of Ayr, and she generally came to market every Wednesday during the summer season, always accompanied by her brother. She pointed him out on the other side of the square near the pillory, which didn't happen to have a resident guest at the time. Duncan had a crutch under one arm and his right leg was deformed. Hugh didn't say anything but Ann could tell from his expression that he was curious.

"Duncan had a horse fall on him when he was but a youngster. It crushed his right leg and it never healed right. Since then he has had to use a crutch, but he learned to ride anyway. He is now an excellent horseman."

Hugh's mind was racing, Ann came to the market on Wednesdays, what about next the week, maybe he could meet up with her again then. He took the chance and asked. She gave him a demure look and said: "Well, if you are going to be here anyway, I suppose we are likely to see each other."

Hugh, his heart jumping, managed to mumble, "Till then." He shakily took her warm hand and, bowing deeply to simulate what he hoped would pass for a chivalric gesture, kissed the back of it.

On the way home he felt so giddy he almost fell off his horse. His face was flushed and his heart was racing. He had to stop at every burn along the way to drink and wash his face in the cool water, just to continue his journey. Blackcraigshire was about 50 miles to the south of Ayr, usually requiring almost two days to cover on horseback. It was dark when he got home on the second day, and he went straight to bed, but could not sleep for thinking of the beautiful Ann. At times he thought he might be dreaming, that she really was an apparition, but the memory of the feel and taste of her soft hand reminded him she was real. He could not wait for the next Wednesday to roll around.

The following day his mother, Mairy, noted his dreamy state. Concerned, she asked if he was sick.

"Nay," he replied. However, when this condition persisted over the next couple of days, Mairy became more concerned. She wondered if he had a fever, and felt his forehead, which seemed unusually warm. She insisted that he lie down and keep a cool cloth across his head until the fever subsided. Hugh refused, and went about his usual chores, but seemed distracted and forgetful.

*Aha!* Mairy thought. *He's met someone. I've seen this before. In fact, I acted the same way when I first met Colin.* So she confronted Hugh: "Did you meet someone, a fair maiden, mebbe?" Hugh's scarlet blush told her all she needed to know.

Finally, it was Tuesday. Hugh was up early, getting himself ready. He wore his best breeches, boots, and shirt for the occasion, plus a plumed hat. His horse, a fine palfrey named "Nubbin," was a handsome, gaited, black gelding. Hugh rubbed him down to a shiny sheen, and the saddlery and tack was freshly cleaned and oiled. He was out to make an impression. Upon leaving he rode at a fast pace and arrived early at the market. Even the farmers and tradesmen had not yet set up their carts and tents to display their wares. Jittery and anxious, Hugh searched for Ann, but found no sign of her. *Och, she's not coming,* he worried, but then realized it was not yet noon. With great effort, he contained himself and strolled about the market in what he hoped would appear a cavalier fashion, but remained nervous.

Finally, he saw her, walking in with Duncan on his crutch, from the far end of the market.

Continuing to feign his casual air, Hugh strolled past, pretending not to see them, then abruptly stopped and said, "Ann, how good to see you again."

She smiled at him sweetly, while discreetly looking him over and thinking, *My, he does clean up rather well.* Sensing that he was the third wheel, Duncan excused himself, saying that he would meet Ann at the mercat cross when it was time to leave for home. Hugh and Ann ambled casually around the market, looking at this and that, chatting aimlessly about frivolous things until Hugh finally decided that it was now or never. *We could go for a ride,* he thought.

"Ann, 'tis such a beautiful day. Would you like to take a ride somewhere?"

"Where might you have in mind?"

"Och, I ken a beautiful place, not too far away." He then added, less truthfully, that his horse was used to riding double.

"I have a well-trained palfrey; he be good at riding double." They could buy some vittles at the market, he said, and he had a flask of wine. "Perhaps a picnic would be nice."

Ann was a little hesitant, but found the idea intriguing, so she agreed, but emphasized that she could be gone for no more than a couple of hours, three at the most.

Hugh purchased a basket from a craftsman, and the two walked about, filling it with delectable fruits, breads, and cheeses. Ann was wearing a long, loose-fitting linen shift, and had a colorful tartan shawl wrapped around her shoulders, cinched at the waist. Her auburn tresses flowed over her shoulders and down to mid-back. Hugh had not been exactly candid about his horse. The palfrey was totally unaccustomed to riding double.

Hugh lifted Ann sideways to sit behind the saddle, as was the fashion for ladies. The horse jumped sideways a little, but then settled down as Hugh placed his foot in the stirrup and started to swing into the saddle. At that, the horse startled, jumping and bucking. Hugh was thrown backward and knocked ignominiously on his butt. A terrible fear rushed to his head that he was likely to find his beautiful Ann sailing helplessly through the air. But that didn't happen. Ann grabbed the reins and threw her leg over the horse's back, pulling it to an abrupt stop.

Hugh was simply flabbergasted. In one short moment he learned two things about Ann Wallace: one, she was certainly not a demure, diffident female, and two, she had the most gorgeous long lithe legs in the world. He finally managed to take the reins and hold the horse still, while Ann, still straddled on the horse's back behind the saddle, her eyes sparkling mirthfully, assured Hugh that everything would be all right.

"Just get in the saddle. I'll scoot up so the horse will think it only has one rider, and we can continue," she said.

Hugh and Ann took the west road out of town, past the bustling quays and the towering masts of the merchant sailing ships, and angled north toward the Irish Sea. The palfrey hit its four beat gait, and the ride was fast and smooth. Hugh was much impressed with Ann's ability to handle the horse and a bit abashed about his fib that the animal was used to riding double.

"Where did you learn to handle a horse like that?" he asked.

"I've have been riding astride for some time now," she said, "whenever my Pa's not around."

As the couple rode on toward the coast, Ann wrapped her arms around Hugh's waist. He felt her warm, firm breasts pressed deliciously against his back. They found a large, spreading oak tree on the cliff top overlooking the sea. Silhouetted above the deep blue waters, the hazy green coast of Ireland shimmered in the distance.

"Bonnie isn't it," whispered Ann.

"Aye. That it be," agreed Hugh.

Little did they suspect the beautiful sight they were gazing at would become, in no more than a couple of generations, the new home for both their families. Under the spreading oak tree, they lay out their picnic, talked, and drank the wine. Ann said that she had mentioned to her father, Earl Dar Wallace, their chance meeting at the Ayr market. The Earl, she said, seemed pleased, stating he well knew and kindly regarded the Henderson family, and had had some kind of business dealings with Hugh's father, Colin, a few years back. He then regaled her with old stories of how the Hendersons were spirited fighting men, and were at the side of her great great-grandfather, William Wallace, at the battle of Stirling.

"I think you and my father would get along well," she confided, with a shy look on her face.

After the picnic, as they stood to leave, Hugh impulsively wrapped his arms around Ann's narrow waist and pulled her close to him, acutely aware of her ample breasts pressing against his chest, and the sweet, flowery smell of her hair. Ann did not resist, but folded her arms around Hugh's neck, and standing on her tip-toes, pressed her body more tightly to his. She looked up dreamily into his eyes, her face flushed, eyes moist, and planted her soft lips upon his in a lingering kiss. They stood in this embrace for a good while, pulses quickening, and hearts beating more rapidly.

But, it was time to go. The two reluctantly hefted themselves back onto the palfrey, disinclined to leave the beauty of the place, but recognizing the need to get Ann back into her brother's custody.

"Let's meet again soon," said Hugh. "I will surely wither and die without you in my arms for so long a time."

Ann, lifted again to the back of the horse, wrapped her arms around Hugh and squeezed him tight.

"There is another market day next week. Can you come?"

"Aye," said Hugh. "Wild bulls could nay stop me. I'll be there."

# 7.
# BETROTHED

ON the next market day, after gathering up orders from his family as to what goods they wanted, and with Ann never off his mind, Hugh mounted Nubbin and set out. He had taken a bath with soapstone in a nearby burn earlier that morning and donned his best garments. He even enticed his mother to braid his hair, and a long pigtail dropped down the small of his back. He again fitted his horse with his best saddlery, and this time, in addition to the usual saddlebags of provisions, including a jug of wine, he added a bedroll. Hugh had the distinct feeling that something special was in store.

Riding her own horse and without her brother along, Ann was accompanied by a bigger, older man, obviously a personal guard. Duncan was busy with other important things, she said, so her father had sent along the man-at-arms, one of the castle guards. Smiling shyly, Ann confided that she had given the guard instructions to tend to his business and let her be, so long as she was back by mid-afternoon. With some trepidation about letting his master's daughter out of his sight for such a long time, he agreed.

She had brought along a basket with which to tote the various delicacies she intended to purchase at the market. The weather was sunny, calm, and warm—a perfect autumn day. They met at the mercat cross, which stood at the edge of the cobblestoned town square, the same place they had first laid eyes on each other several weeks ago. Ann was radiant in a tailored yellow sleeveless gown over a green kirtle, and a jeweled, gold-trimmed leather belt

60

around her narrow waist. Her long, auburn hair was stylishly twisted and wrapped with green ribbons.

They embraced lightly when they met at the cross, each discreetly admiring the looks of the other. The guard excused himself, telling Ann that he was going for a meal at one of the taverns, and Ann could find him there if she needed him. After some casual chatter, Hugh suggested returning to the lovely place overlooking the Irish Sea, where they had been before. Ann agreed, on condition that Hugh let her to pick up a few morsels of food from the market that suited her fancy. His choices had not been bad, she clarified, but they could use a little "variety."

"Good idea," he responded, and accompanied her around the market as she shopped, peeking in bread baskets, examining ripe fruits, nuts, and pungent cheeses.

After shopping, they rode along side by side, engaged in flirtatious chatter and gentle joking. Ann was riding side-saddle, "to please her father," she explained. They arrived at the oak tree on the seaside under a warm sun around noon. Hugh spread his bedroll and they set about laying out the food, with Ann sitting on one side as Hugh reclined beside her, propped on an elbow. The sun lazily moved along it's ordained arc, reflecting off the sparkling blue waters, and the two talked about their lives and dreams for the future until the food was gone and a good dent had been made in the jug of wine.

Ann then suggested they take a walk to "settle our stomachs." "Barefoot would be fun," she said playfully. She pulled the hem of her ankle length gown up over her knees and kicked off her slippers. Hugh again marveled at her long, shapely calves, finely textured, creamy white skin, and fine boned, delicate feet.

"A splendid idea", he allowed, and proceeded to remove his knee-high riding boots and hose. Ann, admiring his long, muscular legs, felt her heart skip a beat.

They walked hand in hand along the high bank through lush green grass by the side of the steep drop-off into the sea. Ann remarked that she had forgotten the wonderful feel of walking barefoot over grass, how the touch of it seemed to caress the soles of the feet. She suddenly dropped Hugh's hand and twirled round and round like a small girl, her gown swirling out, revealing the length of her gorgeous legs, laughing gaily. Hugh gleefully followed her example until both of them became quite dizzy from all the twirling and flopped to the ground side by side, still laughing.

"I can't remember having so much fun!" Ann exclaimed joyously.

"Aye, but the day yet be young," said Hugh, smiling mischievously. Who knew what might happen.

Ann impulsively reached over, hugged Hugh around the neck and planted a big kiss on his cheek. Hugh cupped her face in his hands, looked deep into her sparkling hazel eyes and murmured, "That was very good, but I bet we can make it better."

He gently pulled her down to his side and kissed her full on the mouth. Ann responded in kind, wrapping her arms around his neck, parting her lips slightly and kissing him hard and urgently.

"Maybe we should move back to the bedroll. You'll get grass green on your pretty gown," Hugh whispered.

They got up and sauntered back to the bedroll, Hugh flapping it to release the leftover food bits and crumbs, smoothed it back on the soft turf, and they both happily lay back, side by side. Ann kicked her legs in the air just for the pure joy of it, letting her gown fly up and slide to mid-thigh as she crooked her knees. Hugh lay on his chest beside her and kissed her again, fully and deeply, the tip of his tongue finding hers. Hugh's heart was pounding. Ann was looking up at him through half lowered eyelids, smiling dreamily, hazel eyes soft beneath long luscious lashes.

"Ann, I must tell you something, I cannot hold it in any longer, I love you, I have since I first saw you."

Ann blushed, her cheeks turning pink. She grabbed him around the neck and kissed him hard.

"Hugh, I feel the same. I love you also—very much!"

Hugh felt a lump grow in his throat. His breathing became labored and he coughed to try and clear his chest. *Had he heard right? Ann loved him too!*

He cupped her face in his hands, kissed her forehead, eyes, cheeks and lips. They both rolled toward each other and pressed their bodies together. Ann swung her leg over his hip and tugged at his thigh with her heel. An irresistible urge began building. They both felt it.

Hugh moved his hand onto her bare legs and began caressing them, starting at her knees and moving up her thighs, first on the outside, then the inner side, finally reaching her undergarment. He slid it aside and felt the soft mound of her pubic area. Ann sighed and stiffened a little, whispering throatily.

"I'm ready, but I should tell you I've nay skill at it."

*She is a virgin,* Hugh suddenly realized. He felt a little trepidation, but Ann pulled him down to her. Whispering kind words, he reassured her she need not worry.

"I'll be careful. Just let me know if anything hurts and I'll stop."

Ann spread her long legs, Hugh untied the strings of her undergarment, letting it slip away, and pulled her gown to her waist. He gently rubbed her smooth, firm stomach, then bent down and kissed the insides of her thighs while softly stroking the edges of her crevice, which was ripening and slickening as his kisses came closer. Ann was moaning and thrusting her hips up to meet him, her legs stretched out and her head back with her eyes closed, a look of rapture upon her face. Hugh loosened his trousers, slipped them off and moved up between her legs, covering her body with his, kissing her throat, neck, and ears. Then his stiff shaft found its mark, entered, and slid through the unbroken maidenhead. Ann gasped and Hugh was afraid he had hurt her.

"Did it hurt?" he whispered.

"Nay," she said, "It feels good. Just lie still for a moment while I catch my breath."

Hugh lay still, feeling his organ inside her hot, slick crevice. Shortly, she began to move her hips up and down and in a circular fashion, slowly and gently at first, then progressively faster and more forcefully. Hugh matched her rhythm until they were both moving in unison, groaning and panting, as if running toward a glorious white light at the end of a darkened tunnel, anxiously and urgently needing to reach it. Then they did, in an explosion of pent up desire. Hugh arched his back and muffled a scream, Ann felt dizzy as a sensation of warm pressure spread inside her. They both reached climax simultaneously, bursting out together into a bright light that seemed a lot like Heaven.

Afterwards they lay exhausted but exhilarated, groggy in a euphoric stupor. After a while, Ann asked quietly.

"Did you see the beam?"

"I did," Hugh replied huskily.

"You think we just got a glimpse of heaven?" she asked.

"Aye, methinks we did."

Six weeks later, at the end of October, the great wedding occurred in Ayr, at St. John's Church - two hearts and two families joined as one. As a sort of wedding present to the couple, and to increase their standing in society, Earl Darrow Wallace officially dubbed Hugh Henderson a Knight of the Realm—they were now nobility, Sir Hugh and Lady Ann Henderson. Like most young lovers, after the marriage ceremony and festivities had concluded, they talked excitedly of the wonderful, happy lives they were sure to have together.

As they would later learn, history has a habit of confounding the fondest of dreams.

# 8.
# SPREADING THE WARNING
## GLEN TROOL, LATE 1546

THIS was the time of the "rough wooing" military campaign by England's King Henry VIII. Scotland had long been an ally of France, England's mortal enemy. Henry wanted an alliance with Scotland, to add to his domain and to crush the long-standing alliance of the French with the Scots. Determined to get it, he had proposed a marriage of infants—his young son, the future King of England, Edward VI to the infant Mary, Queen of Scots. This proposal was abruptly and curtly rejected by the Scots. So began Henry's brutal rough wooing campaign.

Henry decided he would force the Scots to reconsider by knocking them to their knees. He would not just go to war, he would decimate them. His troops would burn the farms, kill the men, rape the women, poison the water, crush the farming implements and chop down the fruit trees in their orchards. While he was at it, he would also force them to accept the Anglican form of Protestantism and halt the Calvinist Protestant Reformation in Scotland.

In response, the Scots secretly spirited Mary out of Scotland and sent her to France, where she would become betrothed to the young Dauphin, later to become King Francis II of France. To this affront, the determined and infuriated Henry sent his brother-in-law Edward Seymore, Duke of Somerset, with a vanguard force of several thousand soldiers rampaging across the Scottish borderlands, destroying everything in sight. The Scots did not succumb meekly to these provocations and a full-scale war ensued.

✦ ✦ ✦

Hugh's instinct to leave the lowland and head for the hills had been prescient, and he was right about the English. They were invading, and in the worst sort of way, pillaging, killing and burning every Scottish household they could find. Such had befallen the luckless John Henderson family.

On the way down from Ben Blackcraig after Grannie's remains were given to the earth, Hugh asked Ann, Andy and Innis to linger so he could discuss with them a strategy he had been running through his mind. The English vanguard was but the tip of the spear, he said, sent to spread fear and demoralize the Scottish populace. He expected a much larger English army would follow, probably set its sights on the Scottish capital of Edinburgh. The Scots needed to mobilize opposition quickly. First and foremost, Hugh needed to get word to Baron Andrew Agnew and Earl Dar Wallace about the English advance. It was imperative to organize a rendezvous of the clans to plan a counter strategy. But this needed to be done rapidly, and their horses had been stolen with the rest of the livestock.

Hugh had two other brothers, Richard and Malcom, who lived further away than John had, up near the Ayrshire border. It was not known what might have befallen them, but Hugh hoped they had avoided the recent incursion that brought such disaster to John and himself. He knew each brother had horses, on the backs of which riders could be speedily dispatched to the Agnews at Lochnaw and the Wallace Clan at Blackmor.

Two men would have to be sent. It would be a hazardous and risky mission. First, who knew if the two Henderson brothers still had their horses, or anything at all, including their lives, if the English had found them. Second, travel on horseback over such long distances would take several days. There was no telling what kind of trouble lone riders might run into.

Hugh reasoned that they had only three candidates for the job: himself, Andy and Innis. They were the oldest, strongest, and most experienced. Andy was the spitting image of his Paw, except for having his mother's hazel eyes and wavy brown hair. Having recently finished military training at Irvine, he was a capable and savy warrior. Innis, Hugh's nephew, was sixteen and mature for his age, strong and a good horseman. Innis had no formal education, but like Hugh's Ann, his mother had done her best to provide each child with rudimentary home-schooling. Hugh analyzed the situation aloud, emphasizing that two had to go and one had to stay to protect the family and provide muscle wherever needed.

Ann, Andy and Innis listened attentively, seemingly deep in thought, but offered no suggestions. Finally Ann said, "Aye, it has to be done."

Hugh made his decision.

"Andy, it has to be you and Innis."

All four stood quietly for a few seconds until Andy, with a somber look on his face, stated: "I will go, I'm sure Innis will also."

"Aye," said Innis.

Ann was ridden with anxiety, "It will be a very dangerous mission," she said.

"Aye, it's risky," Hugh acknowledged.

*Risky* was the mildest term Ann could think of. But she was levelheaded and rational by nature. She was the daughter of Earl Dar Wallace after all, and had seen her share of close scrapes.

"Stay away from the main roads, villages and other places of habitation," she instructed the two lads. "People will talk, and the English probably already have spies lined up. Take enough food to keep you going and don't stop to gab with *anyone!*"

Ann was worried about sending the two boys on such an endeavor—but she recognized that youth would be a valuable asset. Hugh was now approaching forty. He was well known and more likely to be recognized, either by the English, or by treacherous Scots borderers who would gladly betray him if the price was right. Andy and Innis were less likely to raise suspicions.

Hugh was also concerned.

"It's a dangerous mission but has to be undertaken. All of southern Scotland is in danger. Be very careful. Don't build any fires at night, and sleep in concealed places."

Ann added, "Innis should take his hunting hound Smartie. He might prove useful. We will keep Trig here to help us with Bossie."

Hugh always turned to Ann for counsel and advice on important decisions, especially those that could affect the family. Ann had a good head on her shoulders; she was as smart as she was beautiful. Plus she was educated, a rarity among Scotland's lowland clans. Her father, Earl Dar Wallace, had sent her to the Glasgow Cathedral School from the time she was seven until she reached seventeen years of age.

Ann started each school year in the late fall after harvest season and boarded there until early spring. The burgh of Glasgow was only some thirty miles distant from Blackmor Castle, the great Wallace clan seat. The Earl, accompanied by two or three of his best men-at-arms, always traveled with Ann to and from school.

Often Hugh would think to himself, somewhat ruefully, that he did not deserve a wife as fine as Ann. She was the great great-granddaughter of a Scottish King and could have had her pick of many Scottish noblemen, but she had chosen Hugh. This made him tremendously proud.

"Keep your eyes peeled," Hugh cautioned Andy and Innis, "There be traitors everywhere. Don't divulge anything to anyone but Baron Andrew Agnew and Earl Wallace, in person! We cannot afford the news you carry to get to loose lips."

As Hugh was issuing these instructions, Ann was thinking, *Maybe we should write a note of introduction for each and conceal it on their persons somewhere. That will prevent any mistake about who they are when they arrive.*

Ann had learned the art of making writing ink from the monks at Glasgow Cathedral, to whom the skill had been handed down over the ages. She kept a supply for use in teaching her own children to read, and later to write. The old family Bible, and the Catholic common book of prayer, had been saved from the attack at the bastle house. These Ann used to teach her children to read, spell and write.

Some proved more adept than others. Andrew, the oldest, took after his father and was much more interested in the military arts than in book learning. He had been a rather indifferent student when he was home, preferring to be outside doing something physical.

The second boy, Joe, was smart enough, but was undependable. He liked to roam, particularly out in the woods. Often Ann would find small animals in his pockets, or worse, in the house, such as field mice, shrews, turtles and sometimes small snakes. Many times the animals were dead or injured.

By contrast the third boy, Jamie, was dependable, sweet and kind. He was diligent in his studies and learned quickly.

But by far, her daughter Ree was her prize student. Intelligent and inquisitive, she loved to learn. She was so quick that Ann soon had her tutoring her own siblings. She was also beautiful. At sixteen she was already a striking figure. Tall and slender like her mother, she had long flowing reddish hair that shined like polished copper when struck by the rays of the sun, and distinct green eyes with a glint of mystery. Her skin was smooth and porcelain white. She was just beginning to blossom into a voluptuous woman. Ree was on her way to becoming a great beauty.

As a part of her teaching, Ann had prepared several large sheepskin parchments, stretched on wooden frames, that they used as writing surfaces. Ink was made from pulverized oak galls mixed with wine and reddish clay. The mixture was then boiled down to produce an ink, virtually indelible if made strong enough. For practice writing on the parchments, Ann made a more diluted version that could be scrubbed off.

Ann wrote the message for the two boys on patches of finely woven linen cloth, addressed to the respective clan chieftains, vouching for the messengers and the news they brought. These patches were sewn inside their tunics and read: *"This be son o' Hugh Henderson. Heed well."*

# 9.
# Two Horses to Ride

ANDY and Innis set off on foot at a loping gait. With occasional short breaks, they could hold this pace for hours. Smartie ran easily out in front, stopping periodically for them to catch up. Each was dressed simply and carried a hooded cape, which would make a warm cover at night, and could be draped over their head, shoulders and torso once they were on horseback. Hugh felt it was too dangerous for them to take a dirk, so each concealed a sharp sgian dubh blade under his waistband. They also carried a knapsack filled with food, mostly sun-dried salmon strips, high in protein, and oatmeal biscuits, enough to sustain them for several days.

As they hurried off, Ann and Hugh stood by, holding hands, watching bravely, but full of sorrow. *May God go with ye*, both prayed silently. Hugh had given Andy and Innis a gold coin each, to be used in case of emergency, or for the purchase of horses if it became necessary. These were large coins from the Roman era, highly sought after and valuable, since they were a known commodity, containing a high grade and standard quantity of gold. The coins had been quickly retrieved from the shitten of the two lads after being swallowed at the bastle house raid, the fibrous vegetable broth they had eaten the next morning proving to be an excellent purgative.

Inheriting the best attributes from both his parents, Andrew Henderson was a well-endowed man. He had his father's physical build—tall, muscular, broad-shouldered, with long legs; plus his mother's honey-brown, wavy hair, hazel eyes, fair complexion, and pouty, pink lips. The military school at Irvine, where his father had sent him when he was twelve, had trained him well; he was an excellent horseman and skilled with the broadsword, dirk and crossbow. Serving as his father's squire, he had seen action in several skirmishes and accompanied his father to jousting tournaments. With his mother's intelligence and his father's savvy, Andy was a natural leader.

Innis was gifted with agreeable features as well. He was not particularly tall like Andy, but more compact, with thick, muscular arms and legs. Innis regularly won the hammer throw and caber toss at the summer market fairs. In fact, he won a fair amount of money at these events. Innis was cool-headed and calculating, not afraid to take risks. Though somewhat reserved, he could be quite pugnacious if riled.

It would be hard to find two more qualified lads for the task ahead. Andy and Innis spent the better part of the first day making their way to Richard Henderson's homestead. Occasionally they stopped at a burn for a drink of water, to rest for a few moments and chew on some nourishment. But mostly, they ran with an easy stride. As dusk was fading into dark, they could see Richard's place in the distance. He had a cruck cottage and corral similar to that of his murdered brother, John. His family consisted of a wife and six children, three boys and three girls.

As they neared, the two lads slowed down. They had been running almost all day and were bone tired and drenched in sweat. They lay on their stomachs at a small burn and eagerly slurped up mouthfuls of the cold clean water.

Suddenly Innis exclaimed, "What be wrong with Smartie?"

Andy saw that the dog was not drinking, but standing still and low, his tail straight out. The tail had stopped wagging, and the dog was sniffing the air. There was a slight breeze blowing their way, and almost simultaneously they both smelled it—smoke!

"Maybe a grass fire," suggested Innis, scanning the horizon.

"No, it smells the same as the fire at the bastle house," said Andy.

"Surely not —," mumbled Innis. Their hearts sank as horrid images came flooding back. They cautiously moved forward. Shortly, through the dimming light, they could make out that the house had collapsed, burned to the ground, and was still smoldering.

*My God*, thought Andy, *the same awful fate has befallen Richard and his family as happened to Innis' family*. The two lads slowed to a plodding walk, no words passing between them, as they contemplated the gruesome scene they expected to find. With great trepidation, they approached closer to the burned-out remains. Each glanced at the other, silently acknowledging the dead, burned bodies they dreaded were there. But there was no stench of death, and no human remains were seen in the debris. They skirted the charred hulk several times, peering intently, trying to make sense of the puzzling scene.

"This be mighty queer," said Innis. "What do you suppose happened?"

"I don't know," replied Andy. "Maybe they were taken prisoner?"

Both felt a spark of hope. If they were captured, at least they might still be alive. There was little time left to look further. Night was on them and there was no moon. With no obvious explanation, the two decided to bed down for the night and further their investigation the next morning. They needed a good night's rest, for they had been running all day and were completely exhausted.

The next day dawned crisp and cold. The two arose, stretching their tired limbs, anxious to see what the daylight might reveal. Both had slept hard, wrapped in their cloaks, bedded down in some thick, dry grass a ways back from the burned-out house. They searched the debris again and raked through it with some long poles fashioned from tree limbs, just to make sure they hadn't missed anything. No dead bodies, either human or animal, were found; nor, for that matter, were there any remnants of household utensils as would usually be at a fire scene, such as metal pots and pans, pieces of furniture, bedsteads and the like.

Searching further, they noted the absence of any farm implements, tack or saddlery. Everything was gone. Foraging military troops ordinarily did not take household articles, as they would be of no value to them. *What in the world could have happened to*

*Richard and his family?* Since there were no human remains, dare they hope Richard's family had somehow survived?

Walking in ever widening circles around the burned house, they noticed hoof prints from farm animals coming out of the corral. There were prints from cows, sheep and at least one horse. Also, human footprints were mixed in here and there, some large, some smaller, some with shoes, some without. The prints were not headed south, as would be expected if the family had been captured by the English, but north, in the opposite direction. That, they realized, was toward Uncle Malcom's place near the Ayrshire border.

Excited by the prospect that Richard's family might still be alive, Andy and Innis struck out toward the home of Malcom Henderson. They followed the trail of footprints, arriving around mid-afternoon. There the two were greeted with great enthusiasm by two families, not just one. After a hearty round of endearments, hugs and backslaps, Andy and Innis sat down with their uncles, along with their wives, to discuss the recent horrid events and the mission upon which they were now engaged.

"We're anxious to hear everything," said Richard. "We be concerned. It's been a long time since we heard from either Hugh or John."

"We have news," said Andy. "It concerns recent happenings and will take some time to tell. But first, would you mind telling us what occurred at your place Uncle Richard? It may be the events are connected."

Both uncles raised their eyebrows.

"Och, you reckon that to be?" Richard exclaimed. "Well, here's what happened with us."

He explained that a man he knew had been returning on horseback from some business in Dumfries. He was nearing the small village of Dalbeattie, not far from Wigtown, where he had planned to stop over to sleep and re-provision. He smelled smoke, and could see an orange glow to the north. He rode that way and found Hugh Henderson's house had burned. Some of the roof sills were still flickering fire. He rode around the house several times to see if there was anything he could do to help, but no one was about.

He did notice hoof prints and fresh droppings from livestock starting at Hugh's barmkin fence. There were prints from many kinds of farm animals, from cows to pigs. Strangely there were also prints of many large, shoed horses mixed in. The trail of prints led south toward the road to Wigtown.

The man said he thought that perhaps Hugh was moving the family to a new place and had recruited some neighbors to help him with the livestock. But he realized it was not a good time of year to start a new household, and wondered what reason there would be to burn the house. He was alarmed that the family might have been attacked and robbed. He hurried on to Dalbeattie and asked around. No one there had seen Hugh's family nor any idea what might have happened.

After lodging in the village for the night, he arose early and proceeded back to Hugh's place, but saw no one, so continued on his journey. After a time, he came upon the home of Hugh's brother John, where he planned to stop over for a quick hello, and ask about Hugh and his family. Dismounting, he found the bashed-in front door and the macabre bloody scene inside. He knew there had a terrible attack. Walking around, he stumbled upon the mass grave and concluded the family had been killed.

Fearing the killers were still about, he had galloped off. As he rode, he noticed a cloud of dust in the distance. Riding closer, he saw a sizeable unit of English cavalry proceeding west, pushing along a herd of livestock. Surmising that the English army had been responsible for what happened to the Hugh and John Henderson families, he hurried on to warn Richard Henderson, hoping the same fate had not befallen him.

Upon hearing the man's terrible news, Richard related, he quickly packed up clothes and furnishings, loaded it all in a wagon, and took his entire family to Malcom's place. Before leaving, he drove his farm animals out of the corral and set the house on fire. A burned out place, he reasoned, would be of no interest to a foraging army, and would perhaps discourage them from pushing further north. He hoped he could return and rebuild later.

"That be the short of what happened to me," said Richard. "Now tell us what happened at John and Hugh's places. It must have been terrible!"

Innis began telling the story of how his family had all been killed by unknown invaders. Before he got far, his face reddened and he coughed, sounding strangled. Tears welled in his eyes and began to trickle down his cheeks. He stood and walked off to the side, his back to the group. Andy realized he was distraught and needed time to re-gain his composure, so took up the conversation. He shared with the uncles the details of what had happened to both families. A large group of horsemen came up to their home, Andy explained. He was on watch, saw them coming up the front road and alerted Hugh.

"Paw ran over and counted at least 20. He assumed they were reivers, clearly too many for us to fend off. We took what weapons and wraps we could quickly round up and escaped out the back way, running into the wood. The horsemen stole all our livestock and set the house on fire. We spent a cold night on the ground, and the next day made our way to Uncle John's. Paw had left our milk cow there to be bred by John's bull. We thought we would stop over for a couple of days and retrieve the cow. Ma needed milk from the cow to help feed her wee twin bairns. ....Och, I guess you've nay heard about them."

The jaws of both men and their wives visibly dropped. After a short silence, Richard, looking incredulous, said, "You mean to say Ann has birthed twins?"

"Aye," Andy answered, "we were all surprised, and, uh, pleased. Anyway, when we got to Uncle John's, around mid-morning, we found th-, well, the horrific scene the man told you about."

There followed a stunned silence as everyone contemplated the gruesome carnage. Finally Malcom said, "You ken it was the same bunch of killers that attacked your place?"

"Aye," answered Andy.

"You said Hugh took them to be reivers," observed Richard, "but the feller who stopped by said he had seen English soldiers."

"Aye, once we arrived at Uncle John's place and saw the situation there," Andy explained, "Paw became convinced the same riders had attacked both places and that they were a unit of English cavalry out foraging and spreading terror. He thinks there will be a big English army headed our way soon."

The two uncles blanched, and looked at each other with a mixture of horror, fear and fury on their faces.

"Balls o' fire!" exclaimed Richard, "If that be the case, none of us er' safe."

Looking at Innis who had returned to his seat, Malcom asked: "Mind telling us how *you* managed to escape?"

Innis, having collected himself, spoke up in a firm voice.

"Pa asked me to go out after moonrise to round up our sheep for shearing the next day. When I left, everyone else was asleep. I took the dog and found the sheep. While herding them back, I heard the pounding of horse hooves coming from around the house, followed by shouting. I could see a bunch of riders out front. It sounded like the front door was being smashed. Other men were rounding up our livestock. Then I heard a lot of screaming. I had the dog chase the sheep and they scattered. A terrible fear arose in me that something really bad was happening at the house, and I ran toward it. Then I realized I had no weapon and couldn't fight that many men, so I, I ran into the wood."

By this point Innis' bottom lip was trembling and he was barely able to get words out. Both uncles and their wives tried to console him, murmuring they knew he had done all he could. Innis coughed again, but tried to go on.

"There, there—was so many. It happened so, fa—fast, … nothing I could do."

His face was again flushed. He got up, turned abruptly and walked out the door. Andy quickly covered once more.

"Innis just needs some fresh air. As you can see, he's been shaken to the core. We found him in the wood the next day and took him with us. Luckily, we were also able to retrieve the milk cow and her heifer."

"Thank God for small miracles," said Richard.

Andy then shared with the uncles the plan Hugh had outlined for a meeting of the clans, and the importance of getting word to

Baron Agnew and Earl Wallace as quickly as possible. It was agreed that Andy would ride southwest toward the Rhinns Peninsula, where Castle Lochnaw was located, to warn the Agnews. Innis would ride to the northeast along the border of Ayrshire, then turn north toward the Wallace fortress at Blackmor.

Innis, his composure recovered, rejoined the group. Andy explained in more detail Hugh's idea for a rendezvous of the clan chieftains at Irvine to discuss the dire situation, and to plot strategy to counter the English advance. He then related the information he and Hugh had gotten from the two English deserters who had so brutally murdered Grannie. The two uncles jumped to their feet.

"What! Ma has been murdered?" This was the first they had heard of it.

"Why didn't you tell us!" Malcom shouted. "What happened?"

Andy quietly told the story.

"It was a few weeks ago, after we were settled at Loch Trool. The milk cow had been out foraging and didn't show up the previous evening. The milk was needed to help feed the twins. Grannie, along with Jamie, went out to look for her."

The two deserters had already stumbled upon the animals, he explained. They slaughtered the calf and were roasting it over some coals. The cow was tied to a tree not far away. Grannie was trying to slip around the men to rescue the cow, but they noticed and hacked her down.

"Without mercy," Andy added, a sharp edge in his voice.

Jamie ran to warn the rest of the family. Hearing his account, Hugh and he had grabbed swords and sprinted off toward the spot Jamie described. They wanted to catch the murderers before they disappeared.

"Thank God, they were still there, Andy said. "Paw and I were able to catch them by surprise and disarm them. Then Paw interrogated them, using methods he thought necessary to loosen their tongues," Andy said with a biting grimace.

It turned out, he said, the two deserters were originally with an advance unit of the English army numbering about 2,000, moving west toward Wigtown. King Henry had sent them to block any Scots army movement from the north, as well as to plunder and terrorize.

"Once we learned all we could, Paw cleaved off both their heads with his broadsword. We left them where they lay."

"Sorry, cowardly bastards," Malcom muttered, his jaw clenched and eyes red with rage.

"We recovered Grannie's body and the cow," Andy continued. "The next day, we buried Grannie atop Ben Blackmor, wrapped in Paw's chieftain cape," he added.

Richard, his face hardened and flushed with bitterness, growled in a low angry tone: "We'll gather up every able-bodied Scotsman from every clan in these parts and smash those English bastards to bits."

# 10.
# LOCHNAW CASTLE

IT would take the better part of two days for Andrew to reach Lochnaw Castle, assuming all went well, and about the same amount of time for Innis to contact Dar Wallace at Blackmor. It was assumed that Baron Agnew and Earl Wallace would ride to Irvine to participate in the council of clan chieftains and help map out strategies for the coming battles. Richard and Malcom had agreed that one of them would also attend the council. The other would stay to help protect the families. It was hoped that Hugh could get there, but that was doubtful because of the distance, and he was presently afoot. Perhaps he could find a way.

The uncles had three grown horses and a six-month-old colt. All three of the grown horses were sturdy and fit. Two of them were fine palfreys, a three-year-old bay gelding and a four-year-old sorrel mare. The third was a Clydesdale, generally used for pulling a cart or for light plowing. However, she was hardy and could be used for riding, able to traverse long distances, but at a slower pace than the speedy palfreys. She was also a mare, mother of the colt.

Andy had the farthest distance to cover and the greatest need to get there quickly, so after some discussion it was decided that he should take the gelding. This was the youngest horse, and at three years of age he was in his prime, muscular and fast, with great durability. Innis could ride the mare, older, not quite as fast and spirited as the gelding, but equally durable. The uncles would wait a couple of weeks; then one of them would proceed on to Irvine on the slower but dependable Clydesdale.

Andy took out one of the gold Roman coins and suggested that he would leave it with the uncles as security for return of the palfreys, or in payment if it became impossible for one or both of them to get back.

The uncles refused.

"We be family, nay payment be needed."

Andy persisted, but the uncles still refused. They were brothers and uncles; no payment was expected, and none would be accepted.

The two palfreys were fed a double portion of oats, saddled, and the two lads sped on their way. Andy, headed to Lochnaw Castle, kept the gelding at a steady canter, alternating occasionally by slowing to a walk. He was covering ground in good time, and the horse was holding up well. At intervals they crossed a burn with cold, rushing water. Here they would both drink, rest a bit, and Andy would allow the horse to graze on grasses and straw along the bank.

Soon, they were out of the hills and entering upon the flatter south Galloway plains. Andy began to make out some rough homesteads scattered about, and after awhile he could see the main road from Dumfries to the Rhinns Peninsula. Late afternoon was coming on as he approached the road, and he noticed a dim trail of dust on the horizon. Quickly closing the gap, he could make out horsemen, maybe a dozen or so, headed east. Andy figured he was just northwest of Wigtown, and this group of horsemen was likely an English Cavalry detachment. There was no cover nearby, and he was out in the open. If any of the cavalrymen looked his way, they could easily see him. He pulled the gelding to a sharp stop. A still figure was less likely to be seen than a moving one.

As he watched, two of the horsemen suddenly broke from the others and headed in his direction, their horses at a full gallop. Andy had no time for a fight. A lone hillock lay to his north, and he knew that a small burn ran behind it, having just ridden from that direction where he stopped for a drink. Wheeling his horse around, he took off at a dead run for the hillock. The gelding was faster than the ponderous cavalry horses and he quickly extended the gap. He rode behind the hillock and guided the horse into the stream, which was concealed on both sides by thickets.

He rode downstream, slowly and carefully so as to avoid loud splashing and muddying the water. The two English cavalrymen circled the hillock a couple of times. Failing to find him, they gave up and returned to the detachment. Andy stayed in the bed of the burn until he was sure he had eluded them and then rode back out onto the open plain. He cut through pastures and fields on his way toward Lochnaw, avoiding the main road.

As dark descended, he came upon a small grove of trees alongside another small burn, which would provide both water and good cover. Here he hobbled the gelding, bedded down and chewed some of the beef jerky strips his uncles had given him. After another day of steady riding, he should arrive at Lochnaw Castle by nightfall.

Late the next afternoon, Andy came over a rise and observed, in the distance stretching before him, a wide, blue bay with green ground rising behind it. This had to be Loch Ryan, which opened onto the Irish Sea and the Rhinns Peninsula beyond. Andy slowed the gelding to a trot and angled south, looking for the neck of the peninsula connecting it to the Scottish mainland. Beyond would be Lochnaw Castle, standing proudly on a high knoll.

After a couple of miles, he saw it, the tall outer wall, constructed of red sandstone several feet thick, encircled by a moat. A great castellated battlement and two towers guarded the castle's front approach and flanks. A marshy lake was in front, fed by two small burns flowing in from the northeast. An additional inner wall protected the main castle. A drawbridge spanned the perimeter moat and heavy doors were set at the main front gate. These fortifications, along with the geographical features, rendered the castle practically impenetrable.

Inside the outer wall was a fairly broad expanse containing a small village with thatched roof homes and shops for virtually every species of craftsmen needed to support a medieval town—blacksmith, butcher, candlemakers, laundresses, clothmakers, saddle and tack makers, et cetera. Also there was a livery barn and stables and a livestock corral. Andy got there just as the drawbridge was being pulled up for the night. Two burly winchmen stood guard and demanded that Andy identify himself and state his business.

"Who ye be lad? State your business."

"'I be Andrew Henderson, son of Hugh Henderson, Laird of Blackcraigshire. I bring an important message for Baron Agnew."

The guard lowered the drawbridge and let Andy pass into the outer courtyard. There, they asked him to dismount and inquired if he had any weapons.

"Only a sgian dubh," he said.

He was searched, and the guards took the sgian dubh. Andy explained he had been instructed that his message could be delivered only to the Baron, in person.

"Bide a wee," said the guard, and hurried off, disappearing into the inner courtyard. After several minutes, he returned.

"Follow me. We'll care for your horse." He returned the sgian dubh.

Andy was led into the smaller inner courtyard, through the massive front doors of the castle to a small parlor near the entry. Here he found Baron Andrew Agnew waiting for him.

"You be the son of Hugh Henderson?"

"Aye, my lord," said Andy.

"You sure enough look like your father," said Agnew.

Andy explained his father had sent him on an urgent mission to deliver a message for the Baron's ears only. His mother had written a note to vouch for him, he added, sewn inside his cloak.

"Your mother be Ann, daughter of Dar Wallace?"

"Aye, she be."

"Well, I'm not surprised she would jot a note. Let's see it."

Andy pulled up his cloak and loosened the patch of fabric, handing it to Agnew.

"Your mother jots well, but I cannot read it."

Appreciating the handwriting, but unable to read the note himself, Agnew sent for his daughter, seventeen-year-old Helen, who was literate. She had spent the last several years at the Glasgow Cathedral School. He had no doubt about Andy's identity, but wanted the note read to him before proceeding with serious discussions.

Momentarily, a young woman skipped into the room with a quizzical look on her face.

"Hello, Father. You wanting something?" she asked brightly.

Sir Agnew explained that the young man standing before her had brought a written note, and he wanted her to read it for him. Then, as an afterthought, he introduced her to Andy.

"This be Andrew Henderson, oldest son of Sir Hugh Henderson, Laird of Blackcraigshire—a good friend and ally."

"It's very nice to meet you, Mr. Henderson," she said, smiling.

"And you as well, m'Lady," said Andy, with a slight bow.

Helen continued gazing at Andy as the Baron asked: "What does the jottin say?"

Helen took the cloth piece in her hand and studied it for a moment, then told her father that it first said that Andy was the son of Hugh Henderson, adding "that you know already," and further, that he brought an important message that should be heeded well.

"What message would bring you all this way," asked Agnew, turning to Andy. Then, realizing that Helen was still in the room, he thanked and dismissed her. Helen left the room, glancing Andy's way with a wink and a sly smile.

Andy gave Agnew a brief synopsis of the terrible events at his family's home, and what they found the next day at his Uncle John's. He also gave him a more detailed account of all that his father had learned from the two English deserters—that a 2,000-strong English army detachment was headed his way. He also mentioned the cavalry group he had encountered on the coast road. Finally, he shared with him the plan to gather important clan chieftains at Irvine to plot strategy against the English forces. Agnew listened carefully and asked a few questions, nodding occasionally and idly twisting the strands of his long brown beard.

When Andy was finished, Agnew looked at him in a friendly manner and smiled. He was already aware of the English Army contingent at Wigtown, he said, having received messages from his brother, Gilbert Agnew, whom he had appointed to serve as sheriff in his stead. He had known of the approach of the English force for several days, he told Andy. He had not heard of the attack on Hugh Henderson's place, nor of the horrible massacre of John Henderson and most of his family. Grim-faced, he expressed to

Andy his sincere sorrow and regret at these events, and asked that his condolences be expressed to the families.

Baron Agnew then stood and paced about the room, his jaw clenched and the color in his face rising. He was in his early 50s and had commanded units of Scottish armies against the English several times. He was greatly respected and considered to be one of Scotland's more able and courageous commanders. Abruptly he stopped, looked over at Andy with a ferocious scowl on his face, shook his fist vigorously and exploded a fury of expletives.

"The bastard English be butchers. The heartless sons-of-bitches have no sympathy or conscience. They brutally massacre helpless women and wee innocent bairns."

The English filth, he swore, would soon be wiped from their country!

After a while, Agnew calmed some, and began to relate to Andy his ideas on how to defeat the English army. The advance force had stopped at Wigtown and were, at that very moment he expected, attacking the town. This was a big mistake, he said. Wigtown was well protected inside a strong wall and was stoutly defended. The relatively small English advance party would never be able to take it, but would get bogged down in the effort, losing men, supplies and strength.

More importantly, from Agnew's viewpoint, they would lose the most valuable commodity of all—time. To take Wigtown, the lead English force would have to await reinforcements or put the town under siege, both of which would take more time and bleed the English significantly. The main prize sought by the English, in Agnew's mind, was clear—Lochnaw Castle. It was the gateway to Glasgow City and the highlands, plus the entire Rhinns Peninsula.

Agnew told Andy how pleased and grateful he was that Hugh Henderson had taken the lead in spreading the news among the clan chieftains, especially to Earl Darrow Wallace. Calling for the meeting of the chieftains at Irvine at this critical time was an inspired idea. Agnew had spent a good deal of time at the Irvine military capital in his younger years, he said, first as a student and later as an instructor. He looked forward to getting back.

He was silent for a moment, still pacing the room, appearing in deep contemplation. His face beet red, he issued a dire prediction.

*"When th' main English Army at lang last gets here, we'll have ae bonnie surpreese awaitin!"*

# II.
# THE ROAD TO BLACKMOR

MEANWHILE, Innis was making good time on the mare. With the hunting hound Smartie loping at his side, he was skirting the west edge of the upland hills of Ayrshire. After reaching the headwaters of the River Clyde, he would turn left and make his way to the great fortress castle at Blackmor, seat of the Wallace Clan and home of the high chieftain, Earl Darrow Wallace. The higher hills to his right were mostly wooded, and in late November, the limbs were bare. Fallen leaves blew across his path in occasional sharp gusts.

At intervals small burns gushed out from narrow glens. Most were shallow enough to ride through, but others had to be searched for crossings, adding to Innis's travel time. The land to his left was mostly bare of forest, interspersed with pastures and fields, populated with small, scattered herds of grazing sheep and cattle, random cottages and squalid-looking peasant hovels. Virtually every home had a roughly cultivated garden, now picked clean and lying barren.

Early winter weather had arrived with force in the higher elevations. Cold blustery winds picked up out of the north as the daylight faded in the milky western sky. A faint, striated purple and orange glow was retreating to the far horizon. It would be a long, frigid, bone-chilling night.

As the weak light faded, Innis slowed the mare so she could better avoid the stony obstacles along the dim path. Soon they reached a sizeable burn that discharged a strong flow of cold water. Thickets of willows and reeds lined the banks. Innis brought the mare to a stop, dismounted, removed his shoes, and led the horse and dog into the rushing stream, where they drank their fill. Knowing the night would be windy and cold, Innis had been scanning the hills for some kind of shelter. Off to his right, he had noticed a clump of large mossy boulders surrounded by short thick bushes and stunted trees. This would provide good cover and shelter from the wind. Leaving the stream, he backtracked and turned up the slope toward the boulders.

Hobbling the mare so she could forage but not wander off too far, he and Smartie scouted the boulder field. They found a large, south-facing rocky outcropping with an overhang. It was surrounded by a roundish perimeter of several smaller boulders and bushes. *"A perfect place,"* thought Innis. He piled up a circle of stones, gathered some dry grass and twigs, took out his flint and built a small fire in front of the overhang. This provided a cozy place protected from the wind for him and the dog. The perimeter proved large enough to hold and conceal the mare as well. All three spent a comfortable night.

Innis awoke the next morning, finding the ground covered with thick frost. The eastern sun's weak rays struggled to pierce a cold, overcast sky. His supply of beef jerky was almost gone. He and Smartie ate the few remaining strips for breakfast. They needed to get going, as it was a full day's ride to Blackmor Castle.

Innis mounted the mare, pulling his hood and woolen cloak more closely about his body, and cinched his trousers tightly with a leather belt. He tucked his sgian dubh beneath the belt, and the small party got underway, stopping at the burn once again to drink and refill his goatskin with water. Innis had no idea when they would find water again after the right turn he expected to soon reach, following a wagon trace northward toward Blackmor. There would be water at the Clyde, but that was at least a half-day's ride away.

Leading the mare through the reed and willow thicket into the cold stream, Innis found that thin frosty ice covered the stems and leaves of the bushes that bent over the rushing water. Truly, it had been a cold night. The mare lowered her head and began drinking.

Smartie lapped up his share, and Innis drank the chilly liquid from cupped hands. After all had drunk, Innis led the mare to the far bank, planning to remount there and resume the ride.

Suddenly, two men stepped in front, blocking their way. Smartie growled, and the mare startled, but did not break away. Innis put his hand on the dog's neck to calm him. The two men were scruffy, dirty, and rough looking, as though they had been out of doors and on foot for a long time. Innis sensed immediately that they were dangerous men.

One was older, with long, scraggly, grayish hair hanging from under his hood, matted with mud and straw. He stood a few feet to Innis's right, near the mare's head, holding a long wooden staff. The other was younger and bigger, with a heavy black beard and dark eyes that squinted malignantly beneath bushy eyebrows. Innis noticed that he had a dirk and scabbard cinched about his dirty tartan. He stood a few feet to Innis's left, resting his hand on the pommel of the dirk.

"What fer be a youthie like ye way out here with such a fine mare?" asked the older man.

"On my way to Blackmor Castle to visit my uncle, Earl Darrow Wallace," replied Innis, trying to keep his voice level. "How far be it to the Clyde?"

By mentioning he was on his way to see his uncle, Innis hoped the Wallace name might give them pause.

"You be a long way off," the younger man said.

"Mebbe we should give ye some help," rejoined the older one, with a leering grin.

Innis was well aware that these men were intent on stealing his horse and likely doing harm to him as well. He had already devised a plan. Turning to his right, the mare concealing the front of his body, he carefully slipped his hand inside his cloak. Gripping the sgian dubh, he silently pulled it from his belt. When the older man stepped forward and grabbed the bridle reins, Innis jabbed the blade into the mare's shoulder, causing her to jump forward and bolt, knocking the older man to the ground and trampling over him for good measure.

At the same instant, Innis charged the younger man with Smartie at his side, covering the few feet before the man could unsheathe his dirk. Innis lowered his shoulder and hit the man in the chest full force, slamming him onto the ground and landing on top of him. Smartie got a firm grip on the man's right arm, biting deeply, snarling and ripping. Innis drove his blade deep into the man's neck, severing his trachea and carotid artery. The man struggled, wheezing and gasping, as a stream of blood squirted from the deep wound. Soon, the struggling stopped and he was still.

As Innis rolled off the man and began getting to his feet, he felt a heavy blow to the back of his head, accompanied by sharp pain and then sudden darkness. The older man had recovered his footing and hit him over the head with the stout wooden staff. Momentarily, he did not know exactly how long, he came to, still groggy, to the sound of furious yelling, growling and yelping.

Smartie had the older man by the leg, biting and growling, staunchly hanging on while the man flayed away with the staff, yelling and cursing, pounding the dog in the head.

Innis scrambled to his feet and charged the man, tackling him and wresting the staff from his hands. Then he got to his feet and beat the man in the head until he stopped moving. Satisfied that both men lay dead, Innis hurried over to Smartie, who had collapsed on the ground and was whimpering pitifully, his legs jerking. He cradled the dog's head, discovering that he was bleeding from the mouth, nose and ears, and panting short shallow breaths. Innis knew the dog was done for. He lifted Smartie in his arms and held him for a long while, looking into his big, brown eyes until the dog was still and the eyes became fixed.

"You be a good dog, Smartie, the best ever," Innis said, tears welling in his eyes.

He found a soft spot of ground near the edge of the stream, broke the staff in half creating two sharp-edged ends, and dug out a hole for a grave. Gingerly and reverently, he lifted Smartie's limp body in, covered him with soil and a layer of large rocks. He dragged the bodies of the two would-be robbers downstream a ways, and secreted them in a patch of willow bushes, certain that they would soon make a grisly feast for the vultures.

Setting off to find the mare, Innis reflected in amazement over what had just happened. He was heartsick over losing Smartie, realizing the loyal dog had saved his life. He was also astonished that he had been able to stave off two grown men who were armed and determined.

*It was more than luck,* he thought. *God was on my side; there must be a reason.*

He found the mare, standing in a small clearing eating dried grass, seemingly unconcerned. She had not gone far. The shoulder wound was still oozing, but did not appear to be particularly serious. Innis mounted up and hurried on. He would have to make good time to reach Blackmor by nightfall.

# 12.
# Winter Takes Its Toll

THE cold front that enveloped Innis on the path to Blackmor had blown in with much force and ferocity upon the small glen at the head of Loch Trool. Hugh Henderson and his second son Joe had managed to construct a stone hearth with a wattle and daub chimney at the rear of the hut, which made cooking easier and provided the drafty structure with a modicum of warmth. However, the cold soon completely froze over the surface of the loch, which required that Ree break holes in the ice to fish for trout, until then their principal source of meat. The fish had become sluggish and uninterested in whatever morsel Ree attached to the end of her hook. The catch soon dropped to zero. Before long, the dried trout strips the family had managed to save up earlier had all been consumed.

To make things worse, what little game there was in the woods had taken cover to survive the cold, and since Smartie had left with Innis, there was not much chance of scaring any up. About the only favorable development was that Bossie had given birth to her new calf and milk production was good. There were many mouths to feed at the little settlement: a cow with calf, a border collie, and seven humans, two of whom were suckling twins. For now there was barely enough to go around. Before long, unless conditions improved, they would be going hungry.

Ann was getting progressively more thin, pale and weak, going without enough food herself, plus trying to breastfeed the twins. Ree, Joe, Jamie and Hugh were also suffering. Something had to be done. Hugh reviewed the remaining options, trying to prioritize.

He came up with a plan—not good, but something. The cold winter weather would last for at least two more months. Meat was the most essential food and they were out. He decided he might have to sacrifice the animals. Bossie's calf would have to go first but its meat would last only a few days. They would need to continue milking Bossie, to keep her from going dry after the loss of her calf. Essentially, her milk would then become the family's only source of protein. But it would only go so far. A last option for additional protein would be the collie, but she was already rail thin and would yield very little meat. *All of these were dreadful choices,* Hugh thought, *but necessity was an unyielding tyrant.*

If they consumed every morsel of meat, bone, and skin, they might get enough protein to see them through for the last couple of months till warmer weather. Perhaps they could gather bark and roots to boil with the sparse supply of meat to stretch the nutrition further. If they were lucky, maybe Hugh and Joe could manage to kill some game to help out, but doubtless things would be very hard for a long spell.

As the days rolled by, the cold did not let up, and the swirling wind continuously sucked the warmth from the drafty hut. The twins developed a raspy cough that settled in their fragile lungs. They were hacking and wheezing, and soon developed a fever, becoming increasingly lethargic. Ann worried herself sick, constantly moaning to Hugh that he should have never brought them to this place. Hugh's rational mind told him he had made the best decision under the circumstances, but emotionally he was ridden with guilt. Joe and Jamie tried to cheer him up, but Hugh was sinking into a deep, unyielding depression.

During the cold nights, Ann and the twins huddled together as close to the hearth as they could without risk that their clothing might catch fire. Hugh had rigged a ring of large stones around the hearth to deflect sparks and provide radiant heat. The rest of the family bedded down in a semicircle behind the ring of stones. Hugh was on the outside, rising before daybreak to add green branches to the fire, that would burn more slowly, adding to the bed of coals. Also he would slice a little meat from the calf's dwindling smoked carcass that was hanging from a nearby tree to prevent predation by wild animals. So far it was the only animal sacrificed. The meat would then be put in the cook pot at the hearth, along with whatever digestible vegetative matter had been found, some water poured in, and the fire stoked.

One morning not long after the twins had gotten so sick, Hugh arose to his chores, careful not to waken his still sleeping family. Once he got the pot filled and the fire going, he reached over and gently shook Ann's shoulder. She stirred, mumbling incoherently, and Hugh went back outside to gather more firewood. Ann instinctively reached for the twins, who were wrapped and lying between her and the stones. Neither of them moved. Ann sat up and lifted the first one, the boy, Malcom. He was stiff and unresponsive. She then frantically reached for the small girl, Helen. She was also cold and stiff. Slowly coming to the realization that both twins had died during the night, Ann moaned, softly at first, then started wailing loudly, finally screaming like a mortally wounded she-wolf. Hugh dropped his load of limbs and rushed inside.

*"The twins!"* Ann screeched, flailing her arms. *"The twins!"*

Hugh knew immediately. Though denied by his fragile psyche, his mind knew. He reached and checked for vital signs, finding what he expected. They had been dead for several hours. Hugh put his arm around Ann's shoulders, but she cast him off.

"Ann, I be so sorry," he whispered.

"Do not touch me," she scolded, "ever again."

By this time, Ree, Joe and Jamie were up, standing back with ashen faces, not sure what to do or say. Hugh stumbled outside, heaving deep sobs, and collapsed to his knees in grief. Finally, Jamie approached.

"Pa, it's not your fault, if not for you we would *all* be dead."

Ann was curled into a fetal position in front of the hearth as Hugh gathered the thin, stiff bodies of the twins and began the long trek to the top of Ben Blackcraig to bury them beside their grandmother. Ann was silent and refused to move when Hugh asked her to go. He realized that there was nothing more he could do to encourage her, so he led the rest of his small, bereaved family up to the higher ground for the sad, final rites. Ann was pale, frail, her skin sallow, all the light gone from her eyes. *My beautiful, vivacious, intelligent Ann,* Hugh thought, his memories returning momentarily to the striking raven-haired beauty he had married, seemingly so long ago. *She's still beautiful,* he thought painfully, *but hovering very near death's door, dying of grief.*

The top of the mountain was shrouded in a ghostly fog, the ancient stone henge barely visible, shimmering like an apparition. One small grave was dug, and the tiny twins were placed in it side by side. After the somber burial, the small band made their way back down through the fog from the top of the mountain, and Hugh Henderson, for the first time in his life, felt that he could not possibly go on.

The rest of the day went by slowly, as in a dream, where forward progress cannot be made regardless of effort. Ann remained by the hearth, her head in her hands, refusing to eat or talk. Hugh and Joe gathered more firewood and reset some game traps. Ree and Jamie stayed inside and did what little they could to comfort their mother. Finally, the night came. No one felt up to preparing food for a meal. They were all dazed, still, and stunned.

Suddenly, after everyone else had finally dozed off, and Hugh was nodding, he heard the clattering, clopping sound of horse hooves and the jinging of bridle chain just outside the hut. *Not just one horse,* Hugh realized, *but several.* Instinctively, Hugh jumped up, grabbed his broadsword and raced outside into the dark, his sword held high, ready to strike. Then he heard a familiar voice ring out.

"Paw, it's me, I'm home!"

Hugh lowered his blade. It was his eldest son, Andy, astride one horse and leading another. In the background, Hugh could make out another person, a big man wrapped in a cloak with a broadsword at his side, also astride a horse. Before he could figure out what was happening, Andy was on the ground, hugging his father and slapping his back.

"Paw, we've brought horses."

Hugh fell to his knees in relief.

"Thank God you've returned. I've been so worried."

Andy knelt beside his father and quickly gave him a short summary.

"Baron Agnew sent us." Pointing at the big man on the third horse, he explained, "This is Harold Douglas, one of Agnew's best fighting men. I told the Baron everything about the English army, and what they have done. The extra horse is for you. The clans are meeting in Irvine. Agnew wants you there."

Hugh stood. Andy had been gone just two weeks, but the family's circumstances had deteriorated badly in that short time. Hugh explained the dire situation to Andy—the death of the twins, the shortage of food, the freezing weather and the state Ann was now in. Andy listened, shaking his head and grimacing. They both sank to a sitting position on the ground and remained silent for a long time.

Finally Andy said: "I don't see how we can take the family from this place."

He then gave Hugh a startling report. The English had ransacked the whole countryside, killing people, pillaging and stealing scores of livestock. Many homes had been put to the torch. To make matters worse, a deadly illness was sweeping the country. Some said it was a return of the plague. Many had been sickened, and quite a few had already died.

Hugh sat in silence, thinking. He agreed with Andy that, as hard as things had become, it was better to stay where they were than to move the family. Where would they go anyway? There was too much danger about, and where else could they find shelter or food. Andy continued briefing Hugh on the military situation. An English advance guard of about 2,000 soldiers was stalled at Wigtown. They had been unable to break the town's defenses and were content to stage a siege and await reinforcements.

Agnew had heard that another 3,000 or so English troops had left Dumfries and were on their way to Wigtown. It would take a week or more for an army of that size to travel such a distance, Agnew surmised. It was unknown whether the reinforcements would enable the English to finally take Wigtown, or if they would be content to continue the siege, or perhaps bypass the town and proceed on toward Lochnaw Castle. In any event, it was imperative that the clan chieftains from Galloway, and the north across Ayrshire, promptly make their way to Irvine to plan strategy for stopping the English. Agnew needed Hugh to be there. He wanted him to command a sizeable unit of cavalry.

Hugh pondered some more. He knew that Andy wanted to go to Irvine, and clearly expected to do so. Hugh badly needed him to act as his squire. But how could the family afford for him *and* Andy to both leave for what would surely be an extended period?

Finally Hugh made a decision.

"We cannot both go. I'm the one that owes fealty to Agnew, not you. I have nay choice, I *must* go, you are not required."

Andy knew Hugh had no choice, but he wanted to be by his father's side anyway, required or not. Andy protested stoutly, as Hugh knew he would. He desperately wanted to join the coming fight. Hugh told him gently that his duty was to become the man of the house while Hugh was gone, and emphasized that the family must not be put in jeopardy. Ann was in a bad way and could not do much. Joe was only 14, still a boy, and Jamie had just turned 12. Hugh had to depend upon his oldest son, Andy, and his daughter, Ree. He had every confidence that they would hold things together.

"Also you'll have the extra horse Agnew sent—for transportation, or in case of some emergency," Hugh said. Then, blanching, he added quietly, "or should you need it for food."

Andy finally relented. His father was right, of course, as he always was.

"I understand, Paw. You be right about the family."

Early the next morning, Hugh left with Agnew's man, Harold Douglas, riding south toward Irvine and whatever fate might be in store.

# 13.
# EARL DAR WALLACE

INNIS arrived at the banks of the Clyde as the weak daylight was fading. He and the mare drank, then crossed the river and headed north. Blackmor lay some five miles in the distance atop a hill overlooking the confluence of the Clyde with the River Nethan. As they neared, the dark castle loomed large, with two rectangular rings of thick surrounding walls, and round bartizan towers at the corners.

The castle keep was expansive, containing some 3,000 square feet, and was a full two stories high. The main entry road followed the south bank of the Clyde, then turned left through two guard towers with a heavy iron gate in between. There it crossed a deep moat to the inner wall, where there were two more guard bastions and a drawbridge. Steep slopes protected the castle on the north, west and south. It was virtually impenetrable from any direction.

Along the road a good-sized village covered the surrounding land for several miles beyond the outer wall. Most of the village buildings were of wattle and daub construction with dirt floors and thatched roofs. It was still very cold, and few people were out as Innis rode by, but smoke rose from almost every chimney, signaling a warming fire inside.

Innis was challenged at the first set of guard towers and told to dismount.

Upon seeing that he was but a young lad, the guards relaxed and asked him his business. Innis told them that he had a personal message from Laird Hugh Henderson of Blackcraigshire to deliver to Earl Wallace. The guards allowed him to remount and ride to the drawbridge, which was some 300 feet away. Behind the tall inner wall and the deep moat, he got a close-up view of the castle towering darkly ahead. Innis stated his business again to the guards at the drawbridge, and they sent one of their members to the castle, which was protected by another heavy iron gate. After awhile he returned and motioned for Innis to follow. Once inside, Innis was led down a huge hallway into a massive dining room where Earl Darrow Wallace was having dinner. He was seated alone at the head of a long, oaken table.

Following his custom, he was dining first, before allowing castle staff, courtiers and other attendants to have their meals.

Innis bowed deeply as he was announced to Wallace, who was holding a large, broiled leg of lamb in his hand and munching on a mouthful. Wallace was a big man in his mid-60s, with an expansive waistline and bristling, reddish-grey whiskers, speckled with bits of loose food. He eyed Innis carefully, swallowed, burped and finally asked what exactly had brought the son of Hugh Henderson all this way for a visit.

Actually, Innis admitted, rather sheepishly, Laird Henderson was his uncle. His own father, Hugh's brother John, had been killed recently by a foraging English patrol. At that, Wallace raised his eyebrows and asked if the message Innis was bringing had anything to do with the English incursion.

"Aye, and more," Innis said.

"Let me hear it then," Wallace thundered.

Innis forgot all about the written message sewn inside his tunic, but Wallace clearly accepted who he was and seemed unconcerned. Innis told Wallace the whole story about the fate of his family, his luck in escaping and being rescued by Hugh, the murder of Granny and Hugh's suspicion that an English invasion was underway. Wallace said nothing, just continued to chew on his food, all the while gazing at Innis with a contemplative look, sometimes using both hands to stuff food into his mouth. Alternately he swilled wine from a big crock jug and ran fleshy fingers through his whiskers.

Finally, the Earl asked, "Hugh's wife, Ann, you ken she be my daughter?"

"Aye, of course," replied Innis.

"She made it through all of this without harm?"

"Aye," Innis replied, "and the rest of Hugh's family did as well. They all escaped before the bastle house was burned."

"Good! I'm very glad to hear it," said Wallace, "but most distressed to hear about Mairy and *your* family."

"Thank you, Sire," Innis mumbled, "You're very kind."

Glowering fearsomely as he slammed his huge fist on the table, the Earl roared, "Kind? Damnation lad, I plan do everything I can to see that the bastard English pay a heavy price for these abominable killings."

Innis said quietly, "I pray so."

Wallace continued, "You say Hugh's house was burned? Where they be living now?"

"Uncle Hugh thought we should get as far away from the English as possible. He led us up to Loch Trool, and we built a thatched hut."

"Good thinking," said Wallace. "You have come quite a distance, lad. Hugh must be considerably worried." Innis did not answer, as it didn't seem a question.

Wallace continued, with a puzzled expression, "Did you see any signs of trouble on your ride up?"

Innis told him about his encounter with the two ruffians who tried to steal his horse. Wallace looked surprised.

"How old you be, lad?"

"Sixteen, but my birthday is coming up in a couple of months," replied Innis.

"Thunner o' Thor. You killt 'em *both!*" Wallace exclaimed incredulously, slapping his open palm on the tabletop with a loud splat, rattling the tableware.

"My dog was a big help," said Innis, looking embarrassed.

Wallace just looked at him in amazement, and finally said that he would be glad to take a small contingent of armed men and ride to Irvine for the chieftain's council. Innis would accompany them, he declared. Undoubtedly they would meet up with Hugh Henderson when they got there.

# 14.
# PERILOUS POLITICS
## SOUTHWEST SCOTLAND, SPRING 1547

A FEW days after Hugh's departure for Irvine, a warm, southerly breeze came up from the Irish Sea, breaking the icy grip of the cold weather that had enveloped the bedraggled crew at the head of Glen Trool. The arrival of the spring of 1547 was a welcome relief. The icy surface retreated from the loch, and trout suddenly became active, snapping up almost anything that appeared the least bit tasty. Ree broke out her hooks and line, found some beetles and worms under rocks around the loch, and started catching trout by the dozens. Jamie joined in, and before long they had more fish than they knew what to do with. Andy put up wooden racks, and soon it was filled with filleted trout drying in the sun.

Ann began to improve, cheered by the return of her eldest son, Andy. She began eating more, helped out around the small hut and recovered some of her lost vigor. They all knew that the warm spell was but an interlude, and they would have to bear a few more cold snaps, but they felt the worst was over.

At Irvine, the clan chieftains began to arrive, among them Baron Andrew Agnew; the Henderson brothers, Hugh and Richard; Earl Darrow Wallace; Earl Gilbert Kennedy of the feared Kennedy Clan; Alpin Fergusson, chieftain of the Clan Fergusson; and James Hamilton, the Second Earl of Arran and Regent for the young Mary, Queen of Scots. Mary's father, King James V, had died when she was only six days old. Arran, as he was generally called, was a skilled military man, trained at Irvine in his early years, and hardened by leading Scottish troops into many battles.

The Council of Chieftains, including many other powerful earls, barons, knights and lords, met in the great hall of the Military Capital Building, a giant, pre-Gothic stone fortress dating back to the times of King David I, who had commissioned it in the 10th century AD. The hall was massive, with giant hearths on each end containing blazing fires. It had only slits for windows, and the inside was smoky and dim. Large candelabras hung from the ceiling holding lighted candles that, even with the hearth fires, provided meager illumination.

Arran and the highest ranked men, including Earl Wallace, Earl Kennedy and Baron Agnew, sat on big chairs lined up on a platform at one end of the hall. The others were seated on benches on both sides of a long table and around the walls. As a knight, and laird of a council shire, Hugh was among these men.

A lot of shouting and wrangling occurred at the beginning, but after a couple of days, a rough order developed and a plan was hammered out. Arran was unanimously selected to be the leader of the whole Scots army. He had the authority to appoint the leaders of the various battle groups. Considering what was then known of the location and movement of the English army, it appeared that most of their troops were still in England.

After two weeks, the council was over, with virtual unanimity of tactics and purpose being achieved among the various lords and chieftains, a rarity in medieval Scotland. They all hurried back to their respective shires to levy every able-bodied man available. They were to gather later at Girvan, a small village on the coast just north of the Rhinns Peninsula, with whatever fighting men they had been able to muster, as quickly as possible.

Arran told them he hoped to have the Scots army assembled and trained in a month. His aim was to get the army ready to intercept the English before they reached Edinburgh. Some lords raised a few dozen men; others came up with hundreds, and a few managed to round up numbers approaching a thousand. All of the knights owned horses, were well equipped themselves and were attended by personal squires. Some also had a retinue of men-at-arms who regularly accompanied them.

Most of the conscripted men, however, had to provide their own equipment, horses and arms, or walk in with whatever they could scrounge up. Arran brought extra provisions and fighting equipment for use by the infantry, such as loads of pikes, halberds and longbows; also, armored vests and helmets, crossbows and extra horses for the cavalry. So did a few of the other more notable and wealthy earls such as Wallace and Kennedy. Under the feudal system, men owed their first loyalty to their clan chieftain, who in turn owed his to the duke, earl, baron or knight under whom he held his vassalage, and ultimately, all owed allegiance to the Scottish crown, here represented by Regent Arran.

The Scottish army assembled at Girvan was a motley group, poorly armed and trained, but united in one very important respect—their lands were being invaded by the hated English. The English army was systematically torching Scots homes along the border, stealing their livestock and murdering their families. In all, an initial 10,000 Scots assembled at Girvan, and more would join them as they made their way to the Rhinns Peninsula, and later, across the coast road east toward Edinburgh.

Andrew Agnew called for Hugh Henderson to join him as soon as he arrived at the council meeting. He advised Hugh that he was in the process of rounding up 500 or so ground forces, and as many cavalry as he could, at Lochnaw Castle. All would gather within the castle walls. They would be well equipped, reasonably well trained, brave and loyal, he said. He was sure that an attack by the English forces was not far off, perhaps imminent—certain to happen before Arran could get the main body of the Scottish army assembled, organized and underway.

Agnew wanted Hugh to leave immediately for Lochnaw Castle so he could lead the cavalry. He had selected other experienced men to command the longbowmen and the pikemen. Agnew had to stay over at Girvan for a few more weeks, as Arran had assigned him to command a large battalion of pikemen, and he had to organize these troops and give them some rudimentary training.

Hugh departed for Lochnaw the next day, accompanied by his brother, Richard, along with Innis as his squire and six of the Wallace men-at-arms. Baron Agnew saw him off and bade him farewell in a most sincere and earnest tone.

"Hugh, my loyal friend, you have ridden by my side in many battles, and never let me down. I trust you more than the Almighty himself. Godspeed."

# 15.
# Preparing for the Fight

THE Henderson brothers, Hugh and Richard, along with their nephew, Innis Henderson, and the Wallace men-at-arms, arrived at Lochnaw Castle three days before the English army got there. First, Hugh and Richard conferred with the two captains Baron Agnew had mentioned would be in charge of the ground forces. They found that the two were impressive men-at-arms, trained at Irvine, and had been in several battles. Hugh was confident in their abilities. Agnew had about twenty other well-trained men-at-arms available who were long-time castle guards and personal aides. Hugh was certain that these men were excellent, versatile fighters. The rest of the forces were conscripts of varying degrees of ability and readiness. Some were well armed and looked competent, while others appeared to have just been pulled from the fields.

Hugh asked the captain of the longbowmen about the skill and training of his archers. What he learned was not comforting.

"They are all brave men, Sire," said the captain, "but as you can appreciate, some are more competent than others. We have a fair-sized armory with a good supply of bows and arrows, and I'll make sure all of them have adequate equipment."

"What about training?" asked Hugh.

The captain explained that the same held true on that score as well—some were well trained while others had hardly any training at all.

"Use the time we have to get them trained as best you can," Hugh ordered, "familiar with formations, rotation firing, the ramparts, and have them practice shooting volleys at various ranges. Also instruct them in the use of flaming arrows. The archers will be one of our most important weapons." The captain nodded.

Hugh then addressed the other captain who commanded the pike squares, "Same with your pikers, captain. Get them ready. We are sure to have some close-in fighting. The pikemen will have to blunt cavalry and massed English ground troops."

Hugh assigned three of the Wallace fighters to the longbow battalion, and the other three to the pikemen. He informed each captain that they were experienced, capable soldiers.

"I suggest you use them in your training exercises and in the front lines when the battle comes. I can assure you Earl Darrow Wallace keeps his men-at-arms well trained. They will be valuable assets."

Then, as an afterthought, Hugh added, "I'm told King Henry has ordered red uniforms for all his soldiers. I guess he believes that will strike fear in the hearts of his enemies, but I think it will make our job less difficult."

He grinned, "They will be easier to spot in the heat of battle."

Hugh explained that he wanted all of the Scots soldiers to wear their everyday shirts over their armor. Most had shirts woven from light colored material—grey or brown, "depending on how dirty they are," he said. That would further distinguish the castle forces from the English. He emphasized that they would be badly out-numbered and he didn't want his men killed or wounded because of mistaken identity.

Finally Hugh asked that his 100 or so cavalrymen be assembled for inspection.

"Have them armed with whatever they have, on their horses, and assembled in the field just outside the front gate in one hour," he commanded.

Hugh, Richard and Innis sat astride their horses facing the shabby cavalry. Hugh was glad that Richard had been the one to ride to Irvine for the chieftains' council instead of his younger brother, Malcom. Richard was a lot like his brother John; he was a brave, skilled Scots horseman, trained at Irvine—a man-at-arms who would someday, Hugh believed, become a knight in his own right.

Most importantly in Hugh's mind, Richard was a smart, strategic thinker, quick to adjust on the battlefield. He had not been in many battles, but Hugh was sure that he would acquit himself well, thinking back at how he had so cleverly moved his whole family, their possessions and a herd of livestock out of harm's way when he learned of the large English foraging force. Burning his house to throw them off track had been a stroke of genius.

Malcom, on the other hand, while very smart, probably smarter than Hugh and Richard combined, was a dreamer, often found under a tree, or on his horse, just sitting and thinking. *Maybe he can become a poet or a bard,* Hugh thought ruefully, *though I doubt such work would feed a family.*

Innis was the spitting image of his father, John—strong, determined and single minded. If a superior asked Innis to do something, he wouldn't have to say it twice and could be sure it would be done properly. Innis was as reliable as the sun was at rising in the east. A perfect squire.

Hugh was on his gelding, a spirited black palfrey with four white stockings, a cavalry horse that was big, but also fast and agile. Hugh preferred palfreys to the heavy "charger" type horses that many knights rode. Chargers, sometimes called destriers, with their great size, were good for lordly jousting tournaments, but real cavalry battles were nothing like the sport of jousting. Hugh prized a horse with speed in acceleration, stopping and turning.

With his broadsword sheathed in a scabbard under his right stirrup, Hugh carried a long dirk at his waist, a cross-bow slung over his shoulder, a large quiver of bolts and a round metal shield. He wore a chainmail vest that covered his arms and upper legs, a steel breastplate and helmet, and vambraces for his forearms and hands. Draped over the armor was his surcoat, emblazoned with the Henderson colors.

Richard was on his big Clydesdale, suited and armed similar to Hugh, but he also carried a spear. Riding a general-purpose rouncy horse, Innis was more lightly armed, carrying extra arms for Hugh and a signaling flag at the end of a long pike pole.

Facing them was a motley array of horses and riders. This was to be Hugh's cavalry. It was even worse than he had feared. Every manner of mismatched man and horse imaginable stood before him. *Back to basics,* he mused with a resigned look on his face. He had noticed about ten or so capable-looking men-at-arms in the ragged group and called them forward. He first determined that all had served in the regular Scots cavalry and had experience in battle.

"We only have about 100 cavalrymen," he told them, "and the English will have 500 or more, and another 2,500 ground forces. That means we'll be badly outnumbered. I don't plan to keep our cavalry cooped up inside the castle walls though. We would get cut to pieces in such tight quarters. I don't know how yet, but I'll get us out in the open so we can fight."

The men sent up shouts of assent.

"I want each of you to be a squad leader. Each squad, including the leader, will number about ten. You will be responsible for keeping your squad together and moving in good order in the right direction." They all nodded.

Hugh continued, "Movements will be signaled by flag. My squire here," Hugh said, pointing at Innis, "will be the flagman. If he falls, then my brother, Richard, will take over. We'll keep it simple. I'll be out in front and call the signals. You watch for them and order your squads to follow."

Hugh then had Innis demonstrate the flag signals they would use and what each meant: (1) side to side—hold in place, (2) front to back—move forward in formation, the faster the wave, the quicker the move, (3) jabbing up and down—charge the enemy en mass.

"You may have noticed," Hugh grinned, "that we don't have a signal for retreat. That's because we never do it."

The men smiled and shook their fists, several letting out war whoops.

"But," Hugh continued, "on occasion we'll need to regroup. Innis has a ramshorn. If he sounds it, immediately regroup around the colors. Understood?"

No one had questions. Decisive—the kind of leader they liked.

Hugh instructed the squad leaders that he wanted each man to carry a crossbow and a large quiver of bolts. The crossbows had limited range, less than half that of a longbow, but the short range did not diminish power. Close quarters would allow deathly fire to both men and horses. The crossbows would have to be reloaded after each shot and Hugh wanted the riders to rotate in a line to produce constant fire. Large round shields would provide protection while reloading. Load and shoot as quickly as possible was the goal. Each cavalryman would need a sword, battle axe or other short weapon to use when fighting became close-in man to man. Finally he wanted one squad armed with spears up front. These men would need larger horses as this would be the "thrust" vanguard. Richard would lead it.

It was time to practice actual maneuvers. Hugh instructed the ten men selected as squad leaders to form up their groups. The rest of the afternoon and all of the next day was spent in training. By the end of the second day, the motley group had begun to resemble a reasonably well-trained and disciplined Scots cavalry. Now all that was lacking was a plan to better even the odds. Hugh, Richard and the captains were working on it.

Scouting reports indicated an English force in excess of 3,000 soldiers was headed their way on the coast road. They were about a day out, with at least 500 cavalry, and the remaining troops were divided between longbow archers, halberdiers and pikers. Accompanying the army were several oxcarts bearing provisions, a herd of livestock, and wagons of hay. Also, there was reported to be a strange-looking, rectangular four-wheeled wagon, armored on all sides, pulled by two teams of Clydesdales.

The English force, all decked out in red uniforms recently ordered by King Henry, had bypassed Wigtown, which was still under siege. Some stayed to help the existing siege forces, which allowed the 3,000-strong contingent to march on toward Lochnaw Castle. Hugh, Richard and the two captains listened carefully to the scouting report brought in by their advance outriders, puzzling in particular over the strange armored wagon. It did not seem reasonable that the English would waste two teams of fine Clydesdale horses to pull a provisions wagon, and why the armor? No one knew.

All agreed that they should make maximum use of the castle's natural defensive features. It would be very difficult for the English to breach the castle walls, and a siege was not likely, as they must know of the gathering Scottish army at Girvan, only a two-day's ride away. Hugh felt that the English strategy would be to take the castle with a quick, forceful, frontal attack. It would likely be accompanied by fusillades of flaming arrows shot into the outer courtyard to set fires and cause panic. Then they would probably try to ram the front gates.

The two captains were confident. They doubted the English could get close enough to ram the gates and did not think they could break through in any event. They felt their longbowmen could cause severe damage to an English force attempting a frontal assault, and their pikemen could prevent a cavalry charge from breaking through the front gate.

Hugh cautioned that the English would have 3,000 professional soldiers against the castle's 500 put-together forces. And he had only about 100 cavalry versus their 500. The Scots were brave soldiers, and the castle defenses were strong, but if the English were able to set enough fires, get a couple of pike squares and a unit of cavalry to the front gate, they might be able to ram through. The two captains glanced at each with arched eyebrows.

The castle forces should be well provisioned, Hugh emphasized, all containers available filled with water and scattered about at critical locations to deal with the fires. Squires should be prepared to quickly bring up spare weapons when needed. The longbowmen, in particular, should have plenty of extra arrows, and pots of pitch so they could set some of them ablaze.

Hugh emphasized that he did not plan to rely solely upon Lochnaw's strong defenses, but to employ an offensive strategy as well. He suggested a rather daring plan: First, should the English stand back beyond longbow range, the Scots should "invite" them to approach the front gates by letting them cross the bridge over the marshy area in front. The idea was to get the English caught in a pincer movement and a withering crossfire.

"Aye, but how do we get behind them?" asked one of the captains.

"I will take the cavalry through the tunnel at the north side wall and circle around," Hugh said.

By taking the cavalry through the tunnel they could ride un-noticed behind the enemy under cover of the reeds and bushes growing along the marsh.

"It might work," one of the captains said tentatively.

"The English probably do not realize our strength," Hugh con-tinued. "They will think we have only a normal-sized defensive force of a hundred or so. That will make them over-confident. I doubt they'll have any trepidation at all in approaching with most of their force. They will not expect a counter attack from outside the castle walls, certainly not cavalry with crossbows. We will have them trapped between the marsh and the outer wall."

The two captains smiled.

*Ae surpreese for th' English.* They liked it.

Hugh continued that he figured the English would have a col-umn of longbowmen approach first, then follow with formations of pikes and halberds. The whole force would be flanked by cavalry. Longbowmen would have kettles of pitch in which to dip arrows, and when they got close enough, they would loose a fusillade over the outer wall. A few of the castle longbowmen, spaced apart, could answer with a spare barrage. This would lead the English to think the castle forces were thin and embolden them to move their pikemen and halberds even more confidently over the bridge for a frontal assault.

By that time, most, if not all, of the English force would be out in the open, Hugh said. He would then swing his cavalry behind them from the far side of the marsh and open up with crossbows. The castle captains could order the rest of the longbowmen up to the parapets. If all went well, the castle forces could cut the English down in a vicious crossfire before they realized the predicament they were in.

"But," Hugh conceded, "as does the weather, reality sometimes brings surprises."

# 16.
# BATTLE OF CASTLE LOCHNAW

THE battle began at dawn the next day. Hugh led his cavalry to the far end of the tunnel. They held there while Hugh, Richard and Innis watched the English movements. The English commander arrayed his army in a broad horizontal line short of the bridge and out of longbow range. Then he sent one squad of about 50 longbowmen across the bridge followed by a unit of pikers. The bowmen loosed a barrage of arrows over the outer wall.

"They're trying to judge our ability to respond," Hugh said. "Just what I expected. I hope our longbowmen remember to fire a weak return."

They did, and the English moved the pike and halberd squares forward and began pushing the main body of their army across the bridge. The pike and halberd squares were in the center, flanked by longbow columns, and two lines of cavalry rode on each side. The entire English force was now across the bridge, out in the open.

Hugh moved his cavalry out of the tunnel behind the cover of the reeds and bushes along the marsh, with Richard on his right leading the lancers, and Innis on his left, laden with extra weapons. They stopped just out of sight as the English drew up en masse about halfway between the bridge and the castle's massive front gate. When there was no response from the castle, the English longbowmen launched a formidable fusillade of arrows over the outer wall, about half of them dipped in pitch and flaming. The castle forces responded with another weak barrage and worked feverishly inside the outer wall to put out the fires.

Then the unexpected happened. From out of nowhere, two teams of Clydesdales, pulling the armored wagon, galloped over the bridge and sped straight toward the front gate. The Lochnaw captains hurriedly deployed the rest of their longbowmen and let loose a heavy fusillade that inflicted significant damage.

Some of the bowmen were instructed to aim at the quickly approaching Clydesdales and wagon. One of the Clydesdales was struck in the chest and fell in its traces, stopping the wagon's progress, but only temporarily, as the lead team was cut loose and the second team lumbered on with the wagon in tow until it was just yards from the gate. Then another of the Clydesdales was felled. The English pikemen, rushing up behind their shields, cut away the second team, then dropped two armored wings from each side of the back of the wagon and started pushing it by hand toward the front gate.

Hugh and his cavalry, drawn up and hidden behind the marsh, looked on in amazement. Richard and Innis were by Hugh's side, with Innis flashing flag signals back to the main force of cavalrymen to hold in place.

"What's the purpose of the wagon," Hugh muttered to Richard. "It's clearly ineffective as a ram; yet the English are moving up as though they expect to break through the outer wall."

Hugh did not have long to puzzle over it. He had Innis signal the cavalry to move quickly and cross the bridge. Then he had Richard advance forward with the squad of lancers on the heavy horses. Hugh and Innis accompanied them. As they were in the process of executing this maneuver, a resounding ear-splitting "boom" echoed over the battlefield.

Hugh could see a big plume of black smoke rising up from the vicinity of the front gate. *That sounded like a cannon,* he thought.

"Look, the gate is splintered and the English are pouring in!" shouted Innis.

Hugh wasted no time: "We've got to charge—now!"

Innis give the signal, and Hugh yelled to his men, "Head straight for the gate!"

Richard, leading the squad of lancers, accompanied by Hugh and Innis, charged forward, closely followed by the main body of the cavalry, piercing with spears, hacking and cutting with swords, and firing crossbows. The English foot soldiers were pushing forward and had their backs to Hugh's cavalry, allowing his horsemen to charge fast and forcefully, inflicting a lot of damage. The English cavalry saw what was happening, and tried to intercept Hugh's horsemen, but their own confused and disordered ground troops effectively blocked most of them.

Hugh lost a few men and horses, but kept moving toward the gate at a rapid pace. When he got there, a number of English ground forces were already inside the outer wall. They were joined in battle with the Lochnaw defenders, who would become badly outnumbered if a more sizeable number of the English got in.

*The front gate break had to be stanched, and fast,* Hugh realized.

A clangor of swords filled the air, accompanied by the piercing of arrows, hacking of swords, and smashing of bodies, both men and horses—an awful amalgam of men screaming, cursing and yelling, horses squealing, metal clanging—the roar of battle.

There was one advantage for the Lochnaw defenders. Their fighters could readily identify the enemy. The red-coated English were easy to spot in the mayhem. As Hugh, Innis, Richard and the rest of the Scots cavalrymen joined the fray, the armored wagon, now inside the outer wall, was being pushed toward the main castle gate and drawbridge. Fighting his way closer, Hugh figured out what was happening. A large cannon was inside the wagon. It was tied down with thick ropes, and a big barrel poked out the front, just as it would from the firing port on a ship.

The English had used it to bust open the outer wall gate and were now busy getting it into position to fire another shot at the main castle gate. If they knocked that gate down, they could get inside the second wall and lower the drawbridge, allowing access to the castle. Once they got inside the castle keep, all would be lost. It had to be stopped.

"Richard!" Hugh cried out over the din of the battle. "The wagon! It's headed for the main gate. They plan to blow it. We've got to stop them!"

Hugh and Richard, followed by Innis, sped toward the wagon, which was about halfway to the gate. Six or seven English soldiers were pushing it, and the cannonmen inside were in the process of reloading. Swords flashing, the three riders slammed their horses into the pushers, and quickly cut them down. Hugh could see the cannon barrel protruding from the front of the wagon, still smoking.

"Innis!" Hugh yelled. "We need to get this wagon turned around and push it back toward the front gate. We can use it as a plug to prevent more English from getting in. Quickly, round up more of our men!"

Innis raced off, and Hugh jumped on the side of the wagon, followed by Richard. They both climbed up and examined the top. It was constructed of heavy boarding spaced a few inches apart. A chained door covered the entry hole and two men were struggling with a big round iron ball. A third was preparing to cram a packet of gunpowder down the cannon's barrel. Innis returned with six men, and Hugh instructed them to turn the wagon around and push it in the opposite direction.

Hollering to Innis over the clamor, Hugh barked, "We need to get inside this thing. It'll take too long to hack through with swords. We need to burn our way in. Quick, bring up a couple of pitch pots. We'll spread the pitch and light the top afire."

Then to Richard, who was guarding his back, "I don't want to kill the men inside just yet; we may be able to put them to our own use."

Soon a couple of Lochnaw archers arrived with pots of pitch and a flaming torch that were handed up to Hugh and Richard. The other men put their shoulders to the wagon, turned it, and began pushing it back toward the front gate. Once the plug was in place, the "wings" were lowered and stanched with heavy timbers.

Scottish longbowmen atop the parapets at the gate towers fired away at the redcoats outside. The plug slowed the number pouring through the gate. The bulk of the English cavalry and ground forces were still outside. Hugh's cavalry forces were rotating, keeping up an almost continuous volley of crossbow fire into the English ranks.

But they could not be held at bay forever. Inside, the pitched battle continued, but the Scots were beginning to get the upper hand.

Meanwhile, Hugh and Richard smeared the pitch on the wagon top and set it ablaze. The three English cannoneers, sure they were about to be burned alive, started groveling and pleading. As soon as a big enough hole was burned, Hugh chopped it open with his broadsword and dropped inside. Richard followed. The cannoneers were not armed and offered no resistance; instead they begged for their lives.

"On one condition," growled Hugh. "If you don't do what I say, we'll chop your ugly heads off." They nodded, eyes wide with fear.

"Is the cannon loaded, ready to fire?" asked Hugh.

"It is," one of them said.

"Then fire it right now," Hugh ordered.

"But it's pointed at our own men," the man protested.

"Aye, it is, but you will fire it, or all of you will lose your heads, and I'll fire it anyway," Hugh growled. "Which will it be?"

One of them grabbed his flint, sparked the powder, and the cannon roared, sending a 12-pound ball hurling through the English columns, tearing many men and horses apart.

"Reload!" Hugh shouted. The three cannoneers looked sick, white as death.

One of them pissed in his pants, the wet stain running down his leg.

"Do it now!" Hugh screamed, brandishing his sword.

The man who had fired said, haltingly, his face ashen, "No. I won't do it."

Hugh brought the broadsword down hard to the top of the man's helmet, cleaving his head open like a ripe melon. He looked at the other two. "Well?"

There were several more balls on the floor. They picked one up, rammed in a packet of gunpowder, rolled in the ball, powdered the touch-hole and fired another round. Again, many English fell, and this time a lot of them broke and ran, some trying to cross the bridge, others plunging into the marsh, all the while being picked apart by the longbows from the parapets and the crossbows of Hugh's cavalry.

By now, the fighting inside was waning, with many more red-coats lying dead and wounded than Scotsmen. The English had been decimated, and they were trapped. An officer stepped forward, waving a white shirt attached to the end of a pike.

"Gentlemen," he said loudly. "You have the day." The fight inside was over.

The two Lochnaw captains climbed up to the cannellated tower atop the castle keep, taking the English officer with them. They waved Baron Agnew's banner and shouted out to the remaining English troops.

"We have 200 of yours, dead or wounded. About the same number are prisoners surrendered by Captain Smith, who stands here beside me. Send out your commanding officer under a white flag. We will release the prisoners and you can collect your dead, upon assurance you will leave and never return. Otherwise, we'll put all prisoners to the sword."

The English commander rode out. The battle was over. Five hundred rag-tag Scots had just defeated a professional English army of 3,000. War whoops and shouts of joy rang out from the victorious Scots, accompanied by a vigorous display and shaking of their weapons.

Hugh grimaced. *This was no time for celebration,* he thought. *A battle had been won, but a war loomed.*

# 17.
# An Aching Heart

KING Henry VIII died suddenly and unexpectedly in London in late January 1547. No one knew whether this would dampen the English throne's enthusiasm for continuing the rough wooing military campaign to force betrothal of Henry's son, Edward, to the young Scots Queen, Mary. There was hope the English might now drop the whole enterprise.

The Scottish commander, Arran, decided to take no chances and continued to build and train a large Scottish army to meet the English if necessary. As it turned out, the English commander, Edward Seymour, the Duke of Somerset, forged ahead with the rough wooing campaign even more vigorously than King Henry had. It was suspected he hoped that a great victory and capture of Scotland's capital, Edinburgh, would make him exceedingly popular in England. He could then turn his regency of the young King Edward into a tacit kingship for himself.

Andrew Henderson and his lonely little family at the head of Glen Trool knew nothing of the events at Castle Lochnaw, nor of the death of England's King Henry III, or of the Scots' preparations for possible war with the English. They all felt desolate, deserted and alone.

Everyone was distraught and anxious over Hugh and Innis. They had been gone for over three months, yet there had been no news. *Where were they? Were they well—alive even?* Such thoughts tortured the heart, but there was nothing anyone could do. They all felt it: Ann, Andy, Ree, Joe and Jamie, although no one said much. It was like an upstream dam. If a crack develops, the whole structure might burst open, inundating all. Everyone realized this, and so they kept their worries unspoken.

The only favorable circumstance was that spring had finally arrived. It was mid-April, and the warmth was there to stay. The grass had greened, leaves had sprouted, dragonflies and other insects had taken to the air, and the trout were biting. The wild animals in the wood were active. Ree had broken out her fishing gear and was hauling in hungry trout by the dozens. Andy and Joe were having good success at hunting and trapping. Food was suddenly plentiful again.

Ann had continued to recover from her horrible grief and was regaining some of her vigor. She could even be heard laughing on occasion. The hut had been repaired and enlarged. Andy continued on his rides to check on tenants and collect rent. Fortunately, none of them had fallen prey to the marauding English forces. They were too far out to be of interest or concern.

Of the thirty or so tenant farming families that lived in the small shire, few had any specie, but most of their livestock had survived the long winter, and the mares, cows, ewes and sows were birthing. Therefore, Andy collected most of the rent in livestock. He now had a small herd of sheep, hogs and cows, one fine gelding and a mare with foal. He was confident that the English forces would stay along the coast and concentrate their efforts on the larger towns. After all, except for the two deserters his father and he had executed late the previous fall, no other English soldiers had been seen anywhere near.

Other than the welfare of his father and cousin, which certainly weighed on him, Andy had another ache that constantly wrenched his heart; he could not get Helen Agnew off his mind. He regularly conjured the image of her that day at Lochnaw Castle when she strolled from the parlor after reading his message to her father and gave him that sly smile. He remembered how his heart almost leaped from his chest, his throat went dry, and when he left, how he longed to see her again.

Finally, the urge became so powerful that he determined he would ride to Lochnaw again. The family was safe, food was abundant, and his mother was regaining her health. Ree, Joe and Jamie were all good hands and could hold things together. In addition he felt certain there would be news of his father and Innis. Baron Agnew had undoubtedly gone to the clan council meeting at Irvine and would have information to share.

He told the family of his decision, couching it in terms of seeking news about Hugh and Innis with no mention of Helen. He said he would be gone for not more than two weeks. Andy was a little surprised when they all readily agreed. He left the next morning at first light, his heart thumping in anticipation.

✦ ✦ ✦

Meanwhile, back at Lochnaw Castle, a handful of English prisoners had been kept, locked up in a strong crib in the stables, including the two cannoneers. Hugh and the captains had decided to keep them as assurance that the English forces, after collecting their dead and wounded, would march on for good. The cannon wagon itself and all the captured arms were retained. When the defeated English troops reached Wigtown, the siege was still ongoing and the townspeople showed no signs of surrender. In fact, Scots raids against the English forces outside the city walls had continued and even intensified. With the loss of the cannon, and many men and arms, there was little hope that the English could break through, so their commanders decided to consolidate forces, abandon the town and march back east to join the main army when it came north.

✦ ✦ ✦

Andy arrived at Lochnaw about mid-afternoon on the second day of his ride. He was recognized by the guards at both gates and was allowed to ride his horse over the drawbridge. After he dismounted and the horse was led away to the stables, Andy eagerly approached the front door. The guards in the keep tower had been watching and had the door open for him as soon as he ascended the front steps. Helen Agnew stood waiting just inside the door.

"Andrew Henderson!" she cried, blue eyes sparkling and white teeth glistening between pouty lips now spread into a wide smile. "How good to see you!"

"Miss Agnew, 'tis good to see you as well," Andy replied brightly, bowing slightly.

Helen, feigning shyness, confessed she realized that Andy was there to see his father, but hoped to get a chance for a short visit with him before he left. Andy blushed and his heart raced. *He hadn't imagined it. Helen was glad to see him.* He managed to control his emotions enough to smile and say that he too would most enjoy a visit, then remembered to inquire of the whereabouts of his father. Helen replied that he was, at that moment, upstairs in the great chamber with her father, Earl Arran, and the rest of the commanders. They were meeting in private, and had left strict instructions to be left alone. Andy looked down the long hallway to the main stairs where he could see two burly armed men standing guard.

"How long have they been meeting?" Andy inquired.

"Several hours," Helen said. "I think they might break soon."

Then, smiling coyly, Helen asked if maybe they, too, could use this time for a private talk. They could slip into the oratory, a small room adjacent to the chapel, just a short walk down the hall. No one would disturb them there, and she had much to tell him.

"Certainly, if you think it proper," said Andy.

Helen led him to the small room, which had a few covered benches facing an altar topped with a silver cross. She closed the door. It was hazy, quiet and still inside, such that they conversed in a whisper. Andy noticed Helen's melodious, sweet, throaty voice.

"Your father is quite the hero," she said softly.

"Och, how so?" asked Andy.

Helen told him the whole story of his father's exploits at the recent battle. She had watched most of it from the castle keep, peeking through arrow slits in the massive tower fronting the main gatehouse. She told Andy of the terrible wagon with the cannon inside that blasted down the outer gate, of Sir Henderson's capture of it, and how he turned it back on the enemy, won the fight and protected them all.

"He changed the battle with that. My father is very grateful, as am I and all in the castle," she said.

Andy just looked at her, a surprised expression on his face, seemingly struck mute. At length, he said, "Whowe, I never heard of such!"

Andy and Helen talked for a while longer, about Andy's family, what each had been doing since they last saw each other, and so on, when they heard heavy footsteps on the stairs.

"They're coming down," she said. "You should go out and greet your father. I'll stay here a bit longer until they've cleared out."

Andy stepped out of the oratory and circled around the short distance to the front entryway. Coming down the hall was a large group of men led by Baron Agnew. Andy could see his father, his uncle, his grandfather and others he did not know walking briskly toward him, still engaged in spirited conversation. Andy stood where he was, and as the group approached, Agnew spied him. He rushed forward, grabbed Andy by the hand in a firm grip, slapped him on the back and thundered: "Andrew Henderson, welcome back to my house! I have much to tell you about your father."

Agnew stepped aside and Hugh wrapped Andy in a great bear hug, kissing him on both cheeks.

"My son! 'Tis so great to see you. I did not expect it!"

Dar Wallace and Richard Henderson stood by, smiling.

"Grandfather, Uncle Richard!" exclaimed Andy. "It's great to see you all so well." Hearty handshakes, backslaps and hugs were exchanged all around as Baron Agnew regaled him about his father's recent exploits.

Provided with his own spacious room, Andy spent his first night at Lochnaw Castle marveling at its formidable construction and appreciating the fine detail that went into the woodwork, paneling, moldings and windows—strong, yet beautiful. His thoughts turned to the burned-out family bastle house. He really needed to get started on the rebuilding, for it was now fully springtime, and it would take several months just to get the foundation down, the walls, doors, and windows put in, and a roof built— and that was assuming he could assemble a decent crew of workmen and manage to finance the project. Several of the tenant farmers still owed back rent and he could perhaps trade work for rent, but it was planting season and would be hard to get them away from their fields.

As he pondered the issue, he recalled the splendid work he had seen on some of the houses in Wigtown. The town had been under siege by the English for several months and had suffered damage, but the English army was now gone. Supplies, especially foodstuffs, were likely quite skimpy. Perhaps he could barter meat on the hoof for construction work by skilled craftsmen. It would be worth a try.

Early the next morning, Andy heard a rap at his door. "Just a moment!" he called, pulling on his breeches and hurrying to the door.

He cracked the door open a bit and was surprised and quite pleased to see Helen Agnew standing there, peeking in at him. She looked freshly scrubbed. Her cheeks were pink, her hair up, and she was clothed in a fresh light green doublet over a matching skirt.

Helen was amused that Andy was not yet dressed.

"Why, 'tis such a fine morning and you are not even dressed," she chided.

"I'm very sorry. I overslept," said Andy, embarrassed.

"You must hurry," she insisted.

Baron Agnew wished Andy to join him right away for the morning meal. Andy quickly splashed his face with cold water from a basin, slicked back his hair, donned his shirt and boots, and rushed down the hall. The Baron was having his breakfast, consisting of pickled sardines, hot porridge, fresh fruits and nuts, in the parlor room.

Hugh, Richard and Innis joined them. They joked good-naturedly, and tried to outdo each other with stories about the recent events. The prime topic was the stunning feat Hugh and Richard had pulled on the English with the capture of the "cannon wagon." All were in high spirits, laughing and boisterous. Andy did his best to join in on the fun, but his mind kept wandering back to the lovely sight of Helen at his door only moments before. He just *had* to see her again!

Once the party broke up, Andy made his way down the stairs and along the long hallway past the oratory where he and Helen had hid the day before. The front of the oratory jutted out a ways into the hall, and as Andy walked by, he heard a soft *Pssst!* There was Helen, looking at him with a mischievous smile. She motioned him to come inside.

"Nobody ever comes in here, except on the Sabbath. Do you have a moment?"

"Aye, of course, for you, always," Andy said.

Glancing about conspiratorially, Helen stage-whispered, "I know a secret. I bet you would be interested."

Intrigued, Andy listened with rapt attention as Helen told him where the cannon wagon was being kept. It was under lock and key in the horse stables. There were armed guards at each end, but she knew a way they could get in and not be seen.

"Would you like to see it?" she inquired. "I can show you. We'll have to be quiet."

Andy was a little apprehensive, but he would be thrilled to get to see the wagon, and of course, he would love to be alone with Helen, so the decision was made. Andy whispered, "I'd love to."

"Come with me then, and be careful," she said. "If anyone sees us, I'll just explain I'm showing you about the grounds."

It was a warm, sunny day in late April. They strolled across the drawbridge into the outer courtyard where the stables were located. Sure enough, there was a guard at either end of the long row of stalls, which were under one roof, backed up to the outside portion of the inner wall. There was a small space between the back of the stables and the wall. Helen led Andy along this space until they came upon a couple of loose boards that led to an inside stall. They crept through the opening and entered the barn.

The light was dim, the air redolent with the musty smell of horse manure, dirt, straw and dust. After they had thoroughly examined the cannon wagon, which was at one end of the row of stalls, Helen took Andy's hand and pulled him along a long corridor where the horses were led in to be rubbed down and fed. Walking carefully to dodge droppings in the subdued light, Andy appreciated the warmth of her small, soft, but sturdy hand and her sweet, earthy smell mingled with the pungent scents of the barn.

Unexpectedly, Helen murmured, "Have you a steady woman in your life?"

After a short pause to consider what she just said, Andy answered, "Nay, I haven't."

"I have no man either," she cooed, happy to hear that Andy was not spoken for.

Helen pushed open the gate to a boose, where the atmosphere was even murkier, but rich with the fragrance of newly mown hay. She tugged Andy inside.

"Let's sit and talk for a moment," she whispered.

A single glowing shaft of sunlight, illuminating motes of floating dust, fell upon one corner of the boose, where a pile of cushy yellow straw beckoned. Talk was sparse, for Helen wrapped her arms around Andy's slender waist, pressing her soft, ample breasts against his chest, her respirations quickening. Andy cupped his hands around her delicate but muscular shoulders, caressing the small of her back, then moved up the nape of her neck beneath her soft, fine-textured, blonde curls. His heart was racing. Helen lifted her head, her cheeks flushed, blue eyes glowing, ripe lips parted.

Andy kissed her fully on the mouth, tasting the sweet saltiness inside. She responded, pressing her body tightly to his, slightly opening her mouth, the hot, wet tip of her tongue probing. They sank in unison upon the pile of hay, still in full embrace, stretching their bodies out, holding each other tight, continuing the kiss.

In short order, Helen had raised one leg over Andy's thigh and they were both rhythmically moving their pelvises against each other.

"Should we?" Andy whispered huskily.

"Shuuch." Helen murmured.

Andy's organ had swelled to such enormous size inside his trousers that it hurt. Helen reached down and began rubbing it, up and down, from outside the stretched fabric. He slid his hand under her fitted doublet and skirt—she wore no underdrawers—and felt her silky soft pubic hair, already wet.

Helen was now moaning and breathing heavily. Suddenly, she sat up and commanded him to turn over on his back. He did as instructed, and she unbuttoned his trousers, letting his swollen pintle free. She took it in her soft hands and stroked it back and forth. Andy was so aroused, he had to stifle a scream.

"Quiet!" she whispered, her hot breath tingling in his ear. Helen then removed her bodice, revealing a linen band with cups. There was a tie string down the front, which she loosened, allowing her rounded breasts to swing free. Andy gasped and felt faint. Never had he seen such a beautiful sight.

Helen pulled her skirt up waist high, straddled Andy on her knees with one shapely, cream-colored leg on each side. She deftly slipped Andy's engorged pintle inside her crevice. It was slick and tight. Both were moaning, moving up and down in rhythm. Heat and urgency built, more and more, until finally, from deep below - an explosion.

They both writhed and shook all over, then lay quiet and still in each other's arms, enjoying the euphoric buzz passing through their brains. When their breathing returned to normal, Helen whispered sweetly: "I felt I was going to die—did you?"

"Aye, aye!" groaned Andy, "but such a sweet death it would have been."

◆ ◆ ◆

Andy returned to Blackcraigshire with his head spinning and his heart about to burst with joy after the thrilling romantic encounter with Helen Agnew. He daydreamed of a time when he would marry Helen, they would have a large family, and eventually build a mansion that would rival the castle at Lochnaw.

Helen, he knew, would require something majestic.

# 18.
# A New Home

BUT, *first things first*, Andy thought. At the moment he needed to get his family out of their pitiful environs at Loch Trool and to a better place. To this end, he decided, they should rebuild the burned-out bastle house, improve and expand it.

He had mentioned this briefly to his father when he saw him at Lochnaw and he was supportive.

Meditating sleepily, he rode along under dappled, sunny skies and considered how he might go about manning and financing such a project. His younger siblings, Ree, Joe and Jamie, were old enough to help (Ree was now 16, Joe was 14, and Jamie was 12). They could pitch in, and his mother, Ann, could ride herd on everybody, manage the household chores and help with the planning. Andy had built up the livestock herd and could sell some at market to raise money, purchase materials and hire some craftsmen. For the more skilled work, he would check around in Wigtown. Many were destitute as a result of the long English siege and would be happy to get some paying work.

Perhaps he could recruit some basic labor from the families of their tenant farmers as well. They could perform work as payment for rent. If all went well, by winter the family should be able to move back into their old home, expanded and improved.

When Andy arrived back at the hut, he had so much news to tell and ideas to share that everyone was giddy with excitement. All were anxious to get on with the building project. Loch Trool had proved a good enough place to hide out but was certainly not suitable for a permanent home. So they packed up and left (except for Joe, who stayed behind temporarily with the border collie to watch after the livestock) and headed southwest down Glen Trool to the bastle house. Andy promised Joe that they would build a rail corral first thing, and he would send Jamie back to help herd the livestock to their new home.

When they reached the house ruins, they found it in much worse shape than Andy had thought. Two walls of the house, the chimney and the pele tower had completely collapsed. Andy had hoped that everything except the roof would be more or less intact, and they could simply make some repairs, put on a new roof, and refinish the interior. Surveying the situation with Ann, Ree and Jamie, it was obvious this would not be possible. A complete rebuild would be necessary. It was nearing dark, so they walked back up the trail to the same copse of large oak trees where they had spent the first night after the attack of the previous fall. The trees grew atop a long, flat rise, affording a view of a large expanse of country-side to the south, stretching toward Wigtown and Luce Bay. Again they would spend the night on the ground among the oak trees.

"So much has happened since we were here last," marveled Ann.

"It just doesn't seem possible," agreed Ree.

Andy and Jamie were silent, remembering—Granny, the two murderous deserters, Bossie and her heifer, the brutal winter, the death of the twins, and the small cemetery atop Ben Blackcraig. Andy's thoughts returned to Helen, his father and Innis. He wondered what the future held in store.

The reverie did not last long for Ann suddenly exclaimed, to no one in particular, "The house must go here!"

"Where?" Andy asked, confused.

"Right here," Ann said firmly, slapping her hand on the ground.

"Why not where it is now?" Ree wondered. "Wouldn't it be easier to rebuild there?"

"Possibly," replied Ann, "but it's safer here, not to mention much more lovely. Look out. We are much higher here, and can see for a long way. We would be secluded amongst the trees, and could spot anyone or anything approaching from a good distance off."

Andy, listening carefully, realized his mother was right. This was the perfect spot.

After the others had gone to sleep for the night, Andy took his mother aside, and for the first time, told her about his romance with Helen Agnew, blurting it out rapid-fire. Confessing that the courtship was short, it was also intense, he declared, without mentioning details. He was deeply in love with Helen and was sure she felt the same about him. He intended to marry her.

This unexpected news came in such a rush that Ann was completely taken aback. She was silent for a long while, looking at her son in amazement. Then slowly, gently, like the stirring of a fragrant spring breeze, the memories of that day long ago, under the branches of a spreading oak on the banks of the blue Irish Sea, came flooding back. *Just like the father, so is the son; what will be must be.*

"We have to build a much bigger and better house than I was thinking," she said.

The next morning, all arose early, ate a quick, cold breakfast of dried trout strips and oatmeal biscuits, and set to work felling tall oak saplings to construct the livestock corral. After two days, the corral was finished enough that Andy sent Jamie back up Glen Trool to fetch Joe and start herding the livestock back. Ann, Andy and Ree talked at length about the new house, what it would look like, what type of construction and materials they could use, where to find workers, and so forth. Scraping off a flat area of ground, the three began drawing rough design outlines with sharpened sticks. At first they stuck with the layout of the old bastle house, but soon each was spotting all manner of deficiencies, ranging from appearance, safety and strength, to convenience and comfort.

They agreed the first consideration should be the availability of materials. The bastle house had been built of stone and timbers. Some of the stone might still be used for fill, but the timbers were all burned. Seasoned timbers would be needed, as opposed to fresh cut trees that would shrink and crack, and these could be acquired at Ayr or Wigtown. A lot of fine limestone rock was nearby and could be quarried. Mortar could be made from a mixture of crushed limestone and oyster shells.

The English siege had taken its toll, as did an earlier outbreak of sickness, thought to be the plague, which had killed about one-quarter of the town's population. This resulted in supplies being plentiful and cheap. Andy only needed to raise some more hard currency. He planned to sell many of his cattle, sheep and pigs at the livestock market at Ayr. He could also barter additional livestock in Wigtown in exchange for supplies and labor. The townspeople were anxious to obtain food and work. *Perhaps I can buy a team of oxen and a sturdy wagon in Ayr,* he thought. *I'll need them to haul supplies.*

After much experimentation with different designs, Ann, Andy and Ree began to coalesce around a house plan along the following lines. The house would be a simple two-story, rectangular structure facing south, with a flat stone floor set in mortar above a gravelled pad. Double stone walls around a timbered frame were slated for the first floor, spanned by a timbered second floor, with plank flooring accessed a by stairwell at the center. The second floor walls would be half-timbered mortar, topped with strong cross-timbers and a pitched-beam, slate-covered roof. There would be a central entryway, a strong oaken front door reinforced with iron bands, and three-story stone pele towers on each end.

The keep would be in the center, with a large great hall and hearth. There would be four bedrooms downstairs on one side, and a parlor and several workrooms on the other. A long hallway would split the second level of the house, with a row of bedrooms and workrooms on either side. At the back, attached to the main structure, would be the kitchen and larder. Out houses would include a milk and malt house, a blacksmith shop, barn, chicken coop, pigsty and dovecote. These structures would be separate, off a ways to the north.

The main barn would be to the side of the house, containing horse stables, cow stalls and the tack and farm implement rooms. A high rock barmkin wall would serve as the corral and protection for the entire complex, and would extend around the main house. The whole spread would be surrounded by trees, and the approach drive would wind up the hill around two switchback curves, which would slow anyone arriving and provide an acoustic warning. As additional protection, a dog kennel would be located near the front entry. No one could approach without warning. Once the building scheme was agreed upon, Ann drew a sketch on parchment as a guide that could be referenced by workers.

Andy sold the livestock at the Ayr market for premium prices, bought a pair of strong oxen and a sturdy wagon, and returned home with a load of wooden support beams. Later he, Joe and Jamie went to Wigtown with the ox wagon, driving a small herd of livestock. There, through a combination of barter and purchase, he was able to obtain mortar supplies, planks, rafters and other building materials. He was also able to hire several skilled craftsmen who were out of work and willing to move to the building site for an extended period of time. Some would bring their entire families and construct temporary housing in their spare time.

Several of the workmen were stonemasons and had their own draft horses. Soon they were at work at the limestone quarry cutting and hauling stone for the walls and slate slabs for the ground flooring. Carpenters worked on the framing. Once the construction started, it proceeded at a surprisingly quick pace. Ann's sketched-out building plan proved valuable. It would not be a fancy house with elaborate flourishes and fenestrations, but it would be strong, durable and functional.

✦ ✦ ✦

Early one morning about daybreak in mid-June, Hugh and Innis rode up. The kennel dogs set off barking loudly, alerting the family camped out in the oak grove behind the rising construction. Only Andy was up, building a fire to warm stiff bodies and start breakfast. He saw the two riders approaching and recognized them immediately. Hugh clattered up, swung off his horse and grabbed Andy in a big bear hug.

Looking around at the construction, he exclaimed, "What's this I see? You be building a castle?"

"Nay Paw, just that our old house was in bad shape and too small. We need something bigger, not a castle exactly, just a larger house," Andy said.

"That be obvious!" declared Hugh, smiling proudly. "By the look of things you be planning something *considerably* bigger."

The commotion awoke Ann, and through sleepy eyes, she recognized her long-gone husband. She sprang to her feet, still in her flimsy nightgown, and ran toward him, jumping barefoot over boards and rock in the process. She sprang on her husband joyously, enveloping him with arms and legs, kissing his face repeatedly. Andy stood discreetly aside as this exuberant display of affection unfolded. Hugh swung Ann around and around in a circle, her legs flying wide, as he had done in days gone by. Soon, they both became dizzy and fell to the ground, laughing and crying at the same time.

Conspiratorially, Andy whispered to Innis, who had also dismounted and was slapping him on the back.

"Innis, a little advise: never fall in love, it makes you daffy!"

As Ann and Hugh rejoiced in their reunion, Innis took Andy aside to fill him in on recent military happenings. Arran, Agnew and the other high military leaders of the Scottish Army had been hopeful, upon hearing of the death of King Henry VIII and the departure of the young Queen Mary to France, that the rough wooing campaign would end. Everything was now in the hands of Edward Seymour, Earl of Hertford and brother of Henry's late wife, Jane. After Henry's death, Seymour had become Duke of Somerset, second in line to the throne behind his nephew, the young King Edward.

Unfortunately, Innis confided, it was believed that Somerset, as he was now called, was even more determined than Henry to bring Scotland to heel. According to Arran's spies in London, he would not only continue the military incursion, but expand and intensify it.

Arran's spies had reported that Somerset was already moving a large English land army of some 30,000 troops up the eastern coast. The troop movement was coordinated with a sizeable naval force sailing up the English Channel. Presumably the navy was being used to transport supplies and war materials for the land forces.

No one knew exactly why Somerset had decided to pursue the campaign with such enthusiasm, but he was a skilled and ambitious military man, and it was suspected he had designs on the English throne himself. A forced alliance with Scotland, accomplished by a great military victory, would make him a hero in English eyes and greatly enhance his claim to the throne. He was already serving as regent for five-year-old Edward and wielded the power of a sovereign. It would be years before Edward reached majority and could assume the throne himself. Who knew what might happen to him in the meantime?

Intelligence provided by Arran's spies indicated the English target was Edinburgh. Once it fell into English hands, the rest of Scotland was sure to follow. Arran's plan was to rush his army to intercept the English when they got closer to Edinburgh and block the advance. In the meantime, Arran had appointed Hugh to lead a special cavalry unit to ride east on a reconnoiter mission. He was to determine the location of the main English army, estimate its strength and capabilities, the number and types of weapons, the time it would take the army to reach Edinburgh and any other useful intelligence. They were now on this mission, Innis said, and could not stay for long—perhaps the rest of the day and overnight.

Due to political considerations, Innis confided, Arran had named two high Scottish nobles of dubious military talent, Archibald Douglas, the Earl of Angus, to head the land forces, and George Home, the Earl of Dunbar, to lead the Scottish cavalry. Arran realized that neither of them, particularly Home, was very adept at military leadership, so he tried to make up for it by selecting more talented and experienced men to lead individual units. For example, Baron Agnew would lead the pikemen, and Hugh would lead a special unit of cavalry, about 200 strong, answerable only to Arran.

While Innis had been imparting this grim information to Andy, Hugh and Ann continued their gay frolicking, joined in by Ree, Joe and Jamie. After things died down a bit, Hugh wanted to examine the construction. Ann, joined by the rest of the family, excitedly showed him around, looking at and explaining the plans as they clambered through the famed-up first floor.

They joyfully spent the rest of the morning looking around the site, marveling at the quantity and quality of the work already finished and trying to envision how the whole thing would look when completed. Hugh had caught glimpses of Andy with Helen at Lochnaw and suspected that a romance was blossoming, a view shared by Baron Agnew. After looking over the ambitious building plans and the substantial construction already underway, Hugh could not resist teasing him a bit.

"Lad, be it possible that you might be building such a fine house for some fancy lassie?"

Andy's face reddened into a full blush. He *did* have a fancy lass in mind for the big house. Ann kept quiet, but could not stifle a grin.

"It's possible." Andy finally said, leaving it at that.

The workmen stayed back a distance to allow the Henderson family to inspect the construction, but when the family finally re-tired to prepare the noon meal, they resumed their work. Hugh and Innis were amazed at Andy's drive and ambition as they watched the workers and craftsmen take on the various jobs with such organization and skill. The bastle house of old was being quickly supplanted by a mansion.

During the meal, Hugh visited with the family about the busi-ness he and Innis were engaged, keeping it rather vague and short on detail. The Scottish commanders at Lochnaw had gotten word of some English troop movement along the eastern coast near Newcastle. He was being sent with a small mounted reconnaissance team to check it out and report back. He thought they would be gone for no more than two or three weeks. They had been in-structed to reconnoiter only, and he did not expect any fighting. Perhaps they could stop off again for a short visit on the way back— and, by the way, they would be leaving at first light in the morning.

Ann was suspicious that more was involved. Hugh had a way of softening troublesome news when danger lurked. But there was nothing she could do; his course was set, and worry would do no good. So she let it be, determined to enjoy his company while she could. As night fell, she enticed Hugh to make his bed with her in a private spot away from the others. He eagerly agreed, and their lovemaking was as passionate as in the early years. Afterward, Ann fell into a deep, contented slumber.

When she awoke, Hugh was gone.

# 19.
## Reconnaissance

HUGH and Innis left at first light, pushing their horses south toward Wigtown. There they met up with the rest of their team of a dozen experienced men. Gilbert Agnew, serving as sheriff, had accommodated the fighting men with great courtesy, providing them with lodging and food, stabling and feeding their horses, and re-provisioned them for the continuation of their fast ride to the east. The English siege force was long gone, consolidated with the brigades that had attacked Lochnaw. They had never broken through the Wigtown walls and fortifications, but had killed a lot of people and caused severe food shortages and much misery.

The last Gilbert Agnew had heard of the English force, it was headed east on the Dumfries Road, he presumed, to meet up with the main body of the invading army. His sources told him the English army was about one-third of the way up the coast between London and Edinburgh, and was making good time because it was being provisioned by a naval force and therefore did not have to move with a large, and slow, supply train.

"We have to hurry," Hugh instructed his men. He emphasized their job was to find the English army, determine its strength, direction and pace of movement. They were also to approximate the breakdown of various types of fighting units, gather any other significant information and report back to Arran. He was just beginning to move the Scottish army out of Girvan. Hugh thought his unit was likely a good bit closer to the English than the English were to Edinburgh, but he first had to find them and then double back to Arran. There was no time to spare.

Gilbert Agnew estimated that the English had probably moved past the Mull of Hull at Kingston. He figured they would encamp for several days while being provisioned by their navy, and would soon be moving toward Scarborough. This is where Hugh set his sights.

After riding hard for a couple of days, Hugh's cavalrymen turned right just past Dumfries and were proceeding south on the Carlisle Road. As they were preparing to eat and bed down for the night, a group of about eight ragged-looking horsemen astride shaggy hill ponies approached. Hugh recognized from their appearance that they were borderers, probably part-time reivers. They were lightly armed and outnumbered, so he was not particularly concerned. The men dismounted and began gabbing in a friendly manner. Hugh asked where they had been and where they were going.

"Where you'se been?"

"Near Kingston," said one of them, who seemed to be the leader. "See'd a big English army going north."

This confirmed the information Gilbert Agnew had provided. The English army had been at Kingston and was proceeding north up the coast.

"How many?" inquired Hugh.

"Plenty!" the man said. "Far as the eye can see. Many ships too!"

Hugh was dubious that the English army and naval group was that large. Scots of the ilk of these men tended to exaggerate.

"Did the English see ye?" Hugh asked.

"A few on horses did, but we got away."

"Why were you there?" Hugh pressed.

"Out on a cold trod to look for stolen cattle," the man said, grinning sheepishly.

*It's not likely these rough-looking men had cattle for someone to steal,* Hugh thought, *more likely they were searching for some to steal themselves.*

Hugh's men had built a large fire and were in the process of roasting some pork strips from a hog they had obtained from a

135

nearby farmer. The newcomers were eyeing it hungrily. There was not enough to share, and Hugh wanted to get on the road as early as possible the next day. He had no time or patience to deal further with these men, so he announced abruptly that he appreciated the information, but could not accommodate any company. The men needed to move on—*swith!* he emphasized.

This brought Hugh's men to full attention, hands on weapons. The ruffians, aware of the odds, quickly mounted their ponies and rode off into the fading light.

"We'll need to post sentries tonight, three shifts. Who'll volunteer?" Three men promptly stepped up.

"We'll be in sight of the English in three days," Hugh said. "Let's get some sleep."

On the morning of the fifth day, they knew that they were near the North Sea coast. It was late summer, and the weather was still hot. The deep blue water of the North Sea, however, was quite cold, and there was often a dense fog that rolled in. As they crawled out of their sleeping rolls, it was so foggy they could see for only a short distance, less than a few yards, and the air had a distinctive salty smell.

Instructing his men to be very careful and keep a sharp lookout, Hugh shouted, "Mount up."

The fog would help hide them, but also would conceal the English. Hugh's men had an advantage though. They were looking for the English, but the English were not looking for them.

The group mounted up and started eastward through scrub trees broken by swaths of open, sandy areas. At length they came upon a long series of hills running parallel to the coast. By now, the fog had lifted. They broke into two groups, and each group ascended a hill.

Hugh warned his men against stopping their horses on top, for to do so would silhouette them against the western sky, making them much more visible. So each group stopped short of the summit, tied their horses, and walked carefully to the top.

"What an amazing view!" Hugh marveled. The blue-black waters of the North Sea stretched off into the distance. White specks floated near the shore and out toward the horizon. *Ships,* Hugh realized, quickly counting about 20 of them.

A road ran along the coast, and Hugh noticed a trail of dust rising in the south.

"The English army," Hugh said in a low tone. "There should be an advance guard a good ways out in front," he continued. "Scan the road forward of the dust."

"There!" exclaimed one of his men, pointing to a distant tree line. Hugh peered intently in that direction. Sure enough, he could make out several red-clad mounted figures, the sun glinting off their shiny helmets. They were moving two abreast in a long line.

"There they are," he said. "English cavalry."

Hugh motioned for the other group to move down the back of the hill they had ascended, and did likewise with his men. Meeting at the bottom, they talked about what they had seen, and how they might go about surveying the English forces further. Hugh decided they should ride south a ways on the inland side of the hills until they were near the main English columns, then ride back up a hill and repeat the process. They proceeded. After topping a hill further south, they could easily make out the English land army stretching off for miles. *Great God!* Hugh marveled. The ruffians from last night had not exaggerated at all.

Stretched out below them was the largest army Hugh had ever seen. They decided to stay where they were, watch and count. The numbers were too much for one man to remember accurately, so Hugh appointed four of his men, whom he knew could count, to quantify the various elements of the army. It took almost the whole rest of the day for the army to pass. They counted over 20,000 men in total; some 6,000 cavalry, 5,000 longbowmen, 8,000 infantry armed with halberds, billhooks and pikes, and a long train of what appeared to be wheeled cannons.

The cannons were not the ship-sized cannon such as in the armored wagon at Lochnaw, but smaller, longer pieces atop two-wheeled carriages, each with a long tongue harnessed to a pair of horses.

"Those are cannon, sure enough," Hugh mulled aloud, "but lighter and more maneuverable. There are scores of them!"

Also, Hugh noticed that one large section of the cavalry was dressed in a different uniform than the standard English garb. These cavalrymen had helmets with plumes and wore blue surcoats and trousers. But it was the weapons they carried that puzzled Hugh. They were not the usual short crossbows favored by most cavalry, but strange-looking objects with long, round rods attached to wooden stocks.

*These men are not English,* Hugh thought. *They must be mercenaries, but from where, and with what kind of weapons?*

"I don't like the looks of that at all," said Hugh. "We've got to figure out a way to get better information."

At the very tail of the army, there were a large number of wooden carts, each pulled by two oxen. The carts had wooden wheels and a long, wooden tongue extending from the front, onto which the oxen were harnessed. Some of the carts were covered, some not. Moving slowly, they were lumbering along in the cloud of dust. Each had a driver who wielded a leather whip, which he occasionally cracked to urge the big beasts onward. A line of horse-mounted cavalry rode along one side.

Hugh surmised that these were supply carts. The ships had to stop and off-load supplies at intervals, whenever the land forces reached the mouth of a river or firth that had a big and deep enough harbor for the ships to move up close to land. The supplies were then offloaded onto the carts.

As the group watched, they noticed that the last cart had fallen behind a considerable distance. Perhaps there had been some kind of mechanical trouble. Whatever the case, there was a large gap between this last cart and the rest of the supply train. The cart had a driver, and there was a lone cavalryman alongside. His only weapon appeared to be a sabre strapped to his side. The cart driver had no weapon other than the whip.

The road wound around curves at places and through wooded areas. The cart would occasionally be completely out of sight from the rest for fairly long stretches. Hugh hatched a plan. Capture this cart at a time when it was out of the sight of the others. If done quickly, they should be able to take it without being seen or arousing suspicion. Hugh was particularly interested in the cavalryman alongside. With any luck they could capture him and squeeze out some good information.

Noticing a curve up ahead in a wooded stretch, Hugh saw that the road was bisected by a deep burn that had been filled with logs to allow passage of the carts. Hugh decided this was the place. They would ride down under cover of the wood to the burn and wait in hiding for the cart.

"We must stop the cart and capture the cavalryman alive," he emphasized.

The oxen had rings in their noses with a rope tied to the ring running back to the driver. This was how the big beasts were controlled. Hugh needed three men—one to ride out and grab the rope, stopping the oxcart as soon as it reached the burn and the others to attack the driver. Hugh wanted them to come at him from both sides, killing him quickly with crossbows. This would distract and confuse the cavalryman, who undoubtedly would charge up to help his comrade. Hugh and his men would surround the cavalryman, seize the reins and hold his horse.

"I will pull him off the horse," Hugh said. "If he draws the sabre, I will take care of that also. I do *not* want him killed. This must all be done fast. Does everybody understand?" They all nodded.

Hugh selected the three who would go with him to execute the attack, and they hurried into position. The rest of Hugh's men stayed hidden further back in the wood to respond only if something went awry. Watching anxiously, Innis stayed with the reserve group.

The attack worked somewhat as planned, though with a couple of surprises. The oxen were successfully stopped, but the driver of the cart lashed his whip at the first of Hugh's crossbowmen to arrive, wrapping the tip of the whip around the man's arm and jerking him off the horse to the ground. The cart driver did not see the other rider, however, who sent a bolt into his chest, inflicting a mortal wound.

The English cavalryman's horse, surprised by all the sudden activity, bolted and ran, with the rider trying desperately to pull him under control. Hugh sped after him, as did his other horseman, soon catching up. Hugh's man managed to get a hold on the horse's bridle reins, pulling the frightened horse's head around as it continued to jump and buck. The English cavalryman was attempting to unsheathe his sabre, but was unable to do so amidst the bucking and spinning of the horse.

Quickly riding up on the other side, Hugh grabbed the cavalryman around the shoulders, and pulled him sprawling to the ground. He then sprang from his horse and had the point of his broadsword poised at the center of the man's chest as he lay, wide-eyed, on the ground. Hugh's comrade also dismounted and was standing near, weapon at the ready.

"Reivers!" the cavalryman hissed through clenched teeth. "You're all cowards."

"That may be, but I wish to have a talk with you, unless you wish to die," Hugh retorted calmly, poking the sharp sword point deeper.

The cavalryman had mistaken them for common reivers. Hugh decided there was no need to disabuse him of that notion unless he refused to talk.

"I don't talk with cowards," the man said, spitting at Hugh.

Hugh withdrew his sword, grabbed the man by the neck of his coat and jerked him to his feet.

"Draw your sabre," Hugh snarled, taking two steps backward. "Then we'll see who's a coward!"

The man did and Hugh let him get the sabre completely unsheathed. Stepping forward, the cavalryman thrust his blade at Hugh's chest. Hugh stepped lightly aside, and brought his broadsword down in a lightning flash upon the man's sword arm, completely severing his hand at the wrist.

The Englishman shrieked, appeared to be reaching for his sabre lying on the ground, but now had no hand with which to grasp it. Hugh kicked him hard in the stomach, knocking him flat on his back. His hand gone and the stump squirting blood, the man looked up frantically at Hugh.

"Sir! I beseech you, don't kill me." The Englishman had suddenly changed from an arrogant braggart to a sniveling milksop.

"You will have to tell me what I want," Hugh said evenly.

"Anything!" the man pleaded.

Hugh instructed his comrade to apply a tourniquet to the man's arm and wrap the stump, and then he proceeded with his interrogation.

"The long line of horse-drawn cannons, what are they for?"

"Artillery pieces," the man said, clenching his teeth and squeezing his stump with his other hand. "They shoot smaller balls than a ship cannon, but over a longer distance."

"How are they used?" asked Hugh.

His face now ashen, the man answered, "In battle, they are brought up to high ground where they can fire over a long distance."

Hugh thought this over for a moment, and then asked, "Where did they come from?"

The man answered weakly, "The Italians. They were the first to make these type guns."

"And the cavalry unit in the blue uniforms?" Hugh asked. "Italian mercenaries?"

The man nodded, his voice now barely above a whisper, "aye."

"The weapons they carry, what are those?"

"Arquebusiers," he moaned. "Smaller powder guns that can be fired by hand."

Eyeing Hugh suspiciously, and despite his pain, the cavalryman asked his own question:

"You be Scottish cavalry?"

"Aye," Hugh answered.

"You haven't a chance," the Englishman said, a thin smile on his lips. "Our army will cut you to shreds."

At that, Hugh's broadsword, which he had been holding point down on the ground as he knelt beside the stricken cavalryman, flashed again. In one fluid movement, he brought the sword down on the man's head, cutting through the steel helmet and cleaving deep into his skull. Blood spurted from the gaping hole in the helmet. The English cavalryman sputtered and fell to his side.

"A brave man," Hugh said quietly, "but too arrogant for his own good."

He instructed his men to release the oxen and overturn the cart. If a unit of the English army came back, they would think there had been an attack by reivers or ordinary outlaws. He also wanted them to gather up anything they could eat on the trip back.

"Hurry! We need to get this report back to Arran!"

# 20.
## Pinkie Cleugh

THE renaissance was in full swing across Europe at this time, starting in Italy and progressing to Portugal, France, Holland and the Germanic countries. In addition to the flowering of the arts, philosophy and natural sciences, great strides were being made in weaponry. In particular, gunpower arms, from cannons to handguns, were multiplying and improving at a fast pace. Also there was innovation in tactics for the use of these weapons. Volley fire had been developed, making it possible to have virtually continuous fire, and massed fire that could inflict multiple casualties instantaneously.

Very little of this progress had penetrated Scotland, however. The Scots were still fighting medieval style, with pikes, halberds, longbows, crossbows, battle-axes and swords. The gunpowder weapons had been introduced in England, and the English army was rapidly assembling a sizable supply and training their armies to use them.

✦ ✦ ✦

Hugh's group sped away. They had all of the intelligence on the size and strength of the English they could safely get. The most important thing now was to get it quickly back to the Scottish army commanders. After four days of hard riding, they met up with Arran's army a short distance east of Dumfries. Hugh went straight to Baron Agnew, informing him that they had found the English army and had important information to share. Soon Arran had his commanders assembled in his tent, and Hugh gave them the startling news.

Everyone was quiet as Hugh related a full summary of the events. After that, there were many questions, punctuated by shouting, expressions of disbelief by some and differences of opinion. Finally, Arran ordered everyone out; he needed to think. After a time, he got word to Agnew and Hugh that he would like to meet with them privately in his tent.

When they returned, Arran was deep in thought, with several maps spread on a table before him. One was of East Lothian, showing in particular the city of Edinburgh, together with the location of other towns and geophysical features of the landscape. Arran wanted to hear more about the English artillery, of which Hugh's men had counted at least 40 pieces.

Arran was a sophisticated man, skilled in the military arts, and had traveled in many areas on the European continent. He was aware of the increasing proliferation of gunpowder firearms. In addition to the Italians, he was aware the Portuguese, Germans, Swiss and French had such weapons. Obviously they were now being supplied to the English.

Arran knew less about the handheld guns, the arquebusiers, as Hugh had said they were called. Logically, he saw no reason that such guns could not be made, and used to dramatic effect, particularly against tightly-packed units of infantry such as the traditional Scot squares of men wielding pikes and halberds. Arran also wondered about the English cavalry—how many, how well equipped? Hugh said his men had counted about 5,000, and they looked very fit. He also described the large unit of mounted Italian arquebusiers.

Arran was worried. He had more of the traditional pikemen, halberd and bow brigades than the English, and they were solid soldiers. His total number of fighting men equaled the English, and maybe exceeded them. But he had only some 2,000 cavalry, and many of them were borderers on hill ponies, not well trained. Plus, they were led by the Earl of Home, a pompous, arrogant man with little actual battle experience. Thank God he also had Hugh Henderson's special unit of cavalry, well trained and dependable, but it only numbered 200. Overall, he was grievously deficient in cavalry strength.

As to firearms, he was even more deficient; he had essentially none. Arran knew that there were some ship-sized cannons inside the walls at Edinburgh Castle. He would somehow have to get them loaded onto wagons or some other means of transport to get them in the field. Still he was worried. In addition to having fewer cannon than the English, his would be heavy and unwieldy. Many of them were of different bores, and shot different sized balls. That was a recipe for confusion during battle.

Arran, Agnew and Hugh discussed these matters at some length, all the while examining the maps to see where and if any advantage could be gained by terrain. Arran felt that he needed to make maximum use of natural barriers if his army was to have a chance.

The main road into Edinburgh from the south ran through the small town of Musselburgh. It crossed the River Esk over a single bridge, built by the Romans when they invaded in about 70 A.D. The Esk was deep and swift at this point, running roughly southwest to northeast. It was the only crossing anywhere near.

This was a pinch point, Arran reckoned, and a good place to stop the English advance. He could array his forces on the slopes of the southwest bank of the Esk, near the bridge, where he could erect fortifications and array the cannons from Edinburgh Castle. His army would be protected by the Firth of Forth on his left, and a large bog on his right. This would be an advantageous position, making it difficult for the English army to punch through to Edinburgh.

Arran had a head start on the English and proceeded eastward with his army toward the River Esk to take up positions. He had time to construct berm fortifications, upon which he spread about the cannons he had obtained from Edinburgh Castle. On September 8, 1547, the English army arrived. The English commander, Somerset, had his army occupy Falside Hill, high ground on the other side of the Esk some three miles east of Arran's main position.

In an outdated chivalric and foolhardy gesture, the leader of the Scottish cavalry, the Earl of Home, led 1,500 of his horsemen across the Roman bridge toward Falside Hill. He took them close to the English encampment and challenged an equal number of English cavalry to a fight. When Home had first presented the idea, Arran considered it a futile maneuver, but reluctantly approved. Somerset, on the other hand, saw opportunity. He allowed Lord Grey, commander of the English cavalry, to accept. Grey met the Scots with 1,000 heavily armored cavalrymen astride large horses, and 500 lighter demi-lancers.

The Scots borderers were lightly armed and most were astride speedy but light Galloway ponies. When the two sides clashed, the Scots were soon badly cut up, put to rout and pursued for several miles. Before it was over, the Scots cavalry had been decimated while the English losses were modest. Hugh's contingent, fortunately, had been held out of this action by Arran. But, right away, because of misguided leadership, Arran had lost almost all of his regular cavalry.

Late that afternoon, Somerset sent an artillery detachment to occupy the Inveresk slopes, a long line of hills on the East side of the River Esk opposite Arran's barricaded main force. Early the next morning he advanced the rest of his army to close ranks with the artillery detachment. During the night, the bulk of the English navy, 30 warships strong, sailed into the Firth of Forth and lay at anchor in a broad bay near the town of Musselburgh. Somerset now had Arran's forces surrounded with men, guns and ships on two sides. There was a bog on the other side of Arran's troops toward the south, and the broad plain of the River Esk ran between the two armies.

Arran was informed of the English artillery and troops opposite him atop the Inveresk hills. Because of Hugh's intelligence report, he was aware of the fearsome firepower of the artillery guns. From his dug-in position Arran's heavy, mismatched ship cannons could not reach the English and would be next to impossible to move. He knew his army was now vulnerable. Considering that his cavalry had been emasculated and his cannons were of little use, his only real strength lay with traditional ground forces. But it would be suicide to send them out to meet the English head-on. They would first have to cross the Roman Bridge and then traverse the broad Esk valley. In the process they could be pulverized by artillery shot and raining arrows. Arran needed a plan. He decided to call in his commanders, including Baron Andrew Agnew and Sir Hugh Henderson, to discuss the situation.

The group assembled in the command tent and Arran explained the predicament. He needed to find a way to neutralize the English artillery staring down on the battlefield. With his cavalry destroyed, he felt he had no choice but to move his army out quickly and cross the Esk. His best chance at victory, he felt, was to force close-in combat, mixing the ranks and thus rendering the English artillery less effective.

Looking at Hugh, Arran asked, "Where do you ken they would array those artillery guns?"

Hugh thought a minute before answering. "They would probably look for a flat area on the high ground as close to the battlefield as possible."

"On your recent surveillance sojourn to the coast, did you learn anything about the range of those guns?"

Hugh thoughtfully ran his fingers through his greyish black chin whiskers.

"Nothing precise, m'Lord, but I was led to believe, on elevated ground such as Inveresk over there, they could cover a broad area. Up to ten furlongs maybe."

Arran's eyes widened. That was over a mile. Shelling could reach all the way to the river. "Lets go outside and get a better look at those slopes," he said.

The commanders followed Arran out of the tent, and they all trained their eyes across the Esk to the high ground beyond. It was mid-morning and a haze of fog still covered the hilltops. Looking north, they could see the dark blue waters of the Firth of Forth. Dim white shapes of the English ships floating on the broad bay could be seen. Across the Esk between the bay and a large roundish hill, they could just make out the church bell tower in the town of Musselburgh. To the south, the hill was connected to a long high ridge that ran several furlongs to another hill of about the same size.

"Yesterday around dusk we had a couple of visitors who lived over yon," Arran said, pointing toward the far south hill. "Twas a man and his grown son. They came in and presented themselves to one of our commanders. Said they wanted to join our army. After being closely interviewed, they were found to be loyal Scots with military training. Since they knew the area, the commander brought them in to see me. I got from them a general description of the layout atop the slopes."

All turned their attention to Arran.

"The men said they were part of a family of seven and lived in a house atop that hill to the south. They had heard the English were advancing with a large army and knew we had advanced our army as well. He figured they would be in the middle of a big fight and decided to vacate the area. The man had relatives in Edinburgh and had already sent his wife there with the rest of the family.

"Where was the English army," asked one of the commanders.

"From what he said, they were marching in on the road coming over from Dunbar on the east coast. The road winds up the south hill, then traverses across the ridge to the north hill. There it splits, with one branch going to Musselburgh, and the other turning south, running along the valley floor to the Roman Bridge."

There was a pause as the men gazed across the valley and tried to envision the geography based on what Arran had said. Finally Baron Agnew ventured a question.

"Sire, I don't suppose you learned anything about the location of the various units of the English army?"

"Nay," said Arran, "I inquired but the man said he had left before the English arrived."

"If I may offer a comment, m'Lord," said Hugh.

"Of course—go ahead."

"Speaking for myself, I agree with your statement that forcing close-in combat is our best choice. But it would be helpful if we had more intelligence, such as where the English have placed their artillery, cavalry, bowmen and various other ground forces. Also a better understanding of the general topography and buildings in the area would be helpful."

"Aye, it would," Arran said, smiling at Hugh, "and I happen to know a man most adept at reconnaissance. Methinks he has just volunteered. Go see those two locals I spoke of and work up a plan. Anything you need is yours. But you don't have long, I expect the English will attack tomorrow."

Soon Hugh found himself staring into the dark brown eyes of a tall bewhiskered man named Clyde Leslie. Hugh told him his mission, emphasizing he had to complete it by nightfall.

Clyde's eyes widened. "Then you have very little time."

" Tis true. Might you have any idea where the English commanders have made their headquarters?"

"I haven't seen with my own eyes, but Fawside Castle is about midway along the ridge. It is set back from the road a good ways. When we vacated our place, there were many people streaming out the front gates, herding animals and carrying whatever personal possessions they could manage. We talked with some of them and were told the English planned to occupy the castle. It is the only fortified position in the area. They hoped it would be left intact when the fighting was over. Not likely in my opinion."

Hugh asked if Clyde knew of anyone in the area who planned to stay put.

"Aye, the parish priest, George Dury. The church is between my place and Fawside Castle. He lives in a small one-room abode attached to the rear of the church building. I stopped by to see if the good father planned to leave, thinking he might like to travel with us. He declined, saying he didn't think the English commanders would allow harm to come to a priest or to a house of worship. He wanted to be available in case any of his parishioners needed assistance once the fighting started. Father Dury is a fine man. I hope he's right that the English aren't apt to do him harm."

"Let's pray he is," Hugh said. "If I can find a piece of parchment, reckon you could sketch out a rough diagram of the road, terrain and buildings you just mentioned?"

"I can try, but understand, I be no artist."

Hugh sent for a sheet of parchment as the two men continued to talk.

"You are confident that Father Dury be a loyal Scot?"

"Aye, I trust him as I would my own son." Then, eyeing Hugh closely, Clyde asked, "Do you plan to go on this mission by yourself?"

"I think it best. I don't have much time. If I take anyone else, it will just slow me down and increase chances of the English finding us out."

"Then you surely don't plan to go in that garb you be wearing. You'll stick out like a black sheep. Folk in our area wear distinctive clothing."

Hugh peered at Clyde, for the first time paying particular attention to his appearance. Clyde was about Hugh's age and size. He wore a grey bonnet made of nubby looking material with a ball on top, and a grey shirt with sleeves cut off at the elbows. It was closed in front with a metal stick-pin. The trouser legs extended to mid-calf. He wore leather-laced shoes with pointy toes.

"I see what you mean," Hugh said. "Your garb is different all right. Local variations I assume?"

"Aye, not so noticeable unless you know what to look for. Men's bonnets and shoes have been made in this style in our area for generations. No doubt the English will have local collaborators. They would notice the difference in your clothing immediately. You and me seem around the same size; I suggest we trade garb."

Hugh nodded and the two men began shucking clothes. "Another thing," Clyde said, "I assume you ride a big cavalry horse?"

"Aye, but not as big as some. I prefer a horse with good size, but also fast and maneuverable. Er, I guess you're about to tell me I need to change horses too?"

"Same problem," Clyde said. "Most everybody in the Inveresk region has a smaller long-haired hill pony."

"I assume you rode in on such a horse?"

Clyde nodded.

"Then I guess prudence dictates that we trade horses too?"

"Aye, that would be safest," Clyde said. "When you get back we can switch again."

"That would be '*if*,' I'm afraid," Hugh winced.

After Clyde had completed the drawing, Hugh was ready to set off. First he paused to tell Innis what he was up to. As Hugh figured he would, Innis wanted to be at his side. In fact he was quite insistent about it. Hugh explained he was sure to be stopped by English troops and challenged. A cover story would have to be concocted.

"Listen," Hugh said, becoming exasperated, "it's hard enough for one person to keep a fib straight, much less two. Besides where would you find a getup like I've got on. Nay, it's safest you don't go."

Innis looked disappointed but didn't protest further. Hugh turned to go. Looking back over his shoulder he called out: "If I don't get back by tomorrow, the trade of horses and clothes I made with Clyde Leslie is permanent. Understand?" Innis nodded.

The hill pony was fitted with a wood-framed saddle with a pelt cover. This apparatus was uncomfortable and the pony had a jarring gait, but Hugh managed to maintain an air of normalcy as he crossed over the Roman Bridge and turned south. If any English scouts were watching, it was not likely he would raise suspicions—just a lone local going about his business. Clyde had told him there was another road coming down the Esk valley that ascended the south hill and intersected the main road near the parish church. Hugh decided he would first stop off there and see if he could talk with Father Dury.

The church was set back in some woods at a Y in the road. Hugh noticed the intersecting road was heavily rutted and riddled by hoof prints from large numbers of men and horses. Evidently the English army had already passed. He pulled up at the back of the church out of sight from the road, and tied the pony to a tree. There was a small dwelling attached to the back of the church. Hugh rapped on the door. After a moment it opened, revealing a tall, serene looking man in a long grey habit. He stood erect and Hugh noticed his body was thick and angular.

*Unusual for a priest,"* Hugh thought, *most are slight and rotund.*

The man gave Hugh a warm smile while looking him up and down with obvious curiosity.

"Father Dury?" Hugh said.

"Aye, but I don't believe we've met. Are you from hereabouts?"

"I'm not," Hugh answered. "I'm with the Scottish army. Name's Hugh Henderson. I got your name from a local man named Clyde Leslie. He and his son have joined our army."

"Och, aye, I know Clyde quite well. He and his family live nearby—or at least they did till a couple of days ago. They came by here with a team of horses pulling a wagon loaded with house-hold goods. Clyde said he heard the English army was invading and a big fight with the Scottish army was expected. He thought the English would occupy Fawside Castle and station their forces up and down this ridge so they would have the high ground. He invited me to go with them."

"He told me the same story," Hugh said.

"You said Clyde and his son joined the Scottish army. What happened to the rest of his family?"

"He said he sent them on to Edinburgh to get them out of harm's way."

"I'm nay surprised. Clyde's a devout family man. Also a strong Scot patriot. You're fortunate to have him. He was right about the English army. They came in right on his heels. It took them all day to pass by. Thousands. I tried to count, but there were too many."

There was a short silence as each man searched for what to say next. Finally Father Dury broke the spell.

"Och, where are my manners. Would you like to come in, Mr. Henderson? My quarters are small, but I can pull up a couple of chairs."

Hugh lowered his head to get under the door-jab and soon they were seated in a small space facing each other.

"I should explain why I'm here," Hugh started.

"Has it something to do with the big battle that beckons?"

"Aye, but first I need to inquire—Clyde said you be a Scot pa-triot as well?"

"Before I took the cloth, I was a member of the Crown's Guard at Edinburgh Castle."

Hugh peered at Father Dury in a new light. He had noticed his height and build, but now he focused on his broad chest and budging shoulders. *In a tight spot, this priest would have more than a prayer to rely upon.*

Satisfied, Hugh said, "When the English passed by, you no doubt noticed a long train of horse-drawn artillery guns?"

"I counted around forty," Dury replied.

"Our army is lacking in heavy guns," Hugh said. "We have only a few old ship cannons from Edinburgh Castle. They are hard to move about. To complicate matters, we've already been in a cavalry fight and lost badly. I'm sure you can appreciate that our situation is dire."

Dury blew out a long low whistle.

Hugh continued, "My task is to reconnoiter the enemy—how their units are arrayed, try to spot any weaknesses."

"And how do you propose to do that?"

"That's why I dropped by. Thought you might have some suggestions. I don't have much time. We expect they'll attack tomorrow morning."

An incredulous expression froze on Dury's face. Finally he said, "I don't know. You are clothed in local looking garb and riding a hill pony so I suppose you won't immediately stick out. But once you get up close to the English forces you're likely to get stopped and questioned. You'll instantly be betrayed by your lowlander accent. The English have local confederates as you probably know."

"Aye, that's a problem I hadn't considered. Any ideas?"

The priest sat in silence for a while, his brow furrowed. "Perhaps I could go along and vouch for you. But how would we get around the accent?"

Hugh considered the problem. "What if I couldn't talk."

"Dumb?"

"Nay, not exactly. We could concoct a story. Let's say I was attacked by bandits and beaten in the head. Made it to your place and you bandaged my wounds. I wouldn't be able to speak except for maybe groaning and moaning."

"I see what you mean, but what if some English guard is suspicious and wants to see under the bandaging?"

Hugh smiled, "We'll just have to make it look convincing."

"How?" Dury inquired.

"Punch me in the face. Concentrate on my nose and jaw. It needs to bruise, bleed and swell."

Three powerful blows did the job. Hugh found himself on his butt on the floor, his nose spurting blood. He took his sgian dubh blade and sliced a deep cut just below his hairline. It also bled copiously. Father Dury pressed a cloth compress to the wounds until the bleeding subsided. Then he tore the bloodied cloth into strips and liberally wrapped them around Hugh's head. The effect was striking. Hugh would easily pass for a casualty from a brutal battle.

"We'd need an explanation for my wounds," Hugh groaned.

"Let's keep it simple," Dury said. "Where you were going and why."

Hugh mumbled through the bandages, "You'll hav, have to piece it together. I'm afraid you made me look too, er, convincing."

Dury laid out possible scenarios, telling Hugh to indicate "yea" or "nay" by shaking his head. Within a few minutes they had worked out a plausible story. Dury had a one-horse buckboard cart. Hugh seated himself in the rear of the cart with his back against the driver seat. Dury laid his staff beside Hugh, tied Hugh's borrowed pony to the back, and they headed out on the road toward Fawside Castle.

Within a few minutes, they began to see English soldiers. Some were herding livestock down the road while others were marching in formation. Several cavalrymen were also seen riding in the direction of Fawside. Soon they were approached by three men astride large cavalry horses. The first wore a plumed helmet and the ornate uniform of an English major. The other was a regular cavalryman. Beside him was a man in civilian clothes.

The major held up his hand, palm forward. "Halt!"

Dury pulled the cart to a stop. "Good morning, Major," he said, doffing his bonnet.

"Identify yourselves and state your business," the English officer intoned in a gruff voice.

"I am William Dury, priest of this parish. This man is the brother of one of my parishioners, a widow woman who lives a few furlongs further out on the Musselburgh road. As you can see, he has been injured. I'm assisting him to his sister's place."

The mounted cavalrymen continued to eye them suspiciously. "How did he get injured?" inquired the major.

"Set upon by bandits," said Dury. "Coming up the west ridge road a few furlongs from my church. He was beaten and robbed by several men. I live in back of the church and he barely made it to my place. I bandaged him as best I could."

The major rode his horse up beside the wagon and unsheathed his sword. Hugh tensed but remained still. The English officer poked him in the side with the point of the sword. "Your name?"

Hugh groaned and made a slurred, indistinct noise, blood oozing from the corners of his mouth.

"His name be Hugh Storey," the priest said. "I know him. He's been up to visit his sister several times. She's been in a bad way since her husband died."

The English officer made his decision. He took a small leather book from inside his vest, tore off a slip and handed it to Dury.

"You may proceed, but do not stop or tarry. If you are challenged again, show them this permission. When you get where you're going, stay put. Likely it'll not be safe around here for the next few days."

Despite the pain in his head, Hugh felt almost euphoric. They had met their first test and passed.

As they neared Fawside Castle, the road grew progressively more noisy and crowded—cavalry units clopping to and fro, foot soldiers marching in cadence, trees being felled and rough corrals built for the livestock. After awhile they reached a roadblock. It was manned by an English officer and several of the blue-coated Italian mercenaries armed with the arquebusier guns Hugh had seen on his reconnaissance foray not so long ago. Dury stopped the cart in a line and they waited their turn. The pause gave Hugh an opportunity to discretely gaze around.

To his left he could see the tower turrets of Fawside Castle. As he had been told, it was back off the road, surrounded by a high, thick rock wall. The front gate was opened wide and Hugh could

155

see lines of artillery cannons mounted on wheeled carriages in the large field fronting the castle. There was a corral filled with horses, and hordes of red-coated soldiers were milling about. The English national flag flew high above the castle keep and battle flags of various battalions fluttered in the foreground. Without question, this was the English army's headquarters.

To his right Hugh could see teams of sawmen felling large trees. Horses were pulling the fallen logs down a rough, newly constructed road along with artillery pieces. Hugh could hear a distinctive chopping, droning noise. He had heard this sound before. It was made by a multitude of men working on the construction of barricades. The clang of axes, grinding of saws, pounding of hammers and jingling of horse harnesses, this sound told Hugh exactly what was going on. Massive fortifications were being constructed, behind which columns of deadly artillery would be spread all along the high ridge opposite tomorrow's battlefield.

From the map Clyde Leslie had given him, Hugh knew that Fawside Castle was in line with the Roman Bridge. *How far down the slopes had the English cleared the trees,* he wondered. Possibly, unless the trees had been cut down for quite a distance, the line of sight for the artillery gunners would be restricted by the tall trees. They would be unable to see the ground at the bottom of the slopes for a sizable distance out toward the Esk. If the Scots could get their ground forces across the bridge and up to the base of the slopes, they would be in this blind spot, protected from the English artillery. This was a critical issue. He absolutely *had* to get a closer look at the fortifications.

As they slowly clopped along in the horse-cart, the numbers of English forces began to thin. They topped a rise in the road and dropped down. Hugh looked around in all directions—no troops in sight. He tugged on the back of Dury's shirt.

"Stop."

"Here? You sure?"

"Aye."

Dury pulled the cart to a stop.

"I need to get out and go back a ways," Hugh half-whispered. "It's essential that I see the exact location of the gun pits."

"You realize you're a dead man if caught."

Hugh nodded. "No choice—got to do it. You go on."

He slipped out of the cart, untied his pony from the back of the cart, mounted and quickly disappeared into the bushes alongside the road. After riding deeper into the wood, a distance he thought would be roughly in line with the gun pits, Hugh turned.

The ground was rough, with boulders and fallen logs scattered about. Fortunately the hill pony proved adept at picking his way through them without making much noise. After a ways Hugh could hear the distant sound of pounding and sawing. He rode the pony a bit closer, dismounted and tied him to a tree in a thicket.

Most of the trees growing on the slope-sides were tall Scottish pines. Mixed in here and there were large deciduous trees with thick trunks and massive limbs covered with leaves. Hugh picked one and climbed it, getting as high up as he could. Looking out he could see several shirtless men busily constructing a log barricade with a dug-out space behind. An artillery piece hitched to a team of horses was nearby. Hugh noticed the trees the men had cut had been formed into a rough semi-circle facing the hillside. Trees further out were left standing. Once the guns were placed in the pit, he realized, the barrels would have to be elevated to fire over the trees.

*My God, not only is there a blind spot along the bottom of the slope, it will be next to impossible for the English gunners to direct fire into it.*

Hugh's pulse quickened. It looked like his hunch was right. The English artillery could fire effectively further out toward the Esk, but closer in would be very difficult. This information needed to quickly be conveyed to Arran and the other Scot commanders.

Then another thought hit him: *Perhaps the fortifications weren't finished. After all, this was the first one he had come upon. Others might have firing lanes of felled trees. He needed to check a few more.*

He moved further downslope, slipped around the fortification and continued south. The sound of men working gradually diminished. Hugh decided to climb another tree. After he reached an adequate height he found an opening in the leaves and looked out. Two more gun fortifications could be seen. Artillery pieces were in place and no firing lanes had been cleared.

Moving around to the other side, Hugh was able to look out over the Esk valley. The Roman Bridge and the road winding beneath the slopes could be seen. *We'll need to get our ground troops across that bridge in the early morning darkness before the English realize what we're up to,* he thought. *Quickly move the men to the base of the slope and charge uphill. This will force the English into hand-to-hand combat. They'll still have the high ground, but it won't make much difference in the wooded terrain. Their big guns will be useless.*

Hugh clambered back down the tree. He dropped from the bottom limb and felt his feet hit the ground. Then all went black.

# 21.
# THE BATTLEGROUND

AFTER a while, Hugh had no idea how long, consciousness slowly returned. As his eyesight cleared he could see ground below him. He was on his stomach bouncing over rough terrain. Trying to move his body to an upright position, he realized his hands and feet were tied. He turned his head. *I'm slung over the back of a horse.* The animal was being led by a tall man in a grey robe. *Father Dury! Why is he here?*

Hugh called out. "Wha,.. what happened?"

Dury pulled up the pony, walked back and loosened Hugh's ties. Hugh was slipped off the pony's back and laid on the forest floor. His head was pounding and the taste of blood was in his mouth. The priest wiped Hugh's face with the hem of his robe, cleaning blood from his eyes and nose.

"You were hit in the head and being dragged by two English soldiers."

"How did you get there," asked Hugh, bewildered.

"I decided to follow in case you got in trouble. I had to stay back a ways so you wouldn't see me and did not plan to intervene unless necessary. I saw the English soldiers slip up as you climbed down from the tree. They whacked you in the head with a battleax, tied your limbs and were dragging you up the slope."

"You rescued me?"

Dury nodded.

"How?"

"I got behind the tree you had climbed. Both soldiers were looking uphill—the direction you were being dragged. I hit one in the head with my staff, knocking him to the ground. The other stepped back and was trying to unsheathe his sabre. I grabbed him around the head, pulled my sgian dubh and cut his throat. Then the first one got up and came at me with his blade. I had to kill him too. It'll take me many years of penance to gain forgiveness in God's eyes for these killings."

Hugh got on his knees and assumed a kneeling posture. Soberly he whispered, "I'm so sorry. I got you into this and now you've saved my life. How can I ever repay such a debt."

"Use the knowledge you got here to help our cause. I held no malice toward these men. I simply had no other choice. Maybe God will understand."

The two men resumed their travel, walking uphill toward the Musselburgh road. After awhile they heard a whinny. Dury's pony stopped, perked his ears and answered.

"That's my pony," Hugh said. "Right where I tied him." Hugh walked shakily over and untied the animal. He turned to Dury.

"This be where we part ways. I know I can never repay all you have done, but I assure you the intelligence we've gained will greatly assist our army."

Dury crossed himself and incanted, "God be with you, Hugh Henderson. You are a brave man."

Hugh mounted his pony and headed through the wood in a northerly direction staying well off the road. Shortly he entered a grove of tall mature pines. The ground was covered in pine needles and the underbrush was sparse. Shafts of suffuse sunlight lit the forest floor. *Rather like entering the nave of a cathedral,* Hugh mused.

To the west he could see the broad Esk valley and the river beyond. Looking north he could just make out whitecaps on the Firth of Forth and the English ships lying at anchor. Suddenly he had a flash of inspiration—*this would be an excellent place to mount a counter-attack. If we could get a sizable force here under cover of darkness, we could get behind the English artillery. We might even achieve complete surprise.* Hugh kicked his pony to a faster pace. He needed to get this intelligence to Arran.

+ + +

Early the next morning well before first light, Arran had Hugh's cavalrymen lead several divisions of pikemen and archers across the Roman bridge. With Innis at his side, Hugh led his cavalry at a fast trot over the plain toward the Inveresk slopes. The infantry marched quick-step behind. When they reached the slopes, they turned north and followed the road toward the bay and the grove of towering pines Hugh had explored the day before. A frigid, salty breeze blew off the bay and a quarter moon could be seen through scudding clouds. The reddish glow of English campfires dotted the tops of the slopes. Baron Andrew Agnew led a rear guard of pikemen, four squares of fifty each. It had taken Hugh's contingent over an hour to cross the narrow bridge and reach the turn.

Behind them, also crossing the bridge and then quickstepping toward the base of the slopes followed 20,000 more Scots troops. Once there they would have protection from English artillery fire. Hopes were high that Hugh's plan would work and the Scots would emerge victorious.

As Hugh's cavalry neared the pine trees, he noticed the English ships were slowly moving. They seemed to be maneuvering into a line closer to shore. *They've pulled anchor, I wonder why,* Hugh puzzled. *Possibly to land more troops? Unload additional supplies?* Hugh didn't have long to ponder the question as his cavalry was already at the wood. He ordered a halt. Here he allowed the ground forces to catch up and for their commanders to issue final instructions. Toward the eastern horizon the stars above Inveresk slowly dimmed. Dawn was creeping nearer.

As the instructions were being given, Hugh guided his horse out onto the open plain and turned his gaze south. The horizon along the tops of the hills had noticeably lightened. The valley below was still dark and Hugh was unable to make out the Scots troops crossing the bridge. A knot of anxiety grew in his stomach. *If our army is still strung out when dawn's light hits the valley floor, we'll be in trouble.*

Hugh rode back to the others. He had more immediate concerns—getting 2,000 ground troops into the wooded grove and moving them up the hill toward enemy positions. He led his cavalry behind the ground troops and motioned urgently for them to enter the wood and move upslope. "As quickly and quietly as possible," he said.

In places the hillside was quite steep. Soldiers lost their footing, slipping and sliding on the pine needles. Disorganization and confusion set in, but still they pushed on, grabbing tree limbs to pull themselves along. Finally, as the first rays of sunlight broke over the hilltops, almost all of the force was in the wood. Hugh's cavalry spread out in a line on the road, with Hugh manning the north flank.

They were preparing to enter the wood and bring up the rear of the battalion. Then something in the bay caught Hugh's attention. He stopped and looked. The English ships were now hugging the coast. Arrayed bow to stern in a long line, the ships were gently bobbing with broadsides facing the shore. Suddenly puffs of smoke appeared all along the line, followed by a gigantic rumbling roar. Hugh had heard this noise before. *Cannon! Holy Hell, they're firing at us.*

A twelve pound iron ball splatted into the ground beside him. Hugh's horse skiddered sideways nearly dislodging him from the saddle. "Get your horses into the wood," he screamed.

They all did, but the situation there was no better. Iron balls pounded everywhere. Trees broke apart and splintered limbs crashed to the ground. Men and horses were getting maimed at an alarming rate. Shouts, cries and curses rang out as men frantically sought cover. Horses screamed and bellowed, jumped, bucked and fell as a fearsome hail of destruction rained down from the skies.

"Up, up!" Hugh screamed. "Move higher—higher."

Slipping, falling, grappling and pushing—men and horses frantically struggled upward. Still the pounding continued. Despite the terrible maelstrom, they slowly moved higher.

Then they stumbled into another kind of barrage. *Arrows!* English bowmen filled the woods above, hidden from view. Some were behind tree trunks and others were in the trees, perched on high limbs. Arrows rained down, picking off the leading edge of the Scots advance one by one. The Scots took cover as best they could. Their bowmen were called forward and answered with arrows of their own. The English were well hidden, enjoyed an uphill position and had superior numbers. The Scots response was mostly futile. Quickly it became apparent that they were in dire danger of getting pulverized.

The Scots commanders called a hurried retreat, turning the troops back down the slope. They'd rather take their chances in a haphazard hail of iron balls and splintered timber than carefully aimed arrows. The retreat became disorderly and turned into frenzied panic. Ground commanders and Hugh's cavalrymen tried to restore order, but their efforts were to little avail.

Only Baron Agnew's pike squares maintained any semblance of discipline. They held their formation and moved further out toward the banks of the River Esk. There they found sparse cover in scrub brush and reeds. Most of the other Scots ground troops fled in a disorderly retreat south down the road or scattered across the broad Esk plain. Many were killed or grievously wounded by the continuing cannon fire from the ships. Hugh had his cavalrymen form up and trot south, through and around the hordes of panicked, fleeing soldiers, hugging close to the tree line.

Up ahead Hugh saw what he had feared all morning. Scots ground forces were stalled at the narrow Roman bridge. Several battalions remained on the other side of the Esk, waiting their turn to cross. Some of those who had already crossed managed to get to the sheltered area at the base of the slopes, while others were out in the open desperately trying to get there. Dawn had broken all across the valley floor and Scots soldiers covered the plain. Some units were in total disarray. Many turned back and were fleeing in panic toward the bridge where they clashed with their own soldiers trying to cross to join the battle. Others threw themselves into the swift river, attempting to swim across, while still others ran into the bog.

Hugh heard another loud rumble. The English artillery atop the high ridge had opened up. Scots soldiers out in the open without cover were helpless. They were falling in droves—some dead, others dying, a few making it to safety. Many men had gruesome wounds—shattered limbs, smashed heads, gaping, torn flesh. Horrific screams, loud piercing cries, curses, angry shouts and mumbled prayers from Scots solders mixed with the anguished squeals and bellows of wounded horses amid the ringing reports from the hilltop cannons. War at its most horrific.

More gunfire rang out, not as loud as artillery, but sharper and coming in volleys. Hugh saw a cloud of dust rising in the south and flashes of reflected sunlight. *The Italian mercenaries with the shiny helmets,* he realized. *They have cut off our south flank and are laying down fire with their arquebusiers. We are now surrounded by gunfire on three sides, and have none to fight back with.*

Hugh looked downstream in the direction Baron Agnew had led his pike squares. The ship cannon and hilltop guns suddenly grew silent. A massive squadron of English cavalry came out of the woods and was charging toward Agnew's pikemen. The pike squares drew up tightly and bristled like giant porcupines. The long sharp pikes impaled the leading edge of the English charge. Horses went down from the piercing stabs, spilling their riders. Scots infantry set upon them with swords and battleaxes.

But the force of the huge English horses combined with a fierce onslaught of sharp lances and swords wore the Scots down. Their squares began to break apart. More English ground troops arrived, slashing with swords and battleaxes to great effect. While the Scots fought valiantly, they were seriously outnumbered. As Hugh watched, they crumbled and a disorderly retreat ensued.

The English cavalry continued its charge up the Esk, heading toward the bridge, cutting down fleeing Scots as it went. Similar scenes were taking place all over. English cavalry and ground troops poured out of the woods and charged the scattered and disorganized Scots from one end of the valley to the other.

Hugh threw his entire remaining unit into the English cavalry charge. Despite the overwhelming odds, he was intent on stopping the English.

"We've got to stop them from plugging the bridge," he shouted.

Formed up tightly with lances and swords, his men spurred their horses across the bloodied battlefield, slashing, hacking and ramming. Suddenly Hugh saw that elements of the mounted Italian mercenaries were arriving and firing away with their arquebusiers. Out of the corner of his eye, he saw Sir Agnew go down, shot in the chest. Agnew got up, seized a discarded broadsword and stood alone, swinging the sword furiously against all who surrounded him.

"Agnew has been hit," Hugh screamed to Innis, "I've got to help him!"

Guiding his horse out of the immediate cavalry battle, Hugh spurred it into a dead run, galloping straight for Agnew. As he flew across the battlefield, he felt a sharp, piercing, sensation in his back, then another in his shoulder. The Italians had him in their sights and were firing away. Arrows from English bowmen whistled in the air. Hugh reached Agnew just as an arrow pierced Agnew's back. The Baron crumbled to the ground. Hugh's valiant horse, shot through by both shot and arrows, stumbled and fell. Hugh landed on the ground at Agnew's side.

Agnew was face down, the arrow stuck deep in his rib cage. Hugh rolled him over. Agnew's eyes were open, and Hugh saw them focus. The two men grasped each other's hands.

"*Fareweel auld freend,*" mumbled Agnew.

Hugh smiled, felt Agnew's hand go slack and saw his eyes fix. Baron Andrew Agnew was gone. Hugh knew that his time had come as well. He looked up and saw a figure on a horse flying pell-mell in his direction. It was Innis.

Hugh tried to move and managed to get to one knee. Charging on foot from the opposite direction, jumping over fallen dead and dying soldiers, was an English infantry officer, resplendent in his red coat and shiny helmet. He was screaming like a banshee and held a lance high above his head.

"*Ye'll nay finnesh me,*" Hugh whispered as the charging figure closed in. He knew his own wounds were mortal, and that he would soon die, but not at the hands of this English officer. Hugh took his broadsword, drove the pommel against the ground, with the blade pointing in the direction of the charging man. Hugh could see his flushed face and his wild eyes, as he leaped into the air. The lance was drawn back, ready to thrust into Hugh's body, but the Englishman's momentum drove him onto Hugh's sword. The sword's blade stabbed the man in the groin, ran up his torso and out his back. As the mortally wounded infantryman slammed on top of him, Hugh's own life flickered out.

Innis slid to a stop, jumped off his horse and rushed to Hugh's side.

"Uncle, Uncle!" he cried. "Please be alive."

Innis rolled the dead Englishman off, and saw that Hugh was gone. A scream, building in Innis's lower stomach, raced up through his chest, came out his mouth and cut through the putrid air, sounding something like a wounded wolf.

*I've got to take him home,* thought Innis. *I cannot leave him here in this terrible place.* Innis knew he had but moments to remount and get out of there, before he suffered the same fate. Instinctively, he pulled Hugh's broadsword out of the dead infantryman's body. He turned to hurry away, then stopped short, as he realized that Hugh's family would want at least a part of him to inter at the cemetery atop Ben Blackcraig. He took the sword and chopped off Hugh's right hand. Grasping the sword and the bloody hand, he jumped on his horse and sprinted off the battlefield.

✦ ✦ ✦

Soon after the battle, chroniclers for both sides surveyed the outcome. There was little doubt. The battle resulted in an overwhelming English victory. Losses to the Scottish Army were appalling—up to 20,000 killed, 10,000 prisoners taken and the loss or destruction of war matériel to support 30,000 troops. The English lost fewer than 2,000 men. It was one of the worst military defeats in Scotland's history and would thereafter become infamously known among the Scots people as Black Saturday.

History would subsequently consider Pinkie as the first major battle between a modern army and a medieval one. Warfare had forever changed. All future wars for several more centuries would be fought with gunpowder guns.

✦ ✦ ✦

None of this was on Innis Henderson's mind as he made his escape. His uncle, the Laird of Blackcraigshire and a knight of the realm, lay dead on the battlefield, along with the bloodied bodies of Baron Andrew Agnew and his brother, Sheriff Gilbert Agnew. The Scots cavalry had been wiped out, as had most of the infantry. Never before in his life had Innis felt so dejected, frail and alone.

Now he had to make his way back to Blackcraigshire and the waiting Hugh Henderson family, to give them this news.

# 22.
# Put to Rest

WHAT *does God want from me?* Innis wondered in his anguish. He was now convinced beyond doubt that the three narrow escapes from death were not just coincidences or mere luck. His father had sent him out to round up sheep late at night, just as English soldiers murdered his whole family? His dog, Smartie, that his aunt had inexplicably sent with him at the last minute, saved him from death at the hands of bandits? His Uncle Hugh, both Agnew brothers, and practically everyone else in his cavalry unit, all better soldiers than he, had just been killed in battle, yet he survived? Yes, God's hand was in it, and now he had to find a way to repay the debt.

Finally, after a four-day ride, stopping only to rest his horse and catch a few hours of sleep, he saw the Henderson house come into view. The rebuilding work was nearly complete, and Innis could not believe his eyes. Standing on a hill in front of him was a great mansion. He stopped for a moment, looking at it in awe. How in the world did Andy and Ann manage to build such an impressive edifice so quickly? But he did not have time to ponder. The most distressing task of his life was now at hand.

It was mid-morning, and Innis could see Andy outside, directing workmen who were putting the finishing touches on the façade of the house. *That's good,* he thought. *It would be* easier *to break the dreadful news to Andy first, without having to face the entire family.* As he neared, he saw that Andy had turned toward him, evidently hearing the hoofbeats of his horse and barking of dogs. Andy was waving both arms, with a big smile on his face. Innis pulled up and motioned Andy to come out to meet him. Andy's expression turned more serious, and he came quickly, with a quizzical look on his face.

"Andy, prepare yourself, for I bring horrendous news," Innis said quietly, still astride his horse. Andy stood rigid and still as the realization sank in that Hugh was not with him.

"There was a great battle with the English near Musselburgh, at a place called Pinkie Cleugh," Innis said, his face ashen. "Your father was killed."

Andy's knees buckled, and he sank to the ground. "No, no—NO!" he cried, progressively louder each time. Innis swung off his horse and knelt on one knee beside Andy.

"He had charged in to try and save Baron Agnew," Innis said, his eyes tearing. "Agnew was completely surrounded by English cavalry and infantry. His entire Scots pike unit lay dead or dying, scattered all about, and the Baron was standing alone, swinging his sword."

Innis waited a few moments while Andy struggled to digest what had just been said, then continued.

"Uncle Hugh rushed in, his horse was killed beneath him, and he himself had been shot many times. Both men fought valiantly, English falling before their swords, but there were just too many."

Again, Innis hesitated so that Andy might comprehend the terrible scene that Innis was recounting.

"I rode toward them as fast as I could, fighting my way in, but it was too late. Both were gone by the time I got there."

The account of the battle had taken its toll on Innis, for his knees buckled and he collapsed to the ground, tears in his eyes. Andy then noticed his father's sword, lashed to the back of the saddle of Innis's horse.

"You brought my father's sword?"

"Aye, aye … I did," said Innis struggling to regain his composure. "It was sticking in an English soldier. I pulled it out and brought it to you, thought you would want it."

"Thank you," Andy mumbled, his face white and tears welling in his own eyes.

Both of them continued sitting on the ground, silently, for a good while, until they felt up to talking again. Innis told Andy that, when he retrieved the sword, he had also severed off Hugh's right hand, with which Hugh had gripped the sword, and had it wrapped in a cloth tied to the horse.

His face still covered with trail dust and stained with tears, Innis expressed his deep regret that he had been unable to retrieve Hugh's body from the battlefield. He had no time he said. "The body was heavy, and English soldiers were everywhere."

Andy nodded. "You did all you could."

By this time, Ann and Ree had come around to the front of the house and had seen the horse, with Andy sitting on the ground talking with someone. Peering closer, Ann exclaimed: "I think that's Innis!"

She and Ree started running down toward them.

"This will be hard," Andy said to Innis. "Let me do the talking. I'll call the whole family together so they will all learn of this at the same time. You just stand by to answer any questions."

They both stood and started walking to meet Ann and Ree, Andy in front with Innis following, leading his horse.

Andy explained that Innis brought news. There had been a battle near Musselburgh, and he wanted the whole family to assemble at the back of the house in a private area, so he and Innis could share the news to everyone at the same time. Filled with apprehension, they all gathered in a grove of tall oak trees out of the sight and hearing of the craftsmen who were still working on the house.

Andy suggested that everyone sit, and they complied—Ann, Ree, Joe, and Jamie. Without preamble, Andy started the sad story.

"There was a great battle. The Scottish Army was outnumbered and outmatched. They fought bravely, but the outcome was a massacre. About half the army was killed, including Paw, Baron Agnew and his brother, Gilbert. Innis barely escaped."

Everyone gasped and sat stunned and mute for awhile, then deep sobs of grief came pouring forth, except for Ann. She suddenly stood, turned and walked away, stopping by a large oak with her back turned, her hands covering her face. Ree went to her mother to try and console her, but was brusquely brushed off. Ann stated she wanted to be left alone.

Once the initial shock wore off, the others started to ask questions, needing to hear the details of what had happened. Andy, assisted by Innis, answered as best he could. Soon Ree asked the inevitable question.

"Where is Paw's body? We need to give him a decent burial."

They all realized that Innis had not brought Hugh's body and were concerned how they could give him a fitting burial without it. Andy explained that Innis, at great risk to himself, had charged in to try to save his Uncle and the Baron, but the battle was so fierce they had both perished before he got there. He had only been able to retrieve Hugh's sword and his right hand. Shock and dismay fell upon the faces of Ree, Joe and Jamie. Andy explained that the defeat was so total and the dead so many, hardly any bodies had been retrieved. They were lucky that Innis had been able to save what he did.

"At least we have a small part of our father to inter. We'll put him alongside Grannie and the twins."

The next day, at daybreak, the family began their sad trek back up the glen to their old place at Loch Trool. Hugh's hand had been wrapped reverently in clean, white linens, and his broadsword cleaned and shined, to be placed in the grave at his final resting place. Since hearing the news, Ann had not spoken a word, her face expressionless and her body rigid. The rest of the family was concerned. Andy asked Ree to stay with her and provide any assistance she might require to make it through the coming ordeal.

They reached the head of Loch Trool about mid-afternoon, rested for a few minutes, then started the climb up Ben Blackcraig. Andy led the way, toting a spade, followed by Ree and Ann, Joe and Jamie, with Innis behind, carrying the sword. When they reached the top, a deep, narrow pit was dug beside the twin's grave, and the wrapped hand and sword were carefully placed inside. Ree recited from memory a favorite verse from the Catholic Book of Common Prayer, and Sir Hugh Henderson was laid to rest for the ages.

Ann still had not said a word nor shed a tear that any of the others had seen. When the grave had been covered over, and Andy said they should start down, Ann finally spoke.

"You all go ahead. I wish to spend a moment alone with my husband. I'll join you in a short while."

Ree looked at Andy, and he nodded acquiescence. The group proceeded down the rocky trail, skirting around the sharp drop-off from the cliff face above. After several minutes of carefully traversing their way down the trail, Jamie suddenly cried out.

"Look, it's Ma! She's standing at the edge of the cliff."

They all looked, and were alarmed to see Ann standing at the very precipice of the sheer drop-off.

Ree called out to her, "Ma! Watch out! There are loose stones there. You could slip!"

Andy had a deeper fear. He took off running as fast as he could back up the trail. Ann held both of her arms high over her head, palms inward, as if in supplication.

Then, as her remaining family watched in horror, Ann Wallace Henderson plunged silently over the cliff face and fell to the stony depths below.

# 23.
# HELEN AND ANDY

THE weather in November 1547 in Blackcraigshire turned out to be perfect, cool nights followed by warm, sunny days. This provided some solace for the Henderson family, now numbering only four, after the deaths of both parents, Hugh and Ann Henderson, within one week of each other.

The four children, along with Innis, had buried Ann beside Hugh, the great love of her life, following her fall from the cliff. All five of them resolved, without anything being said, that Ann's fall was a tragic accident. The word suicide was never mentioned. First, no one knew what was in Ann's mind at the time, so it certainly could have been an accident. Second, Ann's Catholic faith and her teachings to her children dictated that suicide resulted in eternal damnation. No one deserved Hell less than Ann Henderson.

Andy, in particular, though he never said a word about it, had serious doubts whether a place such as Hell even existed. If it did, he felt sure a just God would recognize his mother as a true saint and would never allow her to be banished to such a place. He was confident that they would all see her again someday.

A month had elapsed since Ann's death, and Andy had recovered sufficiently that he was beginning to pine miserably for Helen Agnew. He just had to see her. He worried about how she was doing after the death of her father and uncle. She must feel terribly alone, for she was the apple of Baron Agnew's eye. Her mother, Agnew's first wife, Agnes Stewart, along with a younger brother and sister, had died from the flux when Helen was but ten years of age. She had been an only child until Agnew married his second wife, Rachel Fergusson, a year later. Agnew and Rachel had a son, William, who was now close to four years old. Who would look after Helen and her family, Andy wondered, now that Baron Agnew was gone?

The English army, he suspected, after their overwhelming victory at Pinkie, would consolidate their gains since there was now no Scottish army to oppose them. All of the towns in the borders region were likely to be occupied by the English, and they would surely take Lochnaw Castle.

The expanded house that he and his mother had worked on so diligently in the spring, summer and fall was now finished enough for them to move in. It still needed furnishings and additional interior work, but was essentially complete on the outside. There was more than enough room for the four children, plus Innis, who was living with them. Innis was now 17, still reticent, but had become a strong, tough, experienced man. Ree was 16, a woman in her own right. Joe was 14, and Jamie was 12. Andy felt he could go and spend some time with Helen without any worries about things at home.

Andy left on a cold, clear morning in late November, following the same route that he had taken the previous fall, avoiding the main roads, and keeping a lookout for English troops. Fortunately, none were seen, but he figured the English would return just as soon as they got organized and had a plan in place. Lochnaw would not be safe much longer. After three days of hard riding, Andy arrived late in the afternoon just as a big orange sun was dipping beneath the horizon in the western sky. The lingering golden glow of the sun's disappearing rays backlit Lochnaw Castle such that it resembled, in Andy's imagination, the golden gates to Heaven.

The tower and gate guards now knew Andy on sight and waved him through with a tip of a finger to their foreheads. Someone had hurried to tell Helen of his arrival, for she came bursting out of the heavy front door before he even had a chance to dismount. Andy swung off his horse, and Helen jumped into his arms, squeezing him tight around the neck. Andy swung her round and round in a circle, her legs flying, flaxen tresses unfurled, blue eyes glistening. Helen proceeded to laugh, weep and cover his face with kisses, all at the same time. Neither paid the slightest attention to the gawking onlookers.

Finally, they went back through the front door into the great hall.

"I'm so, so glad to see you!" Helen gushed, squeezing his hand. "I've been so worried."

Andy kissed her full on the lips, not caring who might see, assuring her that he was likewise very glad to see her.

"We're just getting ready to eat our evening meal," Helen murmured in his ear. "You must join us. I want you to meet my step-mother—she's very nice—and my young brother, William, as well."

"Of course," said Andy. "I'd love to. We have much to talk about."

"Promise that you'll be all mine tomorrow?" teased Helen.

"You know I will," rejoined Andy. "I can barely wait!"

Rachel Agnew looked to be in her mid-30s, a good 10-15 years younger than her late husband. She was slight of stature, had brown hair drawn up in a bun, a longish face and dark eyes. She was not beautiful by any measure, but far from ugly. She had an austere aristocratic bearing and tone of voice as she stood to greet Andy, extending a hand. Andy bowed and kissed the back of the proffered hand, as he presumed he was expected to do.

"It's such a pleasure to meet you, m'lady."

Rachel smiled somewhat wanly, but invited him to join them. He noticed a young boy, seated beside Lady Agnew, whom he assumed to be Helen's young half-brother. Taking his seat next to Helen on the opposite side of the table, he addressed the boy, "You must be Master William."

The boy did not respond, just looked at Andy with an expressionless stare.

"Aye, this is William," said Rachel. "He's a little shy around strangers, but warms up once you get to know him."

The meal was soon served, and Andy noticed that the servant staff had dwindled since he was last there. In fact, the castle looked a bit forlorn and lifeless. Andy decided to lead the conversation, as Rachel Agnew did not seem to be going anywhere beyond mere pleasantries.

"I was so sorry to hear of the death of the Baron on the battle-field at Pinkie," Andy said. "I'm told that, at the end, the Baron and my father stood side by side, swinging their broadswords and cutting down English soldiers by the dozens. Very gallant and brave men, both."

At this, Rachel Agnew showed the first hint of emotion.

"I know that my husband and your father were longtime friends, and fought together many times. I appreciate that. But being gallant and brave does not make one any less dead," she concluded with a sudden and surprising upwelling of bitterness.

"'Tis so," said Andy, and promptly dropped the subject.

Andy had learned what he needed to know. Helen was in danger, as were her stepmother and half-brother. Lochnaw Castle was not well guarded. The servant staff had dwindled. Many of the former guards had probably left with Arran's army when they marched eastward to meet the English. Those remaining did not seem to be trained fighters. Something had to be done. He would discuss it tomorrow with Helen.

Meanwhile, news spread across the borderlands of the ignominious defeat of the Scots army at Pinkie. By word of mouth, through returning Scots soldiers who were lucky enough to be among the few survivors, the grisly details of the horrible defeat became known. Such was the case at Blackmor Castle, the Wallace clan fortress in the hills northeast of Ayr. Earl Darrow Wallace had sent a good-sized contingent of fighting men with Arran's army, but his health and age did not permit him to go in person.

By early October, some of his men came straggling back, stunned, embarrassed and despondent. One of them had been a member of Agnew's pikemen, fortunate to be one of the very few who survived the massacre. He had seen the Baron go down and Sir Hugh Henderson's valiant charge to try and save him.

"Both Agnew and Henderson were killed?" asked Wallace, looking shocked.

"Aye, they both fought like demons with their broadswords, cutting down the English right and left, but they were caught out in the open in a vicious crossfire, ship cannon on one side, and artillery on the hills above. They had nay chance."

"What about Hugh's nephew, Innis? Did he die also?"

"I don't know for sure," the soldier said. I've heard that he rushed in on horseback to try and reach them, but I do not know if he survived."

Wallace thanked the man for the information and then sent for his personal guards.

"We must go to Henderson's place," he said, "my daughter may need help."

The men mounted up and headed out early the next morning. It took them three days to reach, and find, Hugh Henderson's place. The group got there the day after Andy had left for Lochnaw Castle. Dar Wallace marveled at the house when it came into view.

"Hugh always told me he had but a modest place," he said. "I did not expect anything as grand as this."

As the men wound their way up the switchback road to the house, they were being watched by Innis, Joe and Jamie. All three were armed with crossbows and were prepared to defend vigorously if necessary.

As the men got closer, Innis shouted, "I know who they are! That big man in the middle is the Earl, Dar Wallace, and the other three are his personal guards."

They all felt very relieved, threw open the front door and hurried out to greet Lord Wallace and his men. Dar was happy to see that Innis was alive and healthy, but distressed to hear the rest of the story. The burial of Hugh's remains on Ben Blackcraig was expected, but the fall of his daughter from the high cliff at the cemetery was both tragic and troublesome.

"Why was she left alone atop the Ben after the burial?" Dar demanded.

"Ma requested it," answered Ree. "Andy asked me to accompany her, and I did, but after the burial, she asked to be left alone with her husband for a short while. We acceded to her wishes.

Obviously, it was a mistake, but she had been so distraught, we thought it might help her."

Dar softened. "A terrible accident," he said, "but Hugh was her husband, and I know how much she always loved him. She deserved a final, private goodbye."

Then, looking about, Sir Wallace inquired, "Where be Andrew, anyway?"

"He's gone to Lochnaw Castle to check on the Baron Agnew's family," said Innis.

Wallace, with a hint of mischief, responded, "You don't suppose Agnew's bonnie young daughter has something to do with it?"

"That be possible," Innis conceded, but did not elaborate.

Ree invited them all in and insisted that they stay the night, apologizing for the lack of beds and furnishings.

"Hell!" Dar thundered. "We've a roof over our heads and walls to keep the wolves at bay. We've no need for more."

✦ ✦ ✦

Back at Lochnaw Castle, Helen, Andy, Rachel and young William had finished up the evening meal. Andy asked to be excused, as he and Helen would like to take a stroll about the grounds to get some fresh air.

"Of course," said Rachel, politely, but somewhat coolly. "I do hope that you'll be able to stay for a few days."

"Tonight for sure," Andy answered, "and perhaps another day or two. I need to travel to Wigtown and check on some business."

"Surely," smiled Rachel, in a dismissive tone, "I do hope that you will pass along our regards to Gilbert's family. I know they must be heartbroken over his death at that dreadful battle, just as we are of Baron Agnew's. I pray that they are doing well."

"I will," said Andy, with an equally token smile, bowing slightly as he and Helen took their leave. "Also I will do my best to attend to any needs they might have."

"Of course," said Rachel.

Andy and Helen left the castle by a side door at the back of the main stairs. They entered into a private courtyard that contained a small fruit orchard and a herb garden that emitted a pleasant, tangy smell. The courtyard was surrounded by a graveled walkway. It was already dark and the air was cool, still and quiet. They walked hand in hand to the back of the orchard to a bench where they could sit and converse in private without fear of being overheard.

Andy enveloped Helen in his long arms and gave her a lingering kiss full on the lips. Helen's body quivered as she pressed her breasts upon Andy's chest.

"Andy, you've no idea how I've missed you," she sighed.

"I think I do," murmured Andy. "I haven't slept since I last saw you."

They kissed again, and Andy gently pushed her back, his hands on her shoulders.

"We've much to discuss, and not much time," he whispered in her ear.

Helen nodded with a look of regret in her eyes.

"I wish we could go back to the straw in the boose. Do you remember?"

"Do I remember?" Andy said, teasingly. "Does a lost calf bawl for its mother?"

Helen smiled up at him and kissed him on the cheek.

"You're no calf, that's for sure. But you're right. We have much to discuss."

They sat down on the bench and began to make plans that, it would turn out, marked the course they would follow for the rest of their lives.

# 24.
# PLANS FOR THE FUTURE

ANDY began first. He spoke of the terrible tragedy that had just befallen them—both their fathers killed in battle. Innis was with them, he told her, but managed to survive. Innis had returned to Blackcraigshire after the battle and shared the whole story. He truly hated to bring Helen more pain, but felt he must tell her also.

"I'm ready," Helen replied, her voice wavering, but strong and determined. "Tell me everything."

Struggling to keep his own emotions under control, Andy related the terrible, almost unspeakable events at Pinkie. Helen listened closely, rivulets of tears occasionally streaming down her cheeks, but she never sobbed aloud. Andy likewise had tears welling in his eyes as he talked, and had to stop momentarily a few times to collect himself.

Finally, he got out the full chronicle of the battle, the remarkable courage and valiant heroism the two men had displayed, especially at the end.

"They were always fighting men," Helen said, brokenheartedly but with a note of pride in her voice, "intrepid Scottish warriors. They did what they were brought up to do, defend our land and our way of life. They were so lucky to die together when the time came."

The eloquence and bravery displayed by Helen at that moment, Andy would never forget. Many times in years to come, his heart would swell and his eyes would tear when the memories of this talk resurfaced.

But Andy was not finished. He had more he had to share.

"Helen, I've more," he said, putting his arm around her shoulder and pulling her tighter to him. "It's about my mother."

"Ann?" Helen gasped. "What?"

Andy told her the story of the burial of his father atop Ben Blackcraig, Ann's fall and the second burial for her. By now they were both emotionally spent, with no more tears to shed. Andy covered the story in an almost catatonic stupor, devoid of outward feelings. Helen listened numbly, scarcely able to comprehend.

After he finished, Helen suddenly stood, pulled Andy to his feet and wrapped him in her arms.

"Your mother—you lost her, too," she stammered.

"Aye..." Andy replied. "Aye."

They stood quietly in the embrace for a long time. Andy's head sank to Helen's shoulder as his whole body trembled and shuddered. Slowly, as they both regained a semblance of composure, Helen spoke to him softly, "We're alone, both of us. Our fathers and mothers are gone. We have only each other."

The realization sank in slowly, as cold honey soaks bread—now they had only each other. Andy raised his head from Helen's shoulder.

"Aye, each other only, forever."

"Each other only, forever," she repeated.

That they deeply loved each other, both had known for some time. But this was something else. Now they were bound together. They both knew it; a deep, permanent union had been joined. But they had scant time to appreciate or ponder it. Plans had to be made, and in a hurry. Andy, suddenly alert, said urgently, "You must go with me. We have to figure out what to do, and we don't have much time."

Helen agreed, suggesting, "You tell me your thoughts first, and I'll respond. We'll keep at it until we have a firm plan."

First, he said, she could not stay at Lochnaw. It would be too dangerous. The English had won. Scotland no longer had an organized army. Those few Scots commanders who survived had all gone home. Arran took a small force to Edinburgh Castle, but not enough to mount any kind of attack on the English. The best he could do was try and hold the castle, and might not be able to do that. Plus, the entire Scots cavalry had been destroyed. The English would occupy all the major towns on the east coast and across the borderlands. It would happen quickly; they would take Wigtown and, most certainly, Lochnaw Castle due to its strategic location. The English could be there in three or four weeks. They could now capture everything they wanted without much trouble.

Helen was silent and her eyes widened as she realized the full enormity of the situation. Andy asked about Rachel and William, and the rest of the castle staff and guards. Helen answered that she did not think Rachel would leave. She explained that William was her father's only living male heir. He therefore stood to inherit the sheriffship of all Wigtownshire by virtue of her father's heritable position as sheriff of Wigtown, a royal burgh.

Her father had vested that office in his brother, Gilbert Agnew, now also dead, but survived by a son, Blair. She thought Blair might have a claim to the sheriffship also, but did not know if it would hold up legally.

In addition to Blair, who was now about 16 years old, Gilbert had left two daughters, Margaret, called "Maggie," and Allison, who went by "Ally." They were about 14 and 12, she thought.

"Nice bairns, all three," she added.

Helen went on to say that she was quite worried about the welfare of all of them. "They must be scared to death. Is there anything we can do?"

"I'll give it some thought," said Andy. "We should help them if we can. Are they still living in Wigtown?"

Helen thought so.

"I think it might be wise to ask Rachel what she wants to do," Andy continued, "first thing in the morning, if possible. I agree she probably won't leave, even temporarily, but she should. Who knows what the English might do to her? The Baron was a known enemy of the English crown after all."

"Aye," said Helen. "We should ask, and I'll do it as soon as I can tomorrow."

Andy then mentioned that they had greatly expanded and improved the old bastle house. It was now much more like a manor house, with a great hall, two levels, and seven hearths. It had 12 rooms in all. Eight of the rooms were heated and could serve as bedrooms. They should have room for all that wanted to go. Unfortunately, he added, they didn't have much in the way of furnishings, so if Rachel were to leave, furnishings and household servants would need to be taken along for her.

"You've done all of that? When?" asked Helen, incredulous.

They had started in the late spring, Andy related, and finished a short while ago. In fact, there were still a good many items to be completed.

"I was going to tell you—but, well, we had so many more important subjects to discuss, I just hadn't gotten around to it yet," Andy said, a little sheepishly.

"It sounds nice," Helen said. "I believe I'll like it."

So that too was settled. Rachel might not leave, but Helen was going with him. Andy was delirious with pleasure. But thinking further, he didn't want to take it for granted.

"Helen, I want you; please know that, I want you forever, and I want you to go home with me now. I want you to be my wife. You just said you would, correct?"

Helen flashed her trademark mischievous smile.

"What? Go home with you, or be your wife, or both? I thought you just proposed. Did I hear wrong?"

Andy looked completely befuddled and embarrassed.

"Forgive me. Aye, I did, but not very well. Let me do it properly."

Taking Helen's hand, dropping to one knee, and looking up at her raptly, Andy spoke earnestly:

*"Helen, my luv, will you mairy me?"*

*"Aye, Andrew Henderson, aye, I will!"*

Andy's face broke into a big smile, tears coming to his eyes once more, this time from joy. Despite all the pain and death, his heart was suddenly full. Helen would his wife. For that one moment, at least, he had never been so happy.

Andy grabbed Helen once again kissing her multiple times all over her face and forehead. At length she pushed him away, for there was much more to decide. If Rachel declined to leave, what about the servants and guards? Rachel had her own favorite and loyal household servants, and Helen was sure they would stay with her. Likewise would some of the guards. But the others?

Helen had a longtime chambermaid and a cook who would insist on going with her, and her father had assigned three men-at-arms to serve as her personal guards. They were steadfast and loyal. She would like for them to go—plus, of course, she and those who accompanied them would want to take personal effects and furnishings. They would probably need three or four wagons for this, Helen thought, and suggested they quickly consult with Harold Douglas, her father's most trusted guard.

"You will remember Harold," she said. "He was the man who helped you take the horses to your father during this past winter when the clans were meeting at Irvine."

"Of course I do," said Andy, delighted to learn that Harold was still there. "A good man, very able and dependable; he would be a real asset. Perhaps we can find him and talk now."

"Yes, let's do that," agreed Helen as they set off in search of Harold.

Soon they found him at the front tower guarding the drawbridge, which had been pulled up for the night. Harold was inside the tower, which served as his living quarters. When Helen called out to him, he groggily responded. Obviously, he had been asleep. He opened the door, invited Helen and Andy inside and lit a small candle. They briefly described the situation to Harold, who immediately understood and agreed with their plan.

"I have been very worried about you, Lady Helen," Harold said. "You are right. No doubt the English will come. You are wise to leave and get as far north of the coast as you can."

Harold said the English were likely to occupy Dumfries, because it was a major crossroad, from both east to west, and north to south—of high strategic value. Also, they would take Wigtown and Castle Lochnaw. With the Scottish army all but destroyed, there was no telling how long they would stay. The English would have little mercy on the people who sided with the Scots. That included Helen, Harold emphasized pointedly. She was an Agnew and her mother was a Stewart, both clans were well known to be longtime Scots loyalists.

"What about Rachel and young William?" asked Andy. "Helen does not think they will leave."

Harold scratched his forehead for a moment. "I agree, Rachel is a Fergusson. I'm sure the English will treat her kindly."

The Fergussons were famous for switching sides when it suited their interests, he explained. They controlled the hill lands to the north, from Dumfries all the way to the mountains east of Ayrshire.

Helen chimed in. She had heard that the high chieftain of the Fergusson Clan, Alpin Fergusson, had sold out to the English for a large sum just recently, to grant their army free access to the coast road.

"From Dumfries all the way to the Rhinns," she said bitterly.

"That was why the English army was able to move, virtually unimpeded, and reach us here at Lochnaw Castle so quickly," Helen said. "The Fergussons could have stopped them, or at least slowed them down, but they did nothing. A handsome sum was paid for that, I'm sure," she said. "Thank God for Andy's father. Without his talent and ingenuity we would have been done for."

Andy recalled the previous fall when he rode to Lochnaw to warn of a possible English invasion. It was true. The English army had been moving freely on the coast road. He had seen them. There had been no signs of Scots resistance whatsoever. And the Fergussons had supplied only a small contingent of fighting men to the Scottish Army in the recent fighting in the east. Most of them were crofters and farmers who probably had no choice in the matter.

"Rachel and William will be fine," said Helen. "The English will treat them royally."

The English would love to establish a stronghold at Lochnaw, she observed, and seize control of the entire Rhinns peninsula. The only Scots who could oppose them now were the Highlanders, and the English would soon be standing in their path, blocking the western coast.

*Aye*, thought Andy. *Rachel is right where she wants to be, pro-tecting her son's claim to the sheriffship of Wigtownshire. There will likely come a time when we'll be forced to oppose her.*

"Harold," Helen implored, "you cannot stay either." The English would not let him live, nor most of the other guards, she feared. "We want you to come with us."

She and Andy then described the new house built at Blackcraigshire at the site of the old burned-out bastle house, and the plans they had formulated.

"We have plenty of room," offered Andy. "The new house is a good ways north of Wigtown and the coast road." It was strongly built, he emphasized, and situated on a hill in a grove of trees. It could not be easily seen from afar, but had good visibility toward the east and south. "We don't have many furnishings, so will need to take some. What do you think?"

Harold Douglas was a big, stocky man with long, black hair. He had a bald spot on top, a heavy beard and mustache, and twinkling black eyes. He looked at the two young lovers for a long moment, as if undecided about what he should do, then broke into a huge grin, his teeth casting a spooky glow in the candlelight.

"I ken I must go and there's no one I'd rather join up with. Baron Agnew bound me for life to protect and defend Lady Helen anyway, so you're likely to have me around for a good while," he said.

Helen and Andy were relieved and pleased to have Harold join them, and told him so. The three of them got down to the serious business of planning the details of their departure from the castle. Harold mentioned that he knew of several other men-at-arms he was sure were planning to leave. He would recruit three or four of the best ones, all good fighting men, who had been very loyal to Baron Agnew. They would be entering a dangerous world, and would need as many skilled fighting men as they could house and support.

Helen would take her two servants. Harold would awaken Andy and Helen at first light. Provisions and furnishings would be loaded and ready to go. They would leave through the side tunnel, as Sir Hugh Henderson had done with his cavalry to such great effect during the battle the previous spring.

Lady Rachel did not normally arise until the sun was at least a quarter up, Harold said, and Helen nodded. Their movements were sure to be noticed by some of the other guards and servants, but they wouldn't know what was going on and would not be likely to awaken Lady Rachel in any event as she did not like to be disturbed early.

Also, Harold continued, they would need some livestock on the hoof, perhaps a small herd of sheep, a few beef, two or three dairy cows, a couple of good border collies for herding and maybe a couple of hunting hounds. Andy said they had livestock at Blackcraig and a collie, but with the extra people, additional livestock and dogs would be welcome.

Harold figured they could fit what they needed into three wagons, each pulled by a team of Clydesdales. They would also need a hay cart. Harold counted up.

"With you and Lady Helen, her two servants, myself, and the four extra guards, we'll have nine in all. Can you accommodate that many, Laird Henderson?"

Andy was taken aback at the strangeness of hearing himself referred to as "laird," but realized it was true; he was now the Laird of Blackcraigshire. He quickly recovered, stating with authority in his voice, "Aye, we can."

Helen looked at him, winked and smiled sweetly.

Harold described the set-up he envisioned for the wagon train: One guard each to drive the three wagons and the cart; Lady Helen's two servants would ride on the wagons. He would get Andy's horse saddled, and have two more outfitted for himself and Lady Helen. The numbers would work out just right. They would need to be out of the tunnel and on the road by quarter sun, when Lady Rachel normally arose.

"That would be the time, m'lady," Harold said to Helen, "for you to inquire whether Lady Rachel desires for herself and William to leave also. As we have said, probably she will not, but you might desire to do her the courtesy of asking."

"Aye, that I will," replied Helen.

At first light the next morning, a foggy and dreary gray day broke, but the plan went smoothly. The wagon train was lined up at the tunnel gate and ready to go by quarter sun. Helen had Andy accompany her as she went to meet with her stepmother. Rachel was in the parlor with William, where she normally had her first meal.

"Helen!" Rachel exclaimed, looking confounded. "You must have arisen quite early today."

"Aye," Helen replied, and then explained their plan, urging Rachel and William to join them. Rachel was clearly taken by surprise, her face blanched and quickly turned reddish as her anger rose.

"You did not even consult me about this," she said, sputtering. "Of course I will not go," she continued, her face getting redder, "and neither will ye. I forbid it!"

Helen stood looking at her stepmother calmly and addressed her in a quiet firm voice.

"I am 17 years old. You have no authority to forbid me from doing anything. I make my own decisions, and I am leaving. The English army will be here soon, but not me. I was born an Agnew, as I am still. My mother was a Stewart. I would not fare well under English occupation."

Rachel was momentarily dumbstruck. Never had she been spoken to in such a manner. Helen finished without further ado.

"So that's your decision, you will stay?"

Rachel did not respond, just continued to sit, glowering.

"Very well, then," said Helen. "I bid you farewell and wish both of you the best."

At that, she turned on her heels and walked out. Andy followed, having never said a word.

# 25.
# THE AGNEW BAIRNS

THE little wagon train headed east on the coast road, three provisions wagons in front, followed by the hay cart and livestock.
Helen rode alongside the wagons, chatting occasionally with her
two servants, a cook named Martha and her chambermaid.
Andy and Harold rode wing on each side of the livestock to keep
them bunched up, getting help from the collies when necessary.
After a few furlongs, all settled into a routine and the train
slowly clopped along.

The road was empty, and there was no sign of English soldiers.
Andy estimated that the trek to Blackcraigshire would take four
nights on the road. They should arrive on the fifth day. At about
one-fourth of the way to Wigtown, they would turn left, leaving
the main road, and proceed northeasterly. He was confident they
could reach the turn by the end of the first day, which they did.
There, they circled the cart and wagons, fed the livestock, hobbled
the horses, built a fire and cooked some food. Harold and his men
cut some good-sized trees nearby and arrayed logs around the fire
for sitting, conversation and eating. Later, they would place the
logs between the wagons to create a corral for the livestock.

The first day of travel had gone well, and everyone was in good
spirits. Once they got a decent fire going, Harold's men slaughtered
and quartered one of the sheep for roasting, and Helen's servants
prepared a big pot of vegetables to boil. Helen and Andy sat a ways
apart from the others so they could talk privately and sneak in a
few affections.

Helen continued to worry about the welfare of her first cousins, the three children of Gilbert Agnew. The mother of the children, Agnew's wife, had died during childbirth several years earlier. It was a breech birth, Helen said, and the baby did not survive either. Helen had been there as a girl when the wife was still alive and recalled they had household servants. She thought she could remember the way to the house. So far as she knew, the three children had no close relatives in Wigtown, so were possibly alone and fending for themselves. Their condition with respect to food, shelter, clothing and overall safety was unknown.

"Andy," Helen said in a soft voice, "I so worry about Uncle Gilbert's bairns. We have not heard anything from them since their father went away with Arran's army. I know nothing of how they're doing."

Andy thought the situation over. The wagon train would have at least three more nights on the road before reaching Blackcraigshire, then getting everyone unloaded and situated at the Henderson house would take another full day. If they were to wait until they got to Blackcraigshire to start the trip down to Wigtown, it would take another two nights. Close to half a fortnight would have passed. Helen was right. The present condition of the three Agnew children was not known, and a lot of bad things could happen if they waited that long.

Abruptly Andy said, "We should go to them now."

Helen was surprised, "But how can we, with all these people, livestock and wagons?" She was anxious to go, but concerned whether they could manage it with everything else they had to do.

Andy thought some more. They had reached the turn, and with no English soldiers in sight, there was no particular danger the rest of the way. The livestock were accustomed to the travel and had been calm and steady. The herd could be placed between the lead and second wagons. The two collies would keep any animals from straying. The wagon group should be able to traverse the rest of the way without trouble. He related his plan to Helen.

"We can ride to Wigtown. We'll take Harold with us. With three good horses, we can easily get there with one overnight on the road, and arrive before noon the next day. There's not time to go to Blackcraigshire first. The others should be able to get there with the wagons and livestock without trouble. The English are sure to come to Wigtown, and soon. Agnew's bairns will not be safe for long. In fact they may not be now."

With concern even more evident on her face, Helen agreed, "Aye, let's do it."

"We will probably need to take the bairns back home with us," Andy said. "They can ride double on our horses if necessary."

Helen looked at Andy closely. "Three more mouths to feed and not much help in return? Are you sure?"

"Aye," said Andy. "We can manage it. Besides they are not small weans. You said the boy, Blair, was 16. They might be more help than you think."

Helen threw her arms around Andy's neck and planted a big kiss on his cheek. "Thank you."

The three arose before dawn, grabbed some bedrolls, hard biscuits, a few cooked strips of mutton from the previous night's meal, mounted their horses and hurried off toward Wigtown. The others with the wagon train moved at a more leisurely pace, downing a good morning meal before getting started. They agreed to meet up again after the third night, just short of the Henderson home.

The three horses were rested and fresh. Andy, Helen and Harold kept up a good canter for most of the day, only stopping occasionally where the road was bisected by a burn to drink water, down some food and rest the horses.

At first, there were few other travelers on the road, but as they got closer to Wigtown, nearing nightfall, they began to meet increasing numbers of people traveling in the opposite direction. A few were alone on horseback, but many were in carts or wagons drawn by horses or oxen, hauling household goods and provisions, some also herding livestock. Most looked to be family groups.

The three riders stopped and chatted for a moment with one such group, inquiring where they had come from and where they were going.

"We came from Wigtown," said the man.

He appeared to be in his 40s and was walking with two older children. A woman near the same age was driving a wagon behind a team of horses, with two younger children seated beside her.

"We left this morning. Everyone in town expects the English army to arrive soon," the man said.

They had heard that the whole Scottish army had been wiped out at a great battle in the east near Edinburgh, he explained, and the town didn't have enough able-bodied men to defend it or withstand another siege. Everyone expected the English would be very hard on the townspeople because of their resistance at the last siege. People were frightened. Most were leaving if able, taking whatever they could with them.

"Where will you go with your family?" asked Andy.

"Ayrshire," answered the man. "I have a brother who lives there. People who have relatives anywhere to the north or west are going to them. We hear the English army is only interested in the towns near the coast."

"Did you have to abandon a home in Wigtown?" Andy asked, eyeing the wagon loaded with home furnishings.

"Aye," said the man. "We got everything we could on this wagon, but had to leave a lot behind."

Helen spoke up, "Gilbert Agnew, the sheriff; we hear he was killed at that battle. Do you know anything about his bairns?"

"Not for certain, but they are still at the Agnew home so far as I know."

He was not aware if any adults were there to look after them, he said. He did recall that Sheriff Agnew had had two house servants but didn't know their present whereabouts.

"Thank you, and God's speed on your journey," Andy said, doffing his bonnet as the two groups continued their separate ways.

That night the three riders turned off the main road and guided their horses to a small wood-covered hill with a burn running beside it. It was a good place to bed down for some rest and sleep. The night air was chilly, but they chose not to build a fire for fear of intruders with so many people about, wrapping their blankets about them for warmth instead. Before nodding off, they talked of what they might encounter the next day.

"We'll easily make Wigtown by noon if we have no trouble," Andy said.

"We'll need to be careful," cautioned Helen. "With so many people leaving and so much fear, we might find a very chaotic situation in town. I think we should go straight to Uncle Gilbert's house."

"Do you remember the way?" asked Andy.

"I think so."

"Ride fast, stop for no one and have our weapons at the ready," Harold said. "I hope not, but we may have to fight our way in, or out—or both."

It was a dark, moonless night, cloudy, with a stiff breeze blowing off Wigtown Bay. The three riders got underway as soon as the dim morning light was sufficient to see for a short distance. The weather was cold and drizzling rain. They turned left at the road and put their horses into a fast canter, splattering mud and keeping their blankets wrapped about them, cinched at the waist, covering their heads. Andy and Harold had their broadswords in scabbards on their backs and dirks belted at their waists—obvious and ready for use if need be.

By mid-morning they were at the town gates, which were open, with people, wagons, horses and livestock streaming out. There was a lot of shouting and cursing as various individuals and groups jostled for position in the muddy street.

"This way," shouted Helen, and the three kicked their horses into a full gallop down a narrow street, plowing around and through groups of people who were pushing out the other way.

"There!" cried Helen, and the three wheeled into a side street. They could see the outline of a large house at the end surrounded by a tall rock wall with a stout-looking double door gate at the entry. It was locked.

Andy rode his horse beside the gate and stood up in the saddle. He was just high enough to see over the top. He saw no one else about, and no sign of life from the house. The windows were dark and looked to be covered from the inside.

"Not much chance of breaking through the gate," Andy called down to Harold.

There was a stout timber inside spanning from one side to the other, held up by heavy iron brackets. They might be able to dislodge it, but would need a length of rope with a metal hook or something similar. One of them could possibly crawl over the top, drop to the ground and remove it, but that could be dangerous, as someone could shoot from inside. Needing in fast and with no time to find and rig up a rope, the more dangerous option seemed the only choice.

Harold volunteered go over the gate and suggested that Andy ride down the wall a ways, look over by standing on the horse and call out to the Agnew children.

"Tell them who we are and that we are here to help," Harold suggested. "Hopefully, they, or anyone else inside, will hear and be distracted just long enough for me to dislodge the timber. If someone sends an arrow my way, well … maybe they will miss," he added with a wry grin.

Andy could think of nothing better. Turning to Helen, he said, "Assuming we get the gate open, I will ride in fast and dismount at the front door. Harold will follow me. I would like you to stay outside the wall until we size up the situation. We will probably have to crash the front door."

"No," said Helen firmly. "I'll go too, the bairns should recognize me."

"But it could be dangerous and …" Andy protested, only to be cut off by Helen. "No, I said that I would go. Now let's get this done. Time is wasting."

Andy and Harold looked at each other and nodded. No use arguing with a woman whose mind was made up. Andy stood in the saddle and hollered out at the house.

"We're here to see Blair Agnew and his sisters. Helen Agnew, your aunt, is with us. We are here to help. Can you come to the door?"

There was no sound and nothing moved. Harold dropped to the ground, lifted the timber and threw open the gate. He sprinted back out and mounted his horse as Andy galloped through the opening to the front door, reining the horse to an abrupt stop and springing down, sword drawn. Harold did the same an instant later, and then the two men kicked the door hard in unison. After the first kick, there was a splintering sound. The second smashed the door wide open.

Standing just inside was a wide-eyed lad of about 16, a dirk in his hand, looking terrified but standing his ground. At that moment, Helen stepped between the two men and stood before the lad.

"Blair Agnew?" she asked.

"Aye," said the lad hesitantly, his voice trembling a little. "And who are you?"

"I am your aunt, Helen Agnew, daughter of Andrew, your father's brother. We just came from Lochnaw Castle," she said, "and are here to offer assistance should you need any."

"Aunt Helen!" Blair cried, still sounding somewhat uncertain. "Is it really you?"

"Aye," said Helen, "where are your two sisters, Maggie and Ally?"

A big smile broke out on Blair Agnew's face.

"Och! Aunt Helen, I can't believe it. We have been so scared. Our father was killed in the war with the English and the house servants have left."

He related that people had been trying to break in. Hearing the commotion outside, he had thought that they also were thieves.

"Until I saw you Aunt Helen," he said, smiling with relief. The sisters, he added, were hiding upstairs.

"Well, go and get them," Helen said, "and put down that sword. You won't need it."

Blair put the sword aside, looking a bit embarrassed, and took off running upstairs to get his sisters. He soon returned, Maggie and Ally in tow.

"Hello Maggie, hello Ally," Helen said, smiling. "I am your Aunt Helen. This is Laird Andrew Henderson and Harold, my father's chief of guards. We are here to help you. Now, why don't we all sit down and work up a plan?"

The three Agnew children were all handsome kids, having the features of both their father and mother, and appeared healthy, though somewhat thin and pallid. Blair was a tall, slender lad with reddish hair, fair skin and blue eyes. He was definitely an Agnew, resembling his father as well as his uncle. Maggie was dark-haired, with brown eyes and a sweet expression, more closely resembling her mother. Ally seemed to be a cross between the two. She had curly blond hair, brown eyes, a round face, and seemed shy.

Andy inquired about the servants. He wondered how many they had and when they left?

Two, a man and a woman, related Blair, explaining, "Da' left them to look out for us, but they left soon after the news of the battle came that he had been killed."

"So you have been fending for yourselves ever since?"

"Aye," said Blair.

"We are out of food," piped up Maggie, the first time either of the girls had spoken.

"What have you been eating?" Helen asked, looking at Maggie.

At first, Maggie related, they had meat and vegetables. George—that was the male servant's name—brought food from the market sometime, but it was scarce. Now they were down to some flour. She could make flatbread, and there was an apple tree in the back, but the apples were mostly gone.

Andy asked if they had horses or a cart or wagon.

"Not any more," answered Blair, "Da' left us two horses and a wagon, but they have been stolen."

"Here's what we'll do," Andy said, explaining his plan. "I have a large house to the north, far from the coast. The English army is coming to take over the town. That's why everyone is leaving. The English will be most unkind," Andy emphasized, "especially after learning you're Sheriff Agnew's bairns. You have to go with us—right now. We'll make a home for you at my place. How does that sound?"

The three Agnews just looked at him, saying nothing, then glanced at Helen. She nodded. "There'll be plenty of room and food. You'll be safe with us."

"But this is our home," protested Ally, starting to cry. Maggie was also sniffling.

Blair addressed his sisters in a firm voice. "We cannot stay here; we've no food. Had you rather starve and maybe be killed by the English?"

The girls looked shocked, and scared.

"Our horses and wagon are gone. Are we to walk?" stammered Maggie.

Andy reassured them. They had three good horses and could ride double. He instructed each of them to gather up a pile of their warmest clothes, tie them tightly in a blanket and not forget shoes. Also, to wear a cloak and something warm over their heads. It was already cold and would get colder at night. For at least two nights, they would be sleeping outside on the ground, he said.

The Agnews rushed off to collect their things. As they were doing this, Helen looked around the house. There were some silver candlesticks and a few other small valuables they could collect and carry on horseback. Everything would be stolen as soon as they were seen leaving, so she collected what she could and tied the items together in a tablecloth. These could be draped in front of the saddle on her horse's shoulders, with roughly equal weight hanging on each side. At least the Agnew children would have something valuable left from their former home.

Meanwhile Harold went out and closed the front gate to secure the horses.

Soon the girls came back down, each with a large blanket crammed full of stuff.

"Too much," Helen said. "You'll need to discard about half from each pack. Remember, it has to fit on the horses."

She started sorting things as the children looked on disappointedly.

"Each of you go and get me another blanket," Helen said.

They did, and she rigged up double packs for each that would drape behind the saddle, similar to what she had done with the valuables.

It was time to go. Andy pushed open the broken front door to go out and fetch the horses.

"THUD—TWANG."

There was a strong vibrating sensation right beside Andy's head. Turning quickly he saw a quivering, just-fired bolt and threw himself back inside, pulling the splintered door closed.

"What was that," shouted Helen.

"A bolt from a crossbow," said Andy, "We're being attacked!"

Harold hurried over, "Where did it come from?"

Andy thought for a moment, trying to visualize the bolt sticking in the door, how it was angled.

"It came straight in, so the shooter must be behind the front gate, or near it," Andy answered.

Maggie and Ally were standing mute, their hands over their mouths, frightened expressions in their eyes.

Blair had turned pale. He realized the danger they were in.

"Thieves," he said. "They're trying to break in."

Andy, Helen and Harold huddled, joined by Blair.

"Any idea how many are out there," Harold asked Andy. "Obviously one man shot the bolt, but there must be others."

They quietly discussed the situation, agreeing that someone needed to get over the wall to find out.

Blair said bravely, "I'll do it."

"No," Andy said firmly. They didn't know how many there were or where. The place could be surrounded.

Helen stood by, rubbing her temple in thought.

"If someone is to go over, we need to create a diversion," she said.

"We can build a fire, create a lot of smoke," suggested Harold.

"They won't know what to make of it and will get together to confer," Andy added, "It will also cause alarm. They are after the valuables in the house and won't want them to burn up."

The house floors were wooden. Helen wondered where a fire could be built without risk of burning the house and themselves in the process. Then Blair spoke up. There was a stable attached to the backside of the house that had dirt floors. There was an inside entrance.

They would need wet straw for smoke, said Harold. Blair confirmed that there was straw in the stable, but it was probably dry.

"Wool blankets," exclaimed Helen, they could pile up the straw and cover it with wet blankets. That would make a lot of smoke."

Blair led them to the stable; Andy and Harold started piling straw while Helen told Maggie and Ally to bring some blankets, then to go back upstairs and hide. Blair and Helen hurriedly gathered a couple of pails of water to wet the piles.

Meanwhile Andy and Harold planned the next move. The stable had shuttered windows on each side that they could open once the fire got going, flooding the outside with smoke. It was a wet dreary day, so the smoke should stay close to the ground.

Harold would then go over the wall in the back, in the expectation that the thieves would gather in front to discuss what to do when they saw the smoke. Andy, Helen and Blair would position themselves at various lookout points around the house—Andy at the front, Helen upstairs by a window and Blair at the back of the house. The fire was lit and fanned, the shutters of the stable flung open and the smoke began to boil out.

Harold took a long board from the stable, leaned it against the wall, clambered up and looked over. Seeing nobody, he dropped to the ground and hurried along the base to a corner, carefully peeking around. Down by the front gate he could see three armed men, one with a crossbow and the other two had dirks. They were engaged in an animated conversation but were too far away for him to hear. He noticed two horses hitched to a wagon near the road. *To carry the plunder,* he surmised. Harold notched a bolt in his crossbow and waited.

Shortly one of the would-be thieves was boosted up to the top of the wall where he was partially concealed by the limbs of a tree. Then a second man was boosted up and quickly dropped to the other side. *They plan to open the front gate and storm the house. I better act fast,* Harold thought. He ran as quietly as he could down the wall, hugging the side, until he was near the bowman on top. The man had not noticed him.

Harold shot a bolt into the man's chest, heard him gasp and watched him tumble to the ground on the other side. The third man wheeled around, saw Harold and drew his dirk. Harold tossed his crossbow aside and charged the man, holding his broadsword high. Just then the gate opened and the second man came out, cursing loudly. Seeing Harold, he too drew his dirk. *Two to one, about right,* thought Harold. Suddenly the second man collapsed, blood squirting from a deep gash that started at the top of his right shoulder.

Harold whammed his broadsword into the third man's sword arm, then brought the sword back around, like a swinging scythe, into the man's neck. The man crumpled, his head nearly severed. Harold spun back around, ready for action, but saw it was Andy standing over the second man, lying lifeless on the ground. The fight was over. The three ambitious thieves were dead.

"Let's get out of here," yelled Andy.

They pulled the bodies of the two dead men back inside the gate to join their fallen companion, re-barred the gate and rushed to the stable to pitchfork out the smoldering straw. Helen and Blair saw what they were doing and ran to help. Once the stable was clear, Helen called the two girls to come down while Andy and Harold rounded up the horses.

In short order, the packs were loaded onto the horses, then the three Agnew children were lifted up—Blair behind Andy, Maggie behind Harold and Ally behind Helen. Then they opened the gate and were off, clomping down the road from the Agnew house, through mud and manure, melding into the growing stream of people leaving town.

"Thank you for saving us," Blair said to Andy in a shaky voice.

The horses now were carrying half again the weight they had before, but they were strong and rested, and did not seem to mind. However, the going would be slower. The group, now numbering six, left the coast road and turned north across the bare country-side as soon as they could. There was no discernible road; they just rode over fields and meadows, following wooded burns where possible. The food provisions were low. There had been none at the Agnew place, and no time to stop and barter. So they shared what they had and drank plenty of water. By nightfall, the food was gone, and they had at least two more days of riding to reach the wagon train, then on to the Henderson house.

Andy and Harold talked over the food situation as they readied to stop for the night. They had seen a few sheep grazing in meadows along the way. They hated to take another poor man's animal, but there was little choice; the Agnew children were already famished and frail.

"I'll do it," Andy said. "Get a good fire going, hidden down in the glen." Harold nodded, and Andy rode off.

The rest of the group dismounted and spread blankets for sleeping, well hidden in a flat meadow alongside the burn. Harold gathered firewood as Andy rode back to collect one of the sheep. He selected a young yearling ram, which would be tender, easy to quarter and roast on a bed of coals. Since it was a male, there would be less loss to the owner. They all filled their stomachs and got a good night's sleep, with extra left over for the rest of the trip.

A new life for the Agnew bairns had begun.

# 26.
# A New Household

AFTER another night on the ground, the group was nearing the outlying environs of Blackcraigshire. They found the wagon trace and saw recently made wheel marks, hoofprints and fresh droppings. Andy figured the wagons had passed and were probably near. The horses were urged to a faster pace, and soon they saw the wagons up ahead. Catching up, they all stopped and discussed the remainder of the trip. With the three Agnews, there were now twelve travelers in the group. Andy instructed the wagon train to move at a slower pace and then galloped off alone to advise his small family of the new arrivals.

As Andy approached, he was immediately spotted by Jamie, who was posted on lookout. Jamie alerted the rest that Andy was coming. They all excitedly ran out the front door and were grinning ear to ear as Andy rode up. Andy jumped down from his horse and gave each a hug.

"How was your trip? Did you find Helen well?" asked Ree, smiling coyly.

Andy, having little time to chat, got right to the nub of the matter.

"Aye, I did. In fact, she is coming along now with some others a ways back down the road."

"Well, it would be nice to have some visitors for a change," Ree said. "How many are there?"

"Let's see," said Andy. "five grown men, three women—that would be Helen and her two servants—then Sheriff Agnew's three bairns, a son and two daughters, so that would be a total of eleven, if I counted correctly."

"What!" exclaimed Ree. "I don't see how we can prepare a meal for that many, including us. There would be sixteen!"

"Don't worry," replied Andy, "we are bringing provisions as well—and something else. We have two wagons full of household furnishings, a herd of sheep, beeves and dairy cows, a hay cart—oh, two more border collies and some hunting hounds."

"Great God!" exclaimed Ree. "Are they planning to stay?"

"Aye, they are."

For a moment, everyone stood in stunned silence. Then Ree tentatively asked, "Er, ah ... how long?"

"A long time, I expect, maybe a year, perhaps several. The English army is occupying the towns along the coast. These are our people. I've brought them here for safety."

Innis wondered about the five grown men Andy mentioned. "Who they be?"

"They are men-at-arms from Lochnaw Castle," Andy said. "You will remember one of them, Harold Douglas, who was the chief guard. He is bringing four of his best men."

They could not remain at Lochnaw, Andy explained, for the castle would undoubtedly soon be taken over by the English army.

"Well, at least we will have no weans to care for," sighed Ree.

Innis appreciated the extra provisions, livestock and dogs, along with five additional fighting men. Ree was excited about the additional house furnishings, hoping that they included some beds. Andy remounted his horse to ride back and lead the group in, first assigning Ree the chore of managing organization of the household goods and placing the various items around the house after the group arrived. Innis was to help with the livestock, wagons and equipment. Also, Andy said, they should gather up as much food as possible. The newcomers would be hungry.

Joe and Jamie set out to gather vegetables to cut up and put in the large iron pot for boiling. There were some dried strips of roasted mutton and beef among the provisions brought in on the wagons, so these would be cut up and tossed into the pot as well.

Ree said she would mix up a big bowl of dough to bake biscuits. Soon a large hearty meal would be ready for everyone.

Most of the new arrivals slept on the floor wherever they could find space on the first night. They were bone tired from the long journey, and all slept well. The next morning, a more extensive organization inside and out got going. The size and configuration of the new house turned out to accommodate everyone quite well. Helen had a bedroom upstairs, nicely furnished with her own things. Another small bedroom next to hers was occupied by her chambermaid.

The two Agnew girls got a bedroom, Jamie and Joe stayed where they were, Andy and Innis continued to bunk together, and Ree had a room near the kitchen that she shared with Martha, the cook from Lochnaw. The five Lochnaw guards slept on the floor in the great hall along with the border collies. The hunting hounds were put in the outside kennel. There were now 16 people in the house, and all would soon settle into roles they were well suited for and contribute to the household according to their talents.

After a couple of days tasks had been assigned, and Andy and Helen finally got some time to themselves. Andy led her up behind the house to the high ground in the grove of oak trees, introducing her to the expansive view across the Galloway countryside with a chivalric bow and sweep of the hand.

*"This is your new abode and estate, m'lady."*

Helen was awestruck.

"It's such a beautiful view," she murmured, squeezing Andy's hand. "And the house," she continued, "it's so big and functional, not to mention lovely! I had no idea."

"Yes, we decided to make it as big as we could," Andy said. "I was hoping to fill it with bairns some day. But considering the many people we have living here now, I guess we'll just have to build on some more when we get started with bairns of our own."

Helen smiled mischievously. "I'm anxious to get started too, but maybe we should get married first. Folks might talk."

Andy laughed, his hazel eyes sparkling. "Perhaps we can practice in the meantime."

They sat down on a bed of leaves. "Maybe we should start that now," Helen teased. "Once we get the technique down, we'll need a really big house. What should we call it?"

"Big house?" mused Andy fatuously.

Helen responded, in a more serious tone, "Actually I like the sound of that, 'Big House' for a house full of bairns."

Andy laughed and kissed Helen on the cheek.

"I think that would be a splendid name, 'Big House' it is."

They then turned to each other, lying face to face on the crunched leaves, and engaged in another of those lingering kisses. It was late fall and the leaves had fallen from the trees, littering the ground in a crisp, soft carpet. The pungent, earthy smell of composting leaves wafted in the breeze. Both felt familiar urges. Helen moaned softly and whispered: "Here? Are you sure?"

Andy realized that while they had some cover and were alone at the time, it might not stay that way. Someone could come looking for them, or just stray by.

"All right," he said, "discretion before valor. We had better wait until tonight. I'll slip up to your room after supper."

At that they sat up and remained silent for a while, enjoying the gorgeous view, the cool air and the tangy smells of autumn.

Without his even really realizing it, the tranquil scene brought back to Andy's memory that terrible night of two years before when the bastle house was attacked and burned. The family had spent a cold night huddled together on the ground on a pile of leaves in this very grove. The only difference, both his mother and father had been alive and in vibrant, good health. Andy sat there, quietly reminiscing as these images flashed in his mind. Momentarily, Helen said sweetly, "You seem deep in thought."

This brought Andy back to reality.

"I'm sorry; I was just thinking of the night two years ago when our house was burned. After escaping, we all slept right here, in this very place. It was so cold."

"Why don't you tell me about it, if it's not too painful?"

"Nay it's not painful," Andy said. I was just thinking of my mother and father, what brave and strong people they were."

"So much has happened. It seems so long ago, but it really wasn't," said Helen. She reminded him that they had first met when he rode to Lochnaw that winter to warn her father of the English advance.

The two laid back and remained still for a while, both engrossed in private thoughts. At length, Helen said quietly, "You were so lucky to have a part of your father brought back to bury. It means a lot to have something tangible to inter and hold dear, a place you can go back to and visit, such as you are able to do with your family at that little cemetery. I so wish I had something of my father."

They talked some more about losing their parents and the importance of some kind of burial or service to commemorate their passing and bring some measure of closure. Helen mentioned that Gilbert Agnew's children must feel the same way.

Suddenly, out of the blue, an idea struck Andy. He said to Helen, "Do you think it would be proper for all of us—you, me, my family, Innis and Gilbert's bairns—to get together and hold a memorial service of some kind to honor them all—Baron Agnew, my parents, Innis's family and Gilbert Agnew? Maybe it would make everyone feel better—sort of symbolically unite us all?"

Helen sat up and looked thoughtfully out over the landscape. "Aye, I agree. It would be nice. After all, we are now one big family. We should consecrate our ties."

Just before the evening meal, Andy called everyone together in the great hall and explained the plan: "It would be a memorial service to honor the recently deceased members of both the Agnew and Henderson clans."

They all looked at him, unsure of exactly what he had in mind.

"Good idea," ventured Ree. "When?"

Andy suggested that it might be fitting to place memorial stones for each family. He said he could get them made at Ayr and could probably have them within a couple of weeks.

Ree, Joe and Jamie agreed, the three Agnew children expressed support, and even Innis appeared enthusiastic. Andy said he would set the plan in motion immediately.

Later that day, the men, including Andy, Innis, Harold, the four Lochnaw men, Blair Agnew and the two younger Henderson brothers, Joe and Jamie, sat down to start working up a plan of defense for the house and surrounding premises. Andy mentioned that he and Helen had decided that the place should be called the "Big House." Everyone laughed.

"It *is* a big house for certain," said Harold, "and everyone here is glad of that. But you never know when trouble might come, and everything works better if you have a plan in place and people know what to do."

"You're right," said Andy. "Why don't we all sit and toss around some ideas."

Meanwhile, Ree, Helen and Martha, the cook, and the two Agnew girls discussed the running of the household and who could best be put to doing what.

At the evening meal, the men, led by Andy and Harold, explained to the entire group the outlines of the plan for defense. An armed man would be stationed at one of the two pele towers on either end of the house at all times, walking the parapets regularly so he could look out in all directions. Shifts would be assigned depending upon who was available. Harold and his four men would do the bulk of the work. Meals would be brought to the guards when they were on duty.

In addition, the fortifications around the Big House would be extended in height, widened and strengthened. A new front gate, constructed of heavy oak and reinforced with iron bands, would be constructed at the front entrance. Eventually, Harold and Andy had agreed, a tunnel should be constructed from the south tower underground below the hill where the oak grove was situated, opening out into the valley on the south side under a canopy of trees near the banks of the River Cree. Any attacking force would likely come from the front, and a tunnel out the back would afford a means of escape. Such a tunnel had once aided Hugh Henderson with his cavalry charge at the battle of Lochnaw. A new kennel and pen enclosure for the dogs would also be built in front, off to one side. Should strangers approach, a chorus of loud barking would be heard.

Helen and Ree had remained silent during the presentation. When the men were finished, Helen said, "Seems you men have been quite busy with your defense planning and I must say it's quite elaborate. You all might like to know that Ree, Martha, Maggie and I are working on a plan for household chores to be assigned to each individual who lives under this roof. In case you haven't figured it out, that includes all of you. When we are finished, we'll let you know. I'm sure every one will be thrilled."

A loud, but good-natured groan was heard around the room.

The next day, Andy started his ride to Ayr to make arrangements for the headstones. He found a mason and contracted with him to construct five stones—one for Mairy "Grannie" Henderson and the deceased twins, one for Hugh and Ann, one for Baron Andrew Agnew, another for Sheriff Gilbert Agnew, and a final one for the murdered John Henderson family, of whom Innis was the only surviving member. Andy would return to Ayr in a week with a cart to pick up the stones and bring them back.

A few days later the integrated family started the familiar trek up Glen Trool to the base of Ben Blackcraig. Blair Agnew, along with one of the Lochnaw guards, had ridden to Wigtown and arranged for the parish priest to come and accompany the group to the small cemetery. A pair of oxen slowly pulled the stout cart with the headstones up the glen, stopping at the location of the former Henderson lean-to. There, the stones were unloaded to be carried by hand on stout timber planks up the final ascent.

As the group trudged slowly up the stony path to the little cemetery, each person was immersed in thoughts of the deaths of family members and the uncertain futures they all now faced. Upon reaching the top, those who had not been there before marveled at the ancient stone henge.

"Is that an old cemetery?" asked Helen.

"Nay, not exactly," replied Andy. "Those slabs are ancient—erected a very long time ago by unknown peoples. We think it was some kind of sacred place, but don't know for sure. Nice to have them though."

Three more graves were dug, and boxes containing cherished artifacts of the two Agnew brothers and the John Henderson family were interred. Included were two silver medallions worn by the Agnew brothers when alive, and a crucifix given to Innis by his mother when he was christened. The graves were carefully covered with dirt, and the headstones sturdily set. As he somberly recited Catholic funeral rites, the priest sprinkled holy water upon the graves.

Words were spoken, first by Andy, followed by everyone else who felt the need to say something. Tears were shed and hugs exchanged amidst murmurs of comfort and endearment.

Everyone felt a small bit better. The departed, so loved and revered in life, had been given proper Christian end-of-life rites and burials. Permanent headstones had been placed to memorialize them over the coming centuries. That the graves were near the primordial circle of stone slabs somehow seemed fitting.

The torch had been passed. A joint family had been spawned and a new generation held its destiny.

# 27.
# CONVERSION

AS the group made its way down Glen Trool to the Big House, Innis lagged behind. He had never been a particularly expressive person, having a laconic manner combined with a taciturn personality. But the experience of the memorial service, together with recurring dreams and thoughts of the many times he had narrowly, and to his mind, inexplicably, escaped certain death weighed heavily on him.

*What is it God wants from me*, he wondered. As he lagged further behind, engrossed in these contemplations, Ree suddenly appeared, walking toward him. He saw her long red hair glowing brightly in the late afternoon sun. Coming near, she said: "We were worried. You were with us coming down from the cemetery, then you weren't. Is everything all right?"

"Aye," he stammered, "I was just thinking ...."

Then Innis abruptly sat down on a large rock and started crying, sheets of tears streaming down his deeply tanned face. A dam had finally burst. Ree sat beside him and put her arm around his shoulder. Innis grabbed her around the neck, pulled her to him, sobbing and shaking so violently he was almost convulsing.

Ree whispered to him softly.

"Innis, I know how hard this has been for you. The murder of your entire family, the many battles, the loyalty you felt for my father, watching him die and unable to help. Nobody could withstand such horror unscathed. I understand; tell me what I can do to help you."

Innis knew from experience that Ree was kind and thoughtful of others. She was also strong and determined and had a streak of fierce independence. If anyone could help him, it was she.

"Ree," Innis said, finally able to break through the shaking and sobbing. "You are the smartest person I know. I trust you completely. I just don't understand what God wants of me."

Surprised and puzzled, Ree looked at him with close attention. What in the world was he talking about? She had never thought of Innis as a pious person. So far as she knew, religious thoughts never crossed his mind. *I had better proceed cautiously,* she thought. *He is overwrought with the emotion of the moment.*

After a short period of quiet, Ree finally gently prodded, "Do you feel that God has spoken to you?"

"Nay," replied Innis. "That's the problem. He has let me live when I should have died—several times—and I have prayed, or tried to, for an answer. God must want something from me, but no answer has come."

Ree was quiet for a while longer, trying to define in her mind what he meant, but remained baffled. So she said:

"Innis, why don't you tell me the whole story."

He did, at length, speaking of the mysteries—why he was spared when his whole family perished; how he happened to be saved from two highwaymen by his dog; why, through a hail of shot and arrows, he survived but his Uncle Hugh and Baron Agnew— far better soldiers—did not.

"It had to be the hand of God," he said, "but why? This has troubled me so—why? I just want to know."

Ree suddenly understood. The poor lad was enthralled, beguiled by this admittedly strange chain of apparent coincidences. He thought it was the work of God, and who was she to say he was wrong. He clearly needed help, and she would do what she could.

Innis was a skilled fighting man, but had little education or experience in the regular affairs of life. From the time he was rescued, he had always been a warrior, most of the time a squire by the side of her father, Sir Hugh Henderson. Her father's death had obviously affected him deeply, as had the massacre of his own family a couple of years before. It was her obligation to help him get it all sorted out. This, she vowed she would do.

"Don't worry, I'll help you, I promise," Ree assured him. "Now lets join the others. We'll have plenty of time to talk about this later."

She did not know how she could help, but she was sure she could figure it out. She just needed more information, but now was not the time. She got him up, and they hurried along to catch up. Innis felt much better. There was no one whose judgment he respected more than Ree Henderson's.

✦ ✦ ✦

A few months later, in the spring of 1548, word came that the English army had indeed occupied Wigtown. Of the townspeople left, many had been ejected from their homes and thrown into the streets to make room for the English troops. Others were forced to live in an attic or basement, or worse, the barn, while the English occupied the main house. The townspeople were pressed into virtual slavery, forced to wait on the English hand and foot, and attempt to satisfy their every whim.

Supplies, livestock and food were confiscated. Those ejected from the town were forced to fend for themselves. Many set up small camps. It was March, and the cold winds of winter had not completely subsided. Food outside the town walls was scarce to nonexistent. Andy sent some of the Lochnaw men to drive a few livestock and a cart or two of early garden vegetables to these camps to help them out. Andy went himself, along with Innis, on some of these missions.

On one such trip, Andy and Innis came upon a camp of about a couple score ensconced on a wood-covered hilltop. It was late on a rainy afternoon when they arrived with a couple of sheep and a meager supply of greens, radishes, carrots and onions. A shabbily dressed older man with long grey hair hanging from underneath a crumpled hat and a thick stubble of whiskers on his face limped out toward them, leaning on a crooked cane. Evidently he was the group's leader.

"Laird Henderson!" he exclaimed, with a hearty grin lighting up his face through the scruffy whiskers. "You be the son o' Sir Hugh Henderson, am I right, the hero o' Pinkie? Andy nodded and started to reply, but the man quickly continued.

"Your companion must be Innis Henderson, the brave Scots cavalry leader who might have won the battle, had he been listened to."

Apparently, stories of the battle had been leaking out and were passed along mouth to mouth, growing in exaggeration with each passing, but Andy and Innis did not mind.

"You do us great honor, not justified, but we thank you anyway," said Andy. "We bring a little food to help you along. Wish it could be more."

The man invited them to come and sit by their campfire. They talked for a while about the war, the situation at Wigtown, how long the English soldiers might stay, and the new religion being preached by John Knox all across the borderlands, from Glasgow City to Edinburgh. The man mentioned that he had heard that a disciple of Knox, a man named Peter Donner, would be preaching at the Ayr market the next week. Knox himself, he said, had gone into hiding because of fear of recriminations from the Pope's Prelate to Scotland, Archbishop David Beaton.

A few days before, he said, he had visited with some folks who had heard Donner preach near Dumfries. They reported he was compelling, a true man of God, and were still ecstatic in their praise of him. Donner preached that a man could talk directly with the Almighty through faith and prayer. A priest was not needed as an intermediary, nor was it necessary to tithe or give the church a portion of one's worldly goods.

"This message," the man said, "created a lot of interest and excitement among many people."

Hearing this, Innis was greatly enthused. This must be the man God had sent to help him find his way. He decided then and there he must go and hear Donner preach. Perhaps Ree could go with him. After all, she had expressed that she wanted to help. He didn't say anything at that moment, but he was excited; soon he might learn the purpose God had for him.

After they got back to the Big House, over the morning meal, Innis sat next to Ree on the bench running the length of the long table in the great hall.

"Ree, could I have a word with you in private as soon as you can take a break from your duties?" he whispered.

Ree could tell from the earnest tone of his voice that it was something important, probably related to the experience she had with him coming back from the cemetery.

"Of course, I'll be in the garden later, digging some carrots and potatoes. You can come out and help me. We can talk then."

When they met, Innis talked in an excited, but hushed manner. He told her of the report he and Andy had heard from the man at the camp of exiled townspeople.

"Do you know of John Knox?" he asked.

"Aye," Ree answered, "I've been hearing a lot about him lately."

"Well, Knox be in hiding. I hear he is being hunted by the Catholic Archbishop Beaton."

Innis then told her of a man named Donner, a disciple of Knox, who had been carrying on his ministry. He was last in Dumfries, and some people at the camp had heard him. They said he was a man of God, very impressive, much like Jesus. He preached that ordinary people, if they had enough faith, could speak directly with God through prayer. God could hear and answer those prayers.

Ree noticed that Innis's face was flushed, his voice sounded dreamy and his eyes looked glazed. She did not say anything, for Innis had moved very close to her, tugging on the sleeve of her smock, his voice hot on her face.

"They say Donner will be preaching at the Ayr market next week. I've decided to go. Please come with me. Don't you see— God has sent him. He can help me learn my purpose. Say you will, I beg of you."

Quickly and abruptly, Ree stood and said, "I don't know if I can. Let me think it over."

She picked up her basket and headed toward the kitchen. Ree was seriously conflicted. True, she had agreed to help Innis with his "problem." But she envisioned this as just talking him through it, not going off with him to hear some unknown preacher spreading a new religion.

On the other hand, Innis was her first cousin, had been a faithful, brave squire to her father in many dangerous battles and had always stood steadfastly beside her and her family. How could she refuse?

Later, Ree confided to Andy the gist of what Innis had told her and of the precarious state of mind he was in.

"He wants me to accompany him to Ayr to hear this preacher, Donner, a disciple of John Knox. He thinks Donner can help him understand what to do."

"I don't know," said Andy. "Knox and Donner are Protestants, a part of this new religion that's sweeping the country. I've heard some tales, ugly things."

Andy warned her that the Catholic hierarchy was up in arms. It was said Cardinal Beaton had already killed several leading Protestants. Going to Ayr to hear the man preach could be dangerous.

"But I promised I would help," pleaded Ree. "He is such a tortured soul. I can't back out on him now."

"Do as you feel you must," said Andy, "but if you decide to do it, be very careful. It might be better for his health to remain a good Catholic."

Ree decided to go, and they left on horseback shortly before midnight, finding their way by the dim light of a waning quarter moon. It was late March 1548, blustery and cold. They left out the back way, heavily wrapped and well provisioned. Ree had been trained to use a light, cavalry-type crossbow from the time she was a young girl, and was an experienced rider. She carried a quiver of bolts and secured her crossbow with a strap across her shoulder, concealed beneath her wrap. She wore a long cloak with a hood, belted at the waist, breeches and boots. Anyone seeing her would think she was a man.

Innis dressed in his usual garb, with an extra heavy coat and hood, his dirk belted to his waist. They kept the horses at a steady canter and arrived at Ayr at dusk the next day. Innis arranged a room at an inn, and they got a decent night's sleep.

The next morning, Innis went downstairs and brought up some food. He had learned that Donner would be preaching at the town square late that evening. During the day, the two walked around the town, passing by and admiring St. John's church with its famous tower where the first Scots Parliament had been assembled by Robert the Bruce in 1315, and where Ree's mother and father had been married all those years ago.

They also strolled along the bustling docks at the wharf area where the river Ayr emptied into the Firth of Clyde. They were impressed by the number of sailing ships and all manner of other boats plying their trade at the docks. Ayr was a busy port town, supported by vigorous trade between Ireland, England, France and the port cities of Scotland.

As the dark of night came on, Ree and Innis made their way to the mercat cross where they figured Donner would position himself so his message would reach the ears of the masses expected to assemble. The night was clear and cold, with the moon expected to rise after midnight. To provide illumination, torches were placed at strategic positions around the square. Soon, a large crowd had gathered. Ree and Innis occupied a favorable vantage point near the cross. After a while, the moon broke the horizon, and a soft murmur started through the crowd.

Fascinated and excited, Ree and Innis craned their necks to look around. They soon spied a break in the crowd, a moving ribbon as people parted to allow a slight, slender figure pass through.

Peter Donner mounted the base of the mercat cross near the pillory. Finally, the gathered crowd could see him well, and the crowd's murmur began again. Physically, Donner was not imposing. He was short, a few inches over five feet tall, weighed maybe 120 pounds, and was dressed all in black. He had long brown shaggy hair, a sparse beard, long face and hawk nose, and there was a shocking pallor about him.

Innis, expecting Donner to have a formidable physical presence as he had heard about John Knox, was disappointed. Ree was merely curious. Then Donner began to speak. Softly at first, he paid homage to the crowd, thanking them for coming. The people strained to hear. There was a pause. Then, like the faint sound of rolling thunder starting far away and drawing ever closer, Donner began his sermon in a stentorian voice.

"How many of you believe the Bible to be the immutable word of God? Raise your hands."

A louder murmur was heard from the crowd and a number of hands were raised.

"How many of you believe that Jesus Christ is the Son of God, born of the Virgin Mary?"

More hands were raised, accompanied by a still louder rumble. Innis joined in enthusiastically. Ree kept her silence.

"How many of you believe that God can forgive your sins, save you from eternal damnation, grant salvation and everlasting life?"

The murmur grew into a low roar. Shouts of "Aye, aye" were heard around the square.

Donner stood quiet for a long moment, raising his thin, frail arms over his head, palms outward toward the crowd, until all was quiet again. He did not speak but looked out at the crowd, his eyes seeming to glow. The crowd grew restless. Then: "Brethren," he thundered, "how many of you pay tithes?"

Many arms went up, then more, and finally a thicket of arms pierced the air.

"How many of you toil the grounds of the diocese, labor for the church and the parish priest? You and all your able-bodied family members, at least one day a week?"

Again, the thicket of arms, accompanied by an angry buzz.

"Do you go to confession, profess your sins to a priest, seeking intervention through him to God?"

A noisy chorus came from the people: "Aye!"

Donner thundered: "The sacraments, the Eucharist, communions, holy orders, penance, confession, unction, and, above all, collection of tithes for the church coffers. How many of you have been taught from childhood that such things were necessary to enter the kingdom of God?"

An angry hissing noise rose from the crowd.

"Brethren in Christ, I have good news. You need not tithe, you need not toil, you need not seek intervention from a priest, you need not take the sacraments. The Bible says nothing of these things. The Catholic high priests just invented them to enrich themselves at your expense."

A loud angry chorus of disgust swept the crowd.

Again Donner raised his arms, palms out, seeking silence. He stood still for a long while. The crowd quieted down. Donner remained silent. Then the buzz started again, becoming progressively louder.

Lowering his voice, Donner asked, "Do you know why you have been hoodwinked all these centuries?" Then louder. "Because the Bible is written in Latin. Ordinary people cannot read it. They can't understand when it is read to them. Only the high churchmen can, and they have never told you the truth!"

The roar became angrier.

Donner stood still and silent again for a moment. Then he yelled, "John Knox has had the Holy Bible translated into Scots. He preaches the gospel to ordinary people. Now he is running for his life. Cardinal Beaton, the Pope's man in Scotland, is hunting him. Beaton is the murderer of James Hamilton, George Wishart and other true believers. At this very moment he is seeking to find and kill John Knox. Simply for telling the truth!"

The roar got much louder and angrier.

"Now, let me quote to you, in your own language, two simple passages from the Holy Bible that will give you understanding,"

The crowd grew quiet—ears cupped in rapt attention, straining to hear. Donner shouted.

"Isaiah 65, verse 44, says, 'Before they call, I will answer; while they are yet speaking, I will hear.' That means God hears your prayers. Even when you do not recite them and no priest is present."

Now the crowd was very quiet, contemplating what he had said.

"And God said this of Jesus Christ, his Son. John 3:16, 'For I so loved the world, that I gave my only Son, that whoever believes in Him shall not perish, but have everlasting life.' "

Another spell of quiet, as Donner let this sink in. Lower, in almost a whisper, Donner continued, "That, my friends, is all you have to do to avoid hell and reach heaven—believe and accept."

His voice rising to a louder cadence, he continued, "Repent your sins, accept Christ and have faith in God." Then still louder, "Anyone can do it; everyone can do it; it only takes an instant, and it lasts forever."

Pushing to a crescendo, "I ask you tonight, do you repent, do you accept Jesus Christ and do you have faith in God? If you do, fall to your knees, for you have been saved."

At first, a few did, then more, then still more, until finally, like an army shot dead in a withering crossfire, everyone in the multitude fell. This included Innis. But Ree remained on her feet. Suddenly, looking around, she realized that everyone else was down. Donner looked into her eyes and moved his lips, whispering silently, *You also.* Ree sank to her knees, not because of what he said, but fearful of standing alone before so many people.

Unnoticed by all the supplicants in the square, a few dark, silent figures stood in the shadows. They were not there to receive the word of God. They were the spies of Cardinal Beaton. They were there to take names and try to determine the identity of the leaders who were supporting this new, and to the Cardinal, very dangerous message.

Innis was ecstatic, still on his knees and blubbering unintelligible words. Ree felt a nervous knot in her stomach. She stood and looked up into the night sky. The luminous shape of a bright waning moon slid silently through clearing clouds. A new cycle was beginning. Some regarded the gradual disappearance of the moon into darkness a sign from the occult. Others, more enlightened, thought it the symbol of a continuum of the natural order. Ree did not dwell upon any of these things. The knot in her stomach had turned bilious.

Donner was finished. "Amen! My Christian brethren, go in peace and may God be with you."

He then abruptly stepped down from the mercat cross and forced his way back through the crowd. Ree noticed, for the first time, that he was flanked, front and behind, by two big, burly men—bodyguards, she assumed. Deep inside, Ree felt a dark foreboding. Something evil was lurking.

Innis grabbed Ree's hand and was pulling her forwards toward the path taken by Donner.

"I want to talk with him!" Innis cried. "I think I understand, but I need to meet him in person. I've some questions to ask."

But it was futile. There were simply too many people packed together. They would never get to him. Already, Donner and the two guards had reached the outward fringe of the crowd and were disappearing into the darkness. Ree jerked Innis back.

"Innis, stop! It's useless; they are already gone."

Innis could see that Ree was right, so they slowed to allow the rest of the people to move on. After the crowd had thinned, two young men about their age walked up. They were clad in long, dirty, grey robes in the manner of the clothing of monks and wore mud-caked sandals. One was tall and very skinny, almost to the point of emaciation. He had dark stringy hair and a scruffy beard. The other was shorter, stocky, with a round face, shoulder-length black hair and a stubble of beard that looked to be several days old. Both had a glazed look in their eyes, as if they had been out on a long drinking binge.

"What an inspiring sermon! Didn't you think so," the tall one said to Innis. "Donner is the best, better than Knox, I think. He so moved the people, just as Jesus did, or John the Baptist. Do you agree?" he asked, still looking at Innis.

"Aye, he did. His spirit filled the square. Everyone was touched. Did you see how they all knelt and prayed?" Innis responded, his eyes still hazy, a giddy smile upon his lips.

Ree pulled the hood tighter around her face and backed away. She did not know these men and had no interest in conversing with them. She only wanted to get back to the Inn, get a meal, some sleep, and ride back to Blackcraigshire first thing the next morning.

The shorter man then said to Innis, "Your companion here, he does not talk?" Then, addressing Ree directly, he said, "What are your thoughts, Sir? Were you not impressed with Reverend Donner?"

Ree pulled her hood back from her head, revealing her pretty face, long red hair, and striking green eyes that looked almost ghostly in the dim light.

"Och! I didn't ken you to be a fair lassie. Forgive me," stammered the short man.

Ree replied, not smiling, "I wrapped myself against the cold. To answer your question, the preacher was well spoken, but we must go. It's getting late."

"Have you time for a beer, maybe?" the man persisted. "We are students of the reformed religion and would enjoy a conversation."

"No, we really have to go, thank you," Ree replied, and turned, walking swiftly in the direction of the inn.

Innis, suddenly stunned out of his stupor, smiled weakly at the two men, and muttered, "Fare you well, perhaps another time," and hurried after Ree.

When they got back to the Inn and had taken a table in the tavern, Ree hissed at Innis, "What's wrong with you—trying to get us mixed up with those strangers! I would never go out for a beer with two men I don't know."

"I'm sorry, Ree. Truly I am. But they came up to us. I didn't feel it proper to just ignore them,"

Ree calmed some. Innis was right; the two men did approach and start the conversation. But there was something about the whole affair that made her feel uncomfortable.

"Innis, I'm sorry. You did nothing wrong. I'm tired and hungry, and it just made me irritable I guess. Let's have some food and get some sleep."

They would leave early the next morning, she said.

Innis, looking embarrassed, finally said tentatively, "Maybe I'll stay over for a couple of days, if you don't mind."

The two men had said they were students of the new religion, he explained. He would like to explore taking some training himself. The message he heard from the preacher affected him and he wanted to know more. Maybe he could look them up, and they could teach him. If they were students, there must be a school or a teacher they went to.

"Would you reconsider and stay over with me?"

"No," said Ree emphatically.

"I admit that I was impressed with some of the things Donner said: the ability to have a personal relationship with God, the simplicity of redemption and salvation. But perhaps it's too simple, too easy. I'm not sure, but I don't want to be rushed into anything. I'm going home, with or without you."

"I'll go with you if you're afraid of going alone," said Innis.

"No, I'm not fearful of that. I'm uneasy about this new religion," Ree said. "I don't think Donner's message will go down well with the Catholics, especially the high churchmen. They have a lot to lose if this catches on. Maybe it's best to stay a good Catholic."

"I am certain that God has led me to this place," said Innis, somewhat mournfully.

He had to stay and see it through.

# 28.

# BETRAYAL

REE left at first light the next morning, her cloak belted securely around her torso and her crossbow at the ready. Very few people were about as she clattered down the cobblestone street out of Ayr and urged her horse into a fast amble. She was anxious to get back home to the Big House.

At the inn, Ree and Innis had shared a room, Ree sleeping on a bed and Innis on the floor. They had slept in their clothes. Ree fell asleep almost immediately, but Innis couldn't get off to sleep right away, still dizzy with ideas about the sermon. He thought more about the conversation he had had with Ree and came to the realization that he could not let her ride back alone. He had brought her there, and it was his obligation to see that she got safely home again. So he decided he would accompany her back, spend the night and return to Ayr in a couple of days. He was sure he could locate the two students and they could help him decide if he should pursue religious training himself.

The next morning, Innis was sound asleep when he was jarred awake by the sound of the door slamming shut. He looked up and realized that Ree had left, taking her cloak and crossbow, and he had not mentioned that he planned to join her.

Panicked, Innis jumped up, pulled on his shirt, trousers and boots, grabbed his cloak and sword, and sprinted down the stairs, out into the gloomy dark morning. He ran to the stable. Ree's horse was absent. *Och! She already be gone,* he thought, as he hurriedly saddled his horse, mounted and galloped off after her.

Innis thought he might catch her by the time he got to the edge of town, but she was nowhere to be seen. Filled with apprehension, he spurred his horse into a dead run and took a right onto the trail to Blackcraigshire. He had covered several furlongs before he saw through the gloom a dim shape ahead. *A horse and rider; that must be her.* He yelled at the top of his voice, "Ree! Ree! Wait up!"

But the figure did not stop or slow. Instead the figure sped up. Innis urged his horse to run even faster. He must catch her.

Ree had noticed the sound of horse hooves behind her when she made the turn onto the trail. She had pressed her horse into an easy gallop, trying to be as inconspicuous as possible, yet put some distance between herself and the unknown rider. She hoped the rider would stay on the road, but when he turned onto the trail, she could see that he was following her, she feared the worst. *A bandit.* She pulled a bolt from her quiver, pulled the bowstring back, cocked her crossbow and kicked her horse into a fast run.

As she topped a rise entering a wood, she felt that the rider was gaining on her. *I must not let the bandit catch me from behind,* she thought, quickly assessing the situation. *It will be difficult to turn and shoot accurately from the back of a running horse.*

She came to a small burn bisecting the trail. Reining her horse, she turned it downstream behind some bushes. Hopefully the pursuing rider would not see her and could continue on the trail. If the bandit did slow or stop, indicating he had seen her, she would be in a better position to protect herself. She stopped, reined her horse around so its head pointed in the direction of the trail. Her crossbow aimed, she was ready to shoot. She pulled out another bolt, placing it under her leg for quick reloading, and waited.

Innis had been gaining on her when Ree dropped below the rise. He expected to be even closer when he topped the rise and could yell her name again. Surely she would hear him this time. As he came over the rise, he could see a long stretch of trail in front of him, but no Ree. She had completely disappeared.

*What the hell? Where did she go?* Innis quickly slowed his horse, looking down for hoofprints. He saw fresh ones go into the burn, but none on the other side. Bending to look closer, he heard a *whump!* Something had hit a tree just beside his head. He had heard that sound before and instantly surmised what was happening.

"Ree! Ree!" He screamed, leaping off the left side of his horse to put something between himself and her.

"Ree—it's me, Innis. Stop shooting!"

Ree rode out onto the trail, the new bolt in her crossbow.

"You fool! I almost killed you. I thought you were a bandit!"

Innis stepped from behind his horse, embarrassed and ashamed.

"I'm sorry, Ree. Forgive me. I didn't want you to have to return alone. I meant to tell you last night, but you were asleep. I planned to go out with you this morning, but didn't hear when you left. I've been running my horse as fast as possible ever since trying to catch up."

As he was blurting all this out, his knees went weak and he sank to the ground, totally dejected. Ree, angry and scared one minute, felt her naturally sympathetic heart turn soft.

"All right, Innis. I forgive you, but don't ever do such a stupid thing again."

"I won't. You can be certain of that," responded Innis weakly.

The two rode on in silence for quite a ways before Innis said, "Ree, let's not tell Andy about this—agreed?"

"Fine with me," she said.

Innis was very relieved. He had been a fool and had done something really stupid. He did not want Andy to learn of it. Andy would take a very dim view of any kind of endangerment to his sister.

They rode on through the morning until about noon when they stopped to rest their horses, drink some water and eat some jerky. They then left, reaching the Big House around mid-afternoon.

The next morning, Innis left again for Ayr. He found that he was not nearly as enthused this time. On the ride in, Ree had explained to him that however much the new Protestant religion might appeal to him, he needed to be careful, for it threatened the existing Catholic order. If he were to talk openly about it, word could get to some priest or vicar, and he might find himself charged with heresy.

As a rule, the Catholic hierarchy did not go after ordinary people, she explained, but if he aspired to spread the Protestant message, he could end up like George Wishart, burned at the stake. He only wanted to learn, he assured her, not preach, so there was no reason to worry.

Innis arrived in Ayr, as before, right at full dark. He selected a different inn this time, closer to the center of town and nearer to the market square.

Once he had paid his fare and stabled his horse, he walked around the street near the square, looking in the windows of taverns, reasoning that the two young students he had met might be in one of them. He knew that politics and religion were often the staples of conversation in such places. After a while he found them, conversing at a back table. He strolled up, trying to appear nonchalant.

"Pardon me, but I believe we've met—at the mercat cross after Preacher Donner's sermon?"

The two young men looked up, puzzled at first. Then one of them smiled. "Och, aye, I believe we have. You were the one with the fair red-haired lassie, right?

"Aye, she be my first cousin. We had heard Donner was speaking and came to hear him," replied Innis.

"Where are you from?" asked the other.

"To the south, two-day ride—Blackcraigshire."

"From your comments the other night, I take it you were impressed with the message Preacher Donner put forth?" said the first.

"Aye, very much," said Innis. "Do you have a moment?"

They both nodded and Innis pulled up a chair.

"You said that you were students of John Knox. I would consider it a favor to hear a little more about him and his teaching."

"Sure. My name is David," said the tall one, "and this is my friend, Alan."

Innis called to the barkeep for a pint of beer for himself and refills for his two companions.

"Your cousin, she's not with you tonight?" asked Alan.

"Nay, she had to go home," answered Innis.

"Where is she from?" inquired David.

"She's from Blackcraigshire also," said Innis. "She's the lady of the house. Her brother, Andrew Henderson, is laird of the shire," he added proudly.

"She seemed a very intelligent educated woman," said David. "Now I understand why."

"Yes, she was educated in Glasgow City, attended the Cathedral School for several years," added Innis. "She's very knowledgeable about everything. I've learned much from her."

Innis justified his lie about Ree's schooling by the fact that her mother, Ann, had attended the Glasgow school and had taught Ree everything she knew.

"Politics and religion also?" asked Alan.

"Aye, and much more," bragged Innis.

"How did she feel about Preacher Donner's sermon? She made favorable comments about it afterwards, as I recall," probed David.

"She liked it, not every part, but in general she thought that he made some good points," Innis agreed.

More rounds were ordered, and the three conversed eagerly.

"Is John Knox himself your teacher?" asked Innis, "Preacher Donner said he was on the run from agents of Cardinal Beaton, if I heard right."

"Nay. Knox is fine," Alan said, conspiratorially. "Donner only says that to get people riled and emotional. We, too, are disciples of Knox, but our teacher is a Master in Protestant tenets. He stays here in Ayr, nearby actually. We attend lectures in his study. Most people are unaware of this, but he is the real leader of the Reformation in Scotland."

"Och, my God!" laughed Innis nervously, already feeling light-headed, "here in Ayr? You're lucky to study under such a man."

"Would you like to attend a few of his lectures?" asked David. "I'm sure we can arrange it. He is always on the lookout for bright converts such as yourself."

"Of course, that would be wonderful," agreed Innis.

"Where are you staying," inquired Alan.

"At the inn around the corner right now."

"That must be expensive," Alan said, confiding that they were rooming in a nearby boarding house.

"We have plenty of room," David added, glancing at his roommate, "and the wife of the owner cooks two meals a day, morning and evening, very good too. We would be glad to have you room with us, right, Alan?"

Alan nodded. "You would only have to pay one-third of the rent. That would be much less expensive than the inn. You could attend the Master's lectures with us. What do you think?"

"Sounds great," said Innis, greatly enthused.

He motioned the barkeep to bring another round, which he paid for. Soon, Innis was quite drunk, along with his two companions.

The next morning Innis awoke with a huge headache in a strange room. He was lying on a pallet on the floor, still in his clothes. His boots were off, and he was covered with his cloak. Groggily, he looked around the bare room. There was a small table with two chairs. Some books were stacked on it beside a half-burned candlestick. The only other furniture was a bed with a straw mattress and a wool blanket. David and Alan were both asleep on the bed, covered by the blanket. Their clothes were piled on the floor.

Innis felt sick to his stomach and badly needed a drink of water. He pulled on his boots and stood up unsteadily. He considered waking his two new companions, then thought better of it. He stumbled out the door and down a short flight of stairs. Finding himself in a low-ceilinged room with a few tables and chairs scattered about, he noticed the smell of cooking food wafting from the back. He walked in the direction of the smell and came upon a tiny, wizened old woman. She had stringy gray hair hanging down to her shoulders above a dirty, drab, threadbare dress and apron.

The woman, her back to him, was busily stirring something liquid and lumpy in an iron pot over the hearth. She suddenly realized he was there, and whirled around, eyes wide with surprise.

"Who be ye?" she stammered.

"My name be Innis. I'm staying with David and Alan in one of the rooms upstairs," Innis replied.

"I don't remember you paying any rent," she said in a high-pitched, crackling voice. "You get no room and no food without pay," she continued, grinning through gapped, yellow teeth and shriveled lips.

"I'm prepared to pay, but please, could I have a cup of water?" Innis pleaded. The woman dipped a cup of water from a nearby bucket, and Innis gulped it down, then another.

"You'll have to pay now," the woman ordered, leading him to a dilapidated cabinet from which she took out a rumpled scrap of paper. "Make your mark. I'll keep up with your expenses."

"I can sign," said Innis, scribbling his signature on the bottom of the paper, and doling out the required amount.

Pocketing the money, the woman replied, "Good. The broth will be done soon."

Innis suddenly felt hot and faint. He hurried outside and vomited. He was immediately better, but had no appetite. He went back up to the room. His newfound mates were now awake but still in bed. After Innis came in, they both yawned, stretched and got out of bed. They were completely nude.

For the first time, Innis got a good look at them, as it was dark when he had initially encountered them, and dim in the back of the tavern the second time. The two men were a couple of years older than he, he reckoned, maybe 19 or 20 years of age. The tall one, David, had sparse body hair, very pale skin, a thin, scruffy beard, and a long angular face with light blue, bloodshot eyes. The shorter one, Alan, was swarthy, with a lot of dark body hair, a short bushy stubble of beard, black eyes and long black oily hair.

*Odd-looking pair,* Innis thought. The two casually pulled on their clothing from the prior day and suggested they all go down for a late morning meal. Innis mentioned that he had already been down and the proprietress was preparing a big pot of broth.

"It was not the most appetizing I've seen," he added.

"Ah, aye, the same every day," said David, "but for what we pay, you can't expect a feast."

After the dreary meal, Innis understood a little better the emaciated state of the two men. Drinking alcohol all night probably did not help, either.

"We go for our classes tomorrow afternoon," David said. "We'll mention you to the Master and recommend that he take on another student."

"Thank you," Innis muttered, wondering what he could do to occupy himself for the rest of the day. He was beginning to wish that he had stayed at the Big House.

The next day was better. For one thing, Innis did not drink himself into oblivion, as he wished to be alert when he met with the Master. For another, the day broke sunny and crisp—a perfect early spring day.

Around mid-morning, Innis walked down past the square to the wharf area. He admired the big sailing ships docked there and the bustle of activity of commerce. Stevedores loaded and unloaded bales and barrels of goods onto carts that they pushed up and down the docks. Fishing boats swung nets bulging with mackerel, cod and other fish common to the area, while fish-mongers haggled over price and dodged swooping gulls. Innis found the frenzy of activity exciting. *Maybe I could go to sea some-day,* he mused.

Time slipped by quickly and soon it was mid-afternoon. Innis walked back to the rooming house. Tomorrow was the day his two new roommates were to take him to meet the Master. David had told him the Master had a large, roomy townhouse at the end of a side street in the wharf area.

The following afternoon, when the three of them walked to the Master's home, Innis realized that he had strolled right past it the previous day and had admired its attractive architecture. The "classes" were held in a library at the back of the house, filled with books. Innis got a chance to glance at a couple of them that were open on a table and noticed they were written in a foreign language, or at least one that he could not decipher. They had arrived late in the day, and the library had a west-facing window that cast a pleasant, golden glow. A lit candlestick stood on the table beside the books.

A big muscular man with a dirk strapped to his waist met them at the door and ushered them to the library. Innis guessed him to be a guard. The Master greeted them from behind an ornate mahogany desk. He too was a big man, but more in a fleshy way than muscular, dressed in a black robe. A long, silver chain dangled from his neck, holding a large, finely crafted silver cross. He had graying dark hair and thin, expressionless lips framed by a strong jaw. He stood and greeted Innis with a slight smile that was not reflected in his cold, black eyes.

"So you are the young man David and Alan told me about. Innis, is it?"

"Aye. I have heard that you are a great teacher," Innis said solemnly, bowing slightly. "Thank you for taking me."

The Master offered each a straight-backed chair lined against the wall.

"I've heard a lot about you from my young charges, also about your young lady, the striking red-haired beauty—sister of the Laird of Blackcraigshire did I hear?" the Master asked soothingly.

"Aye, she be," said Innis in a proud voice. "She has been very influential in my life."

The Master smiled a thin smile, as if his teeth were gritting behind his lips.

"I hear she was educated in Glasgow City for several years?"

"Aye, at the Cathedral School," Innis answered.

"So she was raised Catholic?" the Master said, a slight caustic tone in his voice.

"Not really," Innis said in a half-truth. "There was no church or chapel near our home, the closest being in Wigtown, so we seldom went to services."

"Was not your parish served by a priest?" he asked.

"Yes, but he didn't get up that far very often," Innis said weakly, already feeling uneasy.

"Did you or your cousin seek repentance or take confession on those occasions when the priest came by?"

"Nay, not that I recall," said Innis, "but we very seldom saw him, and he was there but a short time. I was with the Laird's family for not much more than a year, so I really do not know what their religious practices were before that."

"Were you brought in as an orphan?" inquired the Master.

"Aye, my entire family was murdered by English soldiers, and they rescued me."

Looking down at one of his books, the Master asked, barely audibly, "But you could have asked the priest for confession when he came?"

Innis did not answer immediately, as he was becoming confused with all of the questioning. The Master looked directly up at him and said in a demanding tone, "Correct?"

"Aye, I suppose I could have," Innis replied nervously.

*Why was the Master asking me all these Catholic questions,* he wondered. While Innis was pondering this, the Master quickly bored in with an increasingly aggressive interrogation.

"While you were living in the Henderson household, was grace ordinarily said over meals?"

"No, but we did not all sup together. People had various jobs, and all did not come in to eat at the same time," Innis explained, his voice quavering slightly.

"Do either you or your red-haired cousin say Hail Mary prayers at the end of the day at home?"

"I don't, usually. I don't know what Ree does, as she sleeps in her own room."

"So you've never heard her," the Master persisted.

*He must be testing me to determine the strength of my Protestant beliefs,* thought Innis, stating in a firm voice, "Nay."

The Master was quiet for a while, looking at Innis thoughtfully. Suddenly he asked, "Did your cousin always have red hair and green eyes?"

*What kind of question is that?* wondered Innis, before replying, "Aye, ever since I've known her."

The Master suddenly changed tone and topic.

"Tell me, Innis, what did you think of the message you heard from Preacher Donner at the square the other night?"

"I was very impressed," said Innis brightly, much relieved that they were now talking about the subject he expected.

"Tell me about it," urged the Master.

"I've been quite unsettled lately, hoping that God would help me find my calling. Preacher Donner spoke of talking to God through prayer, about finding salvation through faith and redemption. It sounded so fresh, so direct, so...simple," Innis continued earnestly.

That thin, gritty smile again.

"Your cousin, she thought so as well?"

"Och, aye."

# 29.
# HERESY

THE "lesson" lasted for another half hour or so, but the direct questioning of Innis by the Master was over. The Master read aloud several passages from one of the books on his desk in a language that Innis did not understand—Latin, he presumed—and conversed some with David and Alan, but did not address Innis again.

On the walk back to the boarding house, Innis asked his two companions why the Master had questioned him so sharply.

"Och, he does that with every new student," Alan said, "to establish a sort of base so he can better craft your instruction, I think. Don't worry about it; you did well."

The two wanted to stop off at a tavern for some drinks and invited Innis along, but he declined. He had a headache and just wanted to get some food and turn in for the night.

After eating at another tavern and downing a couple of beers to settle his nerves, Innis went back to the boarding house, lay down on his pallet and rapidly fell into a deep sleep. He dreamed he was in a strange place, out of doors, surrounded by a bright light that blinded him, but it was not the sun. Still in this dream-like state, he felt that his arms and legs were being pulled by some strong force, as if he were wrestling with a demon from the spirit world. Feeling as if he was in a trance he could not resist.

Suddenly, he felt a sharp pain in his side that knocked him rolling off the pallet. He opened his eyes. Two burly men stood over him. This was no dream. He tried to scramble and get up, but his feet would not move; neither would his hands. He looked down. His hands and feet were securely tied together. He was helpless.

"Who you be?" he demanded. "What do you want?"

"You'll go with us," one of the men growled.

"Where?" Innis stammered.

"You'll find out soon enough," the man said.

They grabbed his arms, dragged him down the stairs, out of the building and back to the stable. There, Innis was draped over the back of a horse, and a rope was used to tie his hands to his feet underneath the horse's belly. A shroud was placed over his head and he was taken away.

After a long ride, his stomach bouncing painfully up and down into the jarring back of the fast-trotting horse, he was finally taken down and led into a place—a building, he figured, from the hard-feeling stone steps. He was first pulled up the steps, dragged a ways and then taken down some more steps. He heard a metallic creaking sound. The shroud remained over his head and his knees were kicked from behind, sending him crashing to the floor.

"What do you want of me?" he implored.

"You'll keep quiet if you ken what's good for you," came the answer in a snarl.

A moment later, Innis heard the distinctive clang of an iron door being closed and locked.

✦ ✦ ✦

A couple of days later, a lone rider came galloping up to the Big House, the rider waving his arms frantically.

"I come in peace!" he yelled. "Does Lady Mairy Henderson live here? I've an important message for her."

"Stop where you are!" called Joe, who was manning one of the towers. "What kind of message?"

"I don't know. It is written. I was told it was very important and that I should deliver it personally to Lady Mairy," the stranger replied.

"Where did you ride from," asked Joe.

"Ayr," answered the man.

"Who gave you the message?"

"A student in Ayr," he answered. "He studies religion, I think; name be David."

"What is the message?" demanded Joe.

"I can't read it but the student who paid me to deliver it said that Innis Henderson was his roommate. Said he was in serious trouble. He said I should bring this message to Lady Mairy right away."

"Stay there," ordered Joe. "I'll send someone out." Joe ran down the steps of the tower, found one of the Lochnaw men and instructed him to find Andy and ask that he go out and see the man.

Andy hurried out the front door, a dirk tucked under his belt.

"What's this about a message," he asked the man sharply. The man repeated the story.

"Innis, you say? What kind of trouble," Andy asked skeptically. He knew Innis could take care of himself quite well.

"I don't know," the man repeated. "I was only given this note." He removed it from underneath his cloak and held it up.

"Hand it here," ordered Andy, "and keep your hands where I can see them!" When the man hesitated, Andy grabbed his arm and pulled him roughly from the lathered horse.

"I am the Laird of this realm. Mairy is my sister. You will hand it over to me."

The man did, looking frightened. Andy read the note, which was in fine handwriting, certainly not produced by Innis, but had what looked to be Innis' signature at the bottom. The note read, "Innis Henderson has been charged with heresy. He is imprisoned. Catholic authorities will soon decide his fate. Come quickly to explain."

Andy frowned. This, indeed, was a serious situation. He had no doubt that it was true. Innis, infatuated and consumed with the new Protestant religion, had probably blathered all over town, his words finally reaching the wrong ears. The Catholics were still strong in Ayr, in part because Glasgow City was a bishopric with a resident archbishop. The archdiocese included Ayr. Protestants were generally tolerated so long as they kept their views to themselves. However, public advocacy for the Protestant cause was definitely frowned upon.

Something had obviously happened to Innis. Usually a quiet and circumspect man, he had begun actively searching people out to profess his newfound faith—not a good idea. Andy, for his part, didn't care much for religious zealots of any stripe.

Ree was in the kitchen supervising preparation of the mid-day meal. Andy walked in with the note.

"Ree, a man just rode up, asking for you, said he had come from Ayr. He gave me this note." Ree looked at the signature at the bottom and then read the note.

*The script was consistent with that of a learned person,* she thought. She knew that Innis had returned to Ayr in hopes of finding the two students. He wanted them to help him divine the mission God had in mind for him. She, too, had no doubt that the note was authentic.

Andy said drolly, "Methinks he has been blithering about too much!"

Ree replied sharply, "Andy, it's not funny. Innis is in serious trouble. I've got to go and see if I can get him out of it."

"Why you?" Andy asked.

"Innis is a simple soul. You know that. He is honest and loyal, but has had a hard time of it, barely escaping with his life several times. Lately, he has become convinced that these narrow escapes have been miracles from God, and that God has some greater purpose for him. He has talked to me a great deal about this. I have not bothered you with the details. But as you know, that's why we went to Ayr last week to hear that Protestant preacher."

"The note says he has been imprisoned. Do you think that's true?" asked Andy, pointing out that Innis was no preacher and not likely to do any harm to the Catholics. "Why would they bother with someone like him?"

"I don't know," Ree responded, "but Innis was profoundly impressed with the sermon."

After it was over, she related, they had met two students who were studying Protestantism. Innis went back to Ayr to try to find them in an effort to learn more. Somehow, he had gotten himself into trouble.

"I'm sure he *has* talked too much. He was so excited—never have I seen him like that—but he has no real grasp of religious doctrine."

"That's my point," said Andy. "I have heard that Cardinal Beaton's men are chasing after John Knox, but Knox is a highly educated man, not only an impressive preacher, but also a scholar and writer."

He could understand why the Catholic hierarchy would be alarmed at Knox, but they didn't normally chase after barely literate young farm boys like Innis, did they?

"Ayr is in the archdiocese of Glasgow City, and the bishop is intolerant of Protestant ideas," said Ree. "I don't know what he did, but a charge of heresy is quite serious. I'm sure I can help him out. He was born and christened a Catholic, after all. I must go and try."

Andy thought it over. If anyone could get him out of the jam he was in, it was Ree. She was as articulate and informed on such matters as anyone he knew, and her own credentials as a Catholic were unimpeachable.

"All right," he said at length. "I don't like it, but I can see that your mind is made up."

He assigned one of the Lochnaw men-at-arms to go with her. He warned her to dress warmly as it was still cold, and to be very careful when she got there.

Ree and the Lochnaw guard left early the next morning, making good time as they lay down to sleep for only a short while, and reached Ayr by mid-afternoon of the next day. They got a room at an inn and then spent the rest of the afternoon walking the streets in the market area, looking into taverns, searching and asking about the two students. No luck.

The next morning, Ree and her guard walked to the impressive parish church, St. John's. It was a weekday, so there were no worshipers inside. They went down the aisle, past the altar, to a set of back rooms. Ree wanted to talk with the parish priest. Surely if anyone in his parish had been charged with heresy he would have heard about it.

Ree knocked on one of the doors that looked like it might be the chambers of the priest. Momentarily, the door opened and she stood facing a portly man of medium height, in plain priest's raiment. He had a pleasant, ruddy complexion and long, gray hair. He greeted her warmly.

"Father, might I have a private word?" Ree asked courteously.

"Of course," the priest said, smiling.

Ree asked her guard to remain outside, and took a seat inside the chamber. The room was small, but lovely, with stained glass windows, a large table with some books and papers scattered about, a pot of writing quills and a container of ink.

"Excuse the mess, I've been working on my sermon for the Sabbath," the priest said kindly. "Please have a seat. I am Father Francis. What might I do for you?"

Ree did not waste time with further pleasantries. She dove right into the subject that brought her: "I am Mairy Henderson from Blackcraigshire. My brother, Andrew, is Laird of the shire. My mother, Ann, now unfortunately deceased...." here, Ree looked down at her hands folded across her lap and paused. The priest mumbled that he was sorry for her loss. Ree continued.

"She was a Wallace, the daughter of Earl Darrow Wallace of Blackmor. Perhaps you have heard of him."

"Of course, indeed I have—a fine family!" Father Francis exclaimed.

"I tell you this because my mother was educated at Glasgow Cathedral School in her early years."

"Wonderful, wonderful!" Father Francis enthused, "One of the best schools in Scotland. Are you a student?" he inquired.

"No, I would love to take some additional study there," Ree said, "but that's not the reason I came to see you."

"I see—well, if I can be of help in any way, please..." Father Francis said, holding out his hands.

"It's about my first cousin, Innis Henderson," Ree said, looking at him intently, expecting a change of attitude. But there was no change at all in Father Francis' expression. He continued to smile in a fatherly fashion.

"I would love to be of assistance. Tell me what it is you need—or your cousin, that is."

Ree related she had received a note from Innis that he was being held in Ayr on suspicion of heresy by Catholic authorities.

"The note did not say who they were or where he was being held," Ree said.

"What?" said Father Francis, his brow furrowing, and the color draining from his face. He knew nothing of it.

"You said the note mentioned Catholic authorities. Do you know what position they hold?" he asked.

"No, I have no idea, but I can assure you absolutely that Innis is no heretic. He was born and christened Catholic."

"This is very strange," said Francis, stroking his chin. As parish priest, protocol required that a person suspected of such a crime be brought before him for inquiry yet he had heard nothing of it.

"Do you have any idea of the circumstances, why anyone would suspect such a thing?"

"No, not really," Ree ventured, reluctant to get into further details.

"Well, you can be sure that I'll look into it immediately. Surely there is a misunderstanding of some kind. Come back by tomorrow, and I'll share with you anything I find out," concluded Father Francis.

Ree bowed, murmured her thanks, got up and left, feeling quite puzzled but sure the situation would soon be straightened out. She had no doubt that Father Francis knew nothing about it, as he had said. *Now,* she thought, *I must find the two students. If Innis has been successful in locating them, surely they have some information.* Very possibly, one of them wrote the note. The messenger's description of the man who sent the note matched the taller one.

# 30.
# CAPTURE

AFTER leaving St. John's, Ree and the Lochnaw man went down to the Market Square area. The two students, it seemed, liked to drink. She figured they might find them in one of the taverns as nighttime neared and could question them about Innis. A few quaffs of ale should loosen their tongues.

✦ ✦ ✦

In a darkened house further down toward the wharf, two men, in a well-furnished library, talked quietly. One of them was the Master. The other was one of his guards who doubled as a spy.

"Did the bait we put out catch our prey?"

"Aye, Master, it worked perfectly."

The woman came in last night, he related. She had a man with her, a large, well-armed man, a guard, he presumed. They registered at the Boarhead Inn.

The Master smiled. Very good! They now had her where they wanted. But they had to act fast.

"Where are they now?"

"The woman and the man were seen entering the parish church," the guard replied. "They stayed for at least half an hour. One of our spies looked in, but they were not out in the nave. Apparently they went to the back, he guessed to see the priest. They came out and headed in the direction of the market."

*Yes, she went to the priest, thinking he could assist her,* thought the Master, *Cardinal Beaton was wise to keep the priests in the dark about this operation. Only the Archbishop of Glasgow knows that I am en-*

*gaged in this work, but knows nothing of the details. He has no conception of the breadth of our effort.*

"Do you wish that we capture her today?" asked the guard.

"Aye, as soon as possible, but not out in the open," cautioned the Master.

It was not feasible to do it in the market or any other public place where there were people gathered. Too dangerous. The Master looked at his spy, his black eyes squinting in the dim light. "You may need our entire force, so take them all."

First, they needed to dispose of the man with her—her guard, if that's what he was. Then they could more easily handle her.

"I want her brought here. Blindfold and bind her. Take a circuitous route so she cannot keep her bearings."

They needed to complete the mission that night if possible, he emphasized. And the constable should be notified to be available upon a moment's notice.

Ree and the Lochnaw guard went to the market, which was busy on this cold, but sunny, mid-spring afternoon. She had the guard stand on the mercat cross, as preacher Donner had done, so he could see all around and try to spot anyone who matched the description of the two students. Meanwhile she inquired of some of the younger people at the square whether they knew anything about them. Most did not, but one shabby young man about 20 years of age said he had lately been seeing two men of that description hanging around a couple of taverns late at night.

He gave her the tavern names, and she went with her guard to investigate. At one of them, the barkeep said that a couple of ragged-looking young men matching that description had been in his tavern recently with a third man. He described the third man as having a stocky build, long, black hair, shaven, and "a little more tidy."

*Innis*, thought Ree. Taking in a deep breath, she asked the barkeep if he had any idea where they might be staying.

"A rooming house over by the river," he said, describing it and drawing directions on a scrap of paper.

"Thanks," Ree said to the man. Then to her guard, "Let's go."

They walked out the front door of the tavern, then down a series of narrow side streets, Ree looking at the paper to navigate the way. Staying on the same street, they crossed through a couple of intersections.

"We take a right at the next crossing, I think," Ree said.

As they were about to step into the intersection, two large, burly men stepped out and blocked their way. Both had heavy cloaks with hoods pulled over their heads, and dirks strapped to their waists.

"Would you have any money?" one said, menacingly. Ree was about to answer, when she heard a grunt, followed by a loud curse.

"You bastard," shouted her guard. She looked around. There was a third man behind them. Her guard was now gasping, frothy blood leaking from the corners of his mouth. Then he fell forward at her feet. A dirk was buried in his back.

Ree had no time to think; two sets of hands had her head in a vise-like grip. Her mouth was forced open, stuffed with a cloth, and a shroud was crammed over her head. Then her legs were jerked from under her, she was rolled over face-down and bound with strong rope. The men then quickly bundled her into a coach.

Leather straps popped, and the coach clattered off. Ree was terrified. It had all happened in the flash of an eye. *Who were these murderers? Where was she being taken, and why?*

◆ ◆ ◆

Innis was being fed watery broth, bread, and water twice a day, always brought in by the two large men who had taken him. His legs remained bound, and the shroud was kept over his head. When the meager fare was brought, one arm was untied for him to eat with, but the other was kept bound tightly behind his back. The shroud was raised slightly so he could get the food to his mouth.

He could see just enough of his surroundings to know that he was in a cell in the gaol. The room was small, with a rock wall and dirt floor. Smelly straw covered the floor, and he could see the bottom part of an iron door. There was no heat. He had only his clothes and cloak to ward off the cold. Not allowed to leave the cell to relieve himself; he had to feel his way to a corner, and his clothes had become fouled by his own excrement. The fetid smell was so rank, it was all he could do to hold the food down. But he knew he must eat and drink fluids to keep up his strength. *My time will come*, he thought. *Those responsible for my imprisonment will pay.*

✦ ✦ ✦

Father Francis was quite impressed with young lady Henderson, a pretty, well-spoken and sincere woman. Even though he was a priest, he was quite taken with her polite manner, slim figure and creamy complexion, but especially with her glowing red hair and striking green eyes. The tale she had told him about her cousin was odd, to say the least. Such things simply did not happen in his parish without him knowing about it. He had been parish priest for some 20 years.

After Ree and her male companion had left, Father Francis went out and checked his sources to see what he could find out. First, he visited with all of the St. John's church workers. They came from many places around the community and kept their ears to the ground. Usually, one or more of them would know about something like this, but nobody did.

*Very strange*, he thought. Then he walked about town and called on several parishioners. Usually, one could find out about almost anything by surveying them. Still, nothing. He was confident that the young woman was telling him the truth. *What reason would she have to make up such a story?*

He felt a strong compulsion to get to the bottom of it. He decided he would ride to Glasgow City and visit the Archbishop himself. It would take the better part of two days to ride there, arrange a meeting with the Bishop, a very busy man, and return. He had told Lady Henderson to come and see him the next day. If he were to ride to Glasgow City, he would be gone on the morrow, so he needed to get word to her to wait a day.

She had not said where she was staying, but most likely an inn, and there were three in town. He could check, as he was leaving town, until he found the right one. Miss Henderson had said they came from Blackcraigshire, which was to the southeast, so he checked the one in that direction first, the Boarhead Inn. The desk lady smiled when she saw Father Francis enter.

"Good day, Father Francis; how be you this fine afternoon?"

"Quite well, thank you. I'm looking for a young woman, Lady Mairy Henderson from Blackcraigshire. I believe she arrived with her escort last night. I've a message for her. Might she be staying here?"

The desk lady thumbed through her register and shortly exclaimed, "Och, aye, she be."

"Would you be so kind as to furnish me with a slip of writing paper?" Father Francis intoned soothingly. "I wish to leave a note for her."

+ + +

After about half an hour, the coach, having made numerous twists and turns, rumbled to a stop. Two men grabbed Ree and pulled her out. They carried her roughly by her legs and arms into a house. She could see occasional glimpses from underneath the shroud on her head that she was being carried through a door and then back into a darkened room. There, a firm, deep, voice said: "Put her there, on that chair. I want one of you to stay in case you are needed."

"Aye Master," came a reply from one of the men.

*Master?* thought Ree. *I've heard that before, just recently, but where? Oh yes—the other night at the preaching by Donner. The two students. They said that they were studying religion with a Master.*

The man did not address her, and she stayed quiet, taking in everything she could—the polished wood floor, the candlelight, a cool, slightly musty aroma. *Books,* she thought. *That's the smell of old leather-bound books, like in the library at the Cathedral School. I must be in someone's library.* She listened for sounds. The floor creaked outside, and a door opened.

"Has the constable been notified?" she heard the deep voice say.

Another voice, higher, replied, "Aye, he will be here soon."

*Constable?* she thought. *What the hell was that about?* She stayed quiet and still, thinking hard. This had to have something to do with Innis. Was he there?

Certainly not in the same room with her, she was sure of that. *Heresy*, she thought. *Innis had been accused of heresy.* That's what the note said. There had to be a formal charge and a trial to be convicted of heresy. *Is that why she was there, to testify? But they murdered my guard! No, something else is going on. Innis may be in trouble, but so am I.*

After a while, the floor creaked again. Heavy footsteps entered the room. The deep voice said, "All right, we're all here. Let's proceed. Remove the blind."

The shroud was jerked off her head, and the room seemed suddenly very bright. Her eyes tried to adjust. Slowly she began to make out what was around her. She was correct; it was a good-sized library. There were books on shelves along one wall and a table with a candelabra that held three lit candles. A very large man dressed in black sat behind the desk. *Deep voice*, she thought, *probably the Master.*

Another man, well-dressed but quite thin, sat in a chair to Deep Voice's right. *The constable*, she guessed. Standing at the door was a shorter, burly man with bushy eyebrows. He had pulled the hood from her head and was holding it in his hand. He had a salacious gap-toothed grin on his pock-marked face. *One of the murderers*, she surmised.

Ree had a tight knot in her stomach. She felt faint and slightly nauseated. *I've got to keep a hold on myself*, she thought, expecting that Innis would be marched into the room soon.

# 31.
# Interrogation

DEEP Voice finally spoke, looking at Ree with hard, malignant eyes.

"You are Mairy Henderson, known as Ree?"

"Aye," Ree replied cautiously.

"You have a cousin named Innis?"

"Aye."

"The two of you attended a Protestant sermon in the market square last week, delivered by a preacher named Donner?"

"We did," agreed Ree.

"Preacher Donner stood on the mercat cross, and you were right up front, close by?"

"Aye, but what does that have to do with anything?" said Ree, growing tired of these seemingly pointless questions.

Deep Voice rose slowly from his chair, walked to Ree's side and slapped her hard across the face.

"You are only to answer questions, not ask them. Do you understand?"

Ree realized that she was helpless, trapped and bound. She did not reply. Deep Voice returned to his chair. Ree noticed that he had a large, heavy silver chain and ornate cross around his neck, such as those worn by Catholic bishops. She started to ask if he was a bishop, but with her face still stinging, she decided against it.

"You were dressed as a man—breeches and boots—with your head covered by a cloak?"

"I had ridden from Blackcraigshire on a horse, and it was cold," Ree replied, defiant in spite of herself. Deep Voice did not slap her again, although she expected it. He just smirked a thin, conceited smile.

"Och, you like to spar," he sneered. "What was the secret signal that passed between you and Preacher Donner at the end of his sermon?"

"I'm not aware of any signal."

"Eyes were on you, several sets," Deep Voice said. "We saw Donner mouth something to you at the end. You were the only one standing, and you nodded. What was it?"

"I don't remember that," Ree said truthfully.

"You deny it? That's lying," growled Deep Voice.

"I do not deny. I said I did not remember," replied Ree, again in a defiant tone.

"I'm growing tired of your evasion," Deep Voice said, rising from his chair again. "I have an official commission from Archbishop David Beaton, late Prelate for the Pope, to seek out blasphemers, witches and heretics."

Ree said nothing. The knot in her stomach was tightening. Despite gritting her teeth and focusing her mind, a slight tremor had started in her hands.

Deep voice's black eyes seemed to glow as he leaned forward.

"Now, I am going to ask you a series of very important questions. I suggest you consider your answers carefully. Do you accept that his eminency, the Pope, is God's divine representative on Earth?"

Ree swallowed hard before answering. "I accept the Pope is God's representative, but not that he is divine. Only God is divine," answered Ree.

"So you deny the divinity of the Pope?—aye or nay."

Ree thought, *How can I concede this? It goes against everything I stand for, everything anyone in my family has ever stood for—my father, mother, brothers or anyone else.* She stated her answer firmly.

"Aye, I deny it."

"Do you accept the divinity of Mary, mother of Jesus?"

"I accept Mary as the mother of Jesus, but not that she was divine," said Ree.

Do you believe that men, any man or woman, can communicate directly with God through prayer? In other words, do you believe that priestly confession is necessary to reach God and obtain absolution?"

"Aye and nay, if I understand your question," answered Ree.

"Let me clarify for you." Deep Voice smiled like a viper.

"Can you, Ree Henderson, on your own, communicate with God through prayer—Aye or nay?"

"Aye, I think so," said Ree in a firm voice.

"So no priest is necessary—aye or nay?" demanded Deep Voice.

Ree gathered herself and answered firmly, "Aye."

Deep Voice, his black eyes cold as ice, stared intently into Ree's green eyes for a long moment.

Ree stared unblinkingly back into his. Deep Voice then asked, in a measured tone, "Does anyone else in your family, meaning your extended family—grandparents, aunts and uncles, cousins— have bright red hair and green eyes, such as you?"

*What a strange question*, thought Ree. *Why would he ask that?* Then she answered in an assured tone: "I'm not positive, but I've always heard that my grandmother Wallace did—she passed away before I was born."

Now very sure of the trouble she was in, Ree asked Deep Voice, "Where is Innis? Have you already killed him?"

"Nay, he is alive. We have no intention of putting him to death," he replied. The viper smile again.

Deep Voice continued, "You are hereby charged with heresy and suspicion of witchcraft. Do you understand the charges?"

Ree's mind was racing. *I'm charged with heresy and witchcraft? They're not after Innis. It's me! This whole thing was a trap to get me to return to Ayr—but why?*

She answered the question, "Aye, I understand the charges, but I have been Catholic all my life, and I'm certainly no witch. You must know that. I'm totally innocent."

"I think we've heard all we need. Constable, you represent the civil authority in this parish, and I represent the papal authority.

Each of us has a slip of paper and a quill. 'Guilty—aye or nay' is written thereon. Now, let's make our marks."

Ree already knew the outcome. She was not surprised.

"By both state and church, Mairy Henderson, you are found guilty of heresy. The issue of witchcraft is deferred. Your penalty for this crime is death by public burning; do you understand?"

Ree looked down. She did not answer.

"You don't have to answer. The sentence is final," said Deep Voice. It will be executed tonight at the appearance of the full moon."

Ree finally felt panic. *They are going to burn me tonight!*

✦ ✦ ✦

Father Francis rode into the streets of Glasgow City and up to the Cathedral. It was twilight, but the doors were still open. Francis went in and asked the resident priest if he could have an audience with the archbishop as soon as possible, "on a matter of great importance."

The priest said, "He has retired for the night. I can get you in first thing in the morning."

✦ ✦ ✦

It was a clear, cold night. Just before midnight, the bright, perfectly round disc of a full moon was high in the sky, almost directly overhead. There were no clouds and the luminance of the heavenly body lit the whole area.

On the green outside St. John's Church, below the great tower, a long, heavy post had been erected, surrounded by resinous limbs of wood laid crossways. Dry grass had been strategically stuffed in the limbs. Outside the circle of limbs several bags of gunpowder had been placed, to be ignited only if the fire from the wood did not do the job.

Ree was driven over in a coach, still bound, but not blindfolded this time. She was marched to the post and bound to it, from head to toe, by ropes. A strange fleeting thought ran through Ree's mind: *Soon it will be Easter, how appropriate.*

Deep Voice, flanked by the constable, announced himself: "I am Joseph Renfreu, commissioned by Archbishop David Beaton, the Pope's Prelate to Scotland, to act on behalf of the Holy See to seek out and destroy all enemies of the Church, witches, apostates, blasphemers and heretics.

Ree stood silently, moving not a muscle, looking at the gathering crowd. She already knew what she must do.

"Watch, and take note, all of you," bellowed Deep Voice. "Tonight we execute, on behalf of the Holy Catholic Church and the Nation of Scotland, a most vile and insidious prophet of the devil, a heretic, an apostate of God. Remain steadfast in your faith, that you not suffer the same fate."

Ree had been stripped to her undergarments, revealing her young, voluptuous body, which was being ogled by sneering young men pushing to the front.

"Burn! Burn! Burn!" rang the chorus from the assembled, increasingly raucous mob. The fire was struck. The grass ignited and the limbs began to burn around Ree's feet. Ree's voice started low, rising steadily to a crescendo.

"I am being burned by an imposter. Your priest, Father Francis, a man of God you all know. He is not here. Why? Because this murderer, this vile man who claims to act on behalf of Cardinal Beaton, has lured him away."

The flames spread and leaped at her feet, catching the hem of her undergarment on fire. But Ree's voice grew stronger.

"This man, this devil, says I am a heretic. Nay! He is the heretic. I believe in God, I believe that the Holy Bible is the word of God, I believe in Jesus Christ as the Son of God!"

The less strident elements of the mob suddenly grew silent. The crowd grew nearer, the flames leaped higher.

Ree continued, despite the fact that her body was now being consumed by fire.

"I believe that everyone can be saved and go to heaven. Repent, confess your sins, accept Jesus Christ and have faith in God. That's all it takes..."

Deep Voice screamed to his minions.

"Shut her up. Light the gunpowder."

They did, and an enormous explosion of fire immediately muffled Ree's words. In moments, the flames consumed her body. Soon only embers and a pile of ash remained.

✦ ✦ ✦

The following morning, Father Francis had his meeting with the Archbishop at the Cathedral in Glasgow City. He explained he had been told a young man in his parish had been charged with heresy. The man's cousin, a very impressive and intelligent young woman from Blackcraigshire, had come to see him about it. He was convinced there must be some misunderstanding. The young woman was a faithful Catholic, the granddaughter of Earl Darrow Wallace and sister of the Laird of Blackcraigshire, he added. He had found in his years of experience that a little political pressure on the Archbishop was usually effective.

"Another thing, Your Grace," he said to the Archbishop, in a deferential tone, "since this happened in my parish, I would think that I should have been consulted about it."

The Archbishop frowned and looked down at the floor. He had known Father Francis for many years. Francis was one of his best and most dependable parish priests. He liked Francis.

"Let me tell you what I know, which is not much," he finally said.

"Cardinal Beaton, as you know, was a very strong anti-Protestant. He saw the new religion as a threat to the Church in Scotland and wanted to stamp it out. Before his unfortunate death, he issued an official commission to an 'Inquisitor,' let's call him, that gave him authority to mount a vigorous effort to root out Protestant activities. I hear that he has been active here. I don't personally know the man, but I think this is his work. I'm afraid I cannot do much about it. I'm sorry."

Father Francis left, quite sad and dejected, and started his ride back to Ayr. He would not have good news for the young woman, Mairy Henderson, after all.

+ + +

After Ree's execution the night before, two men had met in the darkened library at the house near the wharf. One of them was the Master, Joseph Renfreu. In his hand he held a small purse containing several gold dinars. He held the purse out and jingled the coins.

"Your pay, as agreed. We accomplished a lot tonight—for God, for the Pope and for Cardinal Beaton—may God rest his soul. The

252

instigator, that insufferable witch, is no more, thanks in large part to you, Preacher Donner. We must work together again soon."

The thin, pale man, still dressed all in black, stepped forward and accepted his payoff.

"Knox—have you caught him yet?" he inquired.

"No, not yet, but we are closing in. We will have him soon enough," replied Renfreu.

"Then I'll be on my way. I'm staying in Edinburgh. You know how to find me."

"Aye," replied Renfreu. "Till then."

+ + +

The night before, as the terrible flames finished the consumption of Ree's body, angry murmurs had begun to roll through the mob. Shouts erupted from all over.

"She was no heretic! She is innocent!" yelled a woman. "She's a good Christian!" shouted another. "Where are Beaton's men? They're the ones that should burn!" thundered a man. Then a chant started: "Beaton, Beaton, Beaton!"

Renfreu and the constable had already worked their way through the outside fringe of the crowd, and were near their coach, driver at the ready, by the time the chant began. Renfreu barked, "Get in, let's go." Then to the driver: "Head out in the opposite direction from my house, then loop around. I don't want anyone to suspect where I live."

The coach rapidly rumbled away.

Another man was at the rear of the crowd. He was a trusted cottager farmer of Andrew Henderson's who had come to Ayr to buy some provisions at the market, and heard there was to be a burning of a heretic. He followed the crowd to St. John's Church astride his horse. He stayed back a ways, but could see the terrible scene unfold from over the heads of the gathered people. He saw there was a young woman tied to the post. She looked vaguely familiar, but he was a good distance away and could not see her well. However, when he heard her voice, he was quite sure that it was Ree Henderson. He asked some of the people gathered about.

"We hear it's a woman from Blackcraigshire," someone shouted.

The man did not stay around for the gory finish. He wheeled his horse around and struck out at an urgent gallop. The moon provided just enough light for him to see the road, plus he had come that way many times before and knew the path well. Within several hours he was over halfway to the Henderson house.

The moon was setting, so he stopped for the rest of the night at a small burn that crossed the trail. He and the horse drank their fill of water. He hobbled the horse and tried to get some sleep, but could not. The horrible image of a beautiful young woman being burned alive in front of a boisterous mob was seared into his brain.

By sunup the next morning, he was racing up to the Henderson front gate, shouting at the top of his voice.

"Laird Andrew! Laird Andrew! I must see the Laird! Something terrible has happened to his sister."

The tower guard heard the commotion and the man's words. He went running to fetch someone to go and alert Andy. Shortly, Andy came rushing to the tower and leaped up the steps to the parapet on top. He looked down and recognized the man. It was Charles Raford, one of his most dependable tenants.

"Charles, what's wrong?" Andy shouted.

"Laird Henderson, you should come down. It be terrible news I bring about Lady Ree," Charles said, sounding most mournful.

Andy sprang down the tower stairs, taking three steps at a time, and ran out the front doors to the gate. He opened the heavy gate and stepped out. Charles was soaked through with sweat and his horse was lathered even though it was a cold morning.

Andy feared something bad, but had no inkling how bad it would turn out to be. Charles told him the whole story, his voice cracking, occasionally breaking into heaving sobs, such that Andy could barely make out what he was saying. Finally, he thought that he understood.

"Charles, tell me, is Ree dead?"

"Aye," sobbed Charles.

"Are you absolutely sure it was her?"

"They said that she was from Blackcraigshire. It looked like her from what I could see from far back, and when I heard her voice, I knew it was her."

254

"What did she say?" Andy asked, his face stricken with fear.

"She said she was innocent, that it was a false accusation, the doing of Cardinal Beaton's men. That's all I heard after the fire was lit. I took off and rode all night to get here."

Andy fell to the ground, a piercing scream rising up from his chest and out his mouth.

"My God, no! No, no, no—how much can one family stand?"

Helen came flying to him, wrapping her arms around him, forcing a loud whisper into his ear, "Andy, what is it—tell me, tell me!"

Joe and Jamie were there, too. Andy looked up at them, his eyes clouded, his face stricken and pale, like a dying animal.

"It's Ree," he stammered. "She's been burned at the stake. She's dead. Cardinal Beaton's men did it."

They all sank to the ground, their arms cradling each other, grief so overwhelming that nobody could speak or even cry. Charles was off his horse and standing by, reverently and somber-faced, ready to help if asked. Unexpectedly, a flash swooped through Andy's mind. *Innis. Ree went to Ayr to help Innis. Where was he in all of this?*

Andy struggled to his feet and addressed Charles.

"Did you see Innis?"

Charles thought for a moment.

"Nay, sir, I did not. He was not near Lady Ree, nor did I see him at the market or in the crowd at St. John's."

"This all happened at St. John's?" Andy asked incredulously.

"Aye, sir, it did, on the green. I heard at the market square that something was about to happen and rode out there. I did not see Innis anywhere."

After a while, Andy thanked Charles and he rode off. The rest of the family shuffled back inside, their bodies drooped in sadness. They went into the great hall and sat in silence at one end of the long dining table. Helen's two servants, Harold and one guard, stood quietly at the front door, awaiting any instructions that might come.

Though Andy's body was weak and wracked with grief, his mind began to clear. The guard he had sent with Ree, where was he? He had forgotten to ask Charles about that. And Innis, what had become of him? Had he been killed, too, before Ree, perhaps?

*I've got to find out,* he thought. *I've got to get a hold on myself and go to Ayr—today!*

A terrible wrath was already building in his chest. It had no limits.

# 32.
# WRATH

ANDY quietly got up and left the great hall. Everyone, including Helen, thought that he just needed to go out, get some fresh air and be alone for a while. Instead, as he passed through the door where Harold was standing, he inclined his head. Harold understood and followed. They went to the south tower to talk in private.

"Harold, I've got to get to Ayr in a hurry. The villains who did this will probably clear out of town, if they haven't already."

Harold nodded. He could see the rage in Andy's body, the set jaw, clenched teeth and blazing eyes. He knew that Andy shouldn't go alone. Andy's mind was so inflamed with vengeance that he wouldn't be able to think clearly. Under these circumstances, acting without a cool head was dangerous.

Harold said, not unkindly, "Sire, remember the old saying, 're-venge is best served cold.' Not when you are hot with anger."

Andy gave him a baleful look, "If I wait, the murderers will be gone and no revenge will be possible."

Harold had hoped Andy would invite him to come along. He didn't. Harold decided he would go anyway.

Andy instructed Harold to saddle his best horse, Ned, a sturdy and fast Palfrey, and also one more for a spare. He wanted two fully equipped horses, for he did not intend to stop.

Harold said, "Sire, I will get the horses ready, but we will need a third. I will go with you."

"Nay you are needed here. This is my job. I must do it alone."

Harold protested, even though he was certain it would do no good.

"Sire, there is more to it than just Lady Ree. My man is missing too, as well as Mr. Innis. There is no telling what you might run into. You'll need help."

Andy replied kindly, but firmly, "No, I appreciate what you say, but I must do this myself. Now, let's go to the armory. I'll need additional weapons and armor."

Harold dropped his head in disappointment and concern, but followed Andy to the armory. Andy selected an additional broadsword and extras of the following—mail vests, dirks and scabbards, crossbow, and quivers of bolts. He intended to wear one set of the weapons, and the spares would be carried by the extra horse. He would also wear a steel breastplate and helmet underneath his shirt and cloak. Andy intended to be well armed, with extra protection for his head and upper torso that would also be relatively light and flexible.

Harold assisted Andy in donning his chainmail vest, concealed by a loose shirt under a leather jerkin, breeches and boots, the dirk strapped to his waist in a scabbard, and a sgian dubh tucked inside his boot, covered by the leg of his breeches. He also had a crossbow strapped across his chest, covered by a hip-length cloak.

Andy wanted to look normal in outward appearance. The only visible weapon was the dirk strapped at his waist, which was common and would not raise suspicion. His broadsword was carried in a leather scabbard in front of the saddle stirrup. He anticipated that, once he reached Ayr, he would need to walk about the streets and enter business establishments, such as taverns and inns, without raising alarms. But he would be ready to take deadly action quickly if it became necessary.

Within half an hour, Andy and the horses were ready. Harold had secretly outfitted his own horse as he was preparing the two for Andy and had also requested Martha to put together two sacks of provisions—hard biscuits and dried beef jerky, one for him and another for Andy. He would give Andy about an hour's head start. Then, following, he would keep out of sight until and unless he was needed.

Helen had become concerned when Andy did not return for what seemed an inordinately long time and left the great hall to search for him. She noticed that Harold and Martha were gone too and began to suspect that Andy was up to something. Dread crept into her mind; knowing her husband as she did, she suspected what was going on. Soon, she heard the sound of heavy footfalls coming from the direction of the armory, and Andy strode into view.

"Andy, where have you been? I was worried," she said, concern evident in her voice.

Andy took her arms and started kissing her profusely all over her head, murmuring endearments. She felt the cold, hard armor beneath his shirt, and pushed him away abruptly.

"Don't use that patronizing manner on me. Do you think I don't know what you are up to?"

"I'm sorry, Helen I didn't mean to patronize. It's just that I love you so. You know very well what I've got to do. I wish greatly that I didn't have to go. But this family is now my responsibility. I'm the laird of the estate. I must do as my father would have done. I'm sorry. I know you understand."

Helen broke into deep sobs, pounding Andy on the chest. "Nay, nay!"

She *did* understand, and that was the problem. Her father would have done it; Andy's father would have done it. It was the way of Scottish chieftains.

Finally she visibly relented, straightened up and looked at Andy hard in the eyes.

"You'll take Harold and the other Lochnaw men?" she asked, tears staining her cheeks.

"Nay, I have to go alone. There is no other way. I don't know who did this or why. I'll have to do some discreet investigation to find out. I can't go in with a big group of bodyguards. Everyone would keep mum. Helen, I've thought this through; it's the only way."

"Then promise me you'll be careful. It's dangerous, and I'll die if you don't come back—alive and in one piece," she added.

"Don't worry," Andy said. "I won't take any unnecessary chances. I'll be very careful, and I'll return to you in one piece."

He well knew she would see through these brave assurances. Pushing her gently away, Andy turned and walked out the back way through the gate to where the two horses stood, ready to go. He galloped off, not looking back, his mind and will returning to the terrible task ahead.

After he left, Helen rushed frantically through the house, calling for Harold.

"He's at the south tower," said her chambermaid.

Helen ran that way, calling for him. Harold met her in the back courtyard behind the tower, holding the reins of a saddled horse.

"Harold, you know that Andy has left for Ayr," Helen gasped, out of breath from the rushing about.

"Aye," said Harold.

Then, noticing the saddled horse loaded with weapons, Helen said, "You are going with him, then?"

"Aye, I'll be going, but not *with* him, exactly."

"What do you mean—'not exactly'?" demanded Helen.

Harold explained the conversation he had just had with Andy. He couldn't let him know he was following, or he'd be send back. But he had to stay near enough to help if he got into serious trouble. It would be tricky. Helen nodded, her heart still heavy, but grateful for Harold.

"Harold, bring him back to me alive," Helen pleaded, then added, "yourself also."

Harold gave her a thin smile, then mounted his horse and cantered off on the trail toward Ayr.

✦ ✦ ✦

Innis sat in his fetid cell. He noticed the floor and the walls lighten, and realized the sun was rising. Evidently it would be a clear sunny day outside. Inside his cell, however, it was cold and rancid. He knew nothing of the events of the night before as he sat there thinking: *Are they just going to let me rot in this filthy place? This was the Master's doing. If they think I'm a heretic, why don't they give me a trial. Am I not entitled at least to that. I wish Ree were here. She could get me out of this mess.*

Suddenly there was a creaking of the heavy iron door. It was being opened, Innis realized, but it was not mealtime. He heard footsteps coming toward him, and his hood was jerked off. The two guards pulled him to his feet and unlocked his manacles. The light was so bright that it took a while for his eyes to adjust.

"What's happening," Innis mumbled.

"You be free to go," one of the guards said, "you have been released."

"But why?" Innis asked, disoriented and confused.

"I dinna ken. That be the order we got," said the other guard gruffly, "Now gang while ye can."

"I'd get far away from here as fast as possible if I were you," said the first guard, a bit more kindly.

Innis was so weak and stiff he could barely stand, much less walk. But he gathered himself. This might be his only chance to escape this horrid place. He stood and staggered toward the open cell door, then stumbled down the dark hallway and found the stone stairs. The two guards followed him, not providing any assistance, undoubtedly because he was so filthy they didn't want hands on him.

Innis pushed his legs up the stone steps, and stumbled out into the street. It was about mid-morning, a cold day under a cloudy sky, warmed somewhat by the sun's rays that occasionally broke through. There were few people on the street. Those who were out turned away in disgust as soon as they whiffed his repulsive odor.

Innis looked around trying to get his bearings, finally realizing he was in front of the Ayr Tolbooth, a heavy stone building that housed the offices for collecting tolls from the craft trades, and also for the city council and the constable. The bottom floor served as the gaol, with several dungeon-like cells in the basement where he had been imprisoned.

The Tolbooth was located a couple of blocks from the wharf area. Innis did not know why he had been released, but he was not staying around to find out. He immediately headed toward the quays, and once there, threw himself, clothes and all, off the first dock he came to, plunging into the deep cold water. Despite the frigid water, he stayed in for a good while, thrashing about, rubbing his garments with his hands to remove as much of the repulsive filth as he could. Finally he got out, removed his cloak and shoes, spread them out on the dock in a secluded place to dry and lay down in the sun to warm himself. After he had warmed his body a bit, he removed his trousers and shirt and handwashed them as best he could. He spread them to finish drying and bleach in the sun. Lying naked on the rough planks of the wharf he soaked up the warmth of the sun he had missed for so long. At last his clothing was dry and mostly free of odor, the bleaching having done its job. Innis got re-dressed and headed back toward the market square. He felt in his pocket and found that he still had a few coins, enough for a meal and some beers.

He soon found a tavern, went in and pulled up a chair at a secluded table in the back. He was famished and called for food and a beer from the barkeep. He gulped down his beer and food, continuing to wonder why he had been released. He also began to brood over his two roommates, the traitors who had tricked and betrayed him. He was sure there was a reason he had been imprisoned and then abruptly released. Something must have happened he was not aware of. He decided he would ask around and see if anyone in town knew of anything unusual in recent days.

This could take awhile and what was he to do in the meantime? All he had were the clothes on his back, such as they were, and a few coins. His horse was gone. He was afoot and had no place to stay. But at least he was free. He also had a strong desire to get out of Ayr. Maybe tomorrow, after a night's sleep, he could walk to Glasgow City. He might find work there. He was too ashamed to try to make it back to Blackcraigshire. He had been an ignorant fool—a bawheid—there was no way he could face the Henderson family.

Innis ordered another beer. When the barkeep brought it over he said, "I've been away for a while, working on a ship. Has there been any excitement around here lately?"

"Well, there was a witch burning here a few days ago, a young woman, real bonnie lass I'm told."

Innis felt a chill deep in his bones.

"How long ago exactly?"

"There was a full moon, so about three or four days ago. Happened over at St. John's Church out on the green. A lot of people got pretty upset about it. Apparently the woman claimed she was innocent and was being persecuted by agents of Archbishop Beaton."

The chill in Innis' bones grew colder.

"I don't suppose you remember her name?"

"No, but she had red hair and green eyes, I've heard. That's the main reason she was thought to be a witch. Plus she was a follower of the new religion being preached by John Knox."

Innis was stricken, stunned. He couldn't utter another word. *Ree*, he thought. *That had to be Ree. She must have come back to help me. Oh my God!*

It was him, his stupidity. He caused the whole horrible thing. He staggered out of the tavern, and started making his way over to St. John's Church. When he got there, he went straight out onto the green. There it was, a burned out circle of char and ashes. Ree's remains, he realized, all that was left. Innis felt like screaming but couldn't. He felt he should be angry—somebody should be made to pay for this. But he only felt numb. It was his fault. He had set it all in motion, his idiocy and ignorance. He fell to his knees and buried his face in the ashes.

Trembling mightily, Innis finally arose and started walking, with no particular destination in mind. After he had gone a short way, he abruptly stopped, thinking, *Ree is in those ashes. I should gather a part of her, her essence at least, to take with me. Maybe someday I can return to Blackcraigshire, and she can be buried properly beside the rest of her family.*

However, he had no container in which to carry the ashes, and did not want to insult her remains by depositing them in his pocket or some other place about the disgusting rags he wore for clothes. Then he had an idea. He could walk back to St. John's Church, where the sanctuary was always open during the daytime. Perhaps he could find something appropriate there to hold the ashes.

He entered the front door; it was dim inside, but he could not see anyone else about. He walked down the aisle toward the altar. The light streaming through the large round stained glass window above the apse illuminated the area. There was a wooden podium draped with a clean white cloth upon which rested an open Bible. A golden braided rope was tied around the podium. Surely God— if he existed, which Innis had begun to doubt—would not mind if the cloth and braided rope in this one house of worship were put to such a beneficent use.

No matter—God had turned his back on him, and her. He didn't care. Innis slipped the cloth from beneath the Bible, untied the rope and hurried back out the front door, returning to the burned-out area on the church green. There, he scooped up a double handful of ashes, reverently placed them on the cloth, and tied it with the rope. Then he slipped the small bag inside his shirt and proceeded on his way, he knew not where.

He ambled aimlessly around the streets of Ayr in a near stupor for the rest of the afternoon and into the night. Finally, feeling very hungry again and in need of a beer to dull his senses, he entered the same tavern as before, took the same table at the back and ordered food and beer. He felt in his pocket for coins, took them all out and placed them on the table. After finishing his supper and paying for the food, he asked the barkeep to keep the beer coming until the coins ran out.

✦ ✦ ✦

Andy had kept Ned moving at a steady slow lope, holding onto the reins of the second horse, which soon fell into the same gait. By nightfall, they had covered about one-fourth of the distance to Ayr. Andy could tell that Ned was getting winded and beginning to tire. He stopped at a small burn to allow the horses to drink and rest for a spell, and consumed a couple of biscuits and a few strips of jerky himself. He needed to keep his strength up as well as that of the horses.

It was dark, but he knew that a three-quarters moon would soon be rising. When it cleared the horizon, he remounted on the second horse and continued on, leading Ned. In this manner, the furlongs drifted by until early on the morning of the next day, as the sun rose in a clear sky, he came out onto the road to Ayr and could see the town in the distance.

Andy started planning his approach. He knew that there were two livery stables in town, one on the south side, which was approached by the road he was on, and another on the north side. He decided to stable one horse in each, leaving the extra weapons at the stable with the second horse. He would then walk about town, to the market square and the taverns lining the streets, St. John's Church, and the wharf area, to see what he could find out about Preacher Donner, Cardinal Beaton's men, Innis and the two "students."

After he got the horses stabled and paid up for two days, he walked to the market square. There were not many people out at this time of the morning, but he asked some who were shopping, or wandering about, if they had heard of a young woman being burned at the stake on a charge of heresy a few days before. Several did, and he questioned them about the details, trying to keep the conversation casual, as if he were merely curious.

After talking with several people, he began to piece together what had happened. First, and most important, the executioner in announcing the charge and punishment had identified himself as "Joseph Renfreu, commissioned by Cardinal Beaton." So it was clear that this *was* Beaton's work, evidently set in motion just before the Cardinal's death. Renfreu had been accompanied by the town constable. He must have been in league with Renfreu, possibly paid off, as it was announced the execution was sanctioned by both the Catholic Church and the State. Another important fact was that the parish priest from St. John's had not been seen. It was customary that such public burnings be presided over by the local priest.

The thing that tortured and infuriated Andy the most were reports from several people who heard what Ree had said as she was being burned. She was no heretic. She was a devout Catholic. It was all Cardinal Beaton's doing, carried out by a monster who had been commissioned by Beaton to stamp out the Protestant religion.

This information had raised the heat of Andy's anger to the boiling point. He finally had to go and sit down for a while, drink some cool water from a bucket at the common well in the center of the square and pour what remained over his head. After cooling off a bit, he continued his inquiries, asking if anyone knew where Renfreu lived (no one did), or had seen anyone matching the description of the two "students," or Innis (no one had). *I imagine that the taverns will be the best place to get this last information,* he thought to himself.

✦ ✦ ✦

Harold had seen the trail of settling dust left by Andy's horses as he entered onto the road to Ayr. *That's him,* he thought. *I'd better kick my horse up a notch and close the gap. I need to know where Andy is going to put his horses.*

As he approached the south livery, Harold slowed and stopped his horse in the shade of a large oak. From this vantage point, he could easily see the entry to the livery, but he was well hidden under the tree and not likely to be seen by anyone leaving. After a few minutes passed he saw Andy leave the stable riding Ned. Harold surmised that he had stabled the other horse. Harold continued to follow Andy across town to the north side, where he deposited Ned at the livery there. Harold then saw him walk out, head up the street toward the center of town and the market square.

*He wants to have one horse on each side of town so he can get to them quickly, wherever he might be,* Harold thought.

Harold waited a while until Andy was a good way up the street and then followed cautiously on his horse, keeping a safe distance behind. He saw Andy strolling around the Market Square, occasionally talking to various people. Harold kept back in the shadows with his cloak wrapped tightly around him.

*He's trying to get intelligence on the perpetrators,* Harold surmised. *So far, he's keeping his emotions under control and thinking clearly. Pouring a bucket of water on his head was good, though it may have looked a bit odd, what with the weather so cold.*

Harold intended to stay close, no matter what. He knew Andy was determined to find the perpetrators of his sister's murder, and when he did, anything could happen.

# 33.

# JUSTICE

IT was nearing sunset, and Andy found he was hungry; time to go to one of the taverns to get something to eat, and perhaps garner some information about Innis and the students. He went inside the first one he saw and took a seat near the bar. He ordered some food and a mug of hot cider. When the barkeep came over, Andy indicated that he was a tacksman for a nobleman and was looking for two men, former tenants, who had left owing a considerable amount of back rent. He said he was from Girvan, down the coast, and that the tenants left several weeks ago. He had picked up their trail and heard they had gone to Ayr. The barkeep looked at him blankly. He was prepared to pay a small reward, Andy said, for information leading to their location.

The barkeep looked more interested and asked Andy what the men looked like. Andy described the two students as best he could from what Ree had told him.

"I cannot say for sure," the barkeep said, scratching his head, "but I have seen two young lads about that age that could be them."

The barkeep described them as wearing long, dirty robes like the habits worn by monks and claiming to be religion students.

"That well could be them, trying to mask their identity with the monk disguise" Andy replied. "Do you know where they might be staying?"

The barkeep told him the location of the boardinghouse. He also said that they came in several nights a week, usually late, and drank a lot of beer. He ordinarily had to kick them out around closing time.

He also mentioned that, for several nights, they had a third man with them, about the same age, but better dressed and more tidy; but he had not seen this man for a while. Andy asked how long ago, and the barkeep estimated a couple of weeks. Once the barkeep described the man's appearance, Andy knew for sure it was Innis.

Now he had a lead. From the directions to the boardinghouse given by the barkeep, he figured it was east of the wharf area on the north side of town. Andy paid his bill, left a sizable tip, thanked the barkeep and left. *They may still be there,* he thought. It was not yet dark. He decided to walk quickly to the north livery, get his mount and ride around the area until he found the boardinghouse.

He soon found what he suspected was the place in question. It was on a side street in a row of other buildings. Across the street was a wooded ravine, perfect for hiding his horse. He rode down into the ravine behind some trees and tied the animal to a stout branch.

Removing his broadsword from the scabbard hanging down his back, Andy crossed the street, made sure no one was about and circled the house. It was a two-story, ramshackle affair with a basement. It appeared that there were rental rooms on the first and second floors. There was one large chimney in the front, starting at the basement level. *The main hearth for cooking,* he guessed. The boarding rooms didn't appear to be heated, but most had windows. Some were covered, some not.

Andy walked around to one side and peered in an uncovered window. He was completely taken aback by what he saw and dropped to the ground, out of view of the window, his mind reeling. On a bed to one side of the room were two men. Both were naked, the taller of the two astride the other, humping him from behind.

*My God, they're buggering!* Andy was sure he had found the right men, and now was a good time to attack, as they were obviously indisposed. He found a door to the stairway leading up from the basement and crept to the room. He placed his ear to the door and could hear a lot of grunting, groaning and flesh smacking flesh.

*Good,* he thought. *They're still at it. This will be easy.*

Andy took his broadsword and whacked the pommel hard into the door latch. There was a cracking sound, but the door did not open. He then took the sword in both hands and delivered a powerful overhand blow with the sharp edge into the center. The door splintered and broke apart.

The room was dim. Andy was immediately hit with a dank, sour odor, like that of a rotten melon. By then, the tall man had rolled off the back of the shorter one and they were both cowering on the bed on their knees, holding on to each other. Their faces were white and their eyes wide open with confusion and fear.

Andy considered hacking them both down then and there, but thought better of it. He needed information first. So he turned the broadsword flat-face down and whammed the taller one hard on the top of the head. He moaned and fell off the side of the bed, hitting the floor with a thump, and lay still. The shorter one was frozen in place, his mouth agape as if to scream, but nothing came out.

"Don't make a sound or move a muscle," Andy hissed, "or I will kill you dead right now." The sword hung precariously in the air over the man's head.

"Nod if your head if you understand," Andy said in a low voice.

The man did, and started shaking violently. Andy picked up a dirty tunic from the floor and tore it in two strips, then halved one of them.

"Open your mouth," he ordered. The man did, his eyes almost as big as his mouth.

Andy stuffed one of the strips into the man's mouth and tied the other around his head to hold in the gag. Then he picked up one of the filthy robes and tore it into several long strips, tying the arms and legs of the unconscious taller man, and gagged him in case he came to. He took another of the strips and tied it around the neck of the shorter man, leash-like, and jerked him off the bed. The man crumpled to the floor in a fetal position. Andy kicked him in the side, knocking him sprawling across the room.

"Sit up with your back to the wall. We need to talk," he growled, and removed the gag.

Harold had, by this time, made his way to the window and was peering in. He quickly assessed the situation. *No help needed here,* he thought. *Andy's got it well under control.*

"Do you know a man named Innis?" Andy demanded of the short man.

In a quavering voice, the man whispered, "Ah …Aye."

"He roomed with you and your … companion?"

"Aye."

"Where is he now?"

"I don't know for sure …" the man began. Andy hit him hard in the nose with his fist. Copious amounts of blood started streaming out of both nostrils. The man's eyes were watering, and he was coughing up pink spit.

Andy handed him the dirty gag he had just removed.

"Press this to your nose," he said. "That will slow the bleeding."

The man did as he was told.

"Now, one more time, where be Innis?"

"He was arrested … by, ..by the constable," the man said weakly.

"I asked, where is he?" Andy said, his voice rising.

The man apparently went into hyperventilation, breathing fast and shallow, his chest heaving in and out. Andy waited for a while, never taking his hard eyes off him. Finally, the man's breathing slowed to the point that he could talk, though hesitantly.

The … last I, I, I heard," he stammered, "he, he was in the ga … gaol. "

Andy waited again, thinking, *Shite. I should not have hit the taller one. He might have held up better.* But, he *had* hit the tall one who was still unconscious. He had only the nervous, short one to question.

*This could take all night,* Andy thought, *I guess I should change tactics.* Andy stood up, walked across the room trying to collect himself and then returned to the terrified man. This time Andy laid the sword on the floor and softened his tone.

"Look, you've nothing to fear from me as long as you answer my questions and tell me the truth."

The man visibly, almost imperceptibly, relaxed a little. Andy saw his fists unclench and the pupils of his eyes contract a bit.

"Now, why was Innis in the gaol?"

"He, he was accused of he .. heresy," said the man, his voice getting slightly stronger and more steady.

"Good. See—just relax and answer the questions. It makes it so much easier,"

Andy said soothingly, "Who charged him with heresy?"

"The Master, our teacher and mentor," replied the short man, his voice sounding more confident.

"The Master's name—do you know it?" inquired Andy.

"Aye, it is Joseph Renfreu. He was commissioned by Cardinal Beaton before his death to identify and punish heretics," replied the man.

"Protestants, you mean?" asked Andy.

"Aye, Cardinal Beaton considered this religion an apostasy, an abomination to God. He wanted it stopped. He commissioned the Master to do this work," the man said, a hint of pride creeping into his voice.

"You and your companion, you were helping the Master in this important task?" Andy inquired, realizing that the soft approach worked much better.

"Och, aye, we were his disciples."

"What about Innis? Is he still in the gaol?" Andy pressed, gently.

"Nay, I don't think so. After the red-haired witch was burned, I think he was released."

Andy's rage rose again, almost to the breaking point. His right hand, involuntarily it seemed, reached for the broadsword. Just in time, his brain took over. He got up and walked around the room again. *Calm down*, he chided himself. *There is one more piece of information I really need.*

He came back, kneeled before the man, smiled and addressed him in a calm voice: "I understand. Tell me, the Master, where does he live? Surely such an important man does not stay here in Ayr."

"Aye, he does; not too far from here," the man said proudly. "We take instruction in his library."

"Really? I can hardly believe it," replied Andy, solicitously. "Where?"

"Several blocks away, toward the wharf. He has a wonderful rock house on the corner, with a beautiful study in the back," enthused the man.

That was it. Andy needed no more information and could stand it no longer. But, just in case: "Does the Master live all alone?"

"Nay, he has guards—three of them."

Andy reached for the sword, casually picked it up and turned as if to leave. Then, in a flashing move, he brought the sword swinging powerfully in a horizontal arc, beheading the man instantly. The head rolled across the floor and the man's body remained against the wall for a moment, and then fell forward in a stream of blood.

Andy readied to leave. The tall man was still unconscious. He took his sword and thrust it deep into the man's chest, piercing his heart. Then he left, crossed the street, and descended into the wooded ravine. He sat down on a rock beside his horse.

He had some more thinking to do.

# 34.
# RENFREU

RENFREU'S three guards, assuming they were still there, would be Andy's first obstacle. *Go to Renfreu's house and reconnoiter it first,* Andy reasoned. He mounted his horse, rode it back to the north livery and re-stabled it. Then he armed himself. His dirk was strapped to his waist and the sgian duhh tucked under his belt. The broadsword was sheathed in a scabbard hanging down his back. He donned the chainmail vest and steel helmet, both concealed by his cloak. He was as ready as he could be.

It was now fully dark. In another hour the first quarter moon would rise. This would provide some illumination, but not much. *The situation will just have to work itself out one way or the other,* he thought.

Meanwhile, completely unknown to Andy, Harold was tailing him, only a block behind. Harold hobbled his horse in an open meadow near the north livery, where Andy's horse was stabled, and followed him on foot. He climbed a tree and watched as Andy's dim shape slowly and cautiously circled a stone house on the corner, stopping at intervals to listen and peer into the gloom.

Andy could make out a guard at the front door. He looked to be nodding off occasionally. The guard was standing, alternately leaning his body against the outside wall of the house, then apparently in an effort to stay awake, pacing to and fro in front of the door. *Maybe I could slip close to the guard under cover of darkness, wait until he nodded off, and slit his throat.* But then what? The door was undoubtedly locked. The other two guards were probably inside, not to mention Renfreu. *How would I manage to get in?*

While circling the house, he had found that the only other possible point of entry was a window at the back. He noticed, behind gauzy curtains, the flickering light of what appeared to be three candles, close together, a candelabra probably. There was also a chimney with smoke rising; a hearth inside with a low-burning fire was casting a glow.

*"Renfreu's study,"* he assumed. He could crash through the window and go from there, depending on the situation inside, but there was no assurance that Renfreu would be there, much less that he would be alone. Most likely, the two other guards were positioned at strategic places inside. If he crashed in and Renfreu was not in the room, then what would he do? That would only announce his arrival like a cannon shot, and he would surely be set upon by three heavily armed men.

*Nay,* he concluded. *Bad idea.*

He crept silently around to the front. The light was uniformly dark, black almost, as the moon had not yet risen. A row of sizeable trees lined the street. He climbed one, kneeling on a large limb. He could barely make out the sleepy guard by the front door. *I'll wait,* he thought. *When the moon comes up, I'll be able to see more, plus it will create shadows. Maybe then I can think of something.*

So he waited and watched. Finally, he noticed a slight brightening creeping across the landscape. The moon was rising. The guard's head at the front door was drooping to his chest, and then popping back up. Andy could see him vigorously shake his head, evidently trying to get the cobwebs out and stay awake. Soon, Andy heard a knock, apparently from the other side of the door.

"Thump, thump, thump—pause—thump, thump."

This had the effect of jarring the outside guard fully awake. He rapped three times on the exterior side of the door; it opened, and another guard came out. The first guard went through the open door to the inside.

*Changing of the guard,* Andy surmised. *That's the signal they use.*

The shift for the new outside guard would probably last for several hours. He couldn't wait that long. Slowly, a plan formed. The front door was lit by the moon's dim light, but a tree cast a dark shadow near the side of it. *What if I slip around the house, creep into the shadow, watch until the guard seems distracted or sleepy, then slice his throat with the sgian dubh? I should be able to muffle his mouth to prevent any crying out.*

He could then repeat the knock sequence, which should have the effect of causing one of the other two guards to come out to see what was going on. He could stand against the wall and stab that guard with his dirk. He'd have to act fast to keep the guard from screaming or shouting out. He couldn't afford to alert the remaining guard, or his target, the Master.

Andy dropped silently from the tree, making sure to keep the large trunk between him and the front door. He then slipped into the shadow, the sgian dubh blade in his hand. The guard looked bored, leaning against the wall with one leg bent, foot braced on the wall. A big man with long black hair, he was not walking or scanning with his eyes; in fact, it appeared he was napping.

Andy gathered himself and slipped up on the man from the side as quietly as he could, grabbed a handful of hair, jerked the head back, and simultaneously brought the sharp sgian dubh blade across the man's neck, slicing it from ear to ear. The man opened his mouth as if to yell; nothing came out but a gurgling noise.

Andy quickly released the man's hair and the guard sank slowly to the ground, his arms and legs jerking slightly, and then he was still. *One down, two more to go, then the prize,* Andy thought.

He wiped blood off the sgian dubh with the man's cloak, slipped it under his belt and pulled the guard's body into the shadows. Then he removed the man's cloak and mopped up the blood at the entrance as best he could. He went back to the door and knocked: three raps. Nothing. He repeated it. Suddenly, the door opened and another guard stomped out.

"Jarrod, what's your problem?" the guard said, looking one way, then the other.

His back pressed to the house wall, Andy immediately swung the dirk at the man's throat. But the blade was slightly off mark; it gashed his chin but missed his neck. Andy quickly grabbed the man around the neck in a chokehold, his left arm locked onto his right wrist, fist pressed into the man's larynx. He squeezed as hard as he could to stifle any shout, but the man was big and strong. He seized Andy's arm with both of his hands, swinging around at the same time, getting out of the chokehold. He then rammed Andy hard into the side of the rock house, momentarily knocking the breath out of him, quickly pulled his own dirk and swung it sideways hard into Andy's ribs.

There was a metallic clang as the dirk hit Andy's chainmail vest. The man looked surprised, and Andy feared that he was about to shout, but he didn't. Instead, he raised the dirk and brought it down on Andy's head. It clanged on the helmet under the hood of Andy's cloak, knocking him dizzy.

Before the man could get off another blow, Andy charged him, smacking his steel helmeted head into the man's chest, knocking him sprawling to the ground. Andy then jumped on top of him, one leg on each side, grabbed him by the throat with one hand and pulled the sgian dubh from his belt with the other, stabbing him several times in the chest. The man continued to struggle, trying to get up, but Andy hung on. Finally, his heart repeatedly pierced by the blade, and his windpipe collapsing from Andy's hold on his throat, the man quit struggling and lay still. *Two down.*

The now-dead guard wore a light gray cloak, as did the other guard. Andy's cloak was black. He removed the dead guard's cloak and pulled off his own, laying it over the dead man's body making it almost invisible in the dark shadow. He then donned the gray cloak, pulled his sgian dubh from the man's body and slipped it under his belt. Holding the dirk behind his body, he opened the front door and walked into the black interior. Creeping along what he assumed was a hallway, his back to the wall, Andy peered for any light. All he saw was dark everywhere, as his eyes adjusted to the blackness.

He finally saw a feeble glow near the floor. Then he saw a big whitish figure beside it.

"What the hell's up with Jarrod?" the whitish figure asked in an irritated tone. Andy kept walking, wishing his broadsword was in his hand instead of the dirk.

"Just complaining," Andy said in a low, gruff voice, still walking toward the figure.

"Wait," the figure said. "You're not ..."

Andy plunged the dirk into the middle of the shadowy figure, hoping it would hit a vital organ. The figure shrieked loudly, "You bastard!"

Then, growling oaths, he charged. Andy sidestepped, grabbed the guard by the neck with his left arm, and plunged the sgian dubh into his head, hitting the huge man in the eye. The man screamed louder, stumbled and fell to the floor, face down. Andy managed to unsheathe the broadsword from the scabbard strapped on his back and drove it into the fallen guard's back as he struggled to get up.

The man writhed and jerked, then was still, but he had certainly sounded a loud alarm. Andy crashed the full weight of his body into the door above the faint glow, bursting into Renfreu's study. Renfreu was sitting, seemingly unconcerned, behind a desk with a three-candle candelabra on top. A bed of red coals glowed warmly in the hearth.

"Welcome to my humble abode, Laird Henderson," said Renfreu calmly. Andy was stunned. There he was, standing in the middle of the room, wielding a bloody broadsword, and Renfreu was calm and smiling?

Rattled and momentarily wordless, Andy finally managed to exclaim: "You smile, but I've left a trail of three of your bodyguards dead in my wake. Do you have no regard for them?"

"I'm nay worried," Renfreu said. "God has accepted their souls. What will He do with yours when it knocks on heaven's gate? That will happen soon you know."

Andy recovered some. Renfreu obviously wanted to play a word game; so be it.

"You are nothing but a charlatan you fiendish bastard. Your evil deeds end tonight."

"I'm afraid you are mistaken. Your red-haired sister was the one possessed by the devil." Renfreu said this in a sadistic tone, still smiling.

Rage grew in Andy's chest. Staring balefully into his target's coal-black eyes, Andy exclaimed in a low, clam voice, "She had been Catholic all her life, christened at birth. You must have known that."

"I'm afraid she had strayed and joined the devil's camp," said Renfreu. "She admitted it as she burned."

At this, the rage in Andy's breast was close to explosion, but somehow he managed to hold it in. There were a few additional facts he wanted to know.

"What cause do you have to think she was not a good Catholic?" he demanded.

Renfreu paused. His black eyebrows rose inquisitively and his eyes narrowed.

"Did you not know she was disguised as a man—breeches, boots, and a cloak with a hood covering her head? She brought her companion—Innis, is it—to help incite the crowd at Donner's preaching. My spies saw it all. "

"She was no follower of Donner, or his religion," Andy said, disgust evident in his voice. "She simply accompanied Innis, her cousin, because he asked her."

Renfreu had grown weary of the discussion and decided to end it.

"We determined that your sister was an apostate, a heretic and a witch. She was a leader in the Protestant rebellion. Donner observed her closely. He's trained to spot such people, and he reported this to me. Her punishment was just."

Andy was flabbergasted. Surely he had not heard correctly.

"Donner reported *to you* ?" he asked, incredulously.

"Aye, he is my principal spy. I pay him handsomely for such information. You look surprised. Did you think that I would allow this … this *infestation* to go unabated?"

Renfreu looked at Andy through narrowed ink-black eyes. He was a large man, big girth. He stood easily beside his desk, almost casually, still looking unconcerned.

*Plenty capable,* thought Andy—*and tricky. I need to end this now.*

Andy raised his broadsword.

"Let's see what God thinks of your black soul, for I am about to send it His way."

Renfreu pulled a handheld arquebus from under the desk and pointed it at Andy's head.

"Don't take another step, or I will send a nice round ball into your brain," he said.

This move stopped Andy in his tracks. He knew Renfreu spoke the truth; the weapon could kill him instantly. He stood there, paralyzed, expecting the death ball to plunge into his head at any moment.

Suddenly he heard a *sswiissh* pass his ear, and a thud. Simultaneously, there was a flash and a loud bang. A searing pain pierced his left side and he was knocked backwards. He spun around and fell, his forehead smacking hard on the floor.

The room went black.

# 35.
# FATE

AFTER a while, he had no idea how long, a semblance of consciousness slowly returned and Andy opened his eyes. A big, burly,
bearded face was very close to his, staring at him closely.

"Thank God, Sire. It's me. Don't move; you've been shot."

Andy thought he must be dreaming.

"Harold?" he stammered. "What are you doing here?"

Harold said soothingly, "Just don't move, Sire. I'll tell you all
in good time, but you needn't worry about the evil one; he's dead."

Andy struggled to get up. Harold gently but insistently pushed
him back down.

"Sire, please, be still. You're safe, but you've been shot. I think
your shoulder is broken. We need to take care of that before you
start moving around."

Harold gingerly rolled Andy to his right side so he could inspect the wound more closely. Andy's left shoulder clearly hung
lower than the right one. He was bleeding from a deep wound at
the top front of the shoulder, near his neck. There was another
hole, with less blood coming out, on the back of the shoulder.

"Good. The ball passed through," Harold said, "but it must
have struck your collarbone. I think it's broken. Stay where you
are and grit your teeth. I need to probe the wound."

"Do it then!" said Andy, grimacing.

Harold ran his forefinger along the ridge of Andy's clavicle,
then inside the wound made by the bullet. He felt the fracture,
broken in two places, he reckoned, and displaced. He would

need to get it aligned and immobilized, but first he needed to cleanse it.

"The bone is broken in two places," he said to Andy. "After hitting the bone, the shot ball came out your back. That's good, but I'm going to have to push around on your shoulder to line up the bone up better. Otherwise, it might not heal. This will hurt."

"Get on with it," Andy said, his face white.

Harold looked around the study. He spied a couple of mugs on a shelf. There might be some beer, wine or other kind of spirituous liquid in the room. He walked to the desk, which had been over-turned. There was a cabinet against the wall near Renfreu's crum-pled body. He opened it and saw that there were several dark glass bottles plugged by corks. *Wine*, thought Harold. *Of course—a man such as Renfreu would imbibe fine wine.*

He pulled his sgian dubh from Renfreu's chest wiped off the blood, and pried the cork out of one of the bottles. The smell of strong wine quickly floated up. Then he removed Renfreu's dou-blet and tore the fine linen shirt from his body. He would need that for packing the wounds. He also tore off Renfreu's robe to fashion a sling and went back to Andy.

"Here, take a full swig. You'll need it."

Andy did, and Harold proceeded to carefully pour the wine onto the wounds, front and back, gently daubing them with pieces of linen. Once this was done, he was ready to take on the harder job of aligning the fractured bones.

He told Andy to take another big gulp of the wine and ready himself.

"First, I'm going to push your shoulder into the proper position. Then I'll deeply probe on the broken bone, pressing the pieces into line as best I can. After that, I'll pour more of the wine into the wound. Finally, I will burn both sides of the wound with my blade to cauterize it."

Andy turned his head and saw the sgian dubh resting on the hot coals in the hearth.

"Are you ready?"

Andy nodded.

"Take this roll of cloth in your mouth and clench it as tight as you can."

Andy complied. Soon it was over. All had gone relatively well. Andy was perspiring profusely and his face was ashen. Harold put linen compresses on the wound, tied a bandage around Andy's shoulder, underneath his armpit and over the top. Then he fashioned the sling and tied the left arm tight against his chest.

"Let's get out of here. Do *not* move your shoulder," Harold instructed. He pulled Andy up, draped Andy's good arm around his neck, and walked him out the door. They headed down the street in the direction of the livery.

"How did you learn to be a physic?" Andy asked.

"I'm no physic, but one of my jobs when I was in Baron Agnew's service was to tend to battle wounds. Believe me, I've seen many much worse than yours."

"How did you find me?"

Harold told him the whole story as they were making their way to the stable.

"You did not obey my order!" said Andy in mock seriousness.

"Nay, I didn't," agreed Harold.

"Thanks anyway," said Andy, sincerely appreciative. "But how did you manage to kill Renfreu?"

"The evil one? So that was his name?" said Harold. "I followed you on foot from the north livery and climbed a big tree near the house. I saw you circle it and then climb a tree in front. I also saw the guard outside the door and figured that you would kill him. I had no idea what you would do after that, except that you must have learned the evil one was inside and you wanted to get to him. When you went inside, I followed."

"You saw all that?" Andy said, amazed.

"Aye," Harold explained. He had seen Andy take the first guard from the shadows. He was surprised when Andy knocked on the door, but figured it was a signal.

"I jumped out of my tree at that point and started toward the house."

Harold then saw the guard pull his dirk and start swinging it at Andy. Harold ran toward the action, he said, but slowed when he heard the dirk strike metal.

"I knew you probably still had the armored vest and I was relieved when you threw him to the ground and got the best of him. I must say I was surprised when he did not raise an alarm."

"I was as well," said Andy. "After I got him to the ground, I grabbed him by the throat. He was wheezing, but not loud enough for anyone inside to hear, I guess."

Continuing, Harold related that he saw Andy go inside the house, went in himself, then stumbled and almost fell on the body of the third guard on the floor. Fortunately, he didn't, but he could hear Andy through the half-open door talking to Renfreu. He could tell that Andy was on one side of the room and saw that Renfreu was across from him behind a desk.

"What did you do?" asked Andy.

"I had my sgian dubh in my right hand and my dirk in the other. I was following the conversation between you and Renfreu, firm in the idea that I would step in only if necessary. When I heard Renfreu say he was going to send a ball into your brain, I promptly stepped in and saw that the powder piece was aimed and ready to fire. I threw my sgian dubh at Renfreu as hard as I could. I don't think he saw it coming, for it stuck in his chest, just under the rib cage. At that instant, I heard the piece go off, a loud explosion. The strike of the sgian dubh knocked his aim off, I guess. He almost missed you completely, but unfortunately, hit your shoulder."

"That was the swishing sound I heard coming past my ear," Andy said. "You must be pretty good to stick a blade in a man that far away!"

"I have practiced some," admitted Harold.

"But the blade hit him in the lower chest, you say? It didn't kill him right away then?"

"Nay, it didn't," Harold explained. "I charged him, going over the desk, hit him with my full weight. I came down on top of him. He had dropped the powder piece, and I had lost my dirk, so I pulled the sgian dubh out of his body, got him around the head, and plunged the blade into his temple. Then I got up and hurried over to check on you."

"You saved my life," said Andy somberly. Thank you."

Once they reached the livery and Harold had retrieved his hobbled horse from the meadow, the moon had risen straight overhead. It was just after midnight, Harold reckoned.

"Did you ever find out where Innis is?" he asked.

"Nay," answered Andy.

"Well, I think I might know, if he is still there."

Andy was surprised. "Where?"

"When I was following you to the boarding house, I saw a man in ragged clothes stumbling down a street from the direction of St. John's. He went into a tavern. It looked like Innis."

Andy looked up at the moon, figuring, as Harold had, that it must be nigh on midnight. Most taverns stayed open till after midnight if there were enough customers. They would need to hurry.

"Let's go," Andy said.

Harold urged: "If he be there, you let me handle any fighting. I don't want you to disturb my work on your shoulder."

"Don't worry; I'm in no shape to fight, but let me do the talking," Andy replied.

So it was agreed, Harold would handle the fighting, and Andy would do the talking. They rode to the tavern, tied the horses to a nearby hitching rail and walked through the front door. The place was faintly lit and they saw no customers, but the barkeep was still behind the bar. Then they saw a lone, haggard figure sitting at a table in the back. It was Innis, his head down on the table.

Andy went up to the barkeep.

"That man is my cousin. How long has he been here?"

"Since dark," said the barkeep. "I need to close, but he says he has no place to go. Before long, I'll have to throw him into the street. He is quite drunk and still owes his bar bill."

"How much?" asked Andy.

"Ten pence," the man said.

Andy slapped down a twenty-pence coin. "For your trouble."

They went to the table and Andy shouted, "Innis! Wake up!"

Innis raised his head and looked up, blurry-eyed, trying to focus. He mumbled something unintelligible, and his head fell back to the table.

"Barkeep, could I have a pint over here?" Andy called.

The barkeep brought it over, and Andy poured one-half of it slowly over Innis' head, getting no reaction.

Then he told Harold, "Grab him by the hair, roll his head back, and throw the rest in his face."

Harold did, and Innis opened his eyes, glazed and blinking.

"Get him to his feet and drag him outside. There's a watering tub beside the rail where the horses are tied. Try sticking his head in that and keep doing it until he comes around."

Harold grabbed Innis under the shoulders and proceeded to pull him out into the street. When they got to the hitching rail, he grasped Innis's hair and plunged his head into the tub of cold water, holding it there for a couple of seconds. Innis was sputtering and coughing as his head was pulled out.

"Innis!" Andy shouted again, "It's me, Andy. Talk to me!"

Innis shook his wet head like a dog and slapped himself in the face several times, obviously trying to clear his clouded mind.

"Andy?" he mumbled, looking up and trying to focus his eyes, "What 'er you doing here? Whar I be?"

"Stick his head under again," ordered Andy.

Harold repeated the process. Innis shook his head again, wiped his eyes, and looked at the two men. His vision was better and he was slightly more alert. "Harold—you're 'er too?"

There was a row of large rocks across the street. Andy pointed: "Sit him down over there; we need to talk."

Innis staggered across the street, held up by Harold, who seated him unsteadily on one of the rocks.

"You're drunk," accused Andy. Where have you been?"

Innis just sat mute, looking up at the two men. He made no sound but his eyes began to tear up. Then he started weeping, finally breaking into loud sobs. Andy and Harold stood there, giving him a little time to find a degree of relief. Finally, Innis got a sufficient hold on himself to speak.

"Andy, it all be my fault—Ree—I caused it," he said brokenly. "My best friend, the one I loved the most, I led her here. That's what caused her to die."

"Where is she, Innis," asked Andy quietly.

"They burnt her, Andy. Oh God, they burnt her."

"Where?" asked Andy.

"St. John's, the green," Innis wailed, breaking into sobs again.

Andy waited a while. "Why? Why, Innis?"

"I don't know," whimpered Innis, "but I caused it; I know that. I begged her to go to the preaching. It all came from that."

"How so?"

"Please, Andy, please; I don't know, but it was my fault—my ignorance, stupidity, searching for what does not exist. I don't want to live any more. Please, kill me! Kill me right now! I want to die. Please, Andy, do it!" Innis cried, tears streaming down his face.

Innis dropped to his knees and lay his head on the rock, pleading.

"Andy, bring down your sword. Put me out of my misery, I beg of ye."

Andy was sympathetic and disgusted at the same time. What Innis said was true. His ignorance and foolish religious notions had contributed to Ree's terrible fate, but ignorance did not warrant the death penalty. Andy considered the situation for a while.

*Innis had nothing to do with the evil men who took Ree's life*, he thought.

*I've already wreaked vengeance on them. But I can't just forget this. Innis cannot go back to Blackcraigshire. He has drunk himself into oblivion. How much of his grief is just drunken blabber?*

"Nay, Innis," said Andy. "You must live with what you've done. I'll not kill you."

Innis raised his head from the rock and sat back down, his eyes rimmed with red.

"What did you find at St. John's?" Andy asked.

"Ashes," Innis whimpered miserably, "just ashes. Then he reached inside his shirt and pulled out the sack of ashes tied with the gold-braided cord.

"Here Andy, take this, I scraped up a handful of Ree's ashes. Nothing else was left."

He begged Andy to take the sack of ashes and join Ree's remains in burial with her mother, father and the rest of her family on Ben Blackcraig. Andy took the bag and tucked it inside his cloak. "I'll see that she gets a proper burial."

Innis then noticed that Andy's left arm was tied up underneath his cloak. "What happened?" Innis asked. "Your arm?"

"I came here to destroy Ree's murderers, and I have been successful, with Harold's help. The last one shot me with an arquebus. Harold killed him."

"Wha ..? How many did you get?" asked Innis.

"The plotters and spies," Andy said, "the two students you boarded with, the man they called 'Master.' He was the ringleader, Cardinal Beaton's man. Also his three bodyguards."

"They all be gone?" asked Innis, sounding surprised.

"Yes," said Andy. There's one more, the preacher called Donner. He was in on it. We'll get him, too."

"Donner was in on it? You sure?"

"Yes, he was the main one feeding information to the Master. They used you Innis. You were duped."

"Oh God, how could I be so stupid, so ignorant!" Innis started sobbing again.

"How did you get out of gaol?" Andy asked.

"I don't know. They came around this morning and released me. I asked them why, but they wouldn't tell me," cried Innis.

*You were just the bait. They didn't need you anymore,* Andy thought, but didn't say anything, fearing that it would set Innis off crying again.

Innis continued to sit on the rock, his head in his hands. At length, he looked up and said mournfully, "I know I can never go back to the Big House. I'll leave; I don't know where."

Andy studied him for a while, and then reached a decision.

"Innis, you have no money and no horse. You can't go far."

"I can walk," Innis said.

"Here's the best I can do for you," Andy said.

He related that he had brought some money in case it was needed—a fair amount. He would give Innis half of it. Also, he had brought an extra horse. Innis could take it, too. It was at the south livery. There were some weapons there as well. He would inform the stablemen that Innis would be coming.

"But fix this firmly in your mind, Innis; if I ever see you again, I *will* kill you. You must leave these parts—go far away, to the north highlands or completely out of Scotland. Do you understand?"

Innis said he did, but he did not need anything given to him, he didn't deserve it. Andy emphasized that he was not doing it out of charity, only to give Innis the means to leave and go far away, and never return.

"And Innis, there is one price you'll have to pay. To assure me that you will leave and stay gone, I want you to be recognizable wherever you go. You will have an obvious disfigurement you can't hide. If you come anywhere near Blackcraigshire, I will know it, for you will have no nose. I'm going to cut it off."

Innis looked surprised, but did not say anything. He just nodded.

Andy whispered to Harold, "Hit him hard on the head with the flat side of your broadsword, enough to knock him out." Harold whammed him, and Innis fell off the rock.

Harold held up Innis's head and Andy gripped the tip of his nose while Harold cut with the sgian dubh, starting the blade underneath and cutting up through the skin, flesh and cartilage to the jutting bone. The wound bled and Harold held a cloth compress to it until the bleeding slowed. He then went back inside the pub where the barkeep was just closing up, got a pail of heated water, and laid his sgian dubh on the hot coals in the hearth. He went back out, cleansed the stub of Innis's nose, then seared it with the hot end of his blade. Then he folded another compress in place and tied it with a strip of fabric he had saved from Renfreu's robe.

Andy and Harold carried Innis, draped over Andy's horse, still unconscious, to the south livery and instructed the owner to give him the spare horse and weapons when he came to. Andy also tied a leather coin purse to Innis's belt. Then they left.

Andy was sure he would never see Innis again. Suddenly he felt remorseful and very sad.

# 36.
## SURPRISE

THE two men headed east on the dirt road out of Ayr in the early morning darkness. Neither uttered a word as both were lost in their own thoughts. When they were about halfway to the turnoff to Blackcraigshire, they heard riders rapidly approaching from the opposite direction. The quarter moon was still above the horizon, providing dim light through dark scudding clouds as the shapes of three riders came into view. They recognized them at almost the same instant.

"That's Helen!" cried Andy.

"Also Joe and my man Nathan Douglas," added Harold.

Andy and Harold kicked their horses into a gallop and quickly closed the gap. Helen jerked her horse to an abrupt stop, vaulted off and ran to Andy, grabbing him by the leg, hugging it tightly.

"Thank God, you're alive!"

Andy's horse startled and began stepping nervously in a tight circle, but Andy managed to hold him under control.

Harold pulled his horse to a stop nearby, bantering, "Lady Helen! As promised, I am returning your beloved intact—er, mostly!"

Helen then noticed Andy's left arm was bound around his waist. "You're hurt!"

Andy smiled down at her, "If you'd turn loose of my leg, I'd get down and give you a big kiss."

Helen loosened her grip, looking up at him with an odd mixture of relief, concern and joy. A big kiss was exactly what she needed. Andy grabbed the saddlehorn with his right hand and swung to the ground, pulling her tightly to him, and kissed her deeply. Harold, Joe and Nathan pulled their horses to the side to give the two lovers some room and time to reunite.

"How bad is he hurt?" asked Joe.

"Nothing but a broken collar bone," replied Harold. "It'll heal quickly. Andy just needs to be careful and keep it immobile for a couple of weeks."

Then, louder so Helen could hear him, he added, "That means her ladyship will have to get used to a one-armed lover for a while."

Helen pushed Andy back, retorting in mock seriousness: "Only one arm? Then I'll have to work twice as hard."

Smiling mischievously, Andy said, "I think I'd really like that."

"Believe me, I can do it if you can stand it," teased Helen.

She was looking forward to having Andy all to herself for a while and figured she could last longer than him, one arm or no. With what she had in mind, he would be the one who would require extra stamina.

They all laughed, relieved and happy. Helen walked back to her horse and Andy remounted. Helen gave her reins to Harold and instructed him to lead the horse. She intended to ride with Andy; there was much to discuss. When they got underway, Helen wrapped her arms around Andy's waist, careful to avoid his bound arm, pressed her breasts into his back and snuggled her chin and cheek into the back of his neck.

After they had gone a ways, Helen suggested they should plan Andy's homecoming.

"I'm thinking of some nice surprises. You'd better get lots of rest," she whispered huskily, biting at his ear.

When the moon began to slide behind the trees, they stopped in a small meadow beside a rushing burn, built a fire and prepared to bed down for the night. Helen snuggled up to Andy's right side as he lay on his back, her head resting on his good shoulder. They had bedded down a distance apart from the others, who were still warming around the fire.

"Now, Andrew Henderson, tell me the whole story," she whispered.

Andy shared the entire story as Helen listened, fascinated. What a terrible thing he had been through. She was glad Andy had gotten the master and his confederates, but was still heartbroken over Ree. She was also aware Andy had not mentioned Innis.

"Did you find out anything about Innis?"

"Aye, we did, but that's another story. I'd rather wait to discuss it."

Helen was surprised at this, especially the way Andy had said it—sharply. She decided not to press the matter. He would tell her when he was ready.

The small band awoke the next morning under a panoply of stars fading into a clear dawn, arose and stoked a quickly made fire to warm their stiff muscles. Anxious to get home, they downed some hard biscuits and dried jerky, and started the final leg.

Everyone at the Big House was overjoyed to see them. Maggie, Allie and Jamie gathered some winter vegetables, and Martha brought in a smoked ham from the larder. The vegetables were cut up and put in a big cooking pot, the ham was cut into thick slices and placed on an iron grill, and oatmeal dough was kneaded into loaves. All of the food was arranged on a glowing bed of coals in the kitchen hearth for slow cooking. A delicious meal would be perfect to celebrate the safe return of Andy and Harold. As the meal cooked, the two men regaled the gathered group with the high points of the events at Ayr.

The question of Innis hung in the air. Finally Jamie asked about him. Andy stared down at his feet, looking unsettled, but finally told them the whole story. The men remained silent but nodded quiet acquiescence as Andy shared why he felt he had to do what he did, while Maggie and Allie became red-eyed and teary. It was a hard decision, Andy conceded. He was still ambivalent about it.

"I knew I had to do something—couldn't just let it pass. Innis acted recklessly," he said, pointing out that both he and Ree had cautioned Innis many times to avoid spouting off in public about his religious beliefs.

"The Catholic religion itself is fine," Andy said. "Indeed we all grew up Catholic. But some of the high churchmen have become vain and vengeful, Cardinal Beaton being the worst example. He and his kind have grown rich and powerful using the church, and very jealous of their positions. They put down any perceived challenge forcefully. Innis refused to heed our warnings, putting Ree at risk. As laird of this shire I felt I had to exact some degree of retribution. I'm sorry."

Andy was indeed sorry. His lower lip was visibly trembling as he concluded, and he seemed on the verge of tears. Later, after the meal was finished, Helen pulled Andy aside and whispered: "I know it hurt, what you had to do with Innis. It's not easy being laird. Justice is sometimes a hard thing to mete out. You did the best you could under trying circumstances."

The next day there would be yet another burial at the quickly filling cemetery atop Ben Blackcraig. Ree's ashes would be interred beside Grannie, the twins, and her parents. But that would be tomorrow. For the coming night, Helen had other plans.

After Andy had left for Ayr, Helen was so worried that she constantly had a gnawing in the pit of her stomach and could neither eat nor sleep. At night, after finally dozing off, she had frightening, vivid nightmares of her father being killed, his body pierced by arrows, stabbed and sliced by swords. The image of her father would then mutate in her mind to become Andy, and sometimes Hugh or Innis.

It seemed all the men in her life were dying and it was her fate to be left alone. At times she saw Ree as she was being burned, the flames licking at her body, consuming her clothes, flesh and hair until nothing was left but her open mouth, screaming, her green eyes reflecting the terrible fire. When Helen awoke after these nightmares, she found herself drenched in sweat and shivering, her skin hot as if consumed by fever.

After several nights of this, she decided she had to do something. She talked with Joe and told him of her disturbing dreams. He likewise was worried; everyone was, he said. There had been so much death recently under tragic and frightening circumstances. It was as if a horrible curse had descended upon the whole family. In the back of everyone's mind was a dreadful fear that Andy would be next. Helen had then made up her mind; they would go to Ayr. Joe would go with her along with one of the

Lochnaw guards. She had selected Nathan Douglas, Harold's capable right-hand man, whom she had known for a long time and trusted completely.

The three of them announced at breakfast the next day that they were going. There was much concern, but everyone understood. The fate of the entire family seemed at stake. The relief was enormous when they returned, safe and sound, with Andy and Harold in tow.

Helen's mind focused on one concept above all. She was to be Andrew Henderson's wife. They were now the heads of an extended household. It was their job to protect and nourish the others—and to perpetuate the family. It was this last element that began to weigh most heavily on her. Her mind and body craved it; she desperately wanted Andy to get her pregnant.

As her conscious mind worried on the ride to Ayr, her subconscious was concocting a plan. When she saw Andy and Harold in the road and knew that her prayers had been answered, the plan simply materialized without effort. It was that time of the month when her body was most receptive. Her skin had warmed and her loins were ripe and ready. She decided that she would get Andy in bed and excite him to the point that he gave up a bountiful harvest of seeds inside her.

The next day would be the beginning of Samhain, signaling the end of harvest season and the beginning of winter. Many farmyard mammals bred during this season and gave birth the following spring.

What better time for humans to plant new life?

# 37.
## DREAMS

BEFORE the evening meal, Helen met with her chambermaid and instructed her on preparations for the bedroom. She wanted clean, ironed bed linens, washed in rosewater; the goosedown mattress aired and plumped, scented candles lit and placed around the room and a warm fire built in the hearth. She emphasized that she and Andy should not be disturbed.

After supper was finished, Helen announced that it was time to put the laird to bed.

"He needs time to rest and heal his broken shoulder," she explained with a coquettish smirk. The others had seen Helen's mostly unsuccessful attempts to keep her hands off him and suspected what lay in store.

"Good night, m'Lord!" Joe proclaimed with a deep, stage bow. "May thee rest well, with the most pleasing of dreams."

Helen smiled sweetly at Andy.

"It's bedtime, Sire."

She took him by the hand and led him up the stairs to her chamber. When the door opened, Andy blinked his eyes unbelievingly. He had never seen anything so lovely: the soft light, the comforting warmth, the smell of—roses?

"I feel like the fatted calf being led to slaughter," Andy remarked, his eyes big.

"You are, in a manner of speaking," Helen cooed. "Now, just relax. Remember you are hurt. I'll do all the work."

"As you say, m'Lady."

"Sit here, Sire," instructed Helen, pointing to a chair covered with plump pillows. Andy slowly lowered his tired frame into the soft cushions as Helen sat on a stool before him, pulling off his boots and hose.

"Am I to be subjected to foot torture?"

"Sometimes torture can also be pleasure," Helen whispered. "Sit back and close your eyes."

"Aye, whatever you say," he sighed.

Helen then produced a washbasin and filled it with hot water from a kettle resting on the hearth. She then took Andy's foot and bathed it with a warm cloth. Then she did the same with the other foot. Andy's eyes stayed closed as the warm sensations crept up from his feet, through his muscled calves and thighs. He could not remember ever having had a foot wash before, much less one from such a luscious creature. He felt the pleasing warmth of the room, the softness of the pillows, the tingling in his feet, the aromas filling his nostrils. This was an experience he would not soon forget.

Helen offered him a cup of steaming liquid.

"Here, drink this."

"What is it?"

"It's like hot cider, except with a different flavor. It will soothe your throat."

Andy took the cup and drank.

"You're right; it's good."

Then Helen had him lean back on the pillows and said softly, "Here, Sire. I'm going to cover your eyes. It's to help you relax."

"A blindfold?"

"Aye, you have to trust me. I've another treat in store."

The cares and troubles of recent days gently evaporated from his mind as Helen, glowing like an angel at his feet, looked up and smiled sweetly at him. She wrapped a soft band of linen over his eyes. A deep, satisfying groan, releasing months of accumulated tension, started deep in his stomach and traveled up through his chest and throat, escaping his mouth like the murmur of gently trickling water.

"Helen, Helen," he sighed, "what are you doing to me?"

Helen said, "Och, I've barely started. Now clear your mind and relax."

Andy did so and found himself drowsy—no, not drowsy, but sort of dreamy, like his mind was floating free of his body. His nose took in the smells of rose, mint, safflower, marjoram. ...He became aware that he had never known the names of such scents before. Where did this new-found knowledge come from?

Andy's mind was conjuring up colorful images as he identified each scent—sunrises, blue seas, rose gardens, quiet green forests. Slowly he became conscious of Helen again rubbing his feet, this time with just her hands, which felt warm and smooth—exceedingly smooth, he thought—as she slid her hands over his skin and pressed against his muscles, ligaments and joints. The smells were getting stronger as well, tangy and spicy and sweet. He felt his consciousness fading, drifting as clouds do, but he didn't care; he would just enjoy the ride.

Helen thought to herself, as she looked upon Andy's slack, smooth face, his lips slightly curled at the edges in a blissful smile: *I should have done this before. My stepmother, with her fascination and skill with all manner of herbs and potions, and insistence that I learn about them, left me something valuable.*

She dipped some orange-scented cream from a glass jar with her fingers, rubbed her hands together and moved them up Andy's legs, beginning with his calves, gently massaging the taut muscles, feeling them relax and slacken under her touch. She looked up at him. He still had the rapt smile on his face, the worry lines in his skin were loosening. He was as still and relaxed as if sleeping. It seemed the hot hemp potion was working. *Very good,* she whispered to herself. He needed this after all he had been through. Losing both Ree and Innis, his closest friends. Barely surviving the harrowing ordeal at Ayr. She had found him so wound up she thought he might blow apart.

She moved up to his knees and thighs, using her fingers and thumbs to probe and knead his muscles and sinews under gentle pressure. Andy's moans grew quieter, and she heard a soft hissing sound coming from his mouth and nose. He was beginning to snore.

*He's asleep, time to remove his trousers,* she thought. She removed his belt and unbuttoned the waistband, then gently pulled at the legging. Andy shifted his buttocks, and the trousers slipped off. Helen moved her hands higher, massaging his upper thighs. This restarted the soft moaning, and Helen got the impression that he had partially awakened and was now semi-conscious. From the contented sound of his moans, he was enjoying her ministrations. Soon she reached his crotch, and noticed his pintle had awakened. It was time to get him in bed.

Andy could hear the sound of Helen's soft voice calling him. It seemed like it was coming from inside his head. Slowly he became aware that she was whispering in his ear. He could feel her warm breath and the brush of her lips.

"Andy, I need for you to stand up, remove your shirt and lie down on the bed so I can do the rest of your body."

"Wha...?" he slurred.

"Stand up," she instructed, pulling on his good arm. Andy leaned forward and Helen pulled him to his feet.

"The blindfold, take it off?" he murmured.

"No, not yet. Leave it on for now."

Helen helped him remove his shirt and guided him to the bed, where he lay down on the soft down mattress. Helen sat beside him, placed a cloth over his groin to keep that part of him extra warm and started kneading his stomach. Then she moved to his chest, carefully pressing and rubbing each group of muscles.

Helen admired anew his long, lithe torso and rippling muscles.

"You've so many muscles, this will take a while, so relax and slip back to dreamland," she whispered.

This was not hard for him to do, and soon his soft, snoring sounds rose up from the bed. Andy had visions of lying on a soft pile of leaves, staring up into a clear, blue sky. There were a few cumulus clouds floating slowly by. He became aware that he was in the oak grove on the knoll before the Big House was built.

He heard the voice of his mother, Ann. Rolling his head to one side, he saw her. She was as beautiful and radiant as he had ever seen her. He noticed that her voice was melodious, sweet and strong.

*"This is such a lovely spot, my love. We must build a house here some day."*

Andy wondered if she was talking to him, but then realized it was his father she had spoken to. He rolled his head to the other side, and there sat Hugh Henderson on a pile of leaves, his legs crossed, dressed in a fine kilt and feathered bonnet, his broadsword at his side.

*"Don't worry, Ann. When I return, I'll build you the finest mansion in all of Galloway."*

Ann smiled serenely, through pouty red lips, hazel eyes sparkling under her long, luscious auburn tresses. *"My God, she is so beautiful,"* thought Andy.

Suddenly, he was gazing at the clouds again. The day was warm and sunny. *It must be in the late spring,* he thought. The clouds were more numerous now, and he noticed their changing shapes—a horse, a ship, a wagon, a black coach with silver fittings.

His eyes held on the coach. It was moving; then it stopped. The door opened. Out stepped his sister, Ree, wearing a flowing green gown that matched the color of her eyes. Her red hair glinted brightly off the sun's rays. She wore jeweled slippers.

*"Ma, I'm home!"* she said excitedly, a bright smile on her face.

Ann and Hugh rushed up to greet her.

*"It's so good to have you back,"* cried Ann. *"We've missed you so."*

Andy felt relieved, comfortable inside; his precious sister was back with their parents. They were all happy.

Andy's attention returned to the exotic aromas wafting past his nostrils. They seemed stronger now. He felt Helen's soft hands kneading the back of his neck, then his head. *"Mmmm, that feels good,"* he thought. Then came another sensation: He could feel Helen's breath on his forehead, then her wet lips caressing his face, moving down his chest, pausing at his nipples, where the tip of her tongue drew circles and licked the sensitive tips.

He felt a fullness developing in his groin as her kisses proceeded down his stomach, and then stopped. Suddenly, something hot and tight, yet soft, enveloped his swollen pintle. Andy's conscious state returned.

"Oh, my God!" he moaned.

Helen's breath was in his ear again. This time she was panting hot air.

"Andy, it's time. I want you to lie very still. Remember your injured left shoulder. Don't try to move it. I've tied cloth straps on your right arm and across your neck. Try not to move. I'm taking off the blindfold."

Andy's eyes struggled to focus. Helen's naked body materialized, framed by a soft glow from the hearth. Her long, blonde hair cascaded over her shoulders, and the pupils of her blue eyes were dilated wide as she swung her knee over and straddled him. She then took hold of his engorged pintle and slipped it inside. Leaning forward, she placed the palms of both hands on his chest. He could see her pendulous, round breasts swinging freely over his chest as she began to move her hips back and forth.

Rhythmic contractions moved up from the base of his pintle. It was all he could do to keep from exploding.

"Not yet," whispered Helen huskily. "Just relax and enjoy."

She stopped moving, leaned down and kissed him deeply. He kissed back and tried to rise up to meet her, but found that he couldn't.

"Shhhhh! Be still." She brushed her breasts back and forth across his chest. Andy desperately wanted to raise his body and wrap his arms around her, but could not.

"It's hard," he said.

"Yes, it is," she replied, smiling.

"No, I mean, it's hard to be still," he explained.

"You don't have a choice."

Andy relaxed his upper body and sank back on the mattress. They were both still for a moment, each enjoying the view. Helen straightened her back and, rhythmically, began to move again, her hips rotating up and down and around, slowly at first, then picking up speed. Andy realized that he could move his hips, too, and got in sync, matching her motion. He could feel pressure building from deep inside. He clenched his jaw and tried to forcibly hold it back. They were both now thrusting furiously, up and down, round and round. Andy felt like screaming, but muffled it. Helen was panting and moaning, louder and louder. An explosion was building. They could both feel it. Nothing could stop it; it was inevitable.

"Do it! Do it!" gasped Helen. The Apotheosis was imminent.

Then it blew. Helen could feel it gush up inside. Andy's back arched and he could feel his eyes roll back in their sockets. He could no longer stifle the scream, and it came out, full-throated.

Helen collapsed on his chest, quivering, out of breath. Andy was coughing, and then realized he was straining against the cloth strap across his neck. He relaxed his muscles and sank back down. They both lay there for what seemed a long while, until their breathing returned to normal. Helen loosened his straps and he flung his right arm around her back and squeezed her tightly.

"If that's what it means to be a sacrificial lamb, I'll happily volunteer any time," he mumbled.

"Good, I won't let you forget it," she whispered in his ear.

Andy lay in a euphoric stupor, flat on his back, vaguely aware of a sensation of small bubbles popping in his brain. Helen rolled off and lay on her back at his side, her head cradled in the crook of his right arm. Both were motionless, gazing at the ceiling.

At length Andy murmured, "I've never had such a wonderful dream. What did you do to my head?"

"You mean besides the sex?"

"Aye."

"Oh, something Rachel taught me."

Andy was puzzled. The wondrous experience he just had was something her stepmother had taught her?

"What?"

"I gave you a herb potion. It cleanses the mind."

"Wow! It did that all right," Andy exclaimed, his head still swirling. What was in it?"

"Flouer 'hemp," Helen answered, a smirk on her face.

Andy wondered how a hemp potion could create such an effect. Helen explained as best she could. Rachel was skilled at growing all manner of herbs. She had an herb garden out in the courtyard orchard where they had gone to talk the night before leaving Lochnaw. As a girl, Helen had helped Rachel plant, tend and harvest the herbs. They gathered the leaves, buds and flowers, dried them and placed them in glass containers.

Rachel would boil the dried buds from the hemp plants to make potions, which she sometimes gave to Helen's father, Baron Andrew Agnew, when he was stressed, usually after a battle involving many deaths. Sir Andrew had many frightening nightmares at these times, and Rachel found that the potion would ease his mind.

"I was concerned about you for the same reason," Helen confided. "Also, of course, I had my own selfish reasons."

Andy smiled. "It worked well." Both his mind and body felt refreshed and clean.

"Did you have visions," Helen asked. "Rachel said that Father often did."

"Yes, many beautiful visions. I remember one in particular."

He then told her about seeing his parents beside him and Ree arriving in a black coach, stepping out and joining them. They were so beautiful and happy. He believed they were together in heaven.

"It is such a relief to know that," he sighed, "you cannot imagine how much better I feel. And, to know that I have ye, here on Earth, my heart is so full. I am very happy."

"My sweet Andrew, I am so glad. I could never love you more than I do right now."

A few moments later they both fell into a deep, peaceful sleep.

The next day, during breakfast, Andy shared his vision with the rest of the family, avoiding any mention of what caused it. Ann and Hugh were young again. They were sitting on a pile of leaves in the oak grove where the family had spent that cold night after the burning of the bastle house. Dressed in the finest of garments, they were talking about building a magnificent mansion at that very spot. A beautiful black coach drawn by white horses arrived. Ree, also dressed in glittering finery, got out and joined them. They were all so happy. Andy imagined they were in heaven.

Family members were surprised at this story since Andy was known to be a practical man—not given to fancy. But, as they began to realize he was more complex, his words helped even more to lift the load they all carried.

# 38.

# SEASONS

SOON spring was just around the corner. Andy's shoulder injury had healed and finishing touches were being completed on the Big House. Despite its bitter beginning, 1548 held promise to turn out to be a good year. There was still a chill in the air, but the trees, shrubs and flowers were beginning to bud as the sun's arc lengthened and the days grew longer.

At supper one evening Joe and Ally failed to show up. Helen asked Martha to check and see if they were still in their rooms. She discovered Ally was in her room and asked if she wanted any supper. Ally responded she was not feeling well and would come down later. When she went to check on Joe, he was not in his room. She searched outside and didn't find him there either, and reported what she had found. Andy thought this was strange for Joe was always hungry and came to supper religiously.

"Maybe he is outside at the stables or barn," he said, "He'll show up eventually. Let's go on without him."

Everyone finished, and the table was being cleaned. Joe had not shown. Andy decided to go out and take a walk around. As he was leaving, he met Harold in the entryway. Harold looked at him quizzically, and Andy told him Joe had not shown for supper and he was going out look for him. Harold cleared his throat and heaved a big sigh.

"Nay need for that, Sire, I think I know what the trouble is. Let's go for a ride and I'll tell you."

They decided to ride around the perimeter of the barmkin wall to see if any of the mature female animals had calved.

"What is the trouble?" Andy said with a hint of irritation in his voice.

If it concerned Joe, he had learned from experience, it was often not good news.

"Its not a pleasant matter to talk about," Harold said, "but necessary."

Harold explained that, as he was walking by the stables around mid-afternoon, he heard noises coming from inside. A female voice was sobbing. He stopped and listened and realized it was Ally's voice. "She was begging: "Joe, let me up, please—I don't want to do this."

"Then I heard Joe growl in a gruff voice for her to shut up, he would do as he pleased. This was followed immediately by the smack of flesh upon flesh and a panicked yelp from Ally. I quickly surmised what was happening—Joe was hitting Ally. A rape was going on or about to start. I pushed open the stable door and charged in."

Andy was listening closely, his face getting more flushed by the second. "What did you find inside?"

"I found Ally lying on her back on the ground with her smock pulled up and Joe between her legs with his trousers down. I grabbed Joe by the scruff of his collar, jerked him off and slammed him against the stall railing. Ally jumped up and ran out, with a bloody nose and the back of her smock blotched with horse manure."

"Did Joe offer any explanation?"

"Joe was busy pulling up his trousers, his prick still stiff. He did threaten me—saying this was none of my business and I should keep my mouth shut if I knew what was good for me."

"What happened then?"

"I told Joe that raping a helpless girl *was* my business, and if he took a swing at me and he'd wish he hadn't. He stood there for a moment, his fists clenched, then hurriedly left without another word. I went back inside the Big House to Ally's room, and called to her, asking if she was all right. Still whimpering, she said she was, and just wanted to be left alone."

After Harold confided the story, Andy was furious. His face grew white as a murderous rage built in his chest. Harold had seen that look on Andy's face before and urged him to avoid anything rash.

"Remember, he be your brother," Harold cautioned in a calm voice.

Slowly, Andy's anger subsided a bit and a plan took shape in his mind. It was time for Joe to go for military training at the War College in Irvine anyway, and that would get him away from Ally and out of Andy's hair for a good while.

The training at Irvine traditionally took about two years, with time off to go home during crop planting and harvest seasons. That wouldn't be necessary for Joe as they had plenty of help already. The way Andy was feeling at the moment, he didn't particularly care if he ever saw Joe again. He decided to send Joe off the next day accompanied by two of the Lochnaw men-at-arms to make sure he got there. He would leave the tuition money with the Lochnaw men to be paid to the college commander upon Joe's arrival. Instructions were to be left that Joe was to get no leave to come home except at Lammas and Christmas, or if case of dire emergency. They were also to explain to the commander that Joe was to stay at least through autumn of this year before being released for any reason, and that his training was to be "vigorous and demanding." The commander would understand what that meant.

After the ride with Harold, Andy found Joe back in his room and confronted him about Ally. As expected, he blamed it on the girl, claiming that she "led him on."

Andy was having none of it, becoming even angrier at the obvious lie.

"Did she lead your fists to her face as well?" he thundered.

Joe just stood there, looking sullen.

Barely able to contain his ire, Andy explained that he did not want to hear of Joe being involved in such an escapade again.

"If I do," he growled, "do not expect that I will be as merciful as I am now."

Andy told him that he would be leaving for Irvine early the next morning, and he best get ready.

"I won't go. You can't make me," Joe said defiantly.

"We'll see about that," Andy said.

Glowering, Joe spread his legs in a fighting stance and balled up his fists. That proved to be a big mistake. Andy smacked him with a hard left to the nose, mashing it with a sickening sound, like a ripe melon. Joe staggered back just as Andy slammed him with a right to his stomach, doubling him over. Andy then kicked him hard in the side. Knocked into the wall, Joe crumpled to the floor, his nose bloody and his face contorted into a grotesque sneer. He did not try to get up.

"You will go and you will stay," seethed Andy, "or you will die. Your choice. Now get out of my sight." Early the next morning, sporting a red swollen nose, Joe left for Irvine with two Lochnaw men-at-arms on either side. Andy had already taken Helen aside, apprised her of what had happened, and of his plan for dealing with Joe. They decided not to tell the other family members. It would just get everyone upset and do no good. For the time being they would act as if it was just the normal time for Joe to go for his training.

✦ ✦ ✦

Spring had now blossomed and the days were lengthening. Crops were being planted and grain seeds sown. If the weather cooperated, and the summer was hot with an occasional rain, a good harvest was in the offing. One clear, sunny day in late spring, Andy and Harold rode out around the shire, checking on tenant farmers and crofters to see how things were with them and their families, and also to inspect the condition of their fields. All fields were found to be in excellent shape, likely to produce an abundant harvest.

They got back to the Big House around dusk and handed their horses off to the stable boys to be fed and rubbed down. Andy was hungry, anticipating a big meal. As he walked down the central hall, he could smell inviting aromas from the kitchen. Helen walked out and, seeing him in the hallway, she rushed up to give him a hug and inquire about his day.

They went into the great hall to sit and talk while awaiting the meal. Harold walked by and they invited him to come join them. After some casual chatter about the quality of the crops and the expectation of a bountiful harvest, Harold commented: "Many fiefdoms made a practice of holding big festivals, often spread out over the year to coincide with the seasons. When I was growing up, they celebrated the old Gaelic pagan festivals - Imbolc on February 1 for start of spring, now Valentine's day; Beltane on May 1 for beginning of summer; Lammas on August 1 for start of the harvest season; and Samhain on November 1 for end of harvest and beginning of winter, now Hallowe'en. These were known as 'quarter' days, and all tenant farmers and tradesmen around the shire, along with their families, were invited into the Laird's house for a celebration; and—most important—after harvest, to pay their rent and carried-over debt."

Andy said, as a boy, he had often heard of these seasons, and he liked the last part about tenants paying off rent and debt after harvest.

"So you entice them by having a festival and collect your money at the same time? I like it."

✦ ✦ ✦

After Harold left and she was alone with her husband, Helen said, "I almost forgot. I've got a little secret to share with you."

"Really, what?"

"While you and Harold were out today, I was leaving the kitchen and heard a noise coming from the broom closet under the stairs."

"What kind of noise?"

"Rustling and moaning."

"Rodents?" asked Andy.

"Nay, rodents don't moan silly," chuckled Helen, "I looked through a crack and saw two human bodies stretched out on the floor, embracing and kissing."

Andy did not reply but waited for more explanation.

"After my eyes adjusted to the dim light, I could see it was Ally and Jamie."

"Just kissing," Andy asked, "Er, nothing more?"

"Nay, I don't think so. Both were fully clothed."

"So is there some problem?"

"Not necessarily," Helen responded, "but you do realize Ally is pregnant."

Andy raised his eyebrows in surprise, "Ah … nay, I didn't. I did of course know she had been, er, exposed, but by Joe."

Helen explained the source of her concern. Ally had told her a couple of months ago that her cycles had stopped and she was often sick at her stomach upon awaking. That, Helen knew, was a very reliable sign that she was pregnant. Perhaps Ally had enticed Jamie to have sex so he would think he was the father. Asked about it, Ally stoutly denied she had had sex with Jamie and said he already knew about Joe.

"Have you talked to Jamie about it?" inquired Andy.

"Nay, I thought you should do it. He's your brother after all."

"All right, I'll do it," Andy said with a hint of irritation in his voice.

Reluctantly, Andy went to look for Jamie. He found him helping Martha in the kitchen.

"Lets go out back," he said. Jamie followed.

"I heard about you and Ally necking in the broom closet," Andy said.

" So," Jamie answered, sounding defiant.

"I brought you out here because we need to discuss Ally. She is pregnant. That's because Joe raped her. It's the reason I banished him to Irvine. You realize that do you not?"

"Aye, I know about it," Jamie said, "but I don't care—I love her. I'll help her take care of the baby after it is born. I hope to marry her some day."

Andy rubbed the week's growth of stubble on his chin. There was no reason to doubt the boy. Jamie was a kind, caring person, dependable and hard working. He was 13 and Ally not quite a year older. By the time the baby was born, Jamie would have turned 14 and Ally would be 15. They were not children anymore. Perhaps this would turn out to be good for all. If everything went well, by autumn the family would have a new babe.

"You'd be taking on a big responsibility."

"I'm aware of that too."

‧ ‧ ‧

In no time it seemed, summer was drawing to a close. It had been a near perfect season, lazy, hot days, warm nights and thundershowers spaced out just right to keep the crops healthy and growing. By August everyone was expecting a bountiful harvest, the best in years. The Lammas celebration they had planned for the first of November would be festive indeed, especially for the Henderson household, as their crofters, tradesmen and freeholders would be flush with money and goods from the harvest. All should be in good spirits, with cupboards and storerooms full. There would be plenty left over to pay rent and overdue debt to the laird. Good harvests, particularly of grains, put a smile on everyone's face.

In late November another treat came along. Ally had her babe, an active, healthy girl they named Grace. Immediately everyone started calling her "Gracie." Jamie was as excited by the new arrival as anyone had ever seen him. Before the babe was born, he waited on Ally excessively, always asking if she needed something, worrying that she might be overdoing. He hovered over her so closely that she frequently had to order him out of the room. After Gracie was born, he carried her around like the proudest parent ever, showing her off like a prized colt. His only disappointment was that he desperately wanted to marry Ally, but she kept putting him off.

"Jamie, I love you, I really do," Ally said, "I know you would make a fine father for little Grace, but this is a new experience for both of us. I think we should wait awhile. By next year, if you still feel the same, maybe I'll be ready."

Feeling a hint of hope, Jamie pledged that he would always love her and the baby. He did not want to rush her but wanted her to know he considered Gracie to be his own flesh and blood.

Nothing would make him happier than to formalize their relationship by marriage.

# 39.
## ꓢEW ARRIVALS

IN mid-December, an early cold front from the north descended over Blackcraigshire, accompanied by snowstorms. The Big House and surrounding areas were covered in a foot of the white stuff. While beautiful, it rendered all travel by wheeled vehicles impossible. Fortunately, the residents of Big House had plenty of food and firewood, so they settled in to await more favorable weather.

Late one afternoon, while most family members were in the great room as the evening meal was being prepared, Jamie ran in and shouted to Andy, "Harold says riders are approaching—five of them!"

Andy, followed by Jamie, quickly ran to the west tower, sprinting up the stairs, and mounted the top parapet where they found Harold peering into the snowy gloom.

"They are just now reaching the switchbacks," Harold said.

"Any idea who they are?"

"Not sure," Harold answered. "By the size of their horses and manner of riding, I would say they be military men. They are heavily wrapped against the cold, and I can't see their faces."

Andy looked out and saw five large horses, mixed-breed Clydesdales, most likely. He noticed, too, that the riders all carried broadswords over their cloaks. He called for two of his men with longbows to stand on the parapets so they could draw down on the strangers in case of trouble. He and Harold would meet them at the front gate, and Jamie, armed with a crossbow, would guard their backs from the front door.

Andy and Harold were standing just outside the front door as the riders pushed their horses into the courtyard through the open front gate.

"I know that man!" Harold exclaimed. "The lead rider be Donald Douglas from Lochnaw Castle."

Harold thought the other men were also guards from Lochnaw. Andy stepped forward as the men pulled to a stop.

"State your business and do not touch your weapons. Each of you has arrows aimed at your chest."

"I am Donald Douglas, Laird Henderson. We came from Lochnaw. Harold there can vouch for us."

"Aye, I can," Harold responded, smiling. "What brings you all this way in such weather?"

"We have news, and also wonder if you could put us up for the night."

Harold nodded to Andy, who then agreed.

"Of course. Dismount and come in. Leave your horses. I'll see they are attended to."

The men came in. Andy asked Jamie to get the stableboys to see to the horses and for Harold to show the men to the armory to shed their heavy wraps and weapons. They would then meet in the great hall. Andy went in search of Helen to tell her they had visitors who would require a hot meal and overnight lodging. Wood was added to the large hearth in the great hall, and soon a big fire was blazing.

"Welcome to my house," said Andy. He knew they were cold and hungry and invited them to pull up chairs and thaw out around the hearth. Soon hot food would be brought in. In the meantime Martha would bring each of them a steaming mug of cider. When they were all comfortable, Andy addressed Donald Douglas.

"You said you had news?"

Donald indicated they had left Lochnaw Castle three days earlier. Flashing a wide grin beneath a long, black mustache mingled with sparkling droplets of water from the melted snow, he joked: "Perhaps we should have waited for better weather." They all laughed, and the mood became noticeably more convivial.

Donald launched into his story. Ten days ago a group of a dozen Fergusson clansmen arrived at Lochnaw Castle. They were led by John Fergusson, the youngest son of clan chieftain, Alpin Fergusson. Rachel Agnew, Baron Agnew's widow, was John Fergusson's first cousin. Rachel invited her cousin and the other men into the castle and put them up in grand style. She instructed all the servants and guards that they were her kin and would be staying there for a long while. The servants were to obey all of them the same as they would her.

Two days later, a contingent of English cavalry arrived, numbering about 30. They were obviously expected, as instructions were given to the guards by John Fergusson to let them in, stable their horses and escort them to the castle keep. The next night Donald secretly sent word around for all of the castle guards, some 20 of them, to meet at the front tower. Donald became head guardsman after Harold and Helen left with Andrew Henderson. Like Harold, Donald and many of the guardsmen were Black Douglases.

At the meeting at Lochnaw Castle after the English cavalry arrived, all of the guards agreed that they had no choice but to leave Lochnaw Castle and scatter in small groups to wherever they could find refuge.

"We simply could not stomach being under the thumb of Rachel Agnew and the Fergussons," Donald said. "Not to mention having to bow down to those pompous English cavalrymen."

"What!" joked Harold, "you didn't like boot black?"

Donald gave Harold a disgusted glare, not responding to the jest. Continuing with the story, he explained that he and his men decided to go to Blackcraigshire mainly because they were aware that Harold and his cousin Nathan Douglas had already gone. Also they all kindly regarded Helen Agnew and knew of her wagon train departure with Andrew. Other guards decided to go to relatives and acquaintances across Southwest Scotland, he said. Some were going to the Kennedy clan stronghold at Castle Dunure.

"Please be assured we're all very pleased to have you here," Andy said.

"Thank you, Sire," replied Donald. "We're glad to be here. I have some additional information that might interest you. Several of the guards reported that they had talked with some of Lady Rachel's household servants. The servants said they were very disappointed and concerned at having the English soldiers there, and of the prospect of having to bow and scrape to serve them. Many expressed that they would like to escape. The servants had also picked up some interesting tidbits overheard from conversations between Rachel and John Fergusson."

"I would certainly like to know about anything the servants overheard between John Fergusson and Rachel Agnew," Andy said.

Donald provided a summary of the gossip. They said that when Rachel learned of the deaths of her husband, Baron Andrew, and his brother, Gilbert, at the Battle of Pinkie, she did not seem particularly distraught. She immediately started scheming about how she could assert the sheriffship of Wigtownshire for her six-year-old son, William. She was concerned that it might devolve to Gilbert Agnew's son, Blair, if she did not move quickly. Rachel wanted help in this effort from the Fergusson clan. John Fergusson indicated the clan was willing to help her, but only as a part of *their* overall goal, which was to secure coastal Galloway, from Wigtown all the way to Lochnaw, into the Fergusson fiefdom. The time to mount this conquest was nearing, John Fergusson told her.

In addition, Donald had heard credible reports that the occupying English forces might be called back to England. Edward Seymour, the Duke of Somerset and commander of the English army at Pinkie, had lost influence with the English court. The cost of barracking his soldiers in Scotland had created a significant drain on the English crown's finances. Additionally, the English privy council was dissatisfied with Somerset for failing to press his advantage and take the Scottish capital, Edinburgh, after the victory at Pinkie. There was even speculation that Somerset might be forced to relinquish his regency of his nephew, the young English king, Edward VI.

"In my opinion," Donald said, "a recall of the English troops is likely to create a power vacuum along the borders area, such that it will be tempting for the Fergusson and Maxwell clans to swoop out of their strongholds and push west across Galloway in a conquest campaign. The two clans can assemble a large, well-trained force, plenty capable of defeating almost anyone who opposes them. It is my belief the English cavalry was brought in to help train their horsemen."

There was dead silence in the room as everyone contemplated the dreadful consequences if all of this came to pass.

Andy broke the silence by putting into words what they all were thinking. "I have been worried about the English troops being recalled for some time now. Donald's information confirms those fears. If it were to happen, we here at the Big House would need to be much better prepared than we are now. We stand right in the path of anyone who wants to take over Galloway. I have no doubt that is the ambition of the Fergusson and Maxwell clans. We need more fighting men, horses and arms."

"Sire," Donald said, "You may rest assured that my men and I will join vigorously in any fight that threatens Blackcraigshire. And I have an idea how you might obtain extra horses."

Donald related that he and his men left Lochnaw Castle in the dead of night after everyone had retired. A cold front had come in, he explained, producing snow. As they had gathered their belongings and were getting their horses ready, the snowstorm grew worse. This was fortunate, he said, as it muffled sound and reduced visibility. They were able to leave by the main front gate without attracting anyone's attention. The English cavalry horses were stabled in the barns inside the castle's front wall.

"As we left, we opened the barn gates and drove the horses out the main entrance, then down the road through the snow for a considerable distance. The English will have a hard time finding and catching them. But I believe we can do both."

Andy and Harold listened to Donald Douglas' account with both appreciation and apprehension. The English cavalry horses would help if they could be caught, and Donald and his men would strengthen their fighting force, but much more was needed. Serious thought and planning had to be started immediately.

That night, Andy planned to sleep with Helen in her bed-chamber. For one thing, it was long past the stage where he felt obligated to keep a separate room for the sake of appearances; for another, his room was needed to accommodate the extra men, and finally, he had a lot he needed to discuss with her.

After everyone had eaten and retired for the night, Andy pulled Harold aside. "It sounds like the English troops might leave soon."

Harold scoffed, "I don't know. Those sorry bastards will want to laze around and sup at the feeding trough for as long as they can."

# 40.
# A Plan to Fight Back

AT the top of the stairs, Andy closed the door to Helen's chamber and found her waiting for him.

"Helen, I've much news to tell you. Harold and I just had a long talk with Donald Douglas and the other guards from Lochnaw."

"Och, I know all about that."

"About the Fergussons and the English cavalry?"

"Aye, I was listening at the door. I heard everything."

"You did?" exclaimed Andy, sounding surprised.

"You men—your voices are so loud and carry so far. No wonder you can never keep a secret."

"Well, what do you think?" asked Andy.

"I think 1549 will be an interesting year."

That was a comment Andy did not expect. He was curious about her meaning. Helen explained.

"Look, it's true that Rachel and the Fergussons will have a good opportunity, but we will have a good one, too—even better than theirs, I think."

"I'm afraid I don't follow," replied Andy.

Consider this," said Helen. "The Fergussons want to take all of Galloway, and Rachel wants William to have the Wigtownshire sheriffship. Why are they in any better position to have those things than we are?"

Andy protested, "We're just a small shire up here in the hills. We can't possibly compete with…"

Helen cut him off.

"Yes, we can!" she exclaimed. She was not thinking it could happen in their present condition, she emphasized, "but we can become stronger if we're smart and work at it. We just need to plan and prepare better than the Fergussons," she argued, "and we need to expand—more men, more arms, more people, more fortifications, more livestock, more wealth, more everything."

Blair Agnew had a better claim on the sheriffship than William, she said. William was still just a small boy. Gilbert Agnew had been a very popular sheriff in Wigtownshire. Blair would be, too, if they helped him. And Rachel—she would not be seen as an Agnew, but for what she was—a scheming Fergusson. The Douglases were still feared and respected throughout the south of Scotland. They could bring most of the former guards from Lochnaw on board at the Big House. They already had nine, including Harold, Nathan and Donald.

"Don't you see? We must beat them at their own game, or they will smash us to bits!"

Andy was surprised at the emotion with which Helen had made these comments. Clearly, she had already given the matter a great deal of thought. And, Andy realized, what she said made a lot of sense. There was no question about the Fergussons' desire to take over Galloway and become the preeminent clan in the south of Scotland. If the Fergussons were successful, they would not tolerate a small enemy shire such as Blackcraigshire on their northern border.

"I see what you are saying, and I think I agree," Andy said, "but that is sure a lot to accomplish in a short time."

"Yes, it is," agreed Helen, "but what other choice do we have?"

Andy replied with a wry smile.

"Do nothing and become easy prey?"

Not only did he have the most beautiful woman in the world and the best lover, but also the smartest political strategist. Would she ever stop surprising him?

The next morning after breakfast they all gathered in the great hall. In addition to Helen, Harold, Nathan and Donald, Andy had invited the rest of the family—Jamie, along with Blair Agnew and his two sisters, Maggie and Ally. With the importance of the decisions they were about to make, he felt the entire family should be there. He first shared the news brought by Donald Douglas and the other Lochnaw men, and then began to summarize the plan they had discussed.

Helen knew her stepmother well and was able to shed light on her character and intentions. Rachel was born a Fergusson and was now free to assist her kinsmen with their strategy to take over Galloway. Rachel's main goal, Helen said, was to secure the sheriffship of Wigtownshire for her young son, William.

Harold added his part. At the Big House, he said, they were not particularly strong at the moment, but they had a good opportunity to become stronger. The Lochnaw guards were very loyal to Lady Helen and the Agnew family. They had fought alongside Sir Hugh Henderson, now regarded a hero for beating back the English attack on Lochnaw Castle. Harold brought four men with him and five additional men had come yesterday. All of them were Black Douglases, members of Scotland's most powerful clan for hundreds of years.

"Let me give those of you who might not know," Harold said, "a brief history of the Black Douglases. I think this will give you a good understanding of why we are so lucky to have them on our side."

The Black Douglases, Harold explained, had been one of the most powerful clans in Scotland for centuries. They were defeated a hundred years ago when their stronghold at Threave Castle was overrun by soldiers and clansmen loyal to Scottish King James II. Following the defeat, the king dissolved the Douglas earlship, and all its lands were forfeited to the Scottish crown. With their clan seat and earlship destroyed, the once proud and powerful Black Douglas clan scattered across Scotland. The principal clan leading the plot against them was the Maxwell, supported by its allies, the Fergusson. It was particularly galling to the Douglases that the King had awarded custody of their ancient seat, Threave Castle, to the Maxwells. All remaining Black Douglases, no matter where they ended up, still felt a bitter hatred against these two clans.

"Waw!" exclaimed Helen, "I have heard from childhood that the Black Douglases were a powerful group. That's why my father favored them as castle guards at Lochnaw. But I never knew the story of why."

"Speaking for us all, m'Lady," said Donald, "we Douglases are very pleased to have served at Lochnaw Castle. We have great respect and affection for the Agnew family."

Helen nodded her head. "We have always appreciated it."

Harold laughed, "Now that I have patted myself and my kinsmen on the back, I suppose we'll have to live up to our reputation. Fortunately we have time to prepare for whatever might come. No one expects the Fergussons or the Maxwells to try any serious mischief so long as the English troops are stationed in Scotland. As to the Wigtownshire sheriffship, Blair will have strong support from the Wigtown townspeople and others all across the shire."

Blair stepped forward at a pause in the conversation. He was nervous, but spoke firmly. "Thank all of you for what you have said. To the Douglases, I want to say this. Though I am still young—I will be 18 on my birthday—I am strong and determined to honor my father and take his place as sheriff of Wigtownshire. Also, I want to thank my Aunt Helen, Laird Henderson and Harold. If it had not been for their kindness and bravery in rescuing my sisters and me, we would not be here today."

Helen was seated on the bench running the length of the great table, flanked by Maggie and Ally who were each clutching her arms and looking frightened. Helen smiled, "Why, thank you, Blair. We are so glad to have all of you here."

Andy stressed it was time for Blair to intensify his military training. He could not become an effective and respected sheriff unless he had significant fighting skills like his father. Andy would help when he could, but would assign most of the training to the Lochnaw men-at-arms, with Nathan Douglas in charge. Blair would be outfitted with one of their best cavalry horses, tack, personal armor and weapons. He would be expected to train every day.

Concluding the conversation, Andy emphasized: "We are now part of one big family and must hold together no matter what troubles come. We need to get ahead of the Fergussons and their allies. In that respect, it is important that we reinforce ties with our friends and allies, and develop new ones wherever we can."

Helen and Andy discussed with everyone in the room a general timeline for proceeding with a plan. Andy emphasized anew the need for other allies. "That's something we should work on right away," he said. "First we identify those we might have success with. Donald Douglas mentioned that several of the guards who left Lochnaw Castle were going with the Kennedy clan at Dunure Castle. The Kennedys are known to fiercely oppose anything English. Also they have no regard for the Fergussons after their cowardly double-dealing with the English forces leading up to the battle at Pinkie."

Andy reminded everyone that the Fergussons had promised Arran they would muster many fighting men to join his army, but furnished only a few, and they were simple yeomen, inexperienced and without adequate arms. They had kept their best men at home, all the while taking money from the English for access to the coast road across Galloway.

The Kennedys had furnished several hundred well-armed and experienced troops, most of whom had died at Pinkie. They, and other clans who lost men at Pinkie, still felt a lot of animosity and bitterness toward the Fergussons.

"As some of you know," Andy said, "my aunt, Margaret Wallace, my mother's older sister, is married to Lord Gilbert Kennedy, the Kennedy clan chieftain and the Earl of Cassillis. Lady Margaret is quite similar to my mother, a force in her own right. Perhaps I can arrange to pay a visit to her and the earl, and renew acquaintances."

Helen added that, as a child, she remembered Lord Kennedy coming to Lochnaw Castle to visit with her father. It was her impression that the Agnews got along well with the Kennedys. Since the Kennedy lands joined at the north, she was sure that the Kennedys wouldn't want the Agnew stronghold at Lochnaw Castle to fall into the hands of the Fergussons.

"The Kennedys have a fierce reputation," Andy said, "they are feared and respected. It would be great to have them as allies."

He added, with a wry smile: "With the Kennedy clan chieftain married to a Wallace, and Wallace lands bordering to the northeast, it also seems a good time for Helen and me to visit my grandfather, Darrow Wallace, the Earl of Carluke."

"Before visiting all of these famous relatives of yours, don't you think we should get married?" Helen said abruptly. There was a short silence in the room as everyone looked at her in surprise. She burst out laughing, relieving the tension. They all joined in.

# 41.
# Nuptial Preparations

A COUPLE of weeks after the year 1549 was ushered in, two women named Agatha and Coira arrived at the Big House in a one-horse buggy. The women were there to check on a job they had heard about from Priest Thomas Copeland of Wigtown. He had inquired if they would like to help Laird Andrew Henderson and his betrothed, Lady Helen Agnew, with the planning of a marriage ceremony and celebration. In the back of the buggy were two trunks. The women obviously came prepared to stay for as long as needed.

Agatha, the older of the two, was in her late 30s. She was thin and tall, had prematurely greying long brownish hair done up in a bun and wore a perpetually serious expression. She had lived in Wigtown all her life. The younger one, Coria, was in her mid 20s, with red hair and a round face that usually carried a friendly smile. She was shorter, somewhat plump, and had a bubbly, vivacious personality. Originally from Wigtown, Coria had moved away when she was a teenager and ended up working for a merchant in Glasgow City. When he died, she moved back to Wigtown and joined up with Agatha.

Helen met with the two women. She told them that the marriage ceremony itself would be held on the afternoon of May 1 in St. Ninian's Chapel at Whithorn. The chapel was a small stone building located near a seaside cave where tradition held that the Christian saint Ninian began his ministry in the fourth century A.D. It had a small nave and a simple chancel and altar. Due to the small size of the chapel, which would hold only about 50 standing people, the couple wanted a small, simple exchange of vows attended by family. The Prior at Whithorn, second in rank in the diocese only to the Archbishop of Glasgow, had agreed to perform the nuptials.

Just up the road from the chapel stood Whithorn Priory that served as the cathedral for the diocese of Galloway founded in the twelfth century by Fergus, Lord of Galloway. For hundreds of years, the area had been a famous pilgrimage site, visited by most of the monarchs of Scotland at one time or another. The Cathedral itself was not grand, but was considerably larger than the chapel. Due to the frequent pilgrimages by royalty and other important people, the Cathedral was very generously endowed. It was blessed with an opulent interior and fine stained-glass windows. This is where the couple wanted to hold the reception and feast. Helen would be in overall charge of the entire affair, and volunteered her two nieces, Maggie and Ally, to help in any way they could.

After the newly married couple had had an opportunity to consummate their marriage vows and rest up, they wanted to hold a large gathering at the Big House to celebrate and rejoice. The servants and cottars who worked the shire, the various craftsmen practicing their trades, the men-at-arms and guards, the overseers, the household help, and all their families would be invited. Also the residents of Wigtown who were friends of the Agnew family were to be included. Agnes and Coria were impressed by the quality of the locales for the events and by the amount of work it would require. They settled on a pay rate with Helen and announced that they were ready to get started.

"Och, we have much work to do, and wee time to do it," exclaimed Coria, looking at her cohort, Agatha, with an alarmed expression.

'Then we had better get started!" rejoined Agatha pointedly.

The two women, assisted by Helen and the two Agnew girls, were soon busy with the plans for the wedding and reception. The first thing on the list was to reserve St. Ninian's Chapel and Whithorn Priory for the wedding ceremony and reception. Blair Agnew knew the prior, Androu Ancroft, through the parish priest at Wigtown, Thomas Copeland. Blair and Harold Douglas, head of guards at the Big House, rode to Wigtown to meet with the priest, who promptly agreed to go with them to Whithorn. Priest Copeland believed it would be helpful for him to intercede with the Prior Ancroft, who tended to be overly protective of the priory and chapel.

After all, they were among the most ancient Christian buildings in Scotland and of great historical importance. Fortunately, once the prior learned the identity of the betrothed couple, he had no hesitation. He fondly regarded the Agnew family and knew the story of Hugh Henderson's brave and successful defense of Lochnaw Castle against the invading English a few years back.

"I have no doubt, had Lochnaw fallen to the English, we here at Whithorn would have been next," he said soberly. "It would be an honor to have such a fine young couple as Lady Helen and Laird Henderson married in the chapel, and of course, the priory cathedral can be made available for the reception." The prior assured them that everything would be in fine order and sparkling clean when the grand day arrived, and the parish's priests-in-training at the nearby monastery would be happy to assist in getting things set up and would be available to do whatever else might be needed on the wedding day. Blair and Priest Copeland thanked him profusely for his kindness. Blair also mentioned that two wedding planners the family had retained for the occasion, and perhaps other members of the Henderson household, would be coming by to set up flowers, decorations and make additional preparations.

"Of course," said the prior unpretentiously, inclining his tonsured head in a slight bow, "if they serve Lady Helen they must be quite accomplished."

There was one more piece of business to complete before they left—a minister to officiate the wedding service. Blair had originally inquired of Priest Copeland if he would do it. He said he would be honored to do so, but thought it more fitting to ask Prior Ancroft, since he was a higher official and governed the affairs of the priory. As they were getting ready to leave, Blair asked the prior if he was in a position to officiate the service, mentioning that both Lady Helen and Laird Henderson wished it and had asked him to inquire.

"Of course," answered Prior Ashcroft without hesitation, "I would be delighted."

Another important item was the guest list. Andy and Helen had decided that only family members would be invited to the wedding ceremony itself. First, the chapel where the vows were to be exchanged was small, and second, Helen and Andy wanted a small, intimate ceremony. For the reception, however, they planned to invite a large crowd, including prominent merchants, craftsmen and religious leaders in Wigtown, as well as contingents from the Wallace and Kennedy clans, remnants of the scattered Douglases, and other noblemen, knights, men-at-arms and their ladies who could become important allies. Helen knew a good number of influential people from the Rhinns peninsula, many being former neighbors who did not feel kindly toward her mother-in-law, Rachel Agnew. She also knew people from nearby Portpatrick who had been friends of her father. There were a lot of people to invite.

In years past, most writing had been done by religious orders on parchment or velum. Paper was scarce, although a few bibles and other works on religion had circulated around Scotland since the invention of the printing press by the German, Herr Gutenberg in the 1450s. His development of movable type and a more efficient means of making paper from soaked wood fibers and animal hair made mass production of paper and printed material much more widespread. Coria knew of a print shop in Glasgow City where items such as printed invitations could be produced on fine paper. Such invitations could be made to look very attractive by use of different colored inks and artistic scrollwork, she explained. The custom was generally to send the formal invitation only to the mistress or master of a household with an enumeration of guests indicated, either by name or rank. The mistress or master would see that the word was passed around.

"A wonderful idea," Helen bubbled enthusiastically, "let's do it!"

One other thing was needed from the print shop—notices of the upcoming wedding to be placed in conspicuous public places. This was a requirement of the Catholic Church so that any person who had good reason to object to the marriage could learn of it, along with the place and date it was to occur. Agatha had three posters made. They were tacked up at Whithorn Priory, to the mercat cross in the market square at Wigtown and to the front door at the Big House.

With the wedding plans coming together nicely, Helen and Andy turned their attention to the big celebration to follow at the Big House. They expected a large crowd and planned to put on a festive banquet. Helen wondered if they could arrange some entertainers to liven up the party, such as musicians, jesters, minstrels and jugglers.

Coria came to the rescue. Before joining Agatha, she had worked with a travelling minstrel band and later was hired by a wealthy merchantman in Glasgow City to plan his parties. She would have no problem in arranging jovial entertainment for the crowd by contacting her old friends.

As the big day neared, everyone was busy with the final preparations. Agatha placed an order from a millinery shop in Glasgow City. Included were a large bolt of bright blue silk, another of brown satin, one of white linen and one more of rose colored, richly decorated silk brocade. She also placed an order for several pelts of mink fur from a furrier. All were to be picked up at the same time as the print work.

She, Coria, Helen and Maggie set to work on making the wedding costumes for both Helen and the two Agnew girls. Helen was to have a long, sweeping blue gown, tight fitting at the waist, with a low bejeweled neckline, emphasizing her curvaceous figure. Over the gown they planned a brocade surcoat with mink fur trim and a gold broach with the Henderson coat of arms. She would have a brown satin headdress, also trimmed with fur, with a white veil. Maggie and Ally were to be dressed alike, with white linen gowns and brown satin surcoats.

To save time, and because Agatha seldom made male clothing, Andy went to a tailor in Wigtown. He took Blair and Jamie with him. Agatha sent a drawing of Helen's outfit, and samples of the fabric she was using. The tailor examined the sketch and samples, took Andy and Blair's measurements and told them to return in one week. Upon their return, the clothing was ready to be tried on. Andy was outfitted with a white linen shirt, buttoned down the front with silver studs, and with sleeves sloping to a tight cuff at the wrist. A brown satin doublet served as an overgarment, reaching to mid-thigh, belted at the waist with a broad leather belt, silver buckle and an engraved silver Henderson coat of arms. A traditional Scots blue bonnet with a white, curling swan feather would top it off.

The two boys had linen shirts, brown woolen knee length trousers with white silk stockings, brown leather shoes with a buttoned strap across the top and brown woolen surcoats. Befitting his position as Laird of Blackcraigshire, Andy would also wear a silver-hilted dirk at his waist.

The weather had been beautiful, the trees fully in leaf, and swathes of flowers were bursting into bloom everywhere. Everything had been planned down to the smallest detail. It was sure to be a fabulous event. What could go wrong?

# 42.
# May Day Marriage

THE first day of May was just around the corner, and preparations for the grand wedding and festival were reaching fever pitch. The wedding ceremony was to occur on May Day, the first day of Beltane, which was associated with renewal of the plants and animals of the earth and the beginning of the planting season when seeds sprouted and grew. It was a most propitious time for a wedding. As they were getting ready for bed one night in late April, the wedding just days away, Andy walked up behind Helen and wrapped his arms around her waist, squeezing her gently and rubbing his several day old growth of bristly beard on the back of her neck.

"Mmm, that feels good," she murmured, "but should we—I mean with the wedding so near and all."

Andy let his hands slide to her belly, "I don't feel much there," he teased, "I thought you had already been, ah, exposed. Is there something you haven't told me?"

Helen had been secretly troubled, though never really coming to grips with it. She had so hoped Andy had gotten her pregnant on that night after their return from Ayr. She desperately wanted a baby. Though her cycles had stopped for a couple of months, they had started again and were now regular. She had not noticed any unusual bleeding or pain, so doubted a miscarriage, but it was clear she was not pregnant. Since then they had been having sex of a regular basis, but there had been no signs of pregnancy. She had begun to worry that she might be barren.

Screwing up her courage, she told all of this to Andy. She expected a disappointed response, but Andy just laughed.

"I guess we need more practice. You realize we're getting married at Beltane, the time of new birth, and we're having a big bonfire at Whithorn. We just need to get covered with plenty of smoke and ash—and have a lot more sex."

Helen smiled. She had a wonderful husband. Some, like England's King Henry, beheaded their wives for not bearing children, males in particular. Her husband just laughed it off and requested more sex. That she could give him, and gladly. But still, that small gnawing feeling in the pit of her stomach didn't go away.

Servants, accompanied by men-at-arms from the major families who would be attending, had arrived early to set up large tents. Each had colorful banners with the family colors streaming in the breeze from high poles. Whithorn Cathedral was bedecked with spring flowers and green sprouting stems and leaves, some weaved into garlands and wreaths. A long table, similarly decorated, ran the length of the nave to the chancel. It would be filled with sumptuous foods and drink for the reception to follow the afternoon after a morning wedding. Lighted silver candelabras wreathed with fresh spring flowers and greenery would complete the décor.

Special care was taken with the Chapel of St. Ninian. A long, richly decorated Persian rug runner, borrowed for the occasion from Lady Margret Kennedy, the sister of Ann, Andy's late mother, ran from the entry to the altar. Flowered wreaths lined the walls and altar area. The altar itself was draped with a floor length white silk covering and held a large, colorfully illustrated, open Bible.

The family tents were spread about the priory grounds near the cathedral. A separate smaller tent, with privacy partitions, was erected between the cathedral and the chapel for use by the bride and her attendants in getting her made-up, dressed and coiffed. The groom and his groomsmen would use the family tent for their preparations. After the wedding ceremony in the morning, the festive reception would follow that afternoon, where copious amounts of food and drink beckoned. Later a big celebration for all participants was planned around a huge Beltaine bonfire on a hill over-looking the sparkling blue Solway Firth.

Andy, Helen and their retinue left the Big House two days be-fore the wedding and arrived one day later in the early afternoon. They were amazed at the work that had already been accom-plished, and the quality and beauty of the arrangements. Everything had been exquisitely prepared. Earl Gilbert Kennedy, husband of Andy's Aunt Margaret, had graciously agreed to give the bride away. Andy's grandfather, Earl Darrow Wallace, would serve as Andy's best man.

As soon as they arrived, Helen hurried off to meet with Earl Kennedy and Lady Margaret, and Andy went in search of the Wallace tent to greet his grandfather. He soon saw the massive tent on a nearby rise with the distinctive blue and yellow banner, embellished with a black hawk, talons barred, flying in the breeze. Several coaches were arranged in a semicircle nearby, and horses were grazing inside a makeshift corral. But, Andy noticed, there were no guards at the door of the tent, nor any other sign of human activity. An uneasy feeling developed deep down in his chest. Something was amiss.

As he approached the front entrance, Duncan Wallace, the Earl's son, abruptly walked out of the tent leaning on his crutch, saw Andy and stopped. As he neared, Andy noticed Duncan had a somber look on his face. His eyes were red and his cheeks were pale.

"Andrew, I'm afraid I have bad news," Duncan said "Pa got here, but he got sick this morning. I think it was his heart—prob-ably too much excitement. Anyway I've had some of our guards take him back to Blackmor. Hopefully he will recover, but he might not. He looked pretty bad when he left. We've not told anyone as I didn't want to dampen the occasion."

Andy felt stricken. His throat grew tight and dry, and his knees turned wobbly. He tried to speak but couldn't. Duncan motioned him to a plain wooden bench beside the entrance and they both sat down. There was a long silence. Finally Andy spoke.

"I so hoped he would be able to stand at my side and hand me the wedding brooch. I pray he'll recover. We can't afford to lose such a powerful and caring man."

"I know," Duncan replied. "That was Pa's fondest dream also, to come here and stand by his grandson as he got married. He gave it his best effort, but unfortunately he's not in the best of health. I'm sorry."

"Such a giant of a man, the greatest chieftain I've known …." Andy said, trailing off, a catch in his throat. Duncan then spoke, his voice thin, eyes moist.

"Even though your brain and your eyes say otherwise, you always think they are indestructible."

They both sat quietly for a long while, remembering. Duncan broke the silence.

"I'll serve as your best man if you like, unless you would prefer one of the Henderson uncles."

"No, you are standing in for the Earl now. But I'll understand if you don't want to do it."

"I think that's what Pa would like," Duncan said. "It would be my pleasure."

"Prior Ancroft wants us to have a walk-through rehearsal later this afternoon at the chapel. Are you up to it?"

"Aye, I'll get dressed and meet you there."

The wedding party gathered at the chapel to review the ceremony and rehearse the service. Andy had met beforehand with all of them—Helen, Aunt Margaret, the bridesmaids, Maggie and Allie, and the groomsmen, Blair and Harold to give them the news about Earl Wallace's sudden illness. They were all disappointed, but gamely managed to press forward with the rehearsal. Everyone hoped that tomorrow would bring a better day.

As the wedding party left the chapel and walked toward the cathedral, Andy noticed Lord Kennedy standing out in front. He nodded, and Andy broke off from the group and went over to him.

"Andrew, I just heard about Dar, a real shock. I hope the problem isn't too bad and he's able to overcome it. I understand he was to be your best man."

Andy responded sympathetically, "Aye, a shock to us all. Uncle Duncan has bravely and generously agreed to remain here and serve in Grandfather's stead."

Kennedy nodded and looked at Andy intently. Evidently he had something else on his mind.

"Andrew, I know this is a bad time, but before tomorrow's festivities, there is an important matter I would like to discuss with you. This is probably the only opportunity I'll have."

The main group had moved on, and he and the Earl were now standing alone. "Let's take a stroll," Kennedy said.

They started walking slowly back toward the chapel.

"You are aware, of course, of the ministry of John Knox and the persecution he and other Protestants have suffered at the hands of Cardinal Beaton, the late Archbishop of St. Andrews?"

"Aye," answered Andy. "As you may know, Cardinal Beaton was responsible for hiring Joseph Renfreu, the fake Protestant teacher who entrapped my sister. He had deputized a "master" to charge her with heresy and have her burned at the stake."

"I've heard," said Kennedy, "nasty, cowardly business. I'm pleased you were able to bring justice upon the perpetrators. Truly, a deserving end to those corrupt scoundrels and most courageous on your part." Andy nodded, but did not say anything.

Kennedy continued, "Word is that Knox was captured at St. Andrews by a French military force, and has been impressed into servitude as a galley slave for the French navy."

"I had not heard that," answered Andy.

Kennedy explained, "It was due to the scheming of Mary of Guise, mother of Mary, Queen of Scots. She is an avid Catholic. As you probably know, young Mary is now in France and betrothed to the Dauphine. In my view, we Scots need to be free of both France and England."

"I agree with that," replied Andy.

"Are you aware of a group called 'Lords of the Congregation?'"

Andy answered cautiously, "I've heard of them."

"Good, then you know that the group is composed of some of the most prominent men in Scotland - earls, barons, knights, nobility of the highest order. They have organized to oppose the pope and his evil and corrupt servants in Scotland, such as Beaton and his agents. Much like what is now occurring in England, these men are committed to the Protestant cause and are determined to oppose Catholicism and all its institutions throughout Scotland."

"Yes, I'm vaguely aware of that," said Andy in a neutral tone.

"Something important will be happening soon, and I want you to be aware of it. As you are the Laird of Blackcraigshire and the grandson of a notable earl, himself descended from a famous Scottish king, I am confident I can get you into the group. Personally I would like that very much."

Andy replied carefully, as he had been warned by his grandfather Wallace to be cautious of the wiles of the sly old earl.

"You realize that I'm not very religious."

The Earl nodded, "Religion itself is not a major factor here, although I would observe that your family has suffered greatly at the hands of the high Catholic hierarchy."

Andy's mind flashed painfully back to the terrible fate of his sister and how Renfreu and his students had corrupted the mind of his cousin Innis.

"Truly, it has," he said.

"I'm talking about land, buildings and money—a lot of it," said the earl. "It's a bad time to discuss such matters, but I wanted to give you notice of what's on the horizon so you'll have time to give the matter serious thought."

As they approached an overlook, Kennedy summarized the plan, then cautioned, "You must promise to keep this quiet, agreed?"

Andy nodded.

Kennedy proceeded to tell him that the Lords of the Congregation had decided to move against all Catholic holdings across the Scottish borderlands, from Glasgow City and Edinburgh down to the English border. Included were the many abbeys, monasteries, priories, cathedrals and churches, altogether of incalculable worth. They intended to see a Protestant monarch on the throne in Scotland and to confiscate the Catholic properties. They would then escheat to the Crown. The Lords would be rewarded with a generous fee for "services rendered."

Andy was astounded. He had heard rumors of this for a couple of years but never expected it to actually occur. If the Earl of

Cassillis was confiding this to him, the rumors were true. It was going to happen.

"When will it start?" he asked.

"I don't know. No definite timetable has been set. But fairly soon I think. We can't wait forever," Kennedy replied. "And don't worry, I'll see to it that Whithorn and the chapel are off-limits. Look, I know this is sudden and a lot for you to digest, but think about it and let me hear in the next few weeks,"

"Of course," Andy said, "now if you'll excuse me, I've much to do."

He turned and walked away, his mind spinning as he made his way to the Henderson family tent. Helen was inside with Agatha, Coria and the two Agnew lasses.

"We were just getting ready to go over to the bridal tent. I need to try on my wedding garments and make any needed adjustments," Helen said gaily.

"And you aren't invited," rejoined Maggie, laughing.

Andy smiled, but couldn't get his mind off the just-finished conversation with Lord Kennedy. Helen noticed the worried look on his face.

"Something wrong?" she asked.

"Nay," answered Andy, without conviction.

"I won't be long," Helen said, "then we can talk."

When Helen returned, alone, she said that everything fit beautifully.

"I think you'll like my outfit," she said. "I'm so anxious I'm jumping out of my skin," she continued, radiating a beatific glow. She noticed Andy's long face, and her radiance darkened.

"You're troubled about your grandfather's illness. I know. So am I, but let's try to keep it from ruining our wedding day."

"Aye, that's part of it," Andy said, "but there's more. I just had a strange conversation with Lord Kennedy."

"Tell me about it."

Andy proceeded to tell her the whole story. Helen looked concerned when he finished.

"When do you think this will start?"

Andy said he did not know, but Kennedy had said "soon."

"He said I could have a few weeks to think on it—whether to join with the Protestant Lords. He also made it clear that the main purpose of the endeavor, his purpose anyway, was to confiscate valuable Catholic properties. He clearly expects to become even richer than he is now."

Helen was appalled. "We're getting married tomorrow in St. Ninian's Chapel, the oldest in Scotland, by a Catholic prior. Does he expect to take Whithorn after being a guest here?"

"No, he specifically said that Whithorn and the chapel would be spared."

"What are you going to do?" asked Helen.

"I'm not sure," Andy replied gravely, "I'd rather stay out of the whole affair, but I expect that will be impossible. We'll get dragged in, one way or the other. As you know, I detest the high Catholic hierarchy for what they did to Ree, and to Innis, but the lower ranks of ordinary Catholic believers are a different matter. I was raised Catholic after all, as were you."

"You're right," sighed Helen, "it's not likely we can avoid getting involved."

"Young King Edward of England is an ardent Protestant, as was his father, King Henry," observed Andy.

The English Crown was already expropriating Catholic properties, he said. It seemed the way of the future. But they shouldn't worry themselves about it just now.

"Let's enjoy our wedding."

Helen nodded, "Aye, let's!"

Andy pulled Helen close, she looked up into his face and the sparkle in her blue eyes brightened. He kissed her deeply.

"I love you more than anything," he murmured.

"And I you. We'll get through this somehow," she said, running her fingers through his long, wavy brown hair.

✦ ✦ ✦

May 1 broke sunny and warm. Andrew Henderson and Helen Agnew stood before Prior Androu Ancroft in the semi-circular apse at the back of St. Ninan's Chapel. The fine, richly illustrated

Bible lay open on the altar, the many colors illuminated by the morning sun streaming through the stained-glass windows. Helen's cousin Maggie served as the maid of honor. Andy's Uncle Duncan was the best man. Earl Kennedy gave her away. The vows were said and Prior Ancroft pronounced them man and wife. Andy pinned the brightly sparking bejeweled wedding brooch on Helen's surcoat, raised her veil and gave her a soft kiss. He could feel her heart thumping as he tugged her close.

The troubling events of the day before were temporarily forgotten. There had never been a happier couple. Later, in the early afternoon, the festivities began in earnest. Hundreds of people crowded into the Cathedral at Whithorn, where they happily congratulated the bride and groom, feasted at the sumptuous, luxurious banquet and enjoyed the splendid weather.

Children danced around a maypole, laughing and streaming colorful ribbons behind them, wrapping the pole. Toward nightfall the Beltane bonfire was set ablaze. The newly married couple, still wearing their wedding finery, presided over a joyous celebration that lasted late into the night, fueled by dancing, singing and the imbibing of plentiful spirituous beverages. Tomorrow, heads would pound, but tonight no one cared.

When they finally retired for the night, after the festivities had wound down, Andy and Helen were still giddy from it all and feeling rather amorous. Arriving at the family tent, they found that several family members were already sprawled on the floor to sleep off their very good time.

"What about the bridal tent," asked Andy, "is it empty?"

Helen looked at him, a mischievous smile crossing her lips as she tried to stifle a giggle.

"It should be, why?"

The couple stumbled across the way to the tent, arms wrapped around each other's waist to keep from falling, and plunged inside. Furiously tearing off clothing, they soon stood naked before each other in the moonlight that softly lit the interior with a dim gauzy light. Andy was already stiff. Helen was panting with anticipation, "I want you, husband—now!"

They made love as they never had before. Like two animals in heat, Andy mounted her from behind, plunging deep inside, stroke after stroke, faster and faster, as she pumped her buttocks up and down in a wild, fiery frenzy. Within moments they both climaxed. Thrilled and exhausted, they fell asleep in each other's arms and did not stir again till daybreak.

The next day the Henderson family and all the other wedding guests laboriously packed up their belongings and left. There was another big event waiting after their return to the Big House. They sent the women, Agatha, Coria, Helen and the Agnew lasses ahead with leftover food, drink and decorations. Harold and a couple of the Big House men-at-arms accompanied them. Andy and the remaining men-at-arms would bring the tents later that day. There was still much to do to finish preparations for the Beltane celebration.

Along with the tenant farmer families, there were already a large number of tradesmen who were settling nearby in the shire. Many were younger members of various artisan families of the Wallace clan at Blackmor who were striking out on their own, and others were from Wigtown and surrounding areas. In all, a few hundred people, including children and the steadily increasing band of Big House men-at-arms, were expected to attend.

This was to be a time to tightly bind the loyalties of these people to the laird and to the land.

# 43.

# CLOSE CALL

ONE month before the wedding, a group of men met in the office of the new archbishop at the St. Andrews Cathedral. The office now belonged to Cardinal John Hamilton, appointed by the Holy See in Rome to serve as archbishop and prelate to Scotland following the death of Cardinal David Beaton. Beaton had been murdered at his residence in St. Andrews Castle by Protestant sympathizers, angered by his vigorous campaign to squelch the Protestant cause in Scotland. The men meeting with Hamilton were former disciples of Cardinal Beaton. Included was Peter Donner, an agent of Joseph Renfreu, who had been commissioned by Beaton as a special master to carry out persecution missions against Protestants deemed to be particularly dangerous.

With a few notable exceptions, Cardinal Hamilton was proving not to be as dedicated to the persecution of Protestants as Beaton had been. One of those exceptions involved a plan of revenge for the murder of Master Renfreu and several of his guards in Ayr over a year before. The murders followed the execution, sanctioned by the Catholic diocese, of a Protestant agitator named Mairy Henderson. Convicted of heresy, she had been burned at the stake.

Donner had learned that the killer of Renfreu was Mairy's brother, Andrew

Henderson, Laird of Blackcraigshire. He had recently gotten word that Henderson was planning to marry Helen Agnew at a service to be held in St. Ninan's Chapel in Whithorn on May 1, just a few weeks hence. He was there to implore the archbishop to authorize and finance a mission to hunt Henderson down, capture him, and have him executed for these murders. The wedding seemed to present a good opportunity. Donner emphasized that Henderson had been brought up Catholic but had abandoned the faith and embraced Protestantism. He was doubly dangerous for he was falsely posing as a Catholic and would have his marriage ceremony held at one of the most ancient and revered Catholic sites in all of Scotland.

"This man is most dangerous to our Church," argued Donner. "We must not allow him to go free after committing such heinous crimes and apostasies."

"I am convinced," agreed the archbishop. "You are hereby commissioned to capture this man and bring him here for ecclesiastical trial. I will provide funds for you to hire adequate help. But understand that I want him tried and convicted. I do not want a lynching. Make every effort to avoid any physical harm."

"Aye, of course, your Grace," murmured Donner.

The next night Donner met at his residence in Edinburgh with four highwaymen. Donner had been introduced to them by a friend of his personal guard. Contrary to his promise to Cardinal Hamilton, Donner did not plan to capture Henderson and return him to St. Andrews for trial. He wanted him killed. He had been assured that the highwaymen were more than capable of successfully completing the mission.

Donner paid them one third of the agreed fee at the start, with the remainder due upon completion of the mission. The men decided to travel to Wigtown, visit some taverns and see what they could find out about the details of Henderson's wedding.

On the afternoon of the day following the wedding, Andy and two of his men-at-arms were enroute back to the Big House with a wagon pulled by two Clydesdale horses. The wagon held the tents used by the family at the wedding and some other furnishings. Andy was in the lead, mounted on his favorite horse, a palfrey gelding. The wagon was driven by one of the guards. Another mounted guard brought up the rear. Andy and the two guards were armed with crossbows and broadswords. The wagon driver had a dirk and a long braided leather whip that he occasionally cracked to urge the team of horses forward. They had entered a wooded glade on the dusty "pilgrim's way" between Whithorn and Wigtown.

All of a sudden the guard at the rear brought his horse charging around the wagon, screaming at the top of his lungs, "We're under attack!"

The wagon driver noticed immediately that the man had a crossbow bolt buried in his back. A big splotch of blood stained his shirt. The driver cracked his whip and the two-horse team pulling the wagon lumbered to a slow gallop, stirring up a cloud of dust. Andy looked back and saw what was happening. There were two unknown riders, bandits Andy assumed, bearing down on them from behind. Andy drew his broadsword, wheeled his horse around, and took off to intercept the intruders. The lead bandit had a crossbow slung over one shoulder and was holding a dirk in his hand.

Andy suddenly appeared from the back end of the wagon, seemingly out of nowhere, his broadsword held high over his head. The bandit had little time to react. The two men were closing fast, both horses at full gallop. Andy kept the palfrey headed straight toward the other horse, figuring the bandit's horse might skitter as they closed—he knew his palfrey, a well-trained cavalry horse, would stay on line. Andy could grip the broadsword in both hands and guide his palfrey with pressure from his knees. When they were within a few feet of each other the eyes of the other horse bulged with alarm, and it shied sideways, jostling the rider. Andy slashed his broadsword just above the bandit's shoulders, slicing deep across his neck.

Andy's palfrey had barely slowed when the other bandit appeared out of the dust, closing fast. Andy held his broadsword flat, point aimed forward at the onrushing rider's chest like a jousting lance. As the two horses sped past each other, Andy's sword stabbed the second man square in the stomach, slicing him almost completely in half.

Andy pulled the palfrey to a stop, wheeled him around and took off through the dust left by the speeding wagon. He saw that the second rider had fallen from his horse, and was on the ground beside the road with blood gushing from the giant stomach wound. The first bandit was slightly farther up, slumped over the saddle, blood streaming from his neck. The horse was panicked, shying sideways, as Andy sailed by. That man, too, would soon hit the ground.

Just yards from the wagon, dust stinging his eyes, Andy saw a third man face-down on the ground beside the road, with a whip coiled around his neck. He was not moving. Andy caught a glimpse of the man's riderless horse disappearing through the woods. He instantly surmised what had happened. A third bandit had attacked the wagon, either from the front, or side. The wagon driver had snaked the whip, wrapping it around the neck of the bandit, jerking him off his horse. *There are more bandits,* Andy realized.

As he passed the wagon, he yelled at his driver to slow the team down.

Up ahead there was a sword fight. Two mounted men were wheeling around each other, swords swinging, thrusting and clanging. One of them had a scarlet blotch of blood staining the back of his surcoat, where a crossbow bolt protruded. The man was Andy's guard, fighting bravely despite the painful wound. As Andy reached them, he saw the bandit's horse swing around, presenting the man's back. He closed and stabbed his broadsword deep between the bandit's ribs.

The bandit screamed and spun around facing Andy. But before he could spur his horse forward, he shuddered, coughed and slumped over, then slid to the ground. His frightened horse trotted off. Andy dismounted and pulled his sword from the man's body, wiping the bloody blade on the leg of the man's trousers.

Andy's guard was now slumped in his saddle. Andy ran to him and helped him to the ground where he examined the wound. The bolt had gone completely through the left side of the guard's back and the point was protruding out the front of his torso just below the ribcage.

Andy had the guard sit on the ground and explained the situation.

"The bolt went clean through. I don't think it hit any vital organs, but you are bleeding badly. I'll cut off the back of the bolt and pull the rest out from the front. Get prepared for it will hurt."

By now the wagon had pulled up and stopped. Andy shouted at the driver, "Do you have any wine or whiskey?"

The driver was standing on the front floorboard of the wagon, scanning in all directions to see if there were any other bandits.

"I think we got them all," he yelled to Andy, "er, what did you say?"

"Whiskey or wine or cider, do you have any?"

Looking a bit abashed, the driver pulled a bottle of fine port wine from under the seat.

"Left over from the banquet," he explained, a weak grin on his face.

"Earl Kennedy brought an extra supply, huh?" Andy responded. "Hand it here. We need to pour it in the wound. Also, go back and tear some clothing off one of the dead men, preferably linen. We'll need some cloth to pack and wrap the wound."

There was a barber in Wigtown, Andy knew, who was a decent physic. They could drop the injured guard off there for treatment, and then look up the town marshal. After telling the marshal what had happened, he could conduct whatever investigation he felt necessary. Meanwhile, they needed to hurry on to the Big House. The marshal could reach them there if he needed something more.

✦ ✦ ✦

On May third all the preparations for the Beltaine celebration had been made. The long banquet table in the great hall was decked out with all manner of food and drink. Candelabras, fruits, platters of meat, bowls of fruits, nuts and other delicacies lined the table. Straw was scattered on the floor to soak up spilled drink and food that could be expected once the party was underway. Andy and Helen, outfitted in festive costumes, were poised on seats of honor that had been placed on a dais at the head of the table. At the appointed time, as the sun was setting, the doors were opened and the crowds poured in.

Harold stepped forward and banged a stout wooden staff on the floor to command attention. He intoned in a booming voice: "Citizens of Blackcraigshire and visitors to this realm, I am most proud to introduce our master and mistress, just returned from their marriage at Whithorn, Laird Andrew Henderson and his Lady, Helen Henderson."

A roar accompanied by whistles and vigorous clapping arose in the great hall. Helen and Andy stood, waving to the crowd, and the roar got louder, lasting for a long while. Finally, Andy raised both arms and the crowd quieted down.

"Thank you for coming my good people, and welcome to our realm."

Then, his voice ringing over the crowd noise, "This is the start of a new tradition. Lady Helen and I have decided to have a celebration like this every quarter year, named according to the old gaelic seasons: the Inbolic on February first for the beginning of spring; Beltane on May first for the beginning of summer; Lammas on August first for the beginning of the grain harvest; and Samhain on November first for the end of harvest season and the beginning of winter. All of you work hard for yourselves and your families, as well as for this realm, and you deserve time off from your toils for renewal and celebration. This celebration begins right now. Please—eat, drink and be merry!"

Helen signaled Coria. She opened a side door and in streamed the minstrels, singers and jugglers, dancing around the table in their colorful garb, adding jovial talent to the festivities. The crowd gleefully rushed the table and the party was underway. Harold grinned. This had been his suggestion and it was off to a great start.

Andy and Helen were rejoicing, but Andy felt a vague sense of unease. The bandits who had attacked on the Pilgrim's Way seemed to know Andy's wagon would be coming through at that exact time. It was a busy road after all, and several groups had used it to return home after the wedding. *Why did they pick Andy's group to attack?* It seemed they were much more interested in killing than stealing the wagon or its contents.

Had he been the real target?

# 44.
# Πew Bir⊦h

THE next morning, the newly married couple slept in late, hearts joyous but bodies exhausted and heads pounding. Helen lazily opened her eyes and peered at Andy, her vision still blurry.

"How are you feeling, husband? Are you over all the unexpected excitement from the robbery attempt? Thank God no harm was done to you!"

Andy rolled over, stretched his aching limbs and yawned extravagantly.

"Rather like I've been running all day followed by a gremlin with a hammer pounding on my head," he said, kissing her on the cheek.

"Who do you think the bandits were?" asked Helen.

"I've no idea," Andy said. "Maybe the town marshal can turn up some clues. There were a couple of strange things though. Usually highway robbers pick a secluded spot and lie in wait hoping for an easy target—most often people on foot. Seldom do they go after mounted, well-armed men, unless they know of a very valuable prize. Maybe they thought there was something in the wagon besides tents."

"You don't suppose the high Catholic churchmen had anything to do with it?" Helen asked.

"No, I doubt it," replied Andy, stroking his beard as he considered the question. "Though I've heard from friends in Ayr that they would love to get back at me."

After a while, Helen got dressed and went downstairs to ask Martha to warm some breakfast and bring it up to them, then she rejoined Andy in bed.

"Do you feel up to discussing the talk you had with Lord Kennedy at Whithorn, or do you even remember it after the scare from the bandits?"

"Och, I remember all right. Now's as good a time as any," Andy replied wearily. "I guess we should just think about it in a practical way, what's best for us—you, me and the family. It's pretty clear that Protestantism is the way of the future. It's already taken over in England, and I think it will soon win out here. It seems that there is no way the two groups can learn to co-exist, despite the fact that they are both Christian, worship the same God and read the same Bible."

"It's such a shame," sighed Helen, "so pointless."

"That's why I've never been a big admirer of religion," Andy said, "Although it helps ordinary people, most of the big church leaders are as power hungry as the monarchs. I can't remember a war that didn't involve both the church and the sovereign. It seems they are constantly jousting, causing death and misery to innocent people."

"Sadly, what you say is true," Helen admitted. "Maybe we would be better off to join the Protestant Lords. I don't think we will be able to stay neutral."

✦ ✦ ✦

Toward the end of July, Helen mentioned to Andy that her periods had stopped. He looked startled and asked when she had had her last one. Somewhat coquettishly she replied, "Well, I've not had one since the, ah, before our wedding night."

"Och, we finally got it right?" he shouted, then hesitated, the big smile on his face changing to a slightly worried look.

"You sure you're pregnant?"

Smiling, her cheeks flushed and her eyes moist, she answered, "I think there's a very good chance of it."

Andy grabbed her in a big bear hug, lifting her off the floor, her feet dangling, and proceeded to cover her face with kisses.

"My sweet wife. That's wonderful." Doing some quick arithmetic in his head, Andy exclaimed, "We're going to have a new year's baby?"

Suddenly he felt a pain to his shins. Helen was kicking him and pushing back on his shoulders with her arms, gasping.

"Put me down and quit squeezing so hard."

Andy quickly and gently released his grip and lowered his wife to the floor, a look of concern on his reddened face.

"I'm sorry, I'm just so excited. 'Er, you don't think I did any damage do you?"

Catching her breath, Helen laughed. "No, husband, you didn't. I'm only three months at most. Babies are very durable creatures. You only have to be extra careful after they drop."

"So when exactly do you think …?" he said tentatively.

"I'd guess January," she said.

"Let's go outside for a walk and talk about it. I'm betting on a boy. What should we name him?"

"Not so fast," replied Helen. "Naming a baby takes some time and thought." The couple walked out behind the Big House, up a path to a small grove of oak trees. It was a part of the original area where the Henderson family had spent that long cold night a few years earlier after the raid on the bastle house. They often went there for privacy and to talk about important things away from prying ears. Helen put together a basket of edibles, and Andy grabbed a blanket and a jug of wine. There were significant matters now at hand.

"First things first," Andy said after they were seated.

"How about we name the baby 'Colin,' after my paternal grandfather, ah … if it turns out to be a boy that is?"

"I thought that's what you had in mind," replied Helen with a chuckle. "If we have a boy, Colin it is."

"What if we have a girl," Andy inquired. "Do you have any favorite girl names?"

"Don't rush me," replied Helen in a teasing but meaningful tone. "I like Colin fine for a boy, but would like more time to consider naming a girl."

"You're right, I apologize," Andy replied, trying to sound contrite. "You can have all the time you want, but still, I'm sure it will be a boy."

Helen then moved on to another subject—that of the scheming of her stepmother, Rachel, and Rachel's kinsmen, the Fergussons, to take over Galloway and the Wigtownshire sheriffship. She inquired if Andy had heard anything more about either.

"Nay, I haven't," he said, "and frankly I don't think anything will happen as long as English troops remain garrisoned across the south of Scotland."

"But I thought there was talk that the English may withdraw the troops," Helen said.

"Aye, there is such talk and there's a good chance it might happen, in my opinion. The incursion into Scotland by the French naval force, and the capture of John Knox at St. Andrews, made the English Crown very nervous. The ease with which the French had kidnapped Knox was alarming, Andy said.

"As you know the English have been at war with France for many years and are well aware the French are allies of the Scottish Crown. From what I've heard, King Edward VI fears a massive French/Scots invasion against England's northern border, using Scotland as a land base."

"Do you think that might actually happen? asked Helen, concern on her face. Seems to me it would result in a terrible war."

"True, said Andy. That's why I feel the English are likely to keep troops in southern Scotland for a long time. It will act as a hedge against the French, and also any ambitions by Scottish clans to capture more territory."

"I agree," said Helen with a sigh, "but it's a precarious way to maintain a peace."

✦ ✦ ✦

Winter had arrived and Helen was now quite big. One morning in early December, she and Andy went downstairs to join the rest of the family for breakfast. They found Ally and Jamie on one side of the table holding hands. Their faces were flushed and both looked somewhat embarrassed. Maggie was on the other side with a disgusted look on her face.

"Where's little Gracie?" asked Helen.

Ally said she was still asleep and was being watched by her minder. Helen and Andy sat down beside Maggie, waiting on Martha to have breakfast sent in. There followed a long silence.

"Well, let's not all talk at once," Andy said, looking at the others around the table. He noticed that Ally and Jamie were still holding hands.

"What's up with you lovebirds?' he asked. "You look like two cats that just swallowed someone's pet canary."

Jamie cleared his throat, "Sire, Ally has agreed to marry me. We are betrothed."

Andy and Helen both broke into broad smiles.

"Congratulations to you both. We're so happy for you," cried Helen.

"And you can quit holding hands now," chided Andy. "That might cause a bit of inconvenience in eating your breakfast."

"And wipe those silly grins off your faces," grumbled Maggie, "it's irritating."

"Now Maggie, tone it down," scolded Helen. "They're just happy."

Ally and Jamie continued to hold hands and smile. They were going to get married and they didn't care what others might think.

+ + +

By Christmas Eve Helen was well along with her pregnancy. The whole family, plus everyone else at the Big House and from across the whole of Blackcraigshire, was excited. Helen decided they should cut a holly tree for Christmas, decorate it and place it in the great hall.

"We are all still here, hardy and healthy," she said mirthfully. "Let's make it a Christmas to remember. Everyone grab their wraps and let's go out in search of a tree we can be proud of. I have a feeling that 1550 will bring many wonderful surprises!"

The entire family, including Ally, Jamie and little Gracie, now just over a year old, wrapped themselves against the cold and got in a wagon filled with straw, pulled by two Clydesdales. With Harold Douglas as the driver, they set out in search of the perfect Christmas tree. After a while they found a large holly with bright green leaves, and filled with red berries. It was just the right size to fit in the great hall.

Everyone at the Big House got busy with preparations for a family Christmas celebration. Due to Helen's advanced pregnancy, they had decided they shouldn't invite a large crowd. The residents of Blackcraigshire had been treated to a big Samhain festival just over a month before, celebrating yet another good harvest and the start of winter. They all knew of Helen's condition and would not expect another celebration so soon.

The Henderson family and the residents of the Big House, however, wanted a festive event of their own. Helen could supervise if she wanted—the others would do all the work. The great hall, entryway and front courtyard were decorated with cedar and holly garlands, and candles were placed all around. The holly tree was erected, and the family members richly decorated it with hanging apples, various other fruits, ginger cookies and peppermint candies. Little Gracie was big-eyed, looking excitedly at all the goodies, trying to escape the clutches of her minder to get her hands on them.

When Christmas morn arrived, the sun glistened off an overnight snow through breaks in the clouds. Martha and the kitchen crew, assisted by Jamie, Ally and Maggie, busily put together traditional Christmas treats and a fine supper. When nightfall arrived, a big bonfire was lit out in the front courtyard. Although heavy with her expectant baby, Helen enjoyed the bonfire and decorations, and joined her husband at the head of the great table for the Christmas feast.

January of 1550 blew in with more snowstorms. Everyone was excited to see the blanket of white as it made clean and sparkling the gloomy outside winter environs. Andy and Helen had called in a midwife to help with the baby's delivery and any unexpected complications.

"You don't think all this snow is a bad sign for giving birth do you?" Helen asked anxiously to Andy and the midwife, both standing near.

"Nay," answered Andy, "of course not."

The midwife smiled. *"It's a wonderful sign, m'Lady. Snaw signifies purity. I've ne'er seen a difficult birthin' after a snawfaw. Th' mair th' better."*

"That's good," cried Helen, "For I think the baby's coming any minute now." Indeed he was. Little Colin Henderson made his appearance just before breakfast on January 30, 1550. Colin was a healthy, active boy, big for a newborn. Helen immediately announced that he was the spitting image of his father. Andy didn't say anything for he had a lump in his throat and tears in his eyes. His emotions, however, were betrayed by a proud, wide grin. A new son named after his paternal grandfather. *The next boy we have,* he was thinking, *will have to be named Darrow, after my maternal grandfather.* And he did plan on having many more.

By the time daylight arrived, and the household staff had had their breakfast, Helen and Andy sat at the dais at the head of the long table in the great hall, proudly holding baby Col in their arms and introducing him to all the Big House residents.

Around mid-day, after Helen and the baby had gone to the bedroom for a nap, Andy asked Martha to put together a couple of biscuits with ham, and went to the stable to saddle his favorite riding horse. He told her he was going out to inform some of the shire's more important tenants about little Col's arrival. Instead he headed up Glen Trool toward Ben Blackcraig. He had an unyielding yearn to visit the family cemetery. When he reached the loch he hobbled his horse and began the steep climb up the trail to the cemetery through thick falling snow.

Andy carefully picked his way, constantly on the lookout for lumps and indentations in the deep snow that might signal a large rock or hidden crevice. The last thing he needed was to fall on some concealed obstacle and end up with a sprained ankle, twisted knee or worse. As he gained elevation, it grew colder and the snow lightened to soft, dry, gently floating flakes. He rounded the last bend and stood on the flat plot where the little cemetery lay. Looking up he could see the line of great rock slabs—pale ghosts of an ancient henge enshrouded by a curtain of snow.

"After all these millennia of serving as silent sentries," Andy said aloud, "should some of you have any favorable omens left, I could sure use one."

He looked over at the cemetery and the four engraved headstones he had set over a year ago: one for Grannie Henderson and the wee twins; one for Ann and Hugh Henderson, Andy's parents; another for Baron Andrew Agnew, Helen's father; and the last for Sheriff Gilbert Agnew, brother of the baron and father of the three Agnew bairns, Blair, Maggie, and Ally. Andy selected a large flat stone and positioned it at the foot of his parents' grave. He sat down, bowed his head and was still for a time, snow gathering on his head and shoulders. He felt an irrepressible need to say something but was not sure exactly what. Finally he raised his head, shook the snow from his bonnet and lowered himself to one knee.

"Ma … Paw …I come here today to share some wonderful news and to seek your counsel. First, you are the grandparents of a new baby son just born this morn. The boy's name is Colin, named after his paternal great grandfather, and the proud parents are myself and Helen Agnew Henderson. We were married … well, slightly over nine months ago."

Andy stood and walked around the line of headstones, stopping occasionally to gaze out over the loch and the expanse of Glen Trool. The snow had thinned high up on the Ben where he stood, revealing a sparkling white vista below. News of the newborn had been a pleasure to share. But now he had much more serous matters to discuss. He swallowed to try and loosen the lump in his throat, and went back to his place at the foot of his parents' grave.

"Paw, I wish to thank you and Ma for all the blessings you bestowed upon us bairns, from education, knowledge and independence, to morals and ethics. Sorely do I wish you could have been here on this earth much longer, for I need your counsel and guidance now more than ever. The weight of becoming laird of our shire has fallen heavy upon my shoulders, and I'm afraid I wasn't ready."

Andy stood mute for a long while, trying to organize his thoughts. The horizon above Ben Blackcraig had lightened, casting a gauzy glow as the sun's rays struggled to break through. Finally he said: "Paw, I need to talk with both of you about Ree and Innis."

Andy explained that he realized how fond his father had grown of Innis during the few years he was with them after his escape from the terrible tragedy that befell his family. Andy's father had taken the boy under his wing and made a man of him, training him as his squire as he would his own son. Andy had also grown to care deeply for Innis. They had roomed together, travelled together, hunted together and become more like brothers than cousins. And Ree was the favorite of the entire family, a beautiful woman and a force in her own right.

"I must tell both of you this—Innis fell under the spell of religion, specifically the new Protestant religion, and had begun following a quack itinerate preacher. He got cross-ways with high Catholic authorities and was thrown in the gaol in Ayr. Ree sympathized with his plight and wanted to go to Ayr to help him."

"I realized this could be dangerous and told her so," Andy said. "Still she wanted to help so I agreed. This was a bad mistake. With help from the quack preacher, Ree and Innis were double-crossed by a Catholic agent. Ree was charged with heresy."

Here Andy paused and cleared his throat again. "They burned her at the stake," he finally said, an anguished look on his face.

He raised his head and brushed tears from his eyes. "Innis didn't know anything about it until it was too late."

Andy sat back down on the stone, put his head in his hands and was still for a long time, snow piling again on his bonnet and cloak. He gathered himself for what he knew would be the hardest part.

"Paw, I was full of rage when I heard of Ree's death. A lust for vengeance consumed me. I went to Ayr the very day I learned of it, determined that I would find and kill those responsible. I blamed Innis for getting Ree involved. I was able to wreak retribution against the killers, and then I went to search for Innis. He was in a tavern. He had learned of Ree's fate and drunk himself into a stupor. Still consumed by rage, I banished him from Black-craigshire, gave him some money and a horse and told him to leave

Scotland and never come back or I would kill him. That was bad enough, but then …."

He trailed off, and then fell to his knees, face down in the snow, sobbing. Finally he looked up and let out an anguished wail: "Paw, I cut off his nose."

Andy stood and looked up at Ben Blackcraig and a sky twinkling with gently floating white flakes.

"I had no reason to blame Innis. He was also a victim. And I never came to grips with my own role—I was the one who allowed Ree go to Ayr in the first place. I actually joked about the plight Innis was in. I am absolutely sick to my stomach about it. I lost both my beautiful sister and my best friend. There was a complete failure to think the situation through. I realize that now. I should have been the one to go and help Innis, not Ree. Now look what I've done. Ree is dead—murdered in the most horrible way imaginable. And Innis has vanished. I doubt I'll ever see him again. What a fine laird I've turned out to be."

Snow had piled up on the tops of the headstones like the tall white crests on nun's habits, but Andy was unable to appreciate the peaceful scene. He didn't know what he expected by coming here but felt no sense of redemption or peace. Actually he felt nothing at all. He turned and started the slow trek back down the trail, treading carefully to avoid slipping. As he made his way, he started thinking. *I have a brand new son and a growing family. Absolution is not a gift that can be bestowed. It has to be earned. I need to get back home and take care of my family. That's my job, and it needs tending every day.*

When he reached the bottom, he found Harold standing there holding the reins of two horses. One was his with the hobble already removed.

"Sire, Lady Helen is worried. She asked me to find you and implore you to return home. It'll be dark soon. I followed your tracks, it didn't take long to figure where you'd gone."

Andy nodded, swung into the saddle, and they set off.

THE END

# About the Author

ROGER GLASGOW received his bachelor of science degree in history and political science in 1965 from what is now Southern Arkansas University in Magnolia, and his juris doctor from the University of Arkansas School of Law in Fayetteville in 1969. After a 50-year career as a trial lawyer in Little Rock, he turned to writing. His first book, a memoir published in 2016 entitled Down and Dirty Down South: Politics  and the Art of Revenge, received an "Arkansas Gem" award from the Arkansas Library Association. Broadsword is his debut novel. He and his wife, Jennifer Glasgow, a privacy and technology executive, reside in Little Rock, Arkansas, and Crested Butte, Colorado.

Made in the USA
Coppell, TX
07 January 2023

10591565R00197